WILDE
Katherine Warwick

Grove Creek Publishing

This is a work of fiction. Names, characters, places and incidents are either a product of the author's imagination or are used fictitiously, and any resemblance to actual persons, living or dead, business establishments, events or locales is entirely coincidental.

A Grove Creek Publishing Book / published by arrangement with the author
Wilde © Printing History

All rights reserved
Copyright 2007 by Katherine Warwick

This book may not be reproduced in whole or in part without written permission. For information address: Grove Creek Publishing, 2 South Main St., Pleasant Grove, Ut. 84062

Cover: Jennifer Johnson, Sapphire Designs
Photograph: Rob Ronda www.RobRonda.com
Photograph of Vadim Garbuzov and Kathrin Menzinger
Book Design: Julia Lloyd

ISBN: 1-933963-95-6

Printed in the United States of America

Fairy tales can come true.

WILDE
Katherine Warwick

Grove Creek Publishing

1.

His hips moved in a rhythmic calculated grind. Anna's heart stammered. From the first row, she watched intently. Two dancers engaged in the samba—the Latin dance of love. She didn't look at the woman he danced with – her eyes were locked on him.

One lone guitar strummed – at first slow, tempting, like rain softly stroking a window. Gradually, the trickle became a lilting stream as drums began a thunderous beat. Crossing to center stage, he moved like a tiger: predatory, focused, intent. Heat filled the room. A puissant energy hovered in the air with the promise to electrify and ignite. Muddled voices twisted in whispers of awe. White lights flickered, then dimmed to red-hot pink in time with the music. Somewhere, a glass ball twirled, shooting millions of sparkling stars into circular orbit around the Capitol Theater. Around him.

Anna was taken by his face, finely sculpted with classic lines that both sharpened and eased with the theatrics of performance. His hair was slicked straight back, making it look darker than in the myriad photos and videos she had studied of him.

He was well-formed inside those black pants. Hard legs lunged and slid to the beat. Muscles pressed taut against the sheer fabric of his shirt, melding with the demands of movement. The tapes she had watched did not do justice to the masculine presence pouring from him like streaming lava over the attentive audience.

Anna leaned forward, straining to be closer.

As he danced, he owned both the floor and the woman. Anna's breath stilled. She glanced to see if others were as captivated as she. Every head, all eyes, were focused on the stage.

As the music grew, so did the thrumming in her veins. The woman in his arms, the woman he shared the floor with, was his toy -- his plaything, as he turned and tossed her at whim.

Anna's feet itched to be on the floor, her body yearned to know what it would feel like to dance with him. The past few years of study and waiting were coming to an end, and she could hardly stay in her seat. Easing out a slow, controlled breath, she knew this intense reaction would not do. No one must see her like this – so taken by something she did not possess.

In an effort to slow her racing pulse, she looked at his partner. The woman was tall, languid, lovely, and because she was, Anna's brow lifted in displeasure. Yes, the woman was lovely, but certainly not his equal.

But Anna, would be his equal – at least on the dance floor.

She longed to catch his eye but knew the impossibility of it. He was focused, professional. Perfect. Everything she knew he would be as a dancer. The way his eyes stayed fastened on his partner with a look that spoke of dominance sent a thrilling rush down her spine. Though never given to submission, Anna wanted those eyes to look into hers that way.

She watched the way his hands directed the woman in the steps of the dance, gently yet with enough force to demand complete cohesion.

Guitars threaded the melody. The dancers, now pressed together, slowed to it in sliding dips and lunges. He held the woman's waist and pinned her hip to his before she arched back like water streaming from his hands. Then he brought her up and their bodies fused, faces so close Anna's heart stopped. Would they kiss?

Were they more than dance partners?

The audience applauded, standing in ovation while she continued to sit. Her front row seat allowed her to see that he glowed with sweat. The shirt he wore clung to him as though he had stepped through a mist. The deep V-cut in the front bared glistening taut skin underneath. The very sight sent heat through her system.

He raised his partner's hand before they took their bows and the applause thundered. As he waved, his eyes scanned the audience, found hers and held. Anna knew she had piqued his interest.

She merely tilted her head at him.

His partner tugged his hand, and the tight line holding their gazes broke.

Something deep inside of Anna, something woven with both need and admiration, plucked hard.

Within moments, they would meet face to face.

He gave one last wave to the audience before following his partner backstage.

Because those around her were staring, wondering why she alone was not standing in appreciative applause, Anna rose – then clapped.

A light flashed in her eyes, then another. The photographers smiled, nodding in gratitude before quickly disappearing. All eyes were on her now. It was a feeling she was used to, one she had learned to ignore.

She had but one thing on her mind – to make her way backstage.

Jamie wiped at his brow with a white hand towel an assistant handed to him. The young girl's eyes were wide with admiration and he grinned at her, handing back the towel with a pat to her braided hair.

"You were great, Jamie," she said.

"Thanks." Jamie pulled his sweaty shirt away from his chest in an effort to cool himself and glanced around. "Did you see where Courtney ran off to?"

The girl pointed toward the dressing rooms. "That way."

He tugged one of her braids with a grin.

Crossing the stage, he headed toward the line of doors that were the principal dressing rooms for the Capitol Theater. As with every dance show, there were bodies everywhere. It had been a celebration, not a competition, and so the mood backstage was friendly, not hostile.

"Great job, Jamie," somebody patted him on the back.

Another person elbowed him as he passed. "You guys were incredible."

Jamie nodded, smiled. The routine had been the finale, he and Courtney the guests of honor -- the showpieces. He was pretty happy with the performance. The argument he and Courtney had just moments before going on stage hadn't shown.

Still, his stomach muscles tensed as he approached the dressing room door.

The warm hand on his shoulder relaxed him momentarily. "That was beautiful, bro."

Jamie turned and smiled into the electric-green eyes of his coach, Reuben La Bate. His shaven head glistened chocolate brown and the earring he always wore winked.

Jamie knew better than to say anything. They were around too many people and friendly or not, ears were always ripe for partner problem gossip. He figured if anyone had caught the contention between him and Courtney, Reuben would have.

Reuben glanced over Jamie's shoulder at someone and waved, greeting them with his magnetic smile. Then his eyes slid back to Jamie's. He gestured toward Courtney's dressing room door. "Shall we?"

* * *

They found Courtney sitting in front of the mirror, staring at herself with a blank expression. Neither Jamie nor Reuben said anything for a moment, both navigating how to proceed through the depressively thick air.

Reuben ran a hand along his naked head. Letting out a sigh, he crossed to her. Placing his hands on her shoulders, he kneaded them gently as their eyes met in the mirror. "How you doing, sis?"

Her blue eyes filled with tears.

Jamie's lips pinched and he tentatively approached, standing a few well chosen feet behind Reuben. The three of them looked at each other through the mirror.

She shook her head, glancing at him only a moment, then back to Reuben. "I can't do this anymore." Reuben's expression never changed. He merely kept kneading Courtney's shoulders as he listened. "I can see it in your eyes," she continued, emotion tattering her voice. "He's outgrown me. And I'm tired of feeling like I'm less than he is." She whirled around in her seat, disengaging Rueben's hands. "I'm not less than him. I'm a good dancer."

Jamie began pacing behind Reuben, his nervous hands flicking and snapping out like a gambler with a cramp. "Yes," he shot. "You are."

"Just not good enough anymore?"

Jamie let out a laugh that sounded like it had been his prisoner since before the show. "That's your interpretation, Courtney. Not mine."

She stood her body tense underneath the tight black dress. "That's not what you said before the show."

"I never said that." In two steps, Jamie would have been in her face, had it not been that Reuben blocked him with his body and a palm pressed firmly against his chest.

"Whoa there brother, let's talk about this."

"We have talked about it," Courtney shouted.

Frustrated, Jamie let out a loud groan. "Why do you do this?"

"I'm just saying what you've been tiptoeing around for the last year now."

"The only thing I've been tiptoeing around is your glass feelings," Jamie countered. "I've been afraid to say or do anything for fear you'd shatter to pieces."

Reuben reached out and crimped Jamie's shoulder with the palm of his hand. His electric gaze tagged Jamie with silent warning. "I can see you both have your own ideas about this."

Respectfully, Jamie kept his mouth shut, but jerked his shoulder free.

Courtney's arms crossed her chest tightly, her eyes watered again as she stared at Jamie. "You're heartless."

Jamie's chest rose under a heavy and angry breath, his eyes narrowed. "One of us had to drive the partnership. You haven't had your heart or your brain in it for a long time now."

"And now you want out."

"That is not true."

"It is. You've been critical, pointing out all of my weaknesses, harping constantly—"

"You know I'm only hard on you to help you."

"Help me my—"

"Guys, guys." Reuben drew them both into his sides, looking from one to the other. "Come on. Maybe we should give this some time. Talk about it in a day or two when the engines aren't burning, you know what I'm saying?"

"It doesn't matter anymore." Courtney wrenched herself free, distancing herself from them both. "I'm done." Silence fell with a hollow thud.

Jamie stared at Courtney with the blankness of disbelief. They had been partners since junior high. She had been his friend, almost a sister. They'd been through countless competitions together. Traveled together, screamed at each other, laughed with each other, cried together. The last few years had been difficult on the partnership, yes. But he was committed to ride all of it. Just as he thought she was. Now, it felt like his right side was being ripped away.

"You're just upset. Jake's been gone for—"

"It has nothing to do with Jake," Courtney shouted.

It had everything to do with Jake. For a moment, Jamie wanted to rip the guy's head off and he would have, if the guy hadn't been thousands of miles away at school.

Jamie had tried to warn her two years earlier, when she first became smitten. Dance first, relationships second. It was the way it had to be when you were a competitive ballroom dancer. It was the way he lived. But he'd take the blame if it made her feel better. He wanted to save the partnership.

He took a step toward her, his right hand out as if he were leading her onto the dance floor. She only looked at it and didn't move. "This is what you want. Don't lie about it, Jamie."

"Is it what you want?" He could see she was taken aback with the question. She expected his usual fight -- the fight where he came out winning.

Her shoulders stiffened and she blinked back the anger. "I think it would be best for us both."

Jamie wanted to burst from the inside out. Since he couldn't, he walked the parameter of the tiny dressing room like a panther in a cage. He couldn't believe she was doing this to him – to them, after everything. Theirs had been the one partnership that had endured, beyond all of those in the game. His ego took a hit, but his heart was sore as well.

He looked at her, emotion choking on disappointment. The resolve on her face was stone cold. It was over, and he felt helpless to do anything to change it. Her decision would change both of their lives forever. He contemplated remaining there and fighting it out until she conceded, but knew that would not work this time. Her eyes were devoid of loyalty.

Storming to the door, he flung it open, and ran smack into the shocked face of a woman with granite-green eyes. The weight of her stare crushed him like a boulder. Her gaze was guarded and intriguing. He stole a moment to stare back. Skin pale and smooth blessed a face that lay somewhere between a child's and a woman's. The fascination she wore, he was sure, was due to the fact that she had either been eavesdropping or was a star-struck admirer, now disillusioned from overhearing an argument. She was surrounded by a wide-eyed group, all of them dressed in black. The woman with the smoldering eyes looked vaguely familiar but Jamie was too angry to stop and figure out where he'd seen her, or be cordial.

He made no effort to introduce himself or to see what she and her group wanted, and her brow lifted. Her lips, the only color on her face other than her stormy-green eyes, remained perfectly poised between displeasure and condemnation.

The lot of them stood like a black iron gate, blocking him. And he didn't have time for any of them.

"Excuse me." He plowed through. He heard gasps from the women, grumbles from the men, and he smelled perfume – a heavy, spicy scent on his shoulder as he strode through the back of the theater on his way out. It made him angrier. Now he'd smell her the rest of the day.

Jamie Wilde drove his red truck like a bird with one clipped wing. The freeway was slushy with newly fallen snow but he was too frustrated to allow the caution needed to drive safely. For the moment, his life didn't matter.

Dance mattered.

He was a championship dancer without a partner. He knew what that meant.

Basically, he was screwed.

"I know you're upset." Cheryl sat with her seat belt securely fastened, her eyes round as sapphire pools. "But could you slow down just a teensy?"

"You know what happens when partnerships fall apart," he started, venting. They'd only been dating for a few weeks. She had no idea what happened to dance partnerships that didn't last. "It takes weeks -- months even, to find another compatible partner."

"You won't be finding anyone if we don't make it home alive."

He smiled in spite of the load of frustration on his shoulders. She looked like a two-year-old on a rollercoaster for the first time.

"Sorry." Purposefully, he slowed the car. Out in front of him was grey sludge— in the sky, on the road— it matched the way he felt inside.

"Jamie." Cheryl's voice was the soft pitch of Snow White's. It enchanted her kindergarten students – and him. "I know this is a blow. But there must be hundreds of women who would love to dance with you."

The laugh that escaped him felt good, eased some of the pain refusing to let go. "Hundreds?" He reached over and snuck his arm around her shoulder. Her white-blonde hair was like the sun caught in the dark gloom of the car.

Her eyes remained focused on the road. "Don't you think this requires both hands?" She gestured with a nod toward the snowy stretch of freeway.

Putting both hands on the wheel, Jamie forced his fingers to relax.

"Did you see that woman in the front row?" Cheryl asked after a moment of quiet.

Distracted by his thoughts, Jamie shook his head. It would take months to train someone new, to bring them up to speed. To get the timing perfect.

"I think she was some sort of celebrity," Cheryl continued, still tense against the seat. "All those people around her—like an entourage. People were taking her picture."

"No, I didn't see her." The bubbling in Jamie's nerves wouldn't stop, and only a few things would rid him of the tension. "Wanna hit Bruisers?"

Cheryl shot him a quick look, her eyes still wide as she tore them from the road. "You really feel like dancing?"

"Well I can't go camping in this weather."

"I have school tomorrow. And, call me crazy, but I just want to get home and off these roads. But you can stay for a while if you want. We could watch a movie or something." She reached over and laid her hand on his thigh with a smile.

The overture was appreciated but with the turmoil inside, Jamie could no more think about taking her up on intimacy than driving all night through the blizzard.

He walked her to the porch when they finally arrived at her apartment.

With the door ajar, warmth reached out to him. A raspberry-scented candle was burning inside and the scent snuck out and teased the cool night air. One of her roommates passed, smiled and waved.

Cheryl looked up, eyes sparkling. Her short, blonde hair feathered softly around her face. The invitation was still there and for a moment he debated drowning long-term sorrows in a short-term solution.

"You sure?" she asked.

He shook his head. "I'd be terrible company. I will be until I solve this."

She reached up and stroked the side of his tense jaw. "I'm sorry." Then she lifted on her tip-toes and kissed his cheek.

It relaxed him—temporarily—and he got back in the car with a smile. He'd had so little time for relationships; all of them sandwiched in between the layers of dance that had, in the end, squashed them. This one had lasted longer than the rest, and he was beginning to feel the stirrings of commitment.

No stranger to obligation, it didn't bother him. But with Courtney severing what had been his longest commitment to date, wariness caused him to question if all relationships, professional or personal, were worth the risk.

It was ten-thirty when Jamie pulled up in front of the four-plex where he lived, a new building that looked like a cross between something colonial and something farmhouse with its white siding and red shutters.

His brows synched tight when he saw three large, black Ford Expeditions lined up outside. They had the tell-tale signs of being official vehicles, with quadruple antennas and darkened windows.

He parked his small truck behind the train of them, and two men in dark suits emerged, and stood next to the cars, their hands clasped. Jamie sighed. One of the tenants must be in trouble, and that annoyed him. He'd picked this place because he thought the neighborhood would be free of scum and resulting legal entanglements.

He locked his car and as he walked to the building, noticed the two men move around the black cars to the doors. He heard the doors open, shut, and as he took the stairs up to his apartment he glanced over his shoulder. A group of people was now coming his way and, even in the darkness, he could see that their faces were upturned, looking at him.

Something in their stoic, blank faces caused the hair on his neck to stand for an instant. A scene from a cheesy horror flick flashed into his mind. Nervously, he worked the key in his door, first dropping it, then snatching it up and shoving it into the lock.

The group of strangers was now on the stairs. His heart started thumping. He thrust open the door, then shut it with a relieved sigh, nearly laughing as he leaned heavily against it.

His roommate, Marcus, sat wide-eyed on the couch, doing what Jamie thought must be homework.

"Hey." Jamie pointed his thumb over his shoulder, gesturing. "Do you know who—" A pound at the door stole the rest of the words from his mouth.

"They're here for you, man," Marcus said.

"Me?" Jamie parted the mini-blinds and looked into a flash of six staring faces. "What do they want with me?"

Marcus shook his head. "They've been sitting out there for hours, dude."

"Hours?"

The pounding knock came again and Jamie stared at the doorknob. He took in a deep breath, ran his fingers through his hair and realized he was still in costume. "I've gotta change. Can you?" He gestured toward the door with a nod.

Marcus shook his head. "They're all yours." Then he got up, as if he was leaving.

"Come on." Jamie beat him to the hall. "I can't answer the door like this. Just—" He headed back toward his bedroom. "Just have them sit down and wait."

"They've been waiting, dude," Marcus called even after Jamie had disappeared. "And I don't think they like it," he mumbled as he went to the door.

Jamie stripped and tossed his costume on the bed. Pulling a white tee shirt off a hanger, he simultaneously reached for some well-worn jeans, shredded at the knees. Crazy thoughts ran through his mind. Was Courtney suing him? Did he forget to make a payment on his truck?

He heard nothing from the living room and wondered if Marcus had been killed, if these guys were Mafia-wannabe's. *I live in Utah, for crying out loud, there's no Mafia here.*

He strode to the living room with confidence.

Then he saw her. She was standing in a full-length black coat with a real fur collar in what looked to be cheetah. Her dark hair was underneath a fuzzy black hat, baring only pale skin, deep green eyes and dark, painted lips. Her companions were a mix of men and women, all dressed similarly, in long black coats, dark gloves, and hats. They were all staring at him.

"Hi," he said.

For a moment no one spoke. The woman in the center stepped toward him, her granite eyes sharpening like arrowheads. It was then that Jamie remembered seeing her in the audience at the show – and backstage afterward. Her presence had been undeniable, even as he'd danced and seen her in his side vision -- a dark form with the most ivory-stone skin he'd ever seen.

"Can I help you?" he asked.

A man with ruddy skin stepped out from behind the woman. "You are James Wilde?" His accent was as thick as stew. His black-gloved hands were out in front of his body, ready – for what, Jamie wasn't sure.

"I am." Jamie swallowed an uncomfortable knot.

Marcus stood awkwardly. "Uh, yeah… well, I'm just going to go to the back and – well…you know… be in the back."

No one, except the man who had spoken, watched Marcus leave. Nervously, Jamie shifted his feet, his cold hands squirming in his front pockets.

"May I present Her Royal Highness Anna Zakharov, Princess of the Isles of Slovokia."

Jamie looked from the ruddy-complected man to the mysterious dark goddess in front of him and his face twisted into a smirk. "You're kidding, right?"

When no one moved, he swallowed the laugh. "Is this—" He glanced around. "Is there a camera? You guys from Dancesport?"

"We are from the Isles of Slovokia," the man repeated more firmly. "And this is Princess Anna—"

"I know, you said that. But I've never heard of the place. You guys are actors, right? You're good. I mean you all look really good, you know. You've got the whole, iron-curtain-austere thing down perfectly."

When the group gasped and murmured quietly with each other, Jamie got a sinking feeling in his stomach. The woman with the intriguing eyes had not made a sound, had made no effort to interact with her companions. Slowly she took off her gloves, tugging one finger free at a time and Jamie watched with fascination. As her long, slender fingers emerged, something deep inside of him spun. His eyes lifted to hers.

Extending her hand, she stepped toward him. "I am Anna, James. I have come a long way to meet you."

This woman, the way she spoke; stiff, yet poised in her accent, the way she moved and held herself—she was no ordinary woman, and she certainly was not some actor. Whoever she was, he didn't dare touch her.

Her hand waited in the space between them.

Letting out a laugh innocently high in its pitch, he ran a nervous hand through his hair, realizing it was still slicked hard with gel.

"Uh. Well." Taking her hand, he shook it. It felt fragile in his and surprised him, as she was not a small woman. But then she wore a heavy coat and he had no idea what was underneath. He gestured to the couches. "Would you like to sit down?"

He swallowed as one of the women stepped close, readying for the Princess's coat. Anna slowly unbuttoned the coat and again, Jamie found himself watching her agile fingers. Male curiosity had him wondering what lie underneath the garment. Because the man with the ruddy cheeks was watching him intently, he didn't dare stare, no matter how curious he was.

The black continued, Jamie caught that much all the way down to tight black boots with stiletto heels. She crossed what Jamie observed was one long leg over the other, and sat primly erect.

After placing her coat and gloves in the hands of the waiting woman, she took off her hat, and shook out a cascade of thick, chestnut hair before walking to the love seat and looking at it.

"It's clean," Jamie offered on a laugh, then cleared the frog jumping in his throat. She flipped her long, dark hair over her shoulder and lowered herself onto the couch.

Jamie remained standing with everyone else.

"Anybody else want to sit?" he asked, looking into the blank faces of her companions.

"You are a wonderful dancer, James," Anna started, ignoring those left standing. He edged toward the couch, not sure if he should sit or stand. She gestured for him to sit, so he did.

"Thank you. You were at the show today?"

She nodded. Even though her head moved, her eyes never varied from their intense scrutiny of him. "It was perfect," she said simply. "You were perfect."

His face flushed, and he glanced around at the bank of expressions that made no reaction to her comment. "Thank you."

"I want to dance with you."

"You – excuse me?" Jamie almost laughed. In fact, the air was so stiff he thought he might snap in two if he didn't do something to lighten these people up. He had yet to see any of them smile.

Here was this gorgeous creature from—he couldn't even remember where she had said she was from—saying she was royalty nonetheless, asking to dance with him. It couldn't be real.

"You want to dance with me?" He started to laugh then, the moment, the incident with Courtney, all releasing into hysteria threatening to overtake him.

When she stiffened, when the ruddy-skinned man stepped toward him, flexing his gloved hands, Jamie stopped. Taking a moment to compose himself, he pounded on his chest with his fist. "You want to dance with me."

The bones in her jaw shifted. Her green eyes narrowed. "Mr. Wilde, I told you, I have come a great distance to meet you. I have studied you. I have watched you. It is with great confidence that I have chosen you."

Jamie's humorous demeanor flattened. "What do you mean you've been studying me?"

"I mean that I have made a study of the great American ballroom dance competitors. You are the one I want."

Jamie looked again into the solemn faces of her companions. "You're serious."

"Of course. I am a political emissary of sorts, James. Our country is small. We are one of the world's most exclusive tax havens, known to bankers and those anxious to protect their money. I am here to bring awareness, other than that of banking, to our country.

"Our sibling nation, Russia, has produced many excellent ballroom competitors. Ballroom dance is an interest of mine. I have been dancing since I was a young girl. I want to broaden my training base, and I want to dance with an American. You are well respected and highly anticipated in the world of International ballroom. You will be the best. So I have chosen you."

Jamie was speechless. Again, he glanced around, as if it would all poof into a smoky haze and vanish. "Uh," was all that came out of his mouth. He noticed one side of those perfectly full lips of hers curved up a little.

"It is late." She gave him a courtesy smile and stood. "I am willing to discuss this further tomorrow. We will meet at my home."

"You have a home here?"

"Yes. It is in the Provo river bottoms."

Jamie's head nodded of its own accord. Of course, the river bottoms -- it was the most exclusive area in Provo, laden with mansions, long stretches of property resting behind foreboding gates, protected by stalking Dobermans or other such killer dogs.

He stood, and watched her don her gloves, coat and hat.

"We will meet tomorrow. Noon. I will have a driver come for you."

"I'll drive myself."

"I will send a driver."

"Thanks. But I'll drive myself." Princess or not, he wasn't about to get into one of those Mafioso cars and be driven to a secret destination. He still wasn't sure that this was a hoax. Another glance around for a hidden camera left him looking back into the confused gaze of the exotic woman. "Yeah," he muttered. "I'll drive myself."

"Very well. Vladimir will give you the address." She turned then, and her posse followed her to the door. The ruddy-skinned man scribbled something on a piece of paper that appeared out of nowhere and handed it to Jamie, his expression flat.

Soon, they were all gone. Only Anna remained, standing in the doorway. She extended her gloved hand. "A pleasure to have met you, James."

The leather was cold in his hand, and disguised the fragility he'd felt earlier. When she went to pull her hand free, he held on with a light squeeze. Her eyes opened wide. A pleasant riffling dove deep in his system.

"Until tomorrow, Princess," he said, because he couldn't, for the life of him, recall her name.

2.

Anna wondered how she would hide the look of sooty thumbprints under her eyes from her restless night. Looking at her reflection in the mirror, she shook her head. This would not do. She ran her fingers along the translucency of her cheeks. American women seemed to radiate the kiss of the sun. She, on the other hand, was nothing more than the moon set against the blackest sky. She sighed.

She had not slept well because she had anticipated today – seeing James Wilde again. His face had not left her thoughts, even as she had tried to relax herself with yoga, with incense, with meditation.

It had been more nerve-wracking than any state social function she was required to attend and be charming at, standing face-to-face with him. She expected, after years of watching his taped performances, competitions, and interview pieces, that she could handle meeting him with the practiced precision that was second nature. But when he'd stood on that stage and his body had moved with such impressive grace, she knew meeting him would be a first for her.

She reminded herself that whatever image she had concocted in her head without really knowing him could be terribly inaccurate. Indeed, she had spent countless hours wondering what he was like. His level of skill had given her the idea that he was a perfectionist. Other than that, she had no idea who he really was.

Her mind conjured up someone intense, driven, and, she hoped, romantic, as most men with an interest in dancing were tuned into the finer points of life and relationships, though she warned herself not to dwell on the latter. Theirs was to be a professional relationship. First.

That he had not stopped after the show to meet her properly had been very disappointing. She'd almost demanded that Ivan and Lukov drag him back.

But she'd heard raised voices through the dressing room door, and decided it best not to interfere with his reasons for fleeing.

She'd known Reuben La Bate on sight, and after the other young woman had gone, Anna made him aware of her intentions. Unfortunately, Reuben had no control over James. This alarmed her. In her country, coaches direct the affairs of partnerships. She was surprised that Reuben said she would have to meet with Jamie before any concrete plans could be made.

Anna looked at her watch. She had ten minutes before she met with the staff for their morning meeting at eight o'clock. Ten minutes to choose something that would disguise the circles under her eyes.

She strolled to the room adjacent to her bedroom. It barely fit what wardrobe she had brought with her and she sighed at the inadequacy. They'd had to place many of her accessories in yet another bedroom down the hall. She preferred having everything close at hand.

As she slowly walked along the rows of hanging garments, she thought again of James. In her study, she'd found profuse information about his dance career – but very little about his personal life. Her father's people had done their own search of course, to make sure he would be a respectable choice. They'd preferred Thomas Corwin, from New Jersey, but Anna had chosen James Wilde for specific reasons that even her parents were not aware of.

A smile came to her lips.

She knew well what he wanted in a dance partner and was positive she could give him that. Whether she knew what he preferred in a woman or not, would not stand in her way. If she chose to do more than dance with him, then it would be as she wished.

Anna selected black dance pants that were both comfortable and slim-fitting, the hem of which flared just a little. For her top she chose a white knit shirt with a scoop neckline and long, draping sleeves.

A knock at the door alerted her to the time.

Quickly, she swiped concealer under her eyes, brushed on some blush, and pulled her hair back in a pony tail. Then she answered the door.

Her assistant, Inessa, stood like a timid mouse, her gray eyes lowered behind silver-rimmed glasses. Her black notebook was clutched to her chest. She wore the only thing Anna ever saw her wear; an outfit in head-to-toe grey, with school-girl knee highs, pleated skirt and a cardigan sweater.

"We're ready for you, Princess Anna."

Jamie was relieved to see Reuben's car when he drove down the quarter-mile U-shaped drive to the front of the mansion. He hadn't even looked at the address the ruddy-faced man had given him last night. There was only one house it could be.

It sat like a castle of sorts, smack in the middle of the prestigious neighborhood. A stone arch at the head of the drive towered over his car as he drove past black, wrought iron gates already open for him.

Jamie let out an appreciative whistle. The structure was slate-colored, like a tumultuous storm reflected on the stone walls. Shaped like an H, the wings sprawled east and west. Long narrow windows, each crowned with a lion's head in the upper casing, lined the first and second floors. It looked to be centuries old, even though it was not.

A skittering thrill shot through Jamie and pooled in his stomach.

After he knocked, the front door was opened by one of the men he had seen the night before. The bruiser was dressed in a simple black suit. He wore an earpiece with a wire that disappeared underneath his shirt collar. The large man looked like he might moonlight on the football field.

He stepped aside so Jamie could enter, and touched his ear piece. "Mr. Wilde has arrived." His bullets-for-eyes pinned Jamie. "Follow me, please."

Keeping a fair distance behind the big man, Jamie openly admired the house. The entry was the size of his parents' entire main floor. Tall windows showcased the endless grounds at the back of the property.

Their shoes tapped on tiles inlaid in an Italian design much like a detailed, colorful mosaic. Various gold and crystal chandeliers hung scattered overhead, Jamie noted, as one fixture would not have been enough to light the entire expanse of the room. The chilly air was scented with an exotic spice mix Jamie didn't recognize off hand.

When the big man saw that Jamie was lagging, he slowed. "This way, please," his tone was lined with impatience and Jamie quickly picked up his step as they crossed the area toward two floor-to-ceiling doors from behind which he heard voices.

The big man paused by the outside of the door. Jamie was sure the bodyguard was trying to remind him of their comparative sizes. Then he opened the doors and Jamie was allowed to go in.

The room was large and empty with the exception of a few scattered chairs and a massive stereo system in one corner. Reuben stood in the center, with the princess, dressed in black and white. The other large man, the bookend to the one looming behind Jamie's shoulder, stood flanking the other side of the door.

Reuben's neon grin shot across the room but he remained with the princess. The big man that had escorted Jamie gestured toward her, and Jamie's heart fluttered a little as he strode across the hardwood floor, his feet barely making a sound.

He had thrown on nicer jeans, ones without shredded knees, and a turtleneck sweater in a burnt brown shade he had been told by more than one woman made his dark eyes stand out. Because he felt instinctively comfortable with Reuben, he looked directly at him, and shook his hand.

"Good to see you, bro," Reuben said.

"I didn't know you were coming." Jamie felt the princess scanning him. His armpits began to sweat.

"Yeah, well." Reuben was nervous too, Jamie could tell. He only rubbed his naked head when he was angry, frustrated, or nervous, and he had both hands going at it that very moment. "Anna and I needed to work some things out." Reuben looked from Jamie to the princess.

"Hello, James." Anna tilted her head and extended her hand. "So glad you could join us."

Even more nervous now that she was addressing him, Jamie took her hand. "No problem, Anna." At least now he knew her name. He glanced around the room for a clock. Not finding one, he looked at his watch. "I'm not late."

"No," Anna said, "you are not. We are here now, all of us. Let us begin."

She passed between the two of them and floated toward the chairs, her black dance pants outlining what Jamie thought was a pretty perfect shape. A petite woman in knee socks and glasses instantly stood and vacated one of three chairs, making room.

Anna turned, gesturing toward the seats. "Gentlemen, please."

Both Reuben and Jamie joined her but neither would sit as long as the timid little woman stood nearby. Jamie's brows lifted in question to the woman who merely backed away subserviently, her gaze on the floor.

Without looking at the woman Anna said, "Please be seated, James. Reuben."

After Anna was seated, both men reluctantly sat.

"Where I am from, coaches supervise partnerships." Her voice was deep and rich, like devil's food cake, Jamie thought. "Partners have little to say when it comes to scheduling, arranging competitions, touring, living accommodations, costuming, etc."

Jamie shifted.

"I would like us to rehearse every day, from eight until five," Anna continued. "If necessary, we will work into the evenings. I would like us to prepare for the national and world competitions and disregard anything less prestigious for the time being. Since Latin is your specialty, I would like to focus on those dances. Reuben will be our sole coach, unless I feel that his work is not sufficient. In which case, I will send for Vladimir. I am sure you have heard of him?" She barely paused for Jamie's nod. "But I am sure Mr. La Bate will exceed my expectations.

"Because we will be training so rigorously, I have made room for you in the west wing, Jamie, so the issue of availability will be extinguished. I—"

"Hold on a minute." Jamie sat forward, his hands twitching. He forced himself not to laugh. "I don't mean to be rude, miss – er – Your—"

"Anna. Please, continue."

"Anna. I don't think this is going to work." He looked at her soberly. "I'm sorry."

"Pardon me?"

Jamie sat in awe and fascination at her control, at her demands. "I have students that I teach. That's how I make a living. I can't bag them just because some princess – because you want me to dance with you."

"I am offering you an opportunity, James."

"And it sounds like a great opportunity…for somebody." He looked at Reuben. "Did you agree to this?"

Reuben bit his lip as if keeping a smile at bay. He ran his hands over his head without answering.

"These kids depend on me," Jamie told her, "just like I depend on Reuben. I can't leave them hanging."

"Unfortunately, some sacrifices would have to be made," she said calmly. "There wouldn't be enough time for you to teach and dance to my specifications. However, I am perfectly willing to compensate you for the loss."

Again, Jamie looked at Reuben. "Does she—" he faced Anna, "do you know how much that would cost? We make good money teaching privates."

With the tiniest nod, the hard line in Anna's lips softened. "Yes, I know. I told you, I have been studying you."

Jamie's face pinched with wariness. "Even if I said yes, I'd never agree to a long- term training schedule like you're suggesting."

"Why not?"

"Look, Anna, it's obvious to me that we have different ideas about this. I know how your people practice – like robots. I've seen them." He didn't bother to stop when he saw her stiffen. "And where I agree there needs to be strict discipline in rehearsing, I'm not about to live and breathe it twenty-four-seven." The muscle in her jaw flexed but Jamie bowled on. "Bottom line – I don't want to hate what I do at the end of the day."

Reuben leaned toward him. "I think there's a compromise that could be made here. Consider what she is offering before you jump off."

Jamie looked at Reuben with disbelief. After a sigh, he turned back to Anna. Her expression was like stormy waters under a thick layer of transparent ice. "Go on," he told her.

"There is only one goal, James," she began, her tone frosty, "and that is to be the best. Being the best requires hours of work—"

"I know what it requires," he said, defenses perking up. He knew all about the aching muscles, the music pounding in your consciousness long after rehearsal was over. He'd worked through sickness, through blisters and sprains. More than that, he'd given up everything else; enough time with his family, a social life, and where had it gotten him? Plenty of first place titles, but he'd just been dumped by his partner. He knew the perfect circle could easily be broken, leaving you with a career-altering disaster.

"I'm sorry," she said just as coolly as she had delivered the other speech. "I thought we had the same drive, the same ambition, the same—" She stopped when Jamie stood. He looked down at her.

"I get where you're going with that, and don't do it." He rarely got angry, having learned to control himself with four testy siblings. But his anger knew no bounds when it came to the perfection of his craft. "I have just as much drive and ambition as – well, more than the next guy. Isn't that why you chose me, Your Highness?"

Like mercury in a thermometer, she rose so they were face-to-face. "I am sorry to have made you angry, James. My intention was only to discuss—"

"Only you weren't discussing, you were telling me how it was going to be."

"I, like you, have very distinct ideas about things. Would you like some refreshment?"

Refreshment? Jamie tried to laugh but it caught in his throat. "No. Thanks but, no. You said you studied me. But if you had, you would know that I like to do things my way. I dictate the partnership. It's the way I work. It's gotten me where I am today, and—"

"And that is currently without a partner, is it not?" Anna added.

Jamie took the opportunity to glare. She had spunk. She wouldn't bend like Courtney had. He wasn't sure what he'd expected from a princess, but that firm line of imperialism in her brow hinted that she was dead serious about all of this.

Then there was Reuben. What kind of deal had she arranged with him? That Reuben sat there without jumping to his defense, his fingertips pressed so tight his black skin was turning white at the joints, bothered him.

"You know, I don't dance with just anybody," Jamie began testily, "no offense. I know you're not just anybody in a very real sense of the word. But you've never competed. How do I know you're any—" He stopped himself before he completely insulted her and let out a sigh. "How do you know we would be a good match?"

"I would not have bought this house, moved my staff thousands of miles, if I had not taken you under serious consideration."

The whole idea of being studied and scrutinized bugged him. What, had she flown to a few competitions, followed his career in the trades?

It was he who studied her then, looking openly, brazenly, into her eyes in search of something he wasn't sure of, but had its roots in security and trust. If she'd indeed checked him out, he figured he deserved something similar, a confirmation in his gut at least.

Without warning, he moved himself next to her. Her two bodyguards stepped closer. He ignored them. His chest brushed hers. Along his abdomen, his pelvis, his knees, he felt the tantalizing curves and planes of woman. It pleased him that her eyes opened like a kaleidoscope, and for a moment, emotion flickered there; excitement, wonder, desire, mingling and shifting, coloring her pale skin with a blush. He waited to see what she would do. She didn't move.

Her lips parted and his gaze lowered.

"What are you doing?" she asked. It came out a mere whisper that made Jamie smile.

"Seeing how we fit together." Slipping one arm around her waist, his other deftly scooped her hand, holding it up and out in standard dance position. With the jerk of his right wrist, he pressed against the small of her back and she was flat against him. The left side of his lip curved. Purposefully, he let his gaze roam her with a teasing spark. "I guess you'll do."

Her mouth fell open. Jamie grinned before releasing her and moving back. Out of the corner of his eye, he saw that both of the big men standing by the door had moved considerably closer.

"You have your test Mr. Wilde." Her brow lifted. "I have mine." Like an exotic cat she slithered to the center of the room, turned and stood with her arms out as if expecting him. "Come."

Jamie's teeth grazed his lower lip. The word shot a bolt of heat to his gut. His heart stammered, but he didn't move.

"Come," she repeated.

Willing his feet to move, he crossed to her.

"Shall we Tango?" Anna asked, her body perfectly still in his arms.

"I thought you wanted to concentrate on Latin," Jamie said wryly.

"Tango's standard."

"I'm aware of that. But Tango is what I want – international Tango."

"Yes Ma'am. Rather, yes, Your Highness."

Jamie's hands took command of hers. He felt more strength there than he ever had with Courtney. This was a woman not used to being controlled, at least not on the dance floor.

They started to the left, stepping in unison. She took the turns he pushed at her with her head erect and her body poised. The hard length of her thighs brushed his in and out, in and out, as they strode together. Because the tango was a dance where their stance was hip-to-hip rather than breast-to-chest, he held her in tight -- and felt her resist.

"You're resisting me."

"Your grip is too firm."

"My grip is fine. You need to submit."

"You need to give."

Pulling her in more tightly than he normally would, he meant to make a point. She narrowed her eyes at him. Then she broke their grip and pressed her palms against his chest and pushed. Because he let her go, she stumbled back, and both of the men in suits, the woman in glasses, lunged her direction. Anna held up a palm to stop them, but her eyes remained locked on Jamie.

"Perhaps we are not meant to dance together after all," she said levelly.

Jamie nodded. Flicking out his arms and hands, he turned, and crossed to Reuben. With a shake to Reuben's hand he said, "Call me." Then he began the long walk across the wood floor to the door.

"Where are you going, Mr. Wilde?" Anna demanded.

As he neared the door, the two burly men blocked it, their bodies like boulders. Jamie broke into an amused smile. He turned around, looked at her. "Tell your sumo friends to move, please."

Anna crossed toward him as if she owned all of the time in the world.

"Point taken." She stopped just out of reach. She still had that air of royal pride that dug at him, and ate at him—and baited him.

He kept his jaw set hard, pondering his next move. She was challenging him blatantly, and he liked it. "We do it my way," he said.

"Very well."

When he took a step toward her, she didn't retreat. "And I am not living here."

"But, I—"

"I want my privacy," he said. "Fifty – fifty of any earnings."

"You may have all of the earnings. Money is not my concern."

"Then give yours to one of your orphanages."

"We don't have orphanages in my country." He was within inches of her and still, she had not moved. "I am willing to compensate you," she said.

"Yeah?" They stood face-to-face, and his grin broadened. "Sounds good, but I refuse free room and board."

"A mistake."

He shook his head. "Our personal lives can't touch our professional lives. It's a rule I live by." For a moment, her eyes flickered with something he couldn't read.

"Since you refuse my offer of room and board, a common condition for most partnerships—"

"It's not common when one partner is royalty."

"You are telling me that if I were any other person, you would accept my offer?"

"No." His gaze fluttered over her face.

 "My offer will be four thousand dollars a month."

Letting out a laugh he turned as if ready to leave. "I could work at Mc Donald's flipping burgers for that much."

"For eight thousand dollars a month you could take my offer in full."

He whipped back around. "You'd pay me an extra four just to live here?"

"You misunderstand, James—"

"It's Jamie."

"You misunderstand. Your being here would be a convenience."

He laughed. "A convenience? I'll take seven, for being your partner, on my terms, and living in my own space."

Anna extended her hand. It was then that she gave him the first full smile he had seen on her face. It made him think of a brilliant moon, finally free from the prison of shrouding clouds. He couldn't stop his hand if he wanted to; he reached for hers with the willingness of a boy enchanted by the moon's light. Hers was warm, and he decided the fit was just right.

3.

There were a good many things Anna could waste. Money was the easiest. She loved to shop, to clothe her body in the latest, finest designer-wear from Paris or Italy.

Pampering was another place Anna's money easily disappeared. Daily massages, weekly pedicures and manicures, spa days. All of it was worthy of her family's currency. She indulged in whatever she pleased, whenever she pleased.

Paying Jamie was not a waste money but part of her plan. Anna knew expertise and skill carried a high price tag. She was willing to pay it.

Time was not something Anna would ever waste. Indeed, she preferred nothing more than to have every hour of every day filled.

She insisted they begin training that very day.

Reuben was like a wound-up toy. His energy and enthusiasm took Anna aback, so accustomed she was to the more evenly meted direction of her Russian coaches who ticked like the minute hand of a clock. Reuben was like the second hand.

Jamie too, was tireless. She wasn't surprised.

Pleased with the way their initial work was going, she was not at all annoyed when Reuben's cell phone rang. He excused himself to answer it.

Anna stole the moment to make idle conversation with Jamie, who was going over more advanced steps of samba and rumba. Her heart fluttered as she approached him. The years she had spent studying him through videos and whatever else she could get her hands on had made him something of an enigma in her mind. She intended to change that.

"You pick up quickly, James." Flattery was one of the oldest tricks in the book. In her experience, men devoured it.

He stopped dancing and looked at her. The hair around his face hung in clumps, wet at the tips. Every sharp line and angle in his arms and chest protruded through the wet tee shirt clinging to him.

"I've been at it a long time," he said.

"It shows. Can I tell you again how pleased I am that we will be dancing together?"

She thought she saw vacillation in his eyes, in his body language. He set his hands on his hips. "Well, hopefully it will work out." There would be no hopefully about it, Anna decided. But she nodded agreeably and glanced at Reuben, still on the phone.

Irritation furrowed her brow; Jamie caught it as she watched Reuben. He meant to distract her, do some idle conversing with a princess. "How long did you say you've been dancing?"

"Since I was a young girl. But I have only been instructed in ballroom dance for four years."

"And you've never competed?"

She shook her head. "It has only been recently that I decided I want to compete."

She was still eyeing Reuben, her irritation growing. Jamie wiped at his brow with his forearm and kept talking. "Can we get some water in here?" he asked.

"Yes, of course." Anna called to the woman with the spectacles who had not moved from her seat through the rehearsal. "Inessa, bring us some Evian."

Jamie watched the young woman go, noticing that the two suited men remained by the doors, like imported ceramic bulldogs. "Those guys ever leave you alone?" he asked.

"I don't even notice them." She didn't glance over. "I am so sorry to have neglected your refreshment. I will have water brought in whenever you wish."

Jamie walked, trying to cool off and keep from being faced with the awkwardness of silence with a stranger.

Sneaking a glance at Anna, he wondered what she was like. So far, he knew that she liked to wear black, she had picked him and Reuben, Utah and America, to begin a career in competitive ballroom dance, and she was a lot better dancer than he had expected her to be.

She was a princess. The very idea of it still seemed outrageous. It wasn't as though she didn't fit the bill. She was regal, refined, and seemed to have everyone around her at her beck and call. That she had picked him, an average guy from Provo, was what didn't fit the storybook.

Inessa scurried across the wood floor to them, and Jamie smiled at her, thanking her for the chilled bottle.

"Who is she?" he asked Anna, then he put the bottle to his lips and drank the entire bottle in one long drink.

Anna's eyes widened, watching him swallow the entire bottle. "She's my assistant."

Looking at the young woman across the room, Jamie asked, "How long has she worked for you?"

"Many years. Her mother worked for my mother. They come from a selvikian family."

"A what?"

"A family whose life is spent in the service of the monarchy. It has been so for generations, with each following in the footsteps of the previous generation."

"Huh." Jamie looked at the young woman, hidden behind silver-rimmed glasses; her legs primly crossed at the ankles, and thought she looked like a school girl. "How old is she?"

Anna's tone was threaded with boredom. "Nineteen."

"She's so young."

Anna sighed to show her growing irritation, purposefully looking over at Reuben. Until Jamie strolled over to Inessa and sat himself down right next to her -- then her eyes were locked on him.

He extended his hand to the girl. "I'm Jamie."

The young girl's face blanched white and she kept it lowered. Jamie took Inessa's hand and placed it in his before he shook it with a light chuckle. "Hey, I won't bite."

A smile crept on her lips. "I am Inessa."

"So. Inessa, you like the States?"

"I like them very much, sir."

As if they had known each other for weeks instead of moments, Jamie put his hand on her shoulder. "You can relax, Inessa. In America we're very relaxed, okay?" He gave her shoulder a quick tap, waiting until she looked at him.

After she had, he rose and returned to Anna, who suppressed the urge to lift her brow in displeasure.

Reuben finished his conversation and jogged back across the floor.

Anna couldn't say which set her off, Reuben's lengthy conversation or Jamie's friendly visit with Inessa, but her displeasure had ripened; and she meant to show it. She stood statue-still, chin lifted. "Perhaps we should refrain from personal calls during rehearsal. I think that would be appropriate."

Both Reuben and Jamie looked at each other, then at her. "I have a wife and two kids and they aren't going to make it through one day, let alone three hundred and sixty-five without talking to me at least four to six times – each." Reuben told her.

Anna blinked. "You are joking with me, are you not?"

Reuben laughed then, and it filled the room with its round heartiness. "That's no lie, sis."

"And what about you Jamie?"

"That's why they have voice mail." Jamie tilted his head, gesturing toward the chair where his duffle and phone sat. Anna wanted to ask him if he had anyone significant that would be calling and interrupting their rehearsal sessions, but refrained.

"We must work on that combination we were going over before your phone call, Reuben. Show it to me again."

Slowly counting out the steps, Reuben demonstrated the short combination of steps that Anna thought twisted her feet into a pretzel. Jamie stood watching and the critical heat of his gaze forced her determination.

"Try it this way," Jamie interjected. He stood on her other side and counted out the steps, moving slowly. "Think of it as a two-count with a shuffle first."

Still, her feet would not do as she wished. Her body became tight with frustration, bound by pride. Stiffening, she walked away, giving them her back. When her perturbed gaze landed on Inessa, she strode over to the wide-eyed girl with purpose in her step.

"You may wait outside for me, Inessa. Thank you." Inessa nodded, gathered her clipboard to her chest and quickly exited.

Tight as the face of a drum, Ann circled aimlessly, shaking her head.

When she caught sight of the two men standing at the door and her fists hardened at her sides. "Out, both of you!"

The bodyguards silently vacated the room, leaving only the sound of her angry breath.

Reuben clapped his hands twice, his sign that it was time to get on with things. "Now that we've gotten rid of our audience, let's get to work. Anna?"

She still hadn't stopped, and she didn't look like she was going to. If she'd been Courtney, Jamie would have jumped on her case like a monkey on her back. But they barely knew each other, and the restraint of novelty kept him in check. He could see that, princess or not, Reuben was not changing his crack-the-whip style.

"Starting positions."

"No." Anna's voice was still in shout-mode. "I will work this combination until I get the feet."

Calmly, Reuben approached her. "It's just us here. We're in this together now, remember?" He waited for her to look at him.

As she shifted her eyes to Reuben's, Jamie saw the stark-grey in her gaze soften. She nodded and joined Jamie without looking at him.

"And let's try it with some music." Reuben danced across the floor, his exuberant spirit instantly lifting the mood in the room. "My choice." He shot them both a gleaming grin meant to relax.

Jamie faced Anna, but she kept her gaze just over his shoulder. She looked more like she had taken a leisurely stroll than just danced for four hours. Her hands were dry, her face morning-fresh, and not one stain of sweat darkened her white shirt. And he was as wet as if he'd stepped out of the shower fully clothed.

"You are staring at me," she said, her gaze still off.

"Yeah." He shrugged, smiled. "Just getting familiar with my new partner." He liked the way she lifted her chin, feisty-like. "You run a tight ship here, Your Highness."

"I only require what is necessary."

"And scare the heck out of everybody in the process?" He felt her grip harden. She slanted him a look.

Hissing cymbals sounded the start of the music. Reuben clapped loudly, began calling out the steps. "And one and two, three and four, come in together, tight – tighter. Yes. And three and four."

Jamie liked the way she felt against him. Their heights were complimentary, as if they had been created with each other in mind. To make the most of the sensual illusions in dance, Jamie knew two bodies had to look made for each other. Two halves an audience waited to see come together in perfect unison.

Whatever was inside of her that gave her regal importance, she brought to dance. Jamie felt it fighting him. He didn't mind. It would bring sizzle to their routines that he'd had to artificially create with Courtney, and even then, it had been one-sided. With Anna, the opposition came naturally from the very royal blood flowing through her veins. As if she refused to be possessed or owned by anyone.

Maybe it was the rousing Latin beat that caused his blood to stir, he wasn't sure, but the electricity between them was igniting the air. He wanted to push, to see just how hard he could. Her hands stayed strong, her arms without give, and when the dance ended, the only thing either of them had given was rough breath as it heaved in and out of them both.

Jamie was drenched. He stood looking at her – amazed. She hadn't slowed at all during the practice, and she'd taken every one of his cues as if they had been partners for months. She had kept up with him beautifully; she knew it, was flaunting it in fact, that chin lifting as she zigzagged across from him.

He swallowed the bitterness of pride. He hadn't expected such a performance so quickly. Shock value – she'd used it well. It was something all competitors used to snag the judge's attention and win an audience.

The dance floor was meant to make partners equal, at least to appear equal. But Jamie wasn't ashamed to admit that he preferred owning the floor in his partnerships.

Because he felt challenged, he meant to wear her down. If he couldn't, he'd make a good try of it.

"Again," he said.

The command stopped her, but he didn't catch even the slightest annoyance or hesitation. In fact, the tilt to her head told him she was more than ready to go the distance.

"It's seven o'clock," Reuben said.

"You can go," he told Reuben without taking his eyes from Anna. Then he slowly crossed to her. "She and I will stay and work on it."

Reuben jogged back to the music. "From the top, then."

At this, Anna cocked her head with an amused grin. He matched it with his own. "You're not too tired are you, princess?"

"Of course not." She extended her arms.

He imagined she was a woman used to getting her way. Well, wouldn't this be interesting, he thought, staring down into her eyes.

Over and over he pushed them through the steps, and the hour ticked by. He couldn't believe her tenacity. She'd barely broken into a sweat by the time his patience had worn thin. She was going through the motions professionally – and, as he expected, robotically. She was too stiff and without the emotion needed for Latin. He wanted something human from her.

It was just the imperfection he needed.

"You need to relax, Your Highness."

"I am relaxed."

"You feel like the trunk of a tree."

She cocked her head at him. "Pardon me?"

"A broom, a board, whatever – there's not enough give in your body. There's no passion on your face. Doesn't the music make you feel it?" It pleased him that he'd sent a wrinkle of concern down the middle of her brows.

"Anna." Following their every move, Reuben shook his head. "The steps are perfect but you're too stiff. Think flow, think movement under water."

When Jamie felt her go rigid he said, "It's okay to be corrected."

"I do not mind it coming from Reuben."

He twirled her out, then snapped her back in. "You just don't like it from me?"

"You are not my coach."

He laughed. "I see."

Reuben jogged across the floor to turn off the music.

Jamie looked at her neck, at the flush of pink, and sweat. Her palms had finally moistened in his. Perspiration softened the hair around her face. "Ah, so the princess sweats at last." Her eyes flashed to his. "It's okay to sweat, Anna. In fact, they have floor sweepers at competitions for that very reason. We're human. That's why people watch competition. They come to see the perfect romantic interpretation of one of human nature's most important refinements – dance."

As if his words both pleased and surprised her, she angled her head at him. "Very well put."

He was only momentarily flattered, pressing on to more important issues. "Because of that, the passion has to be there, in the movements, on the face. It's a show."

Reuben let out a sigh. "Jamie's right. You've got the steps, but the passion behind them is what makes dance captivating and beautiful to watch."

"Very well. I will work on that. We will try it again." She readied for Jamie who scratched his head on a laugh.

Satisfied that she was indeed human, and that she knew she wasn't going to stroll into a championship partnership without some sweat and humbling, he was ready to call it a night. "Let's save it until tomorrow," he told her.

"No. I insist."

Jamie and Reuben looked at each other. Jamie appreciated why she didn't want to end a day's practice on anything less than a perfect note. He took position again.

With more determination, he took them through the dances. Cha-cha flowed, even their timing was good. Rumba and samba still begged for emotion and feeling that he couldn't find anywhere on her face. She stepped on his foot during paso dobles. And jive finally drained them both, leaving them gulping for air, swiping at sweaty skin.

Jamie watched her circle. He'd never have to coax her to work, that was obvious. In fact, the only coaxing he'd have to do would be to get her to stop. Even as their breath evened, he could tell by the way she looked at him, with challenge in her eyes; she still had plenty of fire left inside to keep going. If it weren't for his own muscles starting to weep, he'd have kept pushing, just to see how long it took for her to drop. "We don't have to do this, Your Highness," he told her.

Still, she showed no signs of exhaustion. When she firmly shook her head, he knew they were far from done. "But you take your time catching your breath, Jamie."

He wanted to roll his eyes. Fine. If an endurance race was what she wanted, he'd give it to her. They were laying down laws at that very moment. Indeed, he thought she looked completely unfazed by any exertion as she crossed the room to where her bottle of water sat on an empty chair.

Reuben shook his head once, his face taut with thought. "Whew, she's—"

"Fiery, I know." Jamie and Reuben stood shoulder-to-shoulder. "Do you think we can work together?"

"Do you?"

Jamie shrugged. "Skill's there." He swiped the hem of his shirt across his face, watching her primly drink. "Passion's not."

"Doesn't surprise me – given where she's coming from."

"Think it's in her?"

They both eyed her as she delicately patted the back of her wrist to her mouth after drinking.

"Don't know," Reuben said. "We can try."

Both men watched her nimbly tuck stray hairs into place. She had such elegance, Jamie thought, her body simply oozed it. She was almost too untouchable.

"Can you take it?" Reuben asked. Jamie's eyes narrowed but Reuben continued, "I know you're a racehorse, bro. But this kind of demand, day after day can break a man."

Jamie's gaze was fastened on Anna. "Only one of us needs to be broken. How do we look?"

Reuben's smile spread like liquid satisfaction. "Hot."

4.

After Reuben had gone, Jamie and Anna stood alone in the empty room. The windows had been flung open to allow the winter air in. Night had come without notice.

Anna crossed to the music system. Jamie knew dancers walked with grace, but the way she floated over the floor was unlike anything he'd ever seen. He wondered if they taught all royalty that to touch even the floor, was beneath them.

Feeling the first pangs of hunger accompany bone-deep fatigue, he thought about Reuben's comment. If she insisted that they keep a schedule like the one they'd had today, he'd be dead in a week. He wouldn't allow it.

His shirt was hopelessly wet. He wanted to shower, to eat and veg. Because he figured they were finished, he peeled off the drenched tee shirt. The cool air of winter that had eluded him during rehearsal now skimmed his bare skin. His head fell back with pleasurable sigh.

He opened his eyes, shook out his hair and found Anna across the room, staring at him. For a long moment, she didn't say anything.

"It went well today, don't you think?" she finally asked.

Reaching over to where his turtleneck sweater had been flung earlier, he plucked it up with a shrug. "We can do better." Too hot to pull the sweater overhead, he held it bunched in both hands and tentatively crossed to her. "You'll get it down in no time."

"So it had nothing to do with you, is that what you are saying?"

It amused him that she was still uptight. He shrugged, but confidence rode his shoulders. "Well, it wasn't me."

Her eyes narrowed. She went around him and started toward the doors.

"Come on, Anna." They walked shoulder-to-shoulder. "You can't be hard on yourself. It was only our first day."

She came to an abrupt halt at the closed doors. His scent filled her head: sweat, soap and man. He wore confidence in a teasing smile, blocking the doors with his exquisitely cut body. The sight almost stole the anger she was enjoying.

"If I do not demand perfection from myself," she stammered, "I cannot expect it from others."

"Fine, I agree in fact," he said. "Just be real about it. Give yourself some time."

Angling her head with displeasure, she said, "You are right." Another phrase that rarely left her lips and it surprised her that she'd been moved to say it.

As he played with the sweater in his hands, his pectorals shifted, catching her eyes. The skin on his chest was smooth, still glistening with the sheen of perspiration. A tight flutter broke loose low within her.

As if he didn't notice, or didn't care that she'd stared blatantly at him, he opened the bottom of the sweater to slip it over his head. "So, want to go grab some dinner?" After he pulled it on, he ran his fingers through his hair, leaving the unruly waves dangling temptingly around his face.

"We have arrangements to make."

"Fine, let's make them over dinner."

She took the opportunity to open the door, forcing him to move aside. "Arrangements must be made, James."

His stomach growled in protest. "Aren't you hungry?" Her feet barely whispered as she crossed the tile floor with him following. She shook her head. "Well I'm going to turn into a bear if I don't get something fast."

She opened the two doors simultaneously, but he broke her smooth entrance by snagging her elbow. "First, we eat," he insisted.

She covered her shock at the deliberate contact by glancing down at his stomach with a frown. She wasn't accustomed to putting needs before duty. "I will have something brought in if you'd like. Cook can make anything you wish."

"Oh. Well, I guess that'll work."

Anna didn't have to look very far to find Inessa standing dutifully nearby. "Inessa, have cook prepare something for James, please."

Jamie's face contorted into a humorous grin. "You have a cook? You're serious?"

"Just tell her what you'd like." Anna moved behind a wide, mahogany desk without further interest in the subject and began searching through some papers.

"Wow. Okay. How about a peanut butter sandwich on wheat?"

Pausing from the stack of papers she was gathering, Anna looked up. "That is what you would like to eat?"

"Yeah." He fell easily into one of the fat wing-chairs facing her desk but shifted when he realized they wouldn't be comfortable.

Inessa nodded and disappeared out a nearby door.

Jamie wanted to close his eyes, but didn't dare. Anna was still perky, and he was determined to at least make a show of it, even if his body wanted to fold.

They hadn't been followed by anyone into the office, he noted. "Where are Mutt and Jeff?" he asked.

She looked up from the papers on her desk. "Who?"

"Your bodyguards."

Shrugging, she looked back down.

"It really doesn't bother you to have all of these people breathing down your neck every hour of every day?"

"You may look through these papers as you eat, James." She came around the desk and handed him the small stack.

He wilted. "I'll be here all night – what is this?" When he looked up at her, he saw a ghost of a smile on her face.

"Had you accepted my first offer," she began steadily, "your bed, your shower, your reprieve – would be a mere few feet away."

Jamie snatched the pen from her hand. Thumbing through the papers, he skimmed the print – something about his employment being paid in weekly installments, taxes and any other claims to be his responsibility. That he not disclose the arrangement with any other parties without written consent as given by King Nicholas Zakharov or said other.

"Zakharov, huh?" He looked up at her, as if to see for himself that she really existed.

She sat on the corner of the desk in what he thought was a rather casual move for a princess, and nodded, but with the tiniest of smiles, and he resumed scanning the paperwork. The last page was a confidentiality agreement. He was not to disclose to the press, any government or other political leaders, any confidences concerning his association with the Zakharov family in any way. If he was to break the agreement, he would lose any outstanding monies owed him as well as face punishment for said crime as per Slovokian law.

"Hold it." He shoved the end of the pen between his teeth. "What's this punishment by law clause?"

"This is standard in my country."

"Standard or not, I don't want to wake up one day in some castle dungeon in stocks. Or worse." Half grinning, he studied her. "Who's idea was all this, anyway?"

"All what?"

"This contract – America – me, thing." Setting the papers on her desk, he sat forward, elbows on his knees, fingers playing absently with each other.

"Mine." She stood, then walked around to the back of the desk. "I told you, my country would like to broaden its social base. We would like to be seen as something other than the sixth choice for overseas investment opportunities."

"And ballroom will do this because…"

"Because dance is one of the oldest forms of entertainment, is it not? Both socially and for spectating."

"There's no such word as spectating, Your Highness."

She grinned. He rose, and stood across from her, still curious. His eyes flicked over her face. "So what do I call you, anyway?"

"Anyway is not a name, James."

"It's Jamie."

"Is Jamie your given name?"

"No, it's James."

"James suits you. It is strong, masculine."

His smile deepened. "It's Jamie. Is Anna your given name, or is it Princess?"

He had her smiling again and it filled the hunger he felt inside.

She shook her head. "Annika."

A quirked expression lit his face. "Annika? Like Annika Skywalker?"

She frowned. "I think not."

"You refrain from calling me James, and I'll make sure not to call you Annika, how's that?"

The faintest blush colored her cheeks. She snatched the papers and lightly shoved them his direction. "Anna will be fine, Jamie."

Taking the papers, Jamie turned and sat back down just as Inessa quietly snuck in with a plate. Jamie stood again. "Thank you, Nessa. Wow, look at this." Wispy greenery garnished a three-tiered sandwich and an assortment of fruit ready, Jamie thought, to be the focus of a study in oil painting.

Inessa's face turned strawberry-red, her lashes batted; she lowered her eyes and backed away.

"Would you like something to drink, Jamie?" Anna asked.

He had the first bite in his mouth before he'd even sat back down. He shook his head. "This is probably the best peanut butter sandwich I've ever eaten. And what are these? Figs?"

Anna nodded, hiding amusement at his obvious enjoyment of such a simple meal before turning to her assistant. "Inessa, have cook prepare a lightly blackened chicken salad for me please, with watercress and couscous. No tomatoes."

Inessa bowed slightly before turning and leaving the room as quiet as a whisper.

"The princess eats. That's good. I was beginning to worry about your source of fuel."

Anna couldn't help the smile that kept creeping onto her lips. She had not known he had such a charming way about him. Investigations never list such things.

Because he was eating and reading, she took the opportunity to look at him. He reminded her of one of her father's beautiful Ingebred stallions. His dark hair was thick, with the luster of the sable fur on Persius, the only horse she rode. She had felt the strength in his body when they danced. But it was more than that. His disposition was strong, yet willing, teachable yet, she had a feeling there were certain things, as ingrained in the Ingebred that in Jamie no one would ever change.

She liked the warm brown of his eyes; colored with expression that changed with the ease and regularity of the emotions and humor he wore so openly.

The rehearsal had not been disappointing. He was everything she knew he would be. That they would achieve the perfection she envisioned for them would be a natural result of what she now knew was going to be an ideal partnership.

He would be just as tough as she. They would battle, but the opposition would only last until he realized that her way was the best way. That her way was the only way.

He looked up at her and her mind simply stopped working.

"Everything okay?" he asked after an awkward moment.

She stood and adjusted her clothing. "Yes, of course." She was relieved when Inessa came back through the door with a large bowl filled with colorful greens and seared chicken.

Glancing briefly at Jamie, Inessa smiled, handing Anna the bowl. "May I get you anything else, Jamie?" she asked.

Jamie's plate looked as though it had already been washed clean. He grinned and handed it to Inessa who blushed as it passed into her hands. "No. That was great. Thank you."

Anna's brows barely synched. "Thank you, Inessa." She gestured with a tilt of her head for Inessa to leave and the young girl did, shutting the door behind her. "Let us discuss scheduling."

Jamie stood, stretched. "You eat first." He looked at the fire so invitingly leaping in its chamber, and crossed to it.

Anna didn't touch her food. Setting bowl on the desk, she moved closer to Jamie and the fire. "We should practice eight hours each day. We can take a break for lunch at one. Then—"

"Anna, look." Jamie turned to her. The flame warmed the color of his face, danced in his eyes, lit the tips of his hair to gold. "I know you've been used to doing things a certain way but that kind of grind is just not necessary."

"To win national and international competition's it is."

"And how many of those do you have to your name, Anna?" When she turned her gaze to the flames and didn't reply, he said, "I have many. And I didn't earn them all by killing myself along the way. We can have them. But we can still allow time for life."

She looked at him, saw kindness on his face. He couldn't possibly understand how important all of this was to her, how many years she had spent planning. It was more important than winning would be. "This is my life. This is what I want."

He touched her arm lightly and though she had been in his arms, dancing, this touch was as if one of the flames had reached out and burned her. "And we will have it," he said.

"What in your life is more important than dance?" she asked.

For a moment he looked disbelievingly at her. His hand slid back to his side." How about a million other things? Don't get me wrong, dance is important. I haven't gotten where I've gotten by not carefully balancing my priorities and I've made plenty of sacrifices along the way. But there are only so many titles."

Anna could feel her restricted life, her familial circumstances, reaching up from her very bones to choke her. How she envied him. He had done all that she was now setting out to do, and yet he could still do so much more – whatever his heart desired.

"Are you willing to win the titles I am after, for as long as it takes?" she asked.

He contemplated her for a long moment. "Yes."

The word helped to settle her a little but the real comfort she felt came from looking at him – from seeing a surety in his eyes that went beyond words. Suddenly, she was so warm, she began to sweat.

Turning, she took her meal and sat in the other chair, away from the heat of the fire – and him.

He joined her, but remained standing. "It's getting late. I should go."

It was in her nature to ask where, to expect answers. In her world, she was owed everything without question or resistance. That she could only imagine where he would go, what he would do, caused her stomach to knot with uncertainty. She set her food aside and stood, her chin lifting.

"Very good." Extending her hand to him, she forced herself to be cordial and not want for more. "I will see you at nine o'clock tomorrow. Does that give you the time you need to do what ever it is you do in the morning?"

He smiled even though his eyebrows tightened across his face in confusion. He shook her hand. "Nine o'clock should be just fine. See you tomorrow, Anna."

Pride kept her from watching him go. She elected to use her position to call Ivan to escort him to the door. She waited to hear the doors softly shut before she picked up her dinner. The knot in her stomach was still there, and she had the worst feeling that it would remain there as long as she didn't know just what Jamie Wilde was doing every moment of every day.

Before Jamie rolled out of bed, he wondered if he'd just had the most amazing, realistic dream. He'd been asked to dance with a princess. She was beautiful, she lived in a mansion, and she was from some place he'd never heard of.

It had to have been a dream.

Reality was that Courtney was gone, and their partnership was over. So was his career, until he could find himself another partner. The daunting task had him covering his head with his pillow and letting out a groan.

The phone screamed next to his ear and he was glad he'd been buried under the pillow.

"Hello?"

"You gonna do it?" It was Reuben. He'd been in the dream too.

"Do it?"

"Anna – the partnership."

Jamie flipped the pillow off his head and bolted up. The soreness in his legs reminded him that the impossibly long day, had not been a dream. Reality was that he had signed some documents, and now he was dancing with a princess.

"Uh, yeah." Dragging a hand down his face, he threw back the covers and looked at his watch. It was eight-thirty. "Jeez, I gotta hurry. I'm supposed to be there at nine. You?"

"I'll be there. Just wanted to see if you took the bait."

Jamie strode into the bathroom. "Bait?"

Reuben's hearty laugh filled his ear and brought an involuntary smile to

Jamie's lips. "Sometimes I wonder about you."

Jamie turned on the shower, tugged off his boxers. "What?"

"Nothing. See you there."

Jamie looked at the phone before plunking it down on the tile sink. Preferring cold showers over hot, Jamie stood under the icy spray. And thought about Anna.

* * *

When he got to the mansion the ruddy-faced man he had seen in his apartment greeted him and escorted him to the room where they rehearsed. Reuben stood alone by the music system.

"The Princess will be with you shortly," the red-faced man announced. "She is on an overseas phone call with His Majesty."

Jamie stuck his hand out to the man. "And you are?"

"Vladimir Petrenko." Vladimir was just as serious as the bulldogs, Jamie deducted. He wasn't as big, but his dark eyes, his staunch body, were all-business and zero play.

This challenged Jamie, who tended toward teasing with little provocation. He landed a hearty pat on the man's upper arm. "Very good, Vlad. We'll just wait for her until she's finished."

Vladimir's ruddy complexion brightened to pomegranate. His eyes, solid black buttons on his tufted face, shot down to Jamie's hand, still poised companionably on his arm. With a shirk he forced Jamie's arm away. "Excuse me." Then he turned on his heel and left.

Jamie chuckled and crossed to Reuben. "Man, these people are as stiff as Kremlin statues, aren't they?"

"Better keep those iron-curtain jokes to a minimum, bro." Reuben fingered through the CDs shaking his head. "It's a good thing I brought my own music. The stuff she has here wouldn't get a corpse out of the grave."

"What does Gail think of all of this?" Jamie joined him in his browse of the royal CD collection.

"She's happy about the money, not happy about the time commitment. And because I had to put all of my other clients on Saturdays, that pretty much kills my free time."

Jamie pulled out a CD of Russian classics wondering what it might sound like. "You should have taken the room and board option."

"It wasn't offered, and I don't think that would have floated well with my baby. She likes her man by her side at night. And her man likes to be there, you know what I'm sayin'?"

When the door opened, they both turned. Anna paused at the threshold with Inessa behind her. The two suited bulldogs moved past them and entered the room, taking their positions on either side of the door.

"Not again," Reuben mumbled.

"I am sorry to have kept you waiting," Anna began as she crossed to them. "Papa phoned."

Jamie shifted feet. She looked radiant in the hot-pink bodysuit that held her feminine shape with the caress of a glove. She greeted them with a smile he had only seen once in full bloom.

Gesturing with a slender arm, she asked. "Shall we?"

Jamie was ready today. He wore his dance wear: black loose-fitting pants in a light fabric that made the most of air while allowing for optimum movement. His shirt of choice was a regular tee shirt. He kept dozens of them on hand— in white— just for rehearsing. Both his Latin and his Standard shoes went with him everywhere, his tools of the trade.

"Okay." Reuben stood between them. "Let's go over what we did yesterday, then I'll show you some pieces I have in mind for your Latin routines."

Agreeably, they repeated the steps from the day before. Jamie noticed she slid right through the troublesome combination that had bugged her without any clips. It didn't surprise him. He figured she'd probably shut the door when he left last night and headed right back to work. The mood was lighter, more comfortable for them both. Though her demeanor was typically serious and focused, she did smile occasionally. Reuben even had her laughing once when he did a quick tap dance en route to change the music.

The perfection she expected from herself thrived, and if Jamie stopped to take a drink or wipe his face, she continued on alone. Occasionally, she cursed in a language neither Reuben nor Jamie understood, walking in little circles, talking to herself.

There was a general tenseness about her Jamie felt every time they touched. It didn't leave when they separated either – he could still see it in her body, in her face, even if she danced alone.

As the hours passed and Jamie watched Reuben try to get Anna to loosen up, frustration began bubbling under his skin. Surely she had some sort of passion inside of her? Latin dances demanded that innate passion from the dancer and gave it as a gift to the audience in the form of a story. The fervor shared between man and woman was celebrated through steps, expressions, music and mood created by the dance. Jamie wondered if this woman, this flesh and blood statue, had ever been in love. Had she ever been anything but an ornament placed in an elaborate chair with a crown on her head for people to look at?

Jamie let out a sigh. He just might have to pull her off of that rosy, royal perch of hers. She needed to feel human feelings, touch them, taste them, make them hers, before he could use them in their dance.

He strode over to Reuben with his hands forming a T.

"Excuse us, will you please, Anna?" Leading Reuben in a slow head-to-head walk across the room, he voiced his concerns. "She's not getting it." Reuben was already nodding. "It's like she doesn't feel it. She hears the music, but it's getting lost somewhere."

"I agree." Reuben rubbed his head in thought. His eyes lit, and a smile formed where a frown of worry had just been. He jogged back to Anna. "Anna, you got any heavy drapes for these windows?"

Confused, Anna looked around. "I don't believe so. Why?"

"We need light-out shades in here, unless you have another room that we can use in complete darkness."

The confusion on her face was still present. "Not equipped for us to practice in."

"Then we'll need to do something about these windows. Light-out drapes or shades, like the kind they have in hotel rooms. Can you do that for me?" Anna nodded. "As soon as possible," Reuben told her. "In the meantime, we're gonna get dirty."

"Pardon me?"

On a half-jog, Reuben crossed to the music and dug into his CDs.

Jamie grinned.

"You need to work that steel out of your system, sis." Reuben put a CD on and shot her a smile. "And there's only one way to melt steel…with heat."

The base hit loud and hard, thumping so that the chandeliers overhead clinked and shimmied as if ready to break and fall in protest to the floor.

Inessa covered her ears and Jamie ran over to her and snagged her hand, "Come on." Shock drained what little color resided on her face. Her black notebook fell to the ground and she tripped over her feet as he tugged her onto the floor. "Aw, come on, Nessa. This will be good for you, too. Come on."

It was a heavy beat, one that refused to be ignored, one that reached in deep and wouldn't let go. Jamie loved this kind of music. It was his way to unwind; to just listen and respond, his body submitting to the demands of the beat.

Anna's eyes had shot open with the thud of the music, but the sight of Jamie insisting Inessa join them on the dance floor made her blink hard.

When Reuben took her hand, she started. Reuben moved her in front of him. Placing her hands on his hips, he began slow rotations. At first, she snatched her hands back as if she'd been burned but he shook his head, his dark eyes pinning hers, his hands holding hers in place.

"Feel it," he said.

It took only one glance over her shoulder to where Inessa and Jamie stood doing the same thing perfectly and Anna's hips began to swing like a boxer warming up. Determined, she moved in closer to Reuben. "I can do this," she told him.

"You sure can." Reuben smiled.

"You're doing great," Jamie told Inessa. "You like to dance?"

Inessa's head trembled into a wary nod. She kept her smile on him, but she wouldn't stop glancing over at Anna. Jamie had his hands on her shoulders as hers held his hips. "I think you've got it," Jamie's grin spread. "You're a natural."

Inessa radiated and the pure joy made Jamie unable to stop. "Try this," he told her, stepping back. He broke into some simple steps of funk; sharp kicks and squats, with rigid, boxy arms.

She covered her laughing mouth in glee. "That is so good."

"You try it."

"Oh, no, I couldn't."

Jamie slowed the movements so she could follow along. Across the room, Anna had not taken her eyes off of them, and her hips hadn't stopped twirling. There was emotion on her face, but it wasn't the pleasure Reuben was after. Finally, she stopped, setting her hands on her now-still hips. She strode over.

Because the music was so loud, Jamie didn't even notice her standing behind him, but he saw Inessa's glee flatten. She scurried back to her chair, retrieved her black notebook and sat back down.

Catching his breath, Jamie faced Anna with a broad smile. "Hey."

Like the calm before the storm, Anna stood with the fine-tuned appearance of cordiality, but Jamie didn't miss the whirling trouble in her grey eyes. It stupefied him. She was looking at him as if she was trying to decide whether to thank him or behead him, and he wasn't sure which.

"Perhaps we should get back to work."

"Oh, yeah. Sure."

Reuben changed the music and began showing them his ideas for a cha-cha routine. Anna was in awe at the way he moved. Passion glowed on his face with the constancy and beauty of a luminary. He didn't even need music to dance; his limbs moved as if harmonizing to an inner voice, an inner song.

She and Jamie tried the routine. She wondered if she looked as good as she felt. In all of her years dancing, no man had ever made her move with such ease— as if he was leading her through a maze, yet they encountered no obstacles.

Jamie had just the right pressure in his hands when he directed her. She smiled, enjoying the rehearsal, the process of learning. When the darkness of night finally began to shadow the room, a familiar emptiness slipped inside of her, knowing the day was coming to an end.

Reuben left early, having to coach another couple, and Jamie sat in one of the chairs, packing up his shoes. Because she was not anxious for him to leave, Anna dawdled near. "It was a good rehearsal today, yes?"

Noncommittally, Jamie lifted a shoulder, slipping on his street shoes.

"You weren't happy with it?" she asked.

"It was fine." He stood, looking at her. "You're still too uptight -- which is great for standard. You sure you don't want to do standard?"

"I am certain. Standard I know very well." But her ego had been pricked. "I am trying, you know. Was I not any better today?"

"You were." He snatched his duffle bag. "But you're – you're royalty, Anna. Look." He knew he should proceed carefully. "I don't know much about who you are, but from what I understand, emotions, passions -- these are things people in your position are not fond of sharing with the world. Latin is all about those things."

"It's a dance."

"It's way more than that. It's about real passion," he hesitated before continuing, "and love." He studied her reaction. Surely a woman in her position had been in love.

When she crossed her arms and her brow lifted, he figured he'd done nothing to educate her, only annoy her. "You think I know nothing of passion, desire and love? What do you think I am, some sort of detached royal who—"

"I didn't say that at all." He twitched and blew out a breath. "Like I said, I don't really know anything about you. I'm sure you get everything and anything you want."

"Now you make me sound like I am spoiled."

He wasn't making any headway, other than digging a deeper hole for himself. He would try to use the phrase he'd found so difficult to use in his partnership with Courtney, see if it helped any. "I'm sorry." It seemed to work, and her firm chin lowered while the tightness in her arms softened some.

"I have plenty of passion and love," she told him.

Jamie had his doubts—why, he wasn't sure. He wanted to believe her; that would make it easy. "Then you know what it will take for it to look the way it's supposed to."

"Of course."

"Okay then."

They both heard the door open, and turned. Vladimir stood in the threshold, displeasure coloring his face purple. She ignored him until he strode across the floor, boldly standing with the two of them.

"Your Highness," Vladimir began. "May I have a word?"

"Not now." She was not about to lose even one precious moment with Jamie to satisfy Vladimir's questions.

"A moment, please."

"Whatever it is can surely wait, Jamie and I are almost finished."

Vladimir gave a terse nod and backed out the door.

"I should head out anyway; I've got to meet someone in," he glanced at his watch, "a few minutes."

As they walked toward the door, Anna's only thoughts were of who Jamie was meeting and where. "I hope I have not made you late for…your date."

"Not a date." He pushed opened the door, held it as she passed by. "Just hanging with friends."

Vladimir was waiting in the empty entry hall and Anna ignored him, guiding Jamie to the front door where Lukov stood, a fixture of security. "Hanging. Yes, that is a very current expression here in America."

"It's actually hanging out."

At the door, she wished more than anything that she, too, was hanging out with friends. It would be a better alternative than the argument she surely faced with Vladimir.

Jamie waited for Lukov to open the door and the big man reached over with the exact efficiency Jamie noticed the job called for. He was still getting used to the fact that most of Anna's help existed anonymously.

"See you tomorrow." His voice held the thread of uncertainty he got whenever he analyzed the oddness of his new situation with her. He stepped out the door.

"Good night, James."

At the name, he stopped, and glanced over his shoulder at her with a smile both fascinated and uncertain.

Vladimir held the door open for her. Without words, she led him into her office and the door shut with a thud. In her bare dance wear, she clutched her arms to ward off feeling exposed. The room was cool in spite of the dark wood that paneled the walls and the fire she instructed staff to keep continually burning in the fireplace.

"My dear little perushka, you seem to have forgotten your papa's rules."

She wet her lips before pinching them tight. She knew Vladimir took great pride in the fact that he could invade even a royal's space, for his benefit.

"I believe your father insisted on standard ballroom dance because it befits your Royal image better than the more lusty counter part of Latin."

"It was funk, and an exercise, nothing more."

"It was not acceptable."

"It was a means to another end, Vladimir. I will not have a man who knows absolutely nothing about dance telling me what I can and cannot do." She turned, but he wrapped his hand on the bare skin of her upper arm, earning her sizzling glare.

"Your father would not tolerate any guttural exploration, even in the name of dance."

"I will deal with that. You, on the other hand, should be careful on which stones you step. I am sure he would be just as disappointed to find that his confidant has handled his only daughter, the heir apparent, with the casualty of a common thief."

Vladimir released his grip. Anna held her arm up and looked at the branded-white prints his fingers had left on her skin. His eyes narrowed briefly at her. Suddenly, she felt as if he were able to see into her mind, to see the true desires of her heart – and the fragility of her plans were under the harshness of his boot, ready to be crushed. Determination to protect her future rode her shoulders and she passed him with her chin lifted.

It would be good just to get lost in the music. Jamie pushed through the doors of Bruisers and was hit with the thick, moist air of dancing bodies, rich drink and laughter.

Lights flashed in colored streams as the music pumped. He made his way through the crowd searching for Cheryl. Her short, blonde hair would be easy to spot.

Then why were his eyes drawn to all the dark-haired women?

Shaking the odd behavior off, he went to the bar and got a drink, still craning a look around the crowded place. A local dance club, Bruisers was always busy. Like a shot of adrenalin in the system, the local gang he knew from the tight, competitive world of ballroom regularly found themselves drawn to the place, dancing even in off times, unable to get enough. Dancing was in the blood, Jamie had deduced long ago, a hunger that made your bones restless if you didn't satisfy the need.

He felt arms wrap around his waist and turned his head. Cheryl's bright smile seemed to reflect off her white-blonde hair. "Hey." He pressed a kiss on her cheek.

"That's not good enough," she told him and brought his chin around with her fingers so she could kiss his mouth.

He smiled. "That was better."

"I know." Cheryl took his drink, set it on the bar then led him toward the dance floor. They merged into a bobbing soup of people. Even though he'd been hard at it for days straight, there was something about bodies dancing around him that gave him the punch he lacked.

It was good to look at Cheryl's friendly face. The last two women he'd been near had both been on the scale of defensive, with Courtney ready to blame him for the demise of their partnership and Anna with the "her highness" attitude. Cheryl was like putting on a slipper after wearing a tight shoe.

It still bothered him that Courtney had dismissed all they'd done with just a few terse words. In one moment, his life had been dropped on a road he'd had no choice about taking.

Now he was in a contractual arrangement. For a moment, he wondered if he'd acted too quickly, desperate on the rebound. It wasn't the commitment that bothered him; it was that he'd not taken the time to really see if this was a partnership he wanted. What if he found they couldn't stand each other?

Absently, he skimmed the crowd for dark-haired women.

Anna really was different than any other woman he knew. When he had posed the question to her about passion, about desire and love, her green eyes had veiled – perhaps to hide her experience with the opposite sex.

He snickered. It wouldn't be a question of if she'd had boyfriends. Anna probably went through men like fancy hose, slipping them on, then peeling them off, discarding them when she was bored. There would be lots of guys willing to be discarded for whatever Princess Anna wanted.

"You seem distracted," Cheryl shouted over the music.

It was rude to ignore her; he'd done that enough over the past few days. Reaching for Cheryl, he pulled her in close as the song slowed. "Sorry."

"So how is it, dancing with a princess?"

"No different than dancing with anybody else," he said, but that tingle down low in his gut warned him that he was lying.

"Is she nice?" Jamie smiled at Cheryl's girlish enthusiasm. "What's she like?"

He lifted a shoulder. "Like most women, I guess." He looked out over the faces in the crowd, wondering why he wasn't telling Cheryl even he wasn't sure what the princess was all about.

She wrapped her arms around his neck and he closed his eyes, promising himself that he would not think of Anna, of the partnership, or of Courtney.

When he opened his eyes again, his heart jumped. Courtney danced just a few feet away. She hadn't seen him. She looked happy, exuberant even, and for that reason, and because he was still nursing the wound over what had happened, he stiffened.

Cheryl leaned back, looking up at him. "What's wrong?"

"Courtney."

Turning in his arms, Cheryl looked at Courtney now moving in a blissful slow dance with a man she didn't recognize. "Do you know him?"

"No." Jamie eased Cheryl's arms from his neck. "I'll be right back."

Tapping Courtney's dance partner on the shoulder, Jamie smiled. "Excuse me, I need to steal your date for a moment."

The man stopped, frowned, and Courtney's cheerful demeanor vanished. "Jamie, you could wait until I'm done."

He figured he didn't owe her even that courtesy after the way she'd dumped him.

With a smile and a grip, Jamie escorted her off the floor and down a dark hall near the telephones and bathrooms. Here they could communicate without shouting and without an audience.

"You're so rude," she hissed, twirling away from him. "I told you, we have nothing to say to each other."

"You said all that you wanted to say. You didn't even give me a chance to save things. It wasn't fair."

"I don't care if it was fair. I spent ten years in your shadow while you did what was fair—fair for you."

"That's not true. This was a partnership from day one. You and I both know it."

"Only if the decisions were ultimately yours. You're a control freak, Jamie. I got sick of it."

Jamie stepped back with a snag in his heart. When he spoke again, his voice cracked with emotion. "Why didn't you say something a long time ago?"

A tribe of flirty women paused near him as they ventured to the bathrooms. One looked him up and down. "Hey, want to dance later?"

He shook his head, sending the women off with a cold shoulder. "I didn't know you were unhappy."

Courtney let out a sigh. "I know you were only doing what you thought was best for us." There was regret behind her effort to smile. "And you did great for us, Jamie. You did. We went places as a pair I never thought I'd find myself. But—" She glanced out toward the dancing, the lights. "I just think I need a change. For better or worse, you know?"

Still, looking at her was like looking at an extension of himself, at part of his body that was now going its own way. He felt the pain down to the sockets from which she'd ripped away.

Courtney leaned up and placed a quick kiss on his cheek. "I gotta go. I'm here with somebody. Is Cheryl here?"

He tried to swallow the lump in his throat. "Yeah."

"Tell her hi for me." Her smile curved into a light empathetic grin. "You'll be fine, Jamie. You're cream, and you know what they say about the cream. It rises to the top." Then she was gone.

Even though the music blasted, the sadness roving inside of him was as if he'd just lost a loved one. But then he had. Jamie stood in the small hallway, dodging those anxious to make a phone call or use the bathroom. Tonight, the music didn't help. It hurt, pounding into him the sad reminder that nothing stays the same.

He was grouchy the next day. He'd not slept well, finally tanked with the reality of what had happened like a submarine settling over his body.

He was stuck.

He'd signed his life away with Princess Anna. He didn't want to think about it. If there was one thing Jamie hated, it was being trapped, and it was worse being trapped by something of your own making.

But this is your fault, he thought to himself. No one held a gun to your head when you signed those papers.

It had been stupid and rash to give into an absurd fairy tale.

But it wasn't in him to quit.

On the drive over, Jamie wondered just how tough the princess was. Maybe she'd cave under his work ethic. If she did, he was sure she'd rip the contract herself and send him on his way. Then he'd be free to find a more suitable partner without all of the legal and foreign entanglements.

He sat in her driveway looking at the massive house. Anna was in there; proper Princess Anna. Hand-carved like an ivory sculpture. She would give her all to him or he'd be out of there faster than she could say guillotine. His standards would be ruthless. Princess or not, he wouldn't allow anything less than perfection.

He found her with Reuben, the room vacant except for the three of them, the sound system and a handful of chairs. Without as much as a hello, Jamie crossed to the chairs.

"Hey bro." Reuben was at his side in a few easy steps. "You look like something the hound dragged in."

"I'm in a foul mood," Jamie snarled, dropping his duffle on a seat.

Without offense, Reuben smiled and nodded. "I will warn Her Highness."

Jamie snickered, looked across the floor at Anna standing majestically in all white. Like an angel. His breath skipped. Her hair was up in a tight roll, her skin was nearly the same shade as the soft white color she wore. Her arms were poised like a ballet dancer in wait. She tilted her head at him, and those eyes, like the sea underneath a cloud-covered sky, both beckoned and disquieted.

Hastily, he put on his shoes and ripped off his sweatshirt baring his trademark white tee underneath. He was already in a sweat.

He stalked across the floor to her.

At first she just looked at him. He felt her eyes going over his every inch with the intensity of a magnifying glass focusing the heat of the noon sun. It left him feeling ready to run as well as ready to grab her.

"Good morning," she said. But it was more than that. It was: what is wrong with you this morning?

He merely shot her a sharp look. "Let's get to work."

It was going to be some kind of day.

5.

They practiced the new cha-cha routine most of the morning. Jamie was irked that Anna danced without the emotion they'd talked about. She was fluid, smooth, every step was down. But when he purposefully made animated faces at her encouraging her to do the same, all he got in response was plastic-princess.

He didn't know if it was because he was irritable, but he felt too much force in her grip, stiffness in her stance, and figured she was overcompensating for her lack of emotional expression.

"This isn't working." He finally pushed himself away and circled. He checked Reuben, standing just outside the two of them, his chin in his fingers, eyes like green rocks.

"She's too strong," Jamie said.

It didn't ruffle Anna, the statement. She stood more erect and a smile played on her lips. Jamie countered her with a snicker. "Have you studied any of these dances, Your Highness? I know you've studied me. But do you know one thing about the dances and what they mean? What they are supposed to say to the audience?"

She angled her head. "I—"

"I didn't think so."

"You didn't give me a chance to respond."

"Cha-cha is coquettish," Jamie bowled on, "two people teasing each other. But there's no promise of love, no finale with a union in the dance. Still, they dance just close enough to continually bait each other in a friendly way."

"I am baiting, am I not?"

Jamie threw his hands up in the air and let out a groan of impatience.

"I think what Jamie is trying to say," Reuben interjected with calm," is that both of you have the same lure, if you get my meaning."

"I do not understand."

Reuben set gentle hands on her shoulders. "You have an inner strength that is good, Anna. But in dance, even if two partners mirror each other in skill, there must still be a man and there must still be a woman. Two men dancing is…well…it's not what judges or spectators want to see."

Her face flushed and contorted. "Two men dancing?"

Behind Reuben, Jamie stopped pacing, a half-smile working its way on his face. It was the first real emotion he'd seen since he'd first met her, other than that princess superiority she wore like a jeweled cloak.

"Be a woman first," Reuben explained. "Be willing to let him lead."

"I am letting him lead."

Reuben cupped her cheeks, grinned. "And make sure everybody watching you dance knows it. Show us how it feels it be in the arms of a man. See?"

Straightening, Anna nodded and slowly went to Jamie. For a moment, she wore a look of embarrassment and confusion, strung tightly with pride. "Pardon me. I thought I was doing better."

"You are," Jamie said, but without real compliment in his tone. "Just let me do my job and yours will naturally follow."

After they went through the cha-cha routine again, Jamie noticed more give in her body and hands. The routine flowed better and, in spite of his grouchiness, he found himself shedding the cantankerous mood.

They dined in the formal dining room on lunch of their choice, and Anna listened to the two of them discuss the first competition they would enter. In March, Dancesport Nationals were held in Provo, Utah, at the Marriott Center. Couples and teams from around the country came to compete. Though only weeks away, Anna was not at all apprehensive about entering so soon. It was one of the bigger titles, and that was what she was after.

"We will compete," she stated.

"It's too soon." Jamie wasn't looking at her, rather was contemplating how to lift a four-tiered BLT sandwich without it falling apart.

"I do not want to wait."

His eyes shifted from the sandwich to her. "What's your rush? We might not even place."

"Why wouldn't we? You are Jamie Wilde."

Without taking a bite, Jamie set the sandwich down. "That's one of the reasons I want to make sure we're ready. We're still a new couple. It takes time to establish a reputation, to make a name."

"It will not take much time. I am a princess, you are Jamie Wilde. We will be famous for who we are alone." Chin lifted, she took a bite of her salad.

"Don't think it's going to be that easy to sweep the judges off their feet with your title, Anna." Jamie sat back, realizing just what he was up against. She honestly thought they would go in and place their first time out.

"We need some publicity." Setting down her fork, she plucked a cell phone out of her pocket. "Inessa, come to the dining room please." Reuben and Jamie exchanged glances. "I will arrange it." She put the cell phone next to her bowl, and picked up her utensil. "You will see."

She smiled briefly before taking a dainty bite. Jamie wasn't sure why, but he had the feeling that publicity would be like opening a jar of grasshoppers. Just how would it look for the dance world to know he'd signed on with a princess paying exorbitantly for his partnership? The word gigolo came into his mind and, appetite gone, he nudged his plate away.

When Inessa entered she crossed dutifully to Anna and stood, waiting. "Yes, Your Highness?"

"Arrange a press conference with the local and state news agencies."

"Yes, Your Highness."

"Hey, 'Nessa. How's it going?" Jamie rose from his chair and casually reached out, giving her elbow a squeeze. Her head dipped, and she wrote in her notebook without acknowledging him any.

Confusion caused Jamie's face to pull tight, and he didn't miss Anna's stone-cold expression.

"Thank you, Inessa. You may go now." Inessa obeyed the command.

"I want to know what you plan." Jamie figured his stomach could wait, and didn't bother eating lunch. "I won't agree to anything unless you run it by me first. Understand?"

"You already agreed, Jamie." Anna speared another leaf of lettuce. "In your contract."

"I don't remember reading anything about publicity." Setting his cloth napkin on the table, he leaned forward. "Look, if you want me along for this ride, I want to be consulted before anything gets said publicly."

Anna dabbed at her lips with a cloth napkin. "Of course. We are a partnership, are we not?"

She was smiling but it didn't feel right, and Jamie sat back with his eyes locked on hers. He was placing his reputation in her hands, and he didn't like it.

"A little interest in you two as a pair might help," Reuben said. "But be warned, judges have their favorites. Some will like that he's bringing you onto the scene. Some will be loyal to Courtney."

"Even if she no longer dances with him?" Anna's eyes widened with shock.

Reuben nodded. "It will take a long time to show them that you're just as good, just as committed, just as privileged to be in her place."

Anna tossed down her napkin. "That is ridiculous. What about that he is privileged to be dancing with me? Have they no understanding of elitist protocol?"

Reuben shifted in his chair. "There will be some intrigued by your status, Anna. But most have their minds singly on the perfection of dance – with less importance on who is performing it as much as how it is performed."

"I don't believe that." Anna stood and walked to the large windows facing south, toward the back yard. Trees trembled in the cold temperatures and the clouds overhead threatened to drop snow. Her life had been about who she was and where she came from. This was a universal idea, surely. "Jamie has earned his reputation because of who he is. So did Nicole Dubois and Breck Noon. As did Tatyana Breshkov and Igor Valenski or Thomas Curry and Natasha Brand."

"You have a royal title," Jamie began with bite in his tone. "Isn't that enough for now?"

She turned slowly, like a spit under fire. Her eyes were a blaze of warning. "I want the titles for my country," she said. "You have been acquired to help me."

Jamie shot up. "Don't refer to me like some practical expenditure, princess, or you might just find yourself competing against me and a partner of my choice."

"You had your choice, James." She strode directly to him. "For whatever reason – money, notoriety, whim—you made it the moment you signed that contract."

Stepping around the corner of the table, Jamie made sure they were nose to nose. "Yeah, well, you came on strong, lady, with your black clothes and your posse of human guard dogs. What was I supposed to do?"

"Am I supposed to believe I intimidated you? Ha! What kind of a man is intimated by a black cloak? You saw an opportunity to make money and you took it."

Because it was part truth, Jamie stepped away from her, throwing tight fists into the air with a growl that was part frustration, part trapped anger. Moments passed. He stood breathing heavily, unable to look at her. Unable to face himself.

Anna lifted her chin.

Quietly, Reuben stood. "Let's get back to work."

He had nerve, Jamie thought, knowing full well what Reuben was planning. Apprehension stole the color from Anna's face and made her green eyes wide and more colorful. She looked from him, to Reuben. Reuben nodded toward the door, put his palm at the small of her back and escorted her out.

Jamie set his jaw. A deep ache spread throughout his body.

* * *

Anna thought her heart would jump right out of her chest. Jamie hadn't followed her and Reuben, and she glanced out the windows to see if he had left. They stood in the silent, empty room and waited.

She had thought him to be a very mild, even-tempered man. Perhaps this was why Courtney left him. It wouldn't matter if it was. She was not going to let a little thing like temper get in the way of their work.

Anna had learned to live with ill-temperament in her parents, both of whom had a low tolerance for imperfection of any kind. That she could be that way herself was something she knew as well as the onyx flecks in her eyes. It was not a trait she was ashamed of. Her father told her pride was her greatest achievement. That it would set her apart from those striving to keep her beneath the station she was born to inherit.

Still, she was not sure why Reuben was pushing them together when they were clearly in the middle of an argument. An argument, Anna thought with a satisfied grin, she had won.

When the door was finally flung open, her heart skipped. Even across the room, Jamie's dark eyes were hot, fiery, and locked on hers. For a moment he simply stood, seething.

She steadied her shoulders and forced herself to breathe. Jamie's stride didn't slow, even until he was a mere inch from her and she felt his breath on her face. Like a statue he stood in front to her, only his chest moved under the demands of need.

Cautiously, her eyes wandered up his arms, stiff and tense at his sides. His jaw was jagged, the bones exposed, flexing under the pressure of what she knew was great effort to keep his mouth still. He stared out over her shoulder, his gaze struggling not to break.

"Let's try rumba from the top," Reuben said.

Anna ignored a shudder of alarm. Jamie lifted his arms, and the chords and muscles pulled and welded into position. She stared, not sure she should enter his embrace. Blinking back unnecessary insecurity, she wet her dry lips. There was no one that could make her feel weak. There was no one who could make her feel less than what she was – a princess who was going to bring her country into the world on the merit of her own dancing feet. A woman yearning for a life of her own.

She fitted herself next to him.

Moments ticked by. She heard Reuben over by the music, heard the sound system skip before it was ready to hum.

Her heart sung wildly in her chest. Never had a man been able to challenge her with just the power in his eyes. It was exciting, terrifying. She turned away. *This cannot be. He is here for me; he is mine to do with as I please. I will not be intimidated.* As she reminded herself of her power, her position, she expected to feel relieved—but did not.

The music was slow, an ooze of instruments that pulled and drove. The melody was neither soft nor sweet, but slow and sumptuous.

Jamie's hands tightened around hers, his body nudged hers backward with a command she followed.

The music changed and Anna knew Reuben was deliberately slowing the CD to test them. Immediately, her muscles tightened in response as the continual movements of rumba tried every muscle, forcing technique to be expert and unyielding.

Necessity forced her to look up at Jamie. He didn't acknowledge her as he moved them, forcing dependence on him and as her body strove to maintain complete equanimity, her mind went wild with frustration and annoyance. Not sure what he was going to do next, she could only guess where he was taking her.

His hand was on her back, fingertips pressing in as he lowered her into a backbend. Music continued to push. She didn't dare stop, even though the muscles of her abdomen were on fire as he slowly eased her into an arch and then back up again.

His eyes were hard when they finally took hers, sending a flutter through her system that threatened to weaken her. Like the ticking of the second hand, each dip and turn, lunge and sway was done in slow motion.

He brought her around in a spin that muddled her sense of direction, then pulled her hips tight to his and bent over her, forcing her into another tense back-breaking arc, spooned underneath him in the stationary stance until both of their bodies began to tremble and give.

Their faces were within inches of each other – the heat of his breath shot flames from her lips to her pounding heart. She had to look at him, and when she did, triumph darkened his eyes.

When her quaking limbs could take no more, she broke free, stumbling back. Every inch of her shook uncontrollably. This was a battle she could not win. The fact that it had been in the arms of a man she knew now was intent on proving dominance over her, was plain. He was bigger, stronger. She was stunned at the ease with which he had commanded her, as if she were nothing more than a feather on his fingertips.

Reuben turned off the music. Working to compose herself, Anna moved far from Jamie and the hot vacuum surrounding him. She had been taught never to back down or away from anything. Accustomed to men that rarely challenged her, it was not the challenge she didn't care for, but that he seemed to enjoy the very act and was intent on being the victor.

Hearing movement directly behind her, she tensed.

"Again." His voice shot rivulets of fire up her neck.

She kept her back to him only a moment before she turned, giving him her most imperialistic glare. For a brief moment, she entertained refusing. She could call Lukov and Ivan—they would put him in his place. But those were weak responses to a man she had hired to be her partner based on his attention to perfection.

Lifting her chin, she forced her lips into a smile. It was a great feat of will, as just the sight of his unyielding eyes caused her to want to remind him of who she was, and that he would be wise not to forget it.

He held out his hand. In a move meant to sting, she ignored it, brushing past him on her way to the center of the floor.

"Your technique is good, Anna." Reuben slowly crossed to her. She couldn't help but glance Jamie's way, her smile deepening. "You think, man?" Reuben asked Jamie.

Jamie shrugged a shoulder. "I want to do it again."

Reuben's palm pressed flat against his own abdomen to demonstrate. "Remember, Anna, the movement in rumba is centered here. It branches out continually, flowing to the tips of your fingers and toes."

Anna nodded. Jamie crossed to them and stopped to her left. "I will remember that," she managed.

"When are those black-out shades going to be here?" Reuben asked.

"I am working on that as well."

Sighing loudly, Jamie's restlessness and dissatisfaction was obvious. "You're a princess. It's your chance to use your position."

"I've used my position, I can assure you," she snapped, advancing his direction. "Were we in my country, these black-out shades as you call them would be installed. But I am in America. Here people have to make appointments, wait in line behind other customers, whether you are somebody or not."

"Yeah, well, I guess your royal key doesn't open as many doors here as you thought it would, does it?"

Her mouth fell open.

Reuben clapped his hands once. "Okay. Let's take a break, shall we? Sis, what can we do about getting some water?"

Anna shifted her attention to Reuben. "I will summon Inessa."

"Yeah, you do that," Jamie bit out. "Don't go get it yourself."

After a searing moment with their eyes locked, Anna turned and left the room. The door slammed with an echoing thud and Jamie's head fell back. His eyes closed on a weighty sigh.

"Jeez, man, what are you trying to do?"

Jamie shook his head. "This is a mistake."

"It's a little late to decide that now, isn't it?"

"It was stupid—impulsive of me to sign on for this." Jamie's eyes remained fixed on the door. "I mean, look at her. She can do the moves, but it's like watching a mannequin. What do they do to royalty when they're growing up? Lock their souls in some dungeon somewhere?"

Jamie crossed the floor to the empty chairs, his shoulders slumping forward. Reuben stood in thought, watching. Something was up. This was a guy who had stuck through the temperamental, volcanic blasts of Courtney Biggs for ten years. Reuben knew two people could work together if they had to, work well if they wanted to. Sometimes they worked beautifully if they loved each other. Jamie and Courtney had worked well because, overriding everything personal, they wanted to. There was that rare partnership that worked solely based on opposition. Jamie should be used to that; Courtney's ups and downs had been fairly unpredictable.

But Anna was different; their backgrounds were poles apart. Reuben felt sure it was not the first time Anna had dealt with such diversity. But could Jamie handle the on-going challenge of someone unwilling to do what he said simply because he said it?

Reuben studied Jamie's tense demeanor and approached him. The guy needed some serious rest and relaxation. Either that or he needed a woman – probably both. Jamie had always put dance first. That had been hard to watch over the years as Reuben witnessed the endless fallout of Jamie's love life from unintentional neglect.

They talked extensively about this problem, but Jamie figured when the time was right, the woman was right, he'd know it. In Reuben's book, Jamie wasn't opening himself up for anything. Right or wrong, he was as closed in as Anna was without passion. Maybe that could work in their favor.

Reuben sat next to him, pressing his fingertips together, taking in the room, the windows. He would be glad when they were covered and he could force both dancers to drop their defenses and depend on each other. He just hoped the partnership survived until then.

"Something up?" he asked after a time.

Jamie jammed his hands through moist hair. "I'm just irked with myself. Tired. Ornery."

"Okay, that's livable. But don't be so hard on her."

"You know my standards." Jamie's gaze held on the doors. "So should she, if she read up on me like she said she did."

"You come off larger than life, man. Maybe she didn't catch that on tape." Reuben smiled. "Think of oysters, man. What happens when sand just keeps rubbing and rubbing inside of that little ol' shell?"

Jamie tried to smile but couldn't. He let out a groan, sat back, and ran his hands down his face. "But can I stand the sand?"

When the two doors flung open, Jamie's gaze latched onto Anna.

"Think pearl," Reuben whispered. They both stood.

Anna walked toward them with water bottles in hand. She still wore a look of complete annoyance. Jamie's defenses bloomed. What she needed was a dose of reality.

She handed them both a bottle, turned, and went to the center of the room, immediately breaking into the steps they had just rehearsed.

Ripping off the plastic lid of his water bottle, Jamie watched her. She was uptight, even though she was doing movements with flexibility. He saw it in her because he saw it in himself – wearing the strain of perfection like a second skin.

Guilt lodged in his gut like a cramp.

He was doing it again -- pushing too hard, just like he had with Courtney. Like it or not, Anna was his partner and for better or worse, he owed her his support. Pride still had a hold of him but he reluctantly went over, stopping just short of her rotating arms.

"Anna." He watched the graceful curve of her hand as it swept through the air. "Can we talk?"

"Of course."

"Are you going to stop or do I get beheaded by a windmill?"

There was no break in her movement, no acknowledgement of the joke.

"It does not sound like I should stop, James. Your tone is highly agitated, not in the least apologetic as it should be. And you were being sarcastic."

His laugh caught on a snarl. Squeezing the water bottle in his hand, it crackled, popped. He shook his head. The apology would wait. "It's time to get back to work, Your Highness." He thought of Hans Solo, of Princess Leah, and smirked. They'd had to work together. It had been tough and tense, and, he couldn't deny, titillating. Maybe they'd find themselves in a pressurized garbage compactor before this was all over.

* * *

Night came, and with it, heavy snow. As white flakes came down from the sky, mixing with a northwesterly wind, they stirred the air into a blur of hazy white. Anna stood in her bedroom on the second floor and looked out at the long, U-shaped drive.

Jamie was much like the storm brewing; fierce as it swirled and tore, stirring both emotion and defenses, but with an innate necessity and beauty she couldn't ignore.

Like Papa, she thought fondly.

Her father had frightened her as a child, but as she'd grown, she'd learned how to wrap him and his feisty comportment around her little finger. It had made them closer, she thought now, missing both her mother and her father suddenly. The last three months blinked by in a blur.

Would she be able to wrap Jamie around her finger? She figured she would know soon enough. They couldn't spend the hours together without seeing both flattering and unflattering sides of each other.

So far, he'd been what she had expected: determined, driven. She'd been taken back by the power play today but it would not scare her off. Contrarily, as she thought of the way he had ground out their moves a pleasant skittering warmed her.

His eyes seemed to vacillate between teasing and tormenting, unyielding and understanding. Indeed, when he'd looked at her with triumph, she had been deliciously ready to allow him that conquest and any other.

She felt those tremors again and closed her eyes, enjoying them. No man had ever made her feel this way. It was exactly what her girlish fantasies thought a man should summon in a woman.

When the phone rang at the side of her bed, Anna's first thought, and it was ridiculously silly, was that it was Jamie calling to speak with her. Experience had taught her that coincidence rarely coincided with fantasy. Still, it was not her place to answer the phone. One of her staff would do that.

A heavy knock at her door confirmed that neither coincidence nor fantasy was aligned: she recognized Vladimir's demanding pound. She didn't feel like answering the door.

Vladimir entered without permission and she stood back, instinctively wrapping her silk robe tighter around her. "I gave no consent to enter."

He didn't stop respectfully inside the frame, but continued toward her, his black suit stiff, his posture rigid. "Your father is on the phone and that, my lady, takes precedence over your permission." He gestured with an outstretched hand toward the phone sitting on the ornate mahogany side table next to her bed.

She snatched it up, covering the mouthpiece with her hand. "You may leave now, Vladimir."

With a nod, Vladimir turned on his heel and left the room. Taking a deep breath, Anna lowered herself on the side of the bed. "Papa?"

"Annika. Vladimir tells me you are not keeping your word."

"I am, Papa. I—"

"When I approved this I did so based on the fact that your integrity, the integrity and reputation of our country, would not be compromised in any way."

"I would do nothing to compromise either of those."

"Annika." His voice softened. "I know how important this is to you, but do not forget our agreement. It is for the best."

"I have not." Anna bit her lower lip, waiting through a thick silence. She heard her father sigh, could almost see his furry brows meet in a frown over narrowed grey eyes as he scratched at his well-manicured goatee.

"How is your association with Mr. Wilde and Mr. La Bate?"

"They are hard workers. We have our disagreements, I will admit. Jamie is particularly feisty, but nothing I cannot deal with."

"They are both gentlemen? Remembering who you are?"

"Yes." Though she had to admit she liked that neither let her position stop them from treating her just like they would an average American woman.

"Lev wants to see you." Anna fell back on the bed with a moan "He is planning to come over."

"No, Papa. I don't want him here."

"His father and I agree a visit would be appropriate." The irritation in her father's voice sliced with the sharp blade of intended guilt.

"It is too soon." Anna scrambled for a good reason. For her, the very idea was repulsive, and that was reason enough. "I want him to see me when I am ready to compete."

"When will that be?"

Anna cringed, anticipating his response at her lie. "Six months – a year."

"A year?" Her father's voice boomed in such a way that she had to remove the receiver from her ear while he muttered curses in Slovakian. "He will not wait a year to see you, Annika. He is a man. Would you force him into the arms of another because he cannot be with you?"

Anna rolled her eyes. The idea was as preposterous as her marrying the man to begin with. "You would want him here? For me to give him my priceless treasure before our wedding just to keep him?"

More cursing, more huffing slammed into the phone, and Anna was glad there was a large ocean and some even larger continents between them. "Don't mock me, Annika or I will hang up this phone and pay you a visit myself."

It was an empty threat Anna had heard many times before. His duty as a leader came first. His family, his children, fell somewhere below that, and with each year the Isles of Slovokia grew with prestige, Anna, her mother, and her little brother slipped further away from the top of her father's list of priorities.

"Perhaps you should talk to him yourself and explain your reasons."

Anna didn't want to see, nor did she want to talk to Lev and knew her father was only suggesting that so as to further drive the guilt. "I am very busy. Every day I train. I have no time to baby-sit the man."

"Annika," his tone warned that he was losing his patience. "You are adopting American disrespect. Perhaps we will have to bring you back home, where your respect and integrity will be preserved."

Her father never suggested, even in jest, without having given a topic great thought. "I'm sorry, Papa. I'm tired tonight."

"Get some rest. We will speak in two weeks."

Having been suitably set in her time slot, Anna relaxed, knowing that his word was his bond. He would not call her one day before.

Anna hung up the phone and counted her blessings. That she was there was a miracle in and of itself. That she was dancing with a man she admired for his skill, his expertise, one she hoped would play a very integral part in the next phase of her life and career, was another blessing. Someone was watching out for her.

As she turned off the lights and settled herself into the softness of bed, she stared up at the ceiling. Jamie had been incredibly intense of late. She had seen that power, looked deeply into his eyes and seen the passion behind it.

He said she had no passion. It wounded her, but gave her even more determination to show him that she did. Yet she could not ignore the facts: she was a twenty-five year old woman who had never been kissed with anything more than a hurried exploration she had found dull and distasteful.

And as per Slovakian custom and religion, she had yet to give herself to a man. For a royal, that was only allowed within the bonds of marriage. Truthfully, there had been no one that had tested her commitment on that particular subject. Even as a princess, this lack of intimacy did not bother her. Her parents had been navigating both her and Lev in the direction of marriage for years, since family gatherings at the summer house. Lev had been nothing but an annoyance then. He'd grown into an aggravation.

Tradition stunk.

Anna rolled to her side, frustration bubbling in her veins. How could her parents promise her to a man who stumbled with women like a horse on ice? With his money, his status as a single bachelor with a crown, Lev could have any woman – and she had seen the money diggers that had tried to seduce him. He'd fumbled all of those blessed attempts.

Snuggling deeper into the blankets, she forced the insipid vision of Lev from her mind, replacing it with more pleasant thoughts of Jamie. She had a feeling his moods were easily affected by how well he was performing on the dance floor. She liked that it brought spontaneity to each morning.

It made her wonder about his private life. He'd said he didn't mix his professional life with his personal life. She wondered why, when for two people spending hours, days, and months sharing their bodies through dance, a relationship seemed a natural extension.

As she lay in the darkness, his face came to mind and longing, deep and warm, ached within her. He filled the masculine roll of lead distinctly, with long, contoured muscles that enhanced each dance with the power and grace that made the male half of the partnership complimentary to the female. They looked just right together, that she did not need a mirror to know. She felt it when she stood in his arms, where her body met his in the angles and curves, the shadow and light of him.

Trembling through her was an instant sweetness, a yearning that settled in her belly vacant and incomplete. What sort of woman would he find appealing? She was comfortable with Jamie, even with his impudence, his silly rule. A rule she doubted he truly held sacred. A rule she would most definitely challenge. A woman that would bow down for him would not have his respect. Nor, she figured, would they lure him.

She wanted to lure him.

Carefully, she would have to do just the right amount of riling and just the right amount of enticing. It would have to come on like a slow fever, warming him at first before it took him over with a full-blown heat he had no control of.

She smiled.

Somewhere inside, she would find this passion he and Reuben said she lacked. She was sure she did not lack it. She was sure it was inside of her – a fever of her own, one that had been ignited by Jamie.

6.

She seemed different somehow. He'd become more aware of her smile, light sense of humor, her easy agreement with just about everything he said. Her manner toward him was warmer. His suggestions about her stylization were met with agreement, his corrections with thanks.

She was altogether too nice.

Jamie could have sworn she wanted something from him. Almost as if she was flirting. He wouldn't admit that as an acceptable answer. It was so typical to have a thing for your dance partner – it happened all the time. For Jamie, this was not a pattern he was used to, having danced exclusively with Courtney. He'd had a thing for her, back when they were kids, just after they'd partnered. It had been disastrous for their career, sending them both into a zone of flops and failures they had mutually attributed to their romantic feelings. They adopted the "you can't dance and make love," credo, after which their career took off like the lively steps of jive.

Having spent many of his socially formative years in the confines of a dance studio, Jamie never learned to read women. Considering himself a bit backward in this area, he was troubled by Anna's subtle change.

He concluded it was just that they were becoming more familiar, that she was being more accommodating. That and she could see he was right in his opinions ninety-nine times out of one hundred.

Because she was curious about the princess, Cheryl asked to join him for rehearsal Friday. Normally, Jamie shied away from friends watching rehearsals – the familiarity caused him to be unnecessarily anxious. But Anna's extra-friendly behavior had set him on edge and Cheryl's presence might settle some of his confusion.

She leaned up and kissed him as they stood at the door, waiting to be escorted inside.

"I'm a little nervous," she bubbled.

Jamie thought her girlish enthusiasm was cute.

"I've never met royalty before."

He squeezed her hand. "She's just like you and me." But that wasn't completely true, Jamie admitted to himself. Her charisma, exotic beauty, that untouchable aura was a real force that couldn't be disregarded by anyone – even him.

Ivan opened the door, his beady eyes darting to Cheryl. "Hey, Iv. How's it going?" Jamie flattened his palm against the boulder of Ivan's bicep as he and Cheryl passed.

Why butterflies flew in his stomach was beyond Jamie, but when he walked into the dance room and his eyes fell on Anna, talking with Reuben, the butterflies fluttered uncontrollably.

Both Anna and Reuben looked over from the center of the floor. Reuben's smile flashed, as did Anna's fixated stare. It took Jamie by surprise, the piercing look in her eyes over her princess smile.

She wore red today, Jamie noticed as Anna crossed to them, and it seemed to be creeping up her neck and into her face.

"Anna." Jamie readied for her usual cheek-to-cheek greeting but she didn't lean his direction. No, her back was straight as an arrow as she studied Cheryl.

Cheryl smiled and extended her small hand. "It's so nice to meet you," she chirped.

"A pleasure to meet one of Jamie's friends." Anna tilted her head regally, extending a perfectly manicured hand.

"He's said so much about you." Cheryl shook it vigorously.

Only then did the cold granite in Anna's eyes shift to Jamie, causing his gut to crimp. "Has he?"

"I saw you at the Capitol Theater," Cheryl gushed. "I didn't know who you were. I teach kindergarten and my kids are so excited that I get to meet a real princess."

"How lovely. And you are?"

Cheryl looked at Jamie, still staring through narrowed eyes at Anna. After her nudge, he piped, "Oh, excuse me. Cheryl Birk."

"How very nice to meet you, Cheryl."

"Wow, this is just not something that's ever happened to me before."

"I imagine not," Anna said through slightly upturned lips. "Do you dance, Cheryl?"

"Not competitively. And I'm nowhere as good as Jamie. He's amazing. But then, you already know that."

"Yes, James is wonderful." It was that princess smile, Jamie noted, about as sincere as Formica.

Jamie slipped his arm around Cheryl, saw Anna's stormy eyes follow the gesture. Damned if he wasn't completely confused. For the life of him, he couldn't read what Anna was thinking.

"Well." Anna's hands came together at her breasts. "You are here to watch? Then let us get to work. Shall we, James?" She backed toward the center of the room, to Reuben.

"She calls you James," Cheryl squealed. "How cute."

Yeah, when she's ready to behead me. Something was up, and he meant to find out what. He was just getting used to the friendlier, accommodating Anna. This Anna was too closely related to the princess, leaning more toward the attitude of Her Royal Haughtiness, and he didn't like it.

Anna waited with Reuben and tried not to stare at Jamie, bent over, arms on either side of the woman who now sat, looking up into his face with that sparkle and glow of pure love.

Anna's heart took a hit. She'd set out to lure Jamie, even with his principles an obvious barrier. Rehearsals had gone smoother. They'd even enjoyed a few choice moments of laughter along the way. But this girl with her sea-blue eyes and sun-blonde hair, was a new and very real obstacle. The look of affection in her eye was not something Anna could dismiss.

Cheryl pulled Jamie down for a fast kiss but it seemed to take unbearably long to Anna who had to force her gaze away.

"Come on buddy," Reuben called.

On a jog, Jamie was over and stood freshly flushed, Anna thought, from the kiss.

This would not do.

"Let's start with cha-cha," Reuben suggested. "In fact, let's take it from the top and work all the way through."

Anna hoped by the time they got to samba and rumba she would have some resolution to her tumultuous feelings. But the moment she felt his arms slip around her, she knew that would be impossible. She saw everything – the feel of him, the very possibility of him, as nothing more than an elusive ghost in her arms now.

She was mentally worn by the time they reached rumba and their moves were torturously slowed down, intimacy whispering from his body to hers. Every part of the dance besieged her with intensity. His fingers blazed like flame when they grazed her back, her arm, her waist. When he brought her up from a low arch for the last time, their eyes met. A faint line deepened between his brows. He didn't stop, but the concern and wonder in his eyes was in his hands and he finished the dance with a little more urgency.

Anna stood in their final position, with her head against his chest, just over his heart, their hands clasped tightly to their sides in a close expression of love. She closed her eyes. Beneath her head she heard the fierce pound of Jamie's heart. His sweat dampened her cheek. Unconsciously, her fingers twined tightly around his.

Cheryl broke into applause and Anna stepped back, feeling Jamie's confused gaze stay with her. Moving away before he could get a good look at her, she steadied her rampant breath and kept her gaze from the sight playing just at the fringe of her vision.

"That was amazing." Cheryl's arms wrapped around Jamie in a hug that forced Anna to turn for a better look.

"Did you feel it?" Reuben was next to her then, his expression anxious, and drawing her attention away from Jamie. "I saw it in your face, sis. That was a huge improvement."

Anna nodded. She had felt it, and more. Her desire to have Jamie as her own made her take in the dance. The reality that she might never have him had clashed with that need to take, creating the passion she felt so deeply for him.

"It's getting there, guys." Reuben rubbed his hands like a kid anticipating a surprise.

"You guys were great, Anna," Cheryl cooed. "Really great."

"Thank you." Anna's voice, Jamie thought, was void of any emotion, and whatever he'd seen just seconds ago when they'd danced was neatly tucked away now. She was the affable princess again, and it bugged him.

"You look so good together," Cheryl continued innocently. "Way better than Courtney." Cheryl glanced at her watch. "Ooh, I'd better be going. The kids are waiting for me to have lunch so I can tell them all about meeting a real princess." She shook Anna's hand again. "It's been exciting. Thank you."

"You're welcome." Anna gave a gracious nod.

While Reuben went over some of the finer points of the cha-cha routine, Jamie escorted Cheryl across the large hall. Anna couldn't keep her gaze from following them. At last the bubbly blonde was gone and the two doors shut.

As a woman, she could hardly expect Jamie not to be attractive to other women. As a princess used to getting everything she wanted when she wanted it, seeing the one thing she desired in the arms of another was difficult to take. She was dreaming, in fact, to think that her fantasies would become reality.

Anna's heart stung.

She suspected Jamie would be relaxed after having Cheryl observe. Instead, he seemed to slip into a place that was part angry, part bottled-up frustration.

"Are you all right?" she finally asked.

He'd sensed the difference in her body through the continued rehearsal. Earlier, she'd given and he'd taken. It had been the beginning of something – she was finally sharing.

Over the last few hours she'd felt stiff and unyielding again, and the hot and cold, the inconsistency, was not something Jamie could live with. At the end of each rehearsal, he wanted to know where they stood. It would make picking up the next time so much easier if they had an X to mark the spot.

Reuben crossed to the music, turned it off, and packed up his gear. "Let's call it a day."

"But we still have hours left," Anna protested.

"He's right." Jamie hated admitting that he'd had enough, but if he didn't, he knew he'd lose it. That'd gotten him nowhere with Courtney.

"See you Monday." Crossing the floor with his bag over his shoulder, Reuben stopped long enough to pat Jamie's shoulder. "Get some R & R in."

Jamie nodded, and stood alone and weary, in the center of the room as

Anna escorted Reuben to the door. When she came back in, she shut the door behind her. They shared a silent moment staring at each other. Jamie swallowed a knot of uncertainty, then crossed to the chair where his duffle sat. He could hear her light feet coming toward him.

His body tensed.

It was required that he dance with her and under those circumstances, he could look into her eyes, touch her, and know it was permissible. But something inside of him was simmering.

She stood directly in front of him, a red flame, vivid and hot. He didn't dare look at her. His fortification of Cheryl's presence earlier had all but vanished from the room, leaving him mildly annoyed and mystified.

"You sure you don't want to—"

"Yeah," he bit out, sat, and ripped off his dance shoes. "I need a few days off." He took in a deep breath, the air thick between them, and finally looked at her.

Her eyes held concern. Her lips parted as if she wanted to speak. The concern impressed him, but the moist sheen of her mouth only caused unwanted feelings to stir.

He stuffed his dance shoes into the duffle and brought out street shoes. He needed to get out of there, as far away from her as possible, and get his head screwed back on the right way by Monday.

"Something is wrong."

"Nothing's wrong," he snapped. "I just get this way sometimes. You'll get used to it." Slipping on his street shoes, he kept his gaze on what he was doing. "We'll get used to each other's idiosyncrasies." Done, he stood and looked down into her rounded eyes. "We have to."

She followed his hasty exit like a child on the heels of an abandoning parent. "What will you do?"

"I don't know, go in the mountains maybe."

"In this weather?"

"Yeah. Why?" he asked, annoyed that she seemed to care, even more annoyed that he liked it. "Don't you worry your pretty little head, Princess. I was a Boy Scout. I can camp in anything."

"I'm sure you can," she began, following him out into the large entry hall. "But – you signed a contract, and evidently you didn't read the mortality clause."

He stopped, turned. "What?"

"You may not do anything to endanger your life while in the employ of the Slovokian government."

"That's insane." Angry, he flung his duffle across the floor. It spun, finally coming to a stop at Lukov's feet. It seemed the big man appeared out of nowhere, his face like a junk yard dog ready to growl.

Anna waved him away with a shake of her head and a "Shoo." He didn't go. His dark eyes latched onto Jamie in a way that reminded Jamie of who she was and that Lukov's job was to protect her. Anna turned the big man around and gave him a gentle shove through the door before continuing.

"I had to safeguard my investment, Jamie. If anything happened to you, it would directly affect what I was able to do. You see?"

He stepped toward her, thinking about how he could so easily strangle her right there on the spot.

He'd be in the stocks by morning.

Since he could do no such thing, he tensed. "This is just…just great."

He looked at her as if she was a stranger for a moment, his brown eyes darkening, and Anna didn't like it.

Turning, he strode across the room and in a snap, had his duffle and was heading to the front door.

"You mustn't go." She stood regally, her back against the double front doors. His eyes flashed over her face.

"Anna. Look. If I don't go, we'll both pay for it Monday."

"You cannot put yourself in danger."

"I won't be in danger." He reached behind her, his hand skimming her waist, but she moved again, blocking the knob and he pulled back as if he'd been burned.

"I cannot allow it." Anna lifted her chin, her eyes focused on the strain she saw in his face, the way his jaw flexed, eyes flickered, enjoying the warmth swimming low in her belly.

His eyes widened just a little, sharpening with disbelief. "You can't stop me."

"I can and I must," she said firmly. "It is clear to me that you are in distress."

"You're damned right I'm in distress. I need a break."

"You are not thinking rationally and are, therefore, putting yourself and our partnership at risk."

"The only thing at risk right now is my mind, because in two seconds it's going to blow and—"

"Is there a problem, Your Highness?"

Both Anna and Jamie looked over at Lukov, briskly crossing toward them. Backing off, Jamie dropped his duffle to the floor and set his palms up in a gesture of surrender.

"We are fine, Lukov," Anna sighed. "Mr. Wilde and I are talking."

Taking Lukov by the elbow, Anna turned the big man around and gave him a gentle shove toward the back part of the house. "Please, do not disturb us again unless I scream." She waited until the man was gone before facing Jamie again.

Jamie threw his hands up in the air. "Great. You put him on my scent like a hound after a fox."

"He is here to protect me. He is trained to—"

"To bite first, check later. The guy's—"

"Jamie, Jamie." Anna placed her hands on his tense arms. When he stilled at her touch, their eyes locked. Anna's gaze dipped to the full softness of his mouth, then lifted to the dark storm hovering in his eyes. She lowered her voice. "There is only one legal way you can go without breaking your contract."

"Yeah? How's that?"

"If someone from my staff accompanies you."

"No way." Furious, he leaned in close, sending her back against the hard panel of the door. "This is wrong. How could you do this to me? All I want is to go camping – alone. Now, I find that I can't because I signed—" His right hand shot up over her head, planting his fist on the jamb. "I want to see a copy of that contract."

* * *

Jamie's heart tanked. He held the contract in his hands, staring at the very words condemning him. Anna's blood-painted fingernail pointed right to the phrase: …contractee will not engage in any sport, activity, recreation or otherwise, that places said contractee in mortal danger…

"This is ridiculous," he sputtered, tapping the paper angrily. "Nothing is going to happen to me. I'm an experienced camper."

"So were the men—four of them—that were stranded up in the Himalayans last month."

"That was the Himalayans!" He looked into her resigned face. Her brow was cocked over a granite gaze. He closed his eyes. "It's a little thing called reading," he mumbled. "Something you should have done a better job of, Wilde." When he opened his eyes, she was still there, still in devilish red looking at him with her lips tipping up.

He shoved the contract at her, pulled his duffle over his shoulder and stormed out of the office.

"Jamie?"

"I'm going camping."

"But you can't – the contract."

"I'll see you on Monday."

She grabbed a hunk of his sleeve, forcing him back around. "I'm going with you."

His eyes popped open and he stopped. "No way."

"If I accompany you, then the contract remains without breach and you without the consequences of breaching."

Yanking his sleeve free he said, "You are not coming with me."

"You would rather risk the consequences of breaching a Slovokian contract than take a girl camping?"

"You wouldn't last five seconds up there," he told her.

"I have camped before," Anna lied.

"I'm talking snow caves, fifteen below, sleeping bags. Stone soup." She merely nodded. "You've never camped in snow caves," he bit out. "You're idea of camping is the Ritz…or the Plaza. Come on, Anna, you're a princess, for crying out loud. The only boots you've worn are Italian or… or… or Gucci."

"Gucci is Italian," she informed him, enjoying that he was cornered.

"And I have worn boots for many occasions. You decide…me or the guillotine."

"What?!"

"I am joking, of course," she said on a fluttering laugh, entirely at his expense.

Anna thought it fresh that his face was so plain with uncertainty. To settle his concerns, she placed her hand on his arm and again, felt him tense beneath her touch. "You would not be beheaded for breaking a Slovokian contract." Pausing for dramatic effect, she lowered her voice to a soft purr. "I would be the one to assign punishment, and I would not let your head go to such a terrible waste."

He shook his head slowly, eyes fixed on her. "You are one freaky princess."

Then his gaze shifted to her mouth, sending an electric buzz from her lips to her belly. She liked that his look lingered, that when his eyes lifted to hers again, there was more than anger simmering – something fierce, torn and vulnerable.

"I will give you specific instructions," she told him, leading him back to her office. "You will follow them, understand?"

Jamie flipped his hands in the air in a gesture of submission. "Why not? My soul's already been bought. You might as well own the rest of me."

Anna tried not to look utterly pleased. Such an idea was not far off from what she had in mind.

Anna waited for Jamie at the end of the long drive. They'd parted ways an hour ago with him saying that he needed to go home and pick up his camping gear. Anna had little doubt that Jamie would go on without her, the mortality clause and its consequences in regards to breaking the contract was sheer brilliance on her part. She'd quietly packed a small duffle, slipped out one of the side doors unnoticed, and now stood clutching her thick coat around her. She shot frequent glances over her shoulder at the house for any sign of discovery.

It was impulsive and reckless to go, she knew this. Raised with the rigid hand of iron-clad common sense, she could not dismiss the guilt that accompanied an act that broke her father's law, but the fluttering excitement inside dismissed that guilt with the accommodating hand of freedom.

Two bright headlights came around the corner and she ducked behind one of the towering stone lamp posts that flanked the start of the long, circular drive. Taught to be observant, warned to be cautious, she remained tucked there until the car idled. She poked her head out to make certain it was Jamie. He stood half-in, half-out of the driver's side of his truck, looking around. When he found her, a smirk creased his lips.

"Your carriage, Your Highness." Sweeping his arm in a gesture worthy of Cinderella invited into the pumpkin, Jamie's lips twisted into a grin—a grin that flat-lined the minute he laid eyes on her Louis Vuitton bag. "What's that?"

"My suitcase."

"We're going camping, Anna, not to Paris."

"What do you suggest I use, a knapsack?"

"It would be lighter to carry but, hey, you're a strong gal. Go for it." He got in the car and closed his door, rolling down the window. His thumb pointed over his shoulder. "It goes in the back."

Aghast, she didn't move.

"You will not be a gentleman and load it?" she asked.

"I was going on this trip solo, remember? It's you crashing the party. It will be you lugging your bag."

If she hadn't been so stunned and her bones weren't trembling with cold, she would have continued to insist until she had her way. But the fact that he just shot her his spectacular smile and rolled up the window, forced her to hoist the luggage over the side of the truck herself.

Once she was inside, she slammed the door shut and almost laid into him in Slovokian, but the cab was so warm, her trembling body succumbed and her mouth did nothing more than say, "Ah."

They drove in silence and darkness. Anna occasionally checked the side-view mirror for cars that might be following. Relieved there were none, she settled into the seat.

Jamie headed north, taking Canyon Road along the base of the mountains, the two-lane road busy with commuters driving home.

"Do you always drive in silence?" she asked.

"When I need to clear my head – yeah."

When he did not say more, she felt slapped. Her father made her feel that way when he was not pleased and he would say nothing for hours, sometimes days. Her heart snagged. She hoped Jamie was not like that. It was humiliating to have honest attempts at reconciliation shunned.

Suddenly, he reached over, his arm brushing the top of her thighs, his hand working the glove box. The door fell open and golden light streamed onto her lap.

"Music," he told her and put both hands back on the steering wheel without looking at her.

"I thought you liked quiet."

He shrugged. She supposed his detachment was meant to tell her he was not happy she was along. Because it was unacceptable that anyone would not be pleased with her company, let alone a man she had secured as a vital part of her future, her pleasure shifted to annoyance.

"You could be gracious at least," she said.

"I'm forced into taking a tag-a-long on what was meant to be a much needed refresher and I'm supposed to be happy about it?" When he finally looked over, fire smoldered in his dark eyes.

"You could have chosen some other way to loosen up, Jamie," she said testily. "There are many things people do – massages, pedicures, shopping."

He ground out a laugh. "Yeah right. That works for you, maybe. But I've got to sink my body and soul into something, or whatever's hanging on my back will just be there Monday morning."

With her along, Jamie knew he'd not get the rejuvenation he was hoping for. The part of him that had been forced to roll with tag-a-longs being the oldest of five knew he could make the best of it, or make the experience miserable for her.

Or maybe do a little of both.

The mouth of the canyon was massive, a dark crack in whose depth they would be swallowed up. If not for Jamie's headlights, Anna would have felt claustrophobic as the mountain walls flanking the narrow, winding road closed in around them.

He looked so serious, Anna thought, stealing glimpses of him. What was on his mind? Cheryl? In her experience, men did not think of women half as much as women thought of men. Jamie, in his chunky black coat and black turtle neck sweater, could have a lot of women thinking about him.

His cell phone sung a lively tune but he made no attempt to retrieve it.

"Aren't you going to get that?" she asked.

"Nope."

"What if it's important?"

"It's important that no one knows where I am and I keep my sanity."

"Do you tell anyone when you go on these Jeremiah Johnson trips?"

"Jeremiah Johnson?" It pleased her that a grin tugged up one side of his lip. "Uh, no. That would defeat the purpose. How do you know about Jeremiah Johnson?"

"My mother is a fan of Robert Redford."

His phone rang again. Anna squeezed her gloved hands in her lap. No one knew where he was, which meant no one knew where she was, either. When it was discovered that she was gone, it would only take seconds for Vladimir to find out where Jamie's family lived, go there, and question them. They had no idea where their maverick son was. Vladimir would seek Cheryl out as well. The pinch of guilt deepened with her deception. There were no cars on the highway as they took an even narrower road jutting left off the Alpine loop and headed deeper into the crevasse of the mountain. Anna shivered.

She hadn't thought claustrophobia would haunt her on a night that could qualify as a dream. She would be perceived as weak, frightened and childish if he saw her terror for the dark, sky-high, shadowy mountains rising from the earth.

She felt so small.

Jamie pulled into a clearing off the side of the road and didn't even look over at her. "We're here."

He was out in a breath, and Anna forced her own rapid breath to slow. He came around to her door, but opened it without meeting her gaze. When he extended his hand, she grabbed it with more urgency than she liked. But he didn't seem to notice nor did he care that she stumbled slightly when her feet hit the snow.

Dull silence wafted over her, leaving her dizzy. Pressing her back against his car for stability, she decided she would not let on that she wanted to run as fast as she could, out of the soaring grave of the canyon and back into the vast openness of the valley.

Busy unloading the equipment, Jamie didn't see the way she stayed plastered with her back against the car. The cold was unbearable. Immediately her teeth began to chatter. She pulled her coat tight and watched him unload.

He moved without a sound and soon he had a shovel, had settled on a spot a few yards away, and was digging.

"You can wait in the car if you'd rather," he said without as much as a glance.

"No. I'm not at all cold." If he could endure these frigid temperatures, than so could she.

She looked around. Dark sooty shadows seeped into never-ending blackness. Overhead, the moon lit the snow, giving it an almost electrical brilliance as it hung on the tree branches in sagging clumps and blanketed the ground.

"Are there wild animals in these mountains?" she asked.

"Some. Cougars and coyotes mostly." She didn't care for any of them and her feet inched closer to where he stood digging.

"Know how to build a fire?" he asked.

"No."

He stopped and looked over. "You're going to learn." Pitching the shovel upright in the snow, he climbed out of the half-dug hole and strode to her.

She was loosing feeling in her fingers and rubbed her calf-skin gloves back and forth, watching him unload a bundle of wood. Then she followed him to a clearing where it was obvious fires had burned before. Cold seeped through her clothes rapidly; and snuck through her bones to her quaking jaw.

Squatting down, Jamie arranged the wood. "Use small pieces first," he explained, "so the fire catches fast and spreads."

She nodded even though he didn't bother seeing if she understood.

He handed her a small can and a lighter. "This is cheating, but it does the job fast. Open it and pour a little over the logs."

Her cold, stiff fingers would not work, and she winced trying to flick open the tiny lid. Grabbing the can, he flicked it open, then handed it back to her.

"I could have done it," she snapped.

"In about five hours. We'd be dead by then. Pour."

Reluctantly, she did, thrusting her chin up to show her displeasure. "Lighting oil?" she asked.

"Yeah. Now, light it."

The tips of her fingers felt four times their size and she fumbled. "My fingers are so cold I—"

Snatching the lighter from her, he thrust it under the pile of wood. "Light different sections of the fire for an even burn." Then he stood and went back to the truck.

Anna held her stiff hands near the growing flame and squelched a low moan of contentment ready to escape her throat. She wanted to laugh. Any fantasies of romance by the firelight were dashed. He was still mad at her, and the night would be about survival and comfort, rather than seduction and pleasure.

He returned to digging. The fire sent a pink glow to the hard contours of his jaw and brow, the golden brown tips of his hair. Desire hummed deep down near her belly as she watched him work with such concentration. There was so much she wanted to know about him. She wanted him to offer himself freely, because he wanted to, not out of duty to their partnership.

"You are good at this camping," she said, hoping to stir a conversation. The fire was growing before her eyes and her fingers started to feel better.

He stood chest-deep in the snow now, sending large clods over his shoulder as he shoveled. "My family camped – camps."

"You have a large family. That is nice."

"Yeah."

"There is only me and my little brother, Nicolas. He is thirteen." She would tell him about herself whether he wanted to know or not, she decided. "He is a funny boy," she went on. "He likes to play pranks on me. But then I like to play pranks on him also. One time, he pretended to be Spiderman. He tried to make this web and catch me in it. Of course I was so much bigger than him. It was very easy for me to catch him in it. It backfired."

She waited for him to respond but he'd disappeared into the snow.

"Jamie?" Rising, she walked near where he had been. Her heart banged against her chest when all she saw was white. "Jamie?" Panic froze her voice.

Afraid he was buried, she took a step and fell through six feet of hollowed-out snow. Clawing and flailing, she screeched as snow caved in around her.

Grunts came from somewhere beneath her. She felt something that wasn't soft but wasn't hard under her feet. They were a tangle of limbs as Jamie pushed himself up through the snow and tried to grab at her flailing arms.

"Anna, Anna, stop!"

He rose like a snowman, covered in a thick inch of white from head to waist. Instinctively, she threw her arms around his neck. "Thank God. I thought you were buried." She couldn't help that she was shaking.

Jamie ran his hands along the back of her thick coat. "Are you okay?" Anna managed to nod.

"You stepped on our snow cave," he muttered. He climbed out then, shook himself off and reached for her, pulling her up next to him. They stood looking down into what was left of the demolished cave.

"I am so sorry."

He sighed. "Yeah, well…I'll dig another one."

"How about if we just sleep in the back of the truck?"

"Are you kidding? We'd freeze out here. That's the point of a snow cave. The hollowed area keeps your body warmth inside."

She thought about being deep inside a cave of snow and her head swam. She swallowed, and groped for something to steady herself. His car was the safest thing so she went to it as he began digging again.

"Sit by the fire or you'll risk hypothermia," he told her.

She obeyed and her wobbly knees took her back to the fire where she plopped down. "People do this because they want to?" she asked. "You are wet, cold and sleeping in snow. You are surrounded by cougars and coyotes. Who would choose to spend a night like this?"

"We wouldn't be wet and cold if you hadn't stepped like clod-foot onto the snow cave," he said without stopping from his digging.

"Clod foot?" Inside, she was heating up. "You could have marked where you dug, no?"

"With what? You have a Slovokian flag handy?"

"It is not my fault I stepped on the cave!"

"Just stay put!"

She wondered why she'd come along. She could be at home with a nice bath and a warm fire – indoors, where a fire was meant to be. To think she had thought this would be her chance to impress him, to get to know him and hope for romance to bloom. She let out a sigh.

He took off his coat, tossed it her direction. "You are not cold?" she asked after she caught it. She laid the garment over her lap, taking the warmth he had left in it for herself.

"I'm on my second snow cave, remember? Ever dug snow?" He stopped and looked at her.

Afraid he might insist that she learn, she debated telling a lie. "No."

A smirk twisted on his lips. "What I thought. Want to try?"

"No."

"Thought so." He went back to digging. She watched him sink deeper and deeper into the snow until just his head was exposed. The moon lit his face with a white cast that softened it. The anger inside quickly vanished as she marveled that he looked handsome in both light and shadow.

"You and Cheryl, it is serious?" she asked. The rhythm of his digging didn't change with the question. She pressed closer to the flames. "You are boyfriend and girlfriend?"

"You read up on me, you should know this."

"I know about your career in dance, not about your personal life. You don't make love and dance, remember?"

"We're that, I guess." His tone was non-committal and to her surprise, unenthusiastic.

Soon, he emerged, dusting off the fine layer of snow that clung to his clothing. Snow crunched underneath his feet as he crossed to her. For a moment, he stood towering over her. The firelight leapt onto his skin with passionate fingers whose flames danced in his eyes. Her heart banged hard and slow. He was looking at her with such intensity; her whole body warmed under the flare of it. Then he leaned over and plucked his coat from her lap.

"Let's eat." He slipped on the coat.

Anna blinked. Her dry throat demanded she swallow. Forcing herself up, she followed Jamie to the truck.

"Gather some rocks and stones," he told her.

"Rocks and stones?"

"For soup."

"What?"

He pulled a small cast iron saucepan out of a heavy sack. "Stone soup, remember?" Passing her, Jamie hid a grin. It would be most satisfying to see her wander around in search of stones.

"You are not serious."

He couldn't face her; she'd see laughter in his eyes. He busied himself with gathering twigs. "Twigs and stones. The twigs flavor the broth, kind of like a bay leaf. Only, with pine needles and aspen twigs, it has a nuttier flavor. The stones, well, they're the fiber."

"You do not expect me to eat the stones?"

" 'Course not. They just round out the flavor some as it cooks. Now get to it." He waved her away, sneaking a look as she stood, blank-faced, searching the ground. She began mumbling in a language he didn't understand.

After a few minutes, he squatted by the fire, scooped some snow into the saucepan as she watched, then dropped his crushed pine needles and twigs in. The snow melted under the heat of the fire.

"Ah," he began, "there's nothing like stone soup in the winter. Where are your stones?"

She uncurled her gloved palms to expose various rocks. "That's the best you could do?" He took one, held it up in the light. "These black and grey things are no more than gravel kicked off the road. You want to eat gravel, Anna?"

She shook her head. "I don't want to eat any of it. You have it."

"You sure?" Taking her meager offering, he added it to the pot and stirred.

She nodded, clutching her coat closer to her body. He retrieved two speckled blue tin mugs and poured her a cup. The rocks and twigs caught on the lip when he poured the dirt-colored liquid, before falling into the cup with a plop.

He handed it to her. "Princesses first."

Her brows twisted over large, blinking eyes. Taking the cup she sniffed and made a face. "It smells—"

"—Earthy, I know. It's the pine needles. But they have a real clean taste." He poured his cup and waited for her to try it. "Well?"

She brought the cup to her lips as if it would burn her on contact. Then she sipped. Jamie covered a laugh watching her body shudder violently. Her face contorted and she gagged.

"I am sorry," she coughed out. "I cannot eat this. I – I would be ill."

While she shuddered he ditched his concoction in the shadows. The moment she looked at him, he pressed the empty cup to his lips and pretended to drink the contents in one satisfying gulp. "Ah."

He set his cup down, wiped at his mouth, and patted his stomach. "Great stuff. You did a good job with those rocks. I'll have to remember gravel rocks next time. They add a different flavor than the stones, a little grittier." Rising, he all but laughed out loud and went to the truck to dig for the granola bars he'd brought.

He looked over at her, still sitting by the fire, staring with trepidation into the floating muck in her cup.

Stealthily, he ripped open a bar and had consumed half before she turned around and he forced the bar back into hiding, grabbing the foam pad and sleeping bags. He carried them to the cave and stepped down into it. After the mat was down he laid the sleeping bags on top. Then he looked at the two bags, close together. It was going to be tight. His blood warmed, thinking about it. She would be – jeez, she'd be close. He'd just have to ignore her. It would be simple.

Forcing his head back up and out in the clear, he looked at her. She was still sitting by the fire, staring into her mug though he caught her cocking her head all the way back. He jumped out of the cave.

"Did you drink it?"

She nodded. Her body shook with another shudder. Snatching the cup from her, Jamie had to look for himself. It was empty. A hole opened up in his stomach. "Anna. How do you feel?"

She smiled. "Pretty good. It wasn't as bad as I thought."

Jamie closed his eyes. She'd really done it, drunk the disgusting mix. Now she'd probably be sick. He felt awful, guilty – stupid. He'd face who knows what punishment now when her people found out he'd poisoned the princess with stone soup. She'd have to have surgery to remove the stones if they didn't cause a blockage and kill her first.

"I'm tired." She started toward the snow cave.

"Anna, I need to talk to you."

"I was so hungry." She patted her tummy with a content smile. "Now, I will be able to sleep." Delicately she stepped across the snow.

"Anna—"

"One cave?" She looked at him. "We are sharing?"

"You didn't expect me to dig two, did you? Besides, we'll be warmer with two bodies rather than one."

Anna smiled. Jamie's heart plunged. She looked so radiant with the glow of the moon beaming off her face. She'd be bent over, hurling the contents of her stomach within minutes. "Anna—"

"I'm bushed." Stretching slow and cat-like, Anna yawned. Then she began to unbutton her coat. The fire crackled and danced. Mesmerized, Jamie watched her fingers undo each button. He imagined those long, lithe fingers tracing his skin. Anna handed the warm coat to him and he squeezed it in his hands, his jaw locking. Underneath, she wore a sweatshirt with a monkey face on it. "I brought my flannel pajamas. Should I change into them?"

He shook his head, crushing her coat against his body. "Keep your clothes on – you'll need the warmth." And the protection, he thought with frustrated amusement. "Anna. The soup—"

"This is so cozy." Gingerly, she stepped down into the cave. "I didn't think it would really work. You are a genius."

He stood above her at the entrance, watching as she unzipped one of the bags and shimmied into it. She looked up at him. "You were right, it is warm in here. Well, goodnight."

Jamie licked his lips. His arms were tight, his legs wanted to move, and his insides were racing. He'd stoke the fire again before crawling down in there with her. Maybe if he took long enough, she'd be asleep. But what was he thinking? He couldn't possibly let her sleep with rocks in her stomach. He had to get her to the hospital – fast.

He cursed under his breath – so much for a relaxing night away. It would be a three-ring circus once her people knew what he'd done to her and the media caught wind that the Princess was in the ER after a prank by her supposedly trust-worthy American dance partner.

He strode over, slid down next to her, and heard her heavy breathing. She was already asleep, and he blew out a sigh. She laid on her side, her face comfortably smashed, her lips parted like the soft petals of an orchid. He couldn't take his eyes from them, glistening as they were in the moonlight; they tempted him like a ripe piece of fruit.

He had to wake her, had to tell her what he'd done. He touched her shoulder and she groaned, turning onto her back in an arching stretch that had his jaw clenching as he watched her body ripple the sleeping bag.

He dragged anxious hands down his face, frustration building. She settled in the sleeping bag like a feline after a bowl of warm milk. Only he'd tricked her into eating melted snow with rocks and twigs.

"Anna." He shook her gently. "Anna." Her low moan caused something inside of him to pull hard. "Anna, does your stomach hurt?"

She moaned again, and her arms wrapped around herself. Sweat pearled on his brow as he lay next to her with guilt knocking in his head, his heart thudding. "Anna?"

"Oh, my stomach."

He turned her face to his with his fingertips. "Anna, I need to get you to a hospital."

Writhing in the sleeping bag, Anna's face pinched in pain. "Jamie." Her head swung back and forth frantically. Quickly, Jamie unzipped the bag and slipped his arms underneath her.

"Anna." With little effort, she was in his arms like a broken doll and he climbed out of the snow cave. "I – you shouldn't have eaten the soup. It wasn't supposed to be eaten."

"The soup?" she muttered.

He held her close and crossed the snow to his car. "I'm going to take you to the hospital. Hold on. Hold on."

"You told me—"

"It was a stupid prank. It was—"

She slid from his arms, set two feet firmly in the snow and smoothed her clothes, then her hair. Tilting her head, she smiled. "A prank, was it?"

"Wh—you—" He blinked, stammered. Then his eyes narrowed. "You knew all along?"

"Had I not just told you that my little brother Nicolas played pranks on me?"

She looked so smug, so pleased with herself. Pride dented, Jamie turned and went to the snow cave. Her light giggle pricked his ego and he jumped down inside the cave. He didn't bother looking back at her. He ripped off his coat and slid into his sleeping bag, burrowing further into the hole. But he couldn't close his eyes.

"You should be ashamed of yourself," she said, sliding down next to him. Immediately, her warmth filled the tiny space – and him. He kept his back to her. "Making me eat something so disgusting. And to think I wouldn't notice the melted snow with the leaves and rocks right behind you when you got up. Men."

"Goodnight, Anna."

"You were worried about me. I saw it in your face. I was peeking at you."

He flipped over, and they were face to face. Her eyes were inches away, large hollows of black that mystified him. The sweet lushness of her mouth was close enough to taste. Desire swarmed inside, tempting, luring. Every muscle went taut, every pore broke open in sweat. He couldn't take his eyes away from the inviting fullness of her lips.

Flipping back to his other side, he hoped the image of her lying there with that tempting mouth would leave him. You can't dance and make love, he told himself. He repeated it, over and over until his brain dulled with it, his body submitted to the hopelessness of it, and he drifted on to sleep.

Anna heard his breathing change. It went from fast and furious to slow and thick and she knew he'd drifted on. Her own breathing was what kept her awake. She looked up and saw snow, looked down the cave toward her feet and saw black. To her right was white, to her left was white. A crushing, smothering feeling drove her to gulp for air and squirm in the sleeping bag. Tears gathered behind her eyes. She wanted out.

Rising emotions poured over her like an avalanche. Soon, she was clawing her way up and out of the cave and sat, gasping at the entrance. Tears rolled down her cheeks, freezing stripes down her face that brought on a shudder.

Jamie slept soundly and she leaned over and looked at him – a dark shadow lying peacefully in a tomb. She couldn't go back down. But she remembered what Jamie had said about sleeping in the truck.

Her legs nearly gave under duress when she forced herself up. She headed in the direction of the truck, the endless silence opened up around her, making space more unbearable than the closeness of the cave.

"I can do this," she told herself. Still, it was with apprehension that she stared at the place where the cave lay deep. Cougars. Her eyes sweeping the darkness. It would be so easy for one to slink over the snow, jump into the cave, and…she closed her eyes quaking at the bloody vision in her head.

Creeping back to the cave, she looked down at Jamie. If a cougar hurt him, if anything at all happened to him…she took a deep breath. She would stay awake, listen for cougars, and keep Jamie safe. She could do that much.

Anna's lungs burned with every deep, icy breath. Gathering courage, she climbed down into the cave and crawled into the sleeping bag with her eyes focused on Jamie's sleeping face.

7.

She woke to bacon frying, its heavy scent stirring her empty stomach into a ravenous bear just out of hibernation. Anna opened her eyes, saw snow – and screamed. Gulping for air she scrambled out of the cave and stood at the mouth of it, jumping up and down.

Jamie was at her side in a second, his hands on her arms. "Anna, what?" She couldn't find air – or words. "Slow down, breathe, breathe." He took exaggerated breaths, cupped her face so her eyes focused on his mouth as it opened and closed, as her breath worked to mirror his.

The firm grip of his palms at her cheeks, coupled with his eyes, tight with hers, finally calmed her running heart and static breathing. He skimmed his hands up and down her arms. "Better?"

She looked at him through lowered lashes. "I was disoriented."

He'd placed his coat on a rock near the fire and he jogged over, retrieved it, then jogged back. "Here."

With his assistance, she slipped it on. The warmth sunk to her bones. "Thank you." She joined him at the campfire and saw that he'd set out two folding camp chairs. "Chairs, how nice."

"It's the least I could do after last night," he said, avoiding her gaze. Instead, he focused on the bacon and eggs he turned in the pan.

"That smells wonderful. I am very hungry."

He looked up then, eyes somber. "I'm sorry about last night. It's one thing to play around with your brothers and sisters. A princess with a throne and a kingdom is something else altogether."

"I am still just a woman. Like any other."

He shook his head again. "No. You're not."

She didn't like that he saw her in some forbidden light with a deadly moat surrounding her. She would never have him if he could not see her like other women.

"So," she began, watching him fry the eggs. "I am who I am. That does not change things between us. We are still dance partners. Two people," she paused, "a man and a woman."

His dark eyes fastened on hers. Smoke from the fire twisted in front of his face. "You say that," he said, "but we both know it's not true. It's something the whole world knows, Anna. You'll be a queen someday. And I'll just be…" He didn't finish. Something between sadness and regret crossed his face, further mystifying Anna.

He dished up her bacon and eggs, handed it to her.

"Thank you."

"You're welcome."

They ate with the sound of the flowing river rippling through icy rocks. Snow- laden branches dropped thuds of melting snow like hushed bombs throughout the forest. Anna looked up into the grey sky and closed her eyes. It was an exquisite moment, one that would end too soon. It would be unpleasant when they returned. There would be demands and there would be consequences. She had known that the moment she'd instigated the secret reprieve.

When she opened her eyes, she found Jamie watching her, utterly still, his face taut. He held her with a look that was confusion and something else, and her heart beat hard. Was it desire?

She wanted it to be. Not knowing, afraid that it might not be, she stood and took his empty plate, wanting to smooth over something that had not yet happened but upon their arrival home, most certainly would. "Let me help break camp."

His brows lifted and the intensity tethering his face broke. "You haven't camped before."

She shook her head. "But I've read about it – The Campfire Girls Mysteries."

A smile curved his lips. It was the just the sun she needed, knowing the storm would only get darker.

When they emerged from the mouth of the canyon, Anna let out a long-held breath, relieved they were once again out in the vast, open valley. The skies were thick with bulging clouds in grey, white and angry granite. It will snow again, she thought with a sigh. Not that she minded snow. She had grown up with more snow than sun, the Isles of Slovokia, just off the coast in the Crimean Sea sounded temperate in name only. The terrain was similar to that in which she now found herself: tall, overpowering mountains, forests of evergreens, reflective lakes.

She hadn't been at all homesick since she had arrived in Utah. She attributed this to the weather and the similarities in the landscape, and the inherent freedom she felt. Greeting each day thousands of miles away from a responsibility she was trying to escape was euphoric even with the inevitable battle that surely lie ahead.

Turning her thoughts to more pleasant things, she angled herself so that she faced Jamie. "You were born here? In Utah?"

His hair was mussed, like he'd slept hard and dreamt well. A dusting of shadow colored his jaw. A renegade on the run, she thought, then felt guilty. He had no idea what would face them upon their arrival back. The deception gnawed at her, and she decided it would be better to warn him and take his reaction rather than surprise him when everything exploded around them.

"Actually, my brother and I were born in Los Angeles. Mom and Dad moved here when Justin and I were little."

"I would like to meet them, your family."

"Good, cause that's where we're headed."

"Now? Jamie, no, I can't – look at me. I'm a mess. It wouldn't be right."

"You look fine, Anna."

"I cannot make a first impression looking like this. I have not even brushed my hair. I smell like campfire."

"They won't care."

"I insist. You must take me back and let me properly prepare myself."

He looked across the car at her, his eyes sharp. "You're off duty, Anna."

"I'm never off duty, James."

"You are when you're with me." He turned away with a look that meant he was finished, and she was not going to change his mind on the matter.

Anna sat back, arms tucked around her chest, and forgot about bringing up the fact that she'd gone with him last night without alerting her staff. He may have thought that introductions didn't matter, but they did. Showing up without an appointment was not something acceptable in her culture, even among close friends and family. Preparation always made for a more ideal planting ground. She'd been taught that roots were everything. Deep roots ensured healthy loyalty.

Her parents would be mortified if they knew her loyalty had been growing in the western direction of America.

They drove up a winding road, through a neighborhood with tailored homes surrounded by charming white fences. This is where he grew up. The very idea pleased her. It was a family community, she could tell. Houses were close together, the yards filled with snowmen, play sets and sleds.

She was not surprised to see a very inviting home done in red brick and black shutters. An artfully landscaped yard provided the welcoming setting for the house. A half-dozen cars were scattered like toys in the driveway and in front where he parked.

"How quaint." She skimmed the Wilde home with an approving gaze.

Jamie got out and opened her door. "Tell my mom that. She'll love you."

It was loud inside. Someone was playing the piano – and not too well. Warbling chords screamed from somewhere in the house. A little girl with a purple dinosaur tucked under her arm came skipping down the stairs. When she spied Jamie, she squealed and lit up like a lantern.

"Jamie!" Leaping from the middle of the stairs, she jumped with the confidence only love could give her, into Jamie's waiting arms. They spun in a fit of giggles.

"Where are my socks?" A male voice called from above. Anna looked up. A young man nearly Jamie's age emerged with a towel barely hanging at his waist. With a shriek he jumped back behind a wall. "Jeez, Jamie. Why didn't you tell me there was a woman in the house?"

"Get some clothes on Bruce and get down here. My brother, Justin." Jamie started under the arch that led to the back of the house. "Thinks he's Bruce

Lee."

The little girl in Jamie's arms stared at Anna. "I know you."

Anna had hoped no one would recognize her. She smoothed back wayward strands of hair, her face heating. "You do?"

"You're that Princess lady that dances with Jamie."

Jamie kissed Jessica's cheek. "That's right, mite." He set her down as they came into the kitchen.

Anna stopped. It was bright, busy, and a disaster area. A place where real people lived and ate, very unlike the industrial, cold kitchen in the palace or even the tile and stainless kitchen of the mansion. The sink overflowed with dirty dishes. Someone had been making pancakes; the room smelled of dough and burned oil. A bowl with yellow batter that had dried seeping over the edge, sat next to a long black griddle straddling the burners of the island stove. A kitten dangled playfully from a red and white tablecloth that gravity pulled inch by inch toward the floor.

Anna took a step and crunched on something. Looking down, she saw a tiny plastic shoe, along with discarded bites of pancakes and bacon, stuck to her boot.

"Where is everybody?" Jamie asked.

"Around." Jessica was immediately drawn to the playing kitten and gathered the gold and white ball of fluff to her chest. Jamie joined the boy pounding the keys of the piano.

Without stopping, without looking, Jeff said, "Hello."

"Hey, Chopin, I have somebody I want you to meet." Jamie elbowed him, sending the pianist into a frown. For the first time, he stopped, shoving his glasses further up his nose as he turned to face Jamie and Anna. He looked her up and down.

"Anna, meet Jeff. Jeff, meet Anna."

She extended her hand, glad he had called her Anna and nothing more.

"Are you a real princess?" Jessica asked.

Both Jeff and Jessica stared at her, waiting. She smiled her warmest smile, cringing at her disheveled appearance. "Yes. I am."

Jeff whistled. Jessica's mouth formed a perfect "O". She looked at Jamie as if he'd just brought her the most glittering present.

Jamie went into the kitchen and searched for two glasses. There was a half-filled orange juice jug sitting next to two nearly empty gallons of milk on the counter.

"Milk or juice?"

"I am not thirsty, thank you." Anna joined him at the cooking island and looked at the disarray. She had never seen such squalor. But then neither she nor Nicolas was expected to clean up after themselves. Apparently, neither were any of the Wilde children. A maid probably cleaned and cooked for them, she decided. A family of this size would demand such a necessity.

As Jamie drank down his orange juice, she heard voices. A man with dark hair, grey-kissed at the temples, came through a door, his cell phone tucked at his ear. He wore dark slacks and a hunter green shirt.

He waved at Jamie, then his eyes fastened on Anna with a discerning look. "Yes. It would be an excellent option. The rates there are some of the best in the market."

"Jamie?"

The woman who appeared had chocolate-colored hair in morning disarray and Jamie's espresso eyes. She hurried over with a smile. "Justin said you were here." Her hands out and a smile rounding her cheeks, she took Anna to her breast as if they'd been reunited after year's long absence. "You must be Anna." She patted Anna's back with a hearty hand. "How nice to meet you. It's an honor."

"Thank you, Mrs. Wilde."

"Call me Joyce."

"We'll talk on Monday," the man said into the phone. Clicking the device off, he tucked it into the back pocket of his slacks and approached Anna with an extended hand and a cautious grin. "Anna Zakharov? Jack."

Anna shook Jack Wilde's hand. He had warm eyes, but there was sharpness in his gaze that could see through deception – like her father. He shook her hand with the strength of someone she could trust, and someone she didn't want to disappoint.

"You're up early." Jack looked to Jamie.

"Went camping last night."

Jack and Joyce exchanged uneasy glances before Jack moved with edginess to Jamie. It was a posture that had Jamie studying his father. "What?" he asked.

"We had some visitors last night," Jack began. "Late." He looked at Anna.

Her stomach crimped. This was not the way she wanted to be introduced to Jamie's parents, to his family, neatly wrapped in deception. But Jack's pointed gaze would not release her.

"Like who?" Jamie asked.

Jack waited, gaze still on Anna.

"What's up?" Justin cruised in wearing baggy pants and a striped long-sleeved polo shirt. His hair looked like he'd just shaken it dry, hanging to his ears and jaw in a scruffy mop. He gave Anna his best grin revealing a smile, Anna thought, just as enigmatic as Jamie's. "So it's her. How ya doin'?"

Jamie ticked his head Anna's direction. "Anna, Justin, whose butt I can kick in less than zero to five seconds."

Because the attention had shifted to Justin, Anna felt a temporary wave of relief. "Then you and I must talk, Justin," she began smoothly. "I will teach you a way to beat Jamie in less than zero to five. But you must be willing to dance."

Everyone teased and poked good-natured fun at Jamie. It would have relaxed Anna some, if not for Jack's heavy gaze and her own guilty conscience now a leaden crown on her head.

Jamie poured himself another glass of juice with a keen gaze on Anna. "I think you're still figuring out how to whip me in zero to five aren't you?"

With a snicker, Justin wrapped an arm around Jamie's neck in a hold that caused Jamie to choke on his juice and set down his glass. "Any time you need some help bringing this guy down, Anna, you just ask."

Soon, the two were wrestling, falling onto the floor in a knot of thudding limbs and grunts. Nimbly, Joyce stepped over the squirming pile of bodies and started to clean.

Anna glanced at Jack. He was watching his boys with fatherly amusement but she caught him sending her a look that would not be lost in the distraction of Jamie and Justin's tumbling match. She should take Jamie aside and explain her spontaneous acts of the night, but movement out the corner of her eye caught her attention and her intentions were interrupted.

A teenage girl wearing an over-sized tee shirt had appeared. Their eyes met and the girl's widened. She stopped. "Is that her?"

Anna strode over, her hand extended. "I'm Anna."

"Uh, Jocelyn." Jocelyn pulled her shirt down, before fixing tousled hair with her hands.

Jessica ran and jumped into Jocelyn's arms. "She really is a princess, Jocey."

"Oh, yeah?" Carrying Jessica over to the counter, Jocelyn set her down, shooting a disapproving glare at her brothers, still squirming on the floor. "You guys are such retards."

"Do you ride in a carriage?" Jessica asked.

Wandering over from the piano, Jeff snickered. "'Course not. Didn't you see those black cars last night? They look like carriages to you?"

Jack cleared his throat and stopped both sons with the efficiency of a shout. He waited until they stood, red-faced and breathless before he turned to Anna. "Your…friends came by looking for you last night."

Confusion swept Jamie's face. "Friends?"

A sharp silence fell over the kitchen.

"I imagine," Anna began, working to keep her voice level, "that your father is talking about Vladimir and my staff."

"Why would they come here?"

"Probably because they were looking for me."

Jamie's eyes widened. "You didn't tell them you were going camping?"

Accustomed to being stared at, scrutinized, admired, Anna didn't flinch under the heavy stares accompanying the thick quiet now electrified with Jamie's obvious concern. "I did not," she said, lifting her chin. "Perhaps you and I should talk about this privately."

Jamie's eyes hardened. "Anna. I'm – this could be – jeez." Turning, he flicked his hands and arms and paced the tiny space between Justin and the refrigerator. He looked at Jack. "What happened?"

"They were concerned about where she was. Wondered if we knew where you were. I told them I thought you'd headed up in the mountains. Alone."

Jamie let out an angry sigh. "Excuse us." Hard glare on Anna, he jerked his head toward the privacy of the dining room. A single murmur whispered through the air at Jamie's bold actions toward the princess.

Anna passed each family member with her head high, even though she knew very well the misunderstanding didn't shine a flattering light on her at the moment. She looked Jamie in the eye when her shoulder brushed his chest as she went through the door that led to the dining room. Trained to notice and appreciate details of her surroundings, Anna scanned the room curiously. In her mind, she could easily picture formal family dinners here.

"A lovely room," she murmured absently. For a moment she forgot their predicament. In her mind's eye she saw Jamie in a suit and tie, sitting at one of the carved chairs around the long, mahogany dining table. When he didn't make a sound, she looked at him, and found the same hard disproval in his eyes she had seen in the kitchen.

"I am sorry," she began earnestly. "I neglected to tell them I was leaving."

"Neglected?" His face twisted in disbelief. "Look. You know your situation better than I do, but, was that a wise thing, to go without telling anyone?"

"You knew."

He spit out a laugh. "Jeez, Anna, what if something had happened? You put me in a bad spot."

"Regrettably, it was necessary for you to have the privacy you so desired."

He moved away from her, the muscles in his whole body tight as a fist. What had she done? Because he had a pit in his stomach, he knew whatever it was would not be good. He'd seen the look in Vladimir's eyes, the snarl in both Ivan and Lukov's teeth threatening dismemberment if anything happened to her.

"You are worried for nothing, Jamie."

He wanted to believe her, but something in the way she spoke, as if she were trying to convince not only him, but herself, made him doubt the statement.

"Call them," he told her, "right now, so we don't have the National Guard out looking for us. You have your cell phone?"

Lifting her shoulders, she sent him an innocent smile that had him striding into the kitchen. His family waited quietly, pretending to engage themselves in breakfast cleanup. He snatched the cordless phone from the wall.

"Everything all right?" Jack asked. Jamie continued back to the dining room without a word.

Handing Anna the phone, he stood next to her, arms crossed, feet firmly planted.

She dialed without allowing the quivering she felt inside show in her finger tips or voice. "Inessa? It's Anna. Yes, yes, I am fine. May I speak to Vladimir?" Anna lifted her chin and looked directly into Jamie's simmering brown eyes. The doubt she saw there lit her defenses. She hadn't been irresponsible; she'd needed a reprieve, just like him. She'd protected them both by keeping the little getaway secret.

She heard Vladimir clear his throat on the other end. "Where are you?" he asked.

"I am with Jamie, Vladimir and we are perfectly safe."

"You need to return immediately, Your Highness."

"I will be home soon."

"Immediately, or I will be forced to come fetch you at the Wilde home." He paused, his heavy breathing firing into the phone line.

"I will be there shortly." She disconnected the call without letting Vladimir's tone worry her, and handed the phone to Jamie. Caution now darkened his eyes. "Would you drive me home, please? We can discuss this on the way."

Jamie wasn't concerned with what his parents thought as much as why Anna would do such a thing in the first place. He hoped she would explain herself, but they drove in silence. What did he have to say except he was disappointed she'd misled him and utterly shocked that she had. Where his hectic commitment to ballroom dance had not given him a lot of time to spend on women, he'd always thought himself to be a good judge of a woman's character.

He would not have pegged Anna to be dishonest.

Naively, he thought, being royalty and all, she would be forthright to an extreme. Then he wondered if he was just making excuses for a pretty face that was really nothing more than a politician with a crown.

Slanting her a glance, he realized he really didn't know who she was. It made him wonder just what he was doing. "Anna—"

"Let me—"

"Why did you do it?"

"I told you, you could not go alone."

"Yeah, but you still could have let them know." When she didn't answer, he figured he knew already. If her staff had known, the two of them wouldn't have gone anywhere. He wasn't sure how to proceed. Still feeling the fresh sting of deceit, he frowned. "This whole thing stinks."

"I will make sure things are right. You will see."

Though he really wasn't as worried about himself as he let on, he was concerned that her honesty would now be an issue of trust between them. He believed honesty was the glove of commitment.

They pulled up to the house and stopped just through the open gates.

"Great," Jamie muttered when he saw the dozens of news and police vehicles. He swallowed the nub in his throat. "Oh, brother."

"Don't worry." She patted his arm, then pulled down the lighted mirror on the passenger visor and frowned at her reflection. "I will take care of everything."

"I don't suppose there's a back way into this place."

Anna shook her head, smoothed her hair as best she could and swung the visor back up. Those casually loitering around the front door had taken notice of them and were scurrying up the drive in their direction.

"Crap." Jamie turned, his arm grabbing the back of the seat as he readied to back the car out. The heavy gate had already swung shut. He let out a fast breath. "Any suggestions, Your Highness?"

Though her stomach was a web of knots, Anna spoke confidently, "Drive on."

He shot her a glare.

Once they pulled up to the door, the car was surrounded like a dead carcass being scavenged. Questions were screamed through the windows, lights flashed in their eyes. Navy-uniformed police officers broke through the crowds and stood near the car. One leaned close, shouting through the noise. "Are you ready to come in, Your Highness?"

Anna nodded.

The doors were opened, and both she and Jamie were escorted to the front door of the house among a ticker-tape of questions and more snapped photographs. Once inside, Jamie broke free of the officer's grasp with the shrug of impatience.

Vladimir stood in the center of the hall, his hands clasped behind his erect back. Lukov and Ivan stood beside him.

As if nothing out of the ordinary had occurred, Anna turned to the two policemen that had followed them inside. "Thank you again for your swiftness in coming to our aid. Your attentiveness to my safety is appreciated. You are most efficient. Again, I thank you, but my staff is fully equipped to take over security from here." When they didn't make a move to leave, she turned to Vladimir. "Is there some reason these gentlemen are not following my orders?"

Vladimir's lips quivered and he slowly stepped toward her. "They have remained at my request." He shot a steely look at Jamie. "Until this is settled."

Anna turned back to the officers. "My good gentlemen." Taking two of them by the elbows, she led them toward the front doors with a congenial smile on her face, and the other officers followed. "Your service, though thorough, is no longer needed. I am sure, in fact, that your service could be put to better use somewhere else in the city at this moment. As the supreme dignitary for the Isles of Slovokia, I am the only one in authority to dismiss or retain your services."

Neither of the officers even gave Vladimir a second glance, so taken with Anna's smooth and convincing delivery to the front door. Jamie's eyes narrowed and the crimp in his gut tightened. The officers smiled, shook her hand and left without further question as if she'd blown fairy dust in their eyes and blinded them.

Anna faced Vladimir. "You were undermining my position and my authority."

"Let us talk about this in private, Anna."

Jamie's wary gaze caused Anna an uncomfortable crimp in her stomach. "Jamie had no knowledge of my plans." Vladimir rolled his eyes but Anna ignored him. "You will not cause trouble for him."

"He has done that for himself." Unfazed, Vladimir crossed to the office. "Ivan, Lukov, tell the media I will make an announcement in fifteen minutes."

Anna's eyes widened when the two, burly men readied to do Vladimir's bidding. "You will not make an announcement without my approval."

He spun around. "You were gone. We did not know where you were. You left the results of that foolish decision in my hands. It is still in my hands, and I will make the final remarks to the press."

"I am home and I will make the remarks." Intent to do just that, Anna whirled around but Vladimir snagged her by the upper arm.

Vladimir's eyes narrowed on Anna. "You may want to freshen up before you face the press, Your Highness." Something passed between Anna and Vladimir that Jamie couldn't read, but it left a vicious vibe in the air.

"Jamie, please wait for me in the rehearsal room," she told him.

Jamie nodded. He had to trust that she knew what she was doing, that she could handle the man. There was an ugly familiarity in the air and he figured this was not their first disagreement.

He stood in the rehearsal room alone, peeking out one of the windows at the lingering press, huddling in the cold. The police had gone, and he was glad. It cut a hole inside of him somewhere he couldn't identify, near his heart, to think that Anna dealt with this kind of frenzy on a regular basis. Even worse was the idea that he'd played a part in it, even unwittingly.

Part of him, the part that had seen her handle the pressure with the ease of a party hostess, had the feeling the tricky nature of what she did was done more out of duty than love.

Vladimir was clearly displeased with the overnight events and he couldn't say he blamed the man. With the press in full frenzied force, the stirrings of trepidation he felt inside weren't something he could ignore.

When he heard steps, he turned. It didn't surprise him to find Vladimir coming his direction looking like he might have a gun hidden somewhere in that black suit. Because Anna was upstairs for a time, he readied for a face-off.

"I will speak with out interruption," Vladimir's tone cut the silence like the blade of a knife. He spoke only after stopping purposefully close. "You placed her Royal Highness in a very dangerous position last evening. There are those who would take advantage of any opportunity that she is vulnerable. Her welfare is primary to the welfare of her country, as she is next in line to the throne." Vladimir's face gradually turned crimson. "You put her, her future, the very future of her people, in jeopardy with your irresponsible behavior."

Jamie understood what had happened was irresponsible and he was willing to take his part of the blame, but more than the reprimand darkened Vladimir's eyes – the threat went far deeper.

He worked to keep his patience and ego in check. "I would never do anything to jeopardize her safety. And just for your information, I had no idea that Anna hadn't cleared her getaway with you guys."

Vladimir let out a sharp laugh of disbelief. "Perhaps Her Highness will be looking for a new dance partner; one willing to remember who she is. One who will remember their station."

Jamie's jaw locked. His lips twitched to keep from breaking into a self-defensive snarl. Forcing a grin, he sent a companionable slug to Vladimir's upper arm. "No problem, Vlad. Whatever Anna wants." It almost pleased him, the slight bulge in Vladimir's eyes, the fine mist of perspiration webbing the man's forehead.

Jamie turned, crossed to the music and dug out his CDs. Out the corner of his eye, Vladimir stood in the same place, fists hanging opening and closing at his sides. Ah, vintage Van Halen. Since he was stressed, Jamie knew a good funk dance would help kick the fight out of his own fists.

The bass pounded a rhythmic, savage beat matching Jamie's nervous frustration. Jamie had danced for countless tough judges, but as he looked across the floor at Vladimir, he doubted he'd find any less critical than this. Still, his blood sang when David Lee Roth screamed and the lyrics demanded that he run with the devil.

The grin spreading across his face wasn't something he could stop. Neither was the surge thundering through his body like a frenetic storm. He slid across the floor and began to let loose in a routine of jumps and kicks, punches and twists, dips and floor rolls. He didn't bother seeing whether Vladimir stayed, he didn't care. The part of him that gave itself freely to the music was gone, lost in the words, lost in the beat – in exorcising his soul.

A final set of handsprings across the floor landed him at Anna's feet. Playfully, he bowed, before circling her, catching his breath. She broke out in a grin, applauding.

Vladimir stormed from the room.

"Very well done." Anna had changed into a soft brown velour sweat suit. She'd pulled her hair back into a pony tail and looked breathtakingly fresh and unfazed, Jamie thought, by the trouble they were in.

"You ready to face the sharks?" he asked, flicking out his hands and arms.

She strode across the floor to the music and turned it down some. "Certainly. I'll only be a few minutes. You can continue dancing, if you wish." Then she swept toward the doors in what would have been an elegant exit, except Jamie wasn't about to be left behind.

"Wait a minute." Jamie jogged up next to her. "I want to be there."

"That really is not necessary. I clean my own messes."

"So do I and I'm going to be there." He stayed shoulder-to-shoulder with her.

It was clear by the sharp look in his brown eyes that he was not in the mood to negotiate. Where Anna preferred to take care of issues herself, she appreciated that his integrity demand his participation. "Very well."

Jamie looked down at his clothing, wrinkled and dirty; and ran a hand along his face with a grimace. "I look like shiz."

"Shiz?"

"I'd never swear in front of royalty." He sent her a flash of teeth, glittering eyes that teetered between teasing and tempting. She loved a mussy man. Anna doubted anyone would care what he said at the press conference if he smiled like that.

"Shall we?" When he held the door open for her, she realized all of this would find its way back to her father. But that was what she wanted.

8.

Jamie wasn't sure if Provo was lacking for juicy news, or if it really was a big story, but the missing princess headline ran for two days with him starring as the bad guy. And his bad guy image didn't stay locked up on the TV screen or on the cover of the newspaper. The phone in his apartment rang off the hook with both nosey friends and back-biting associates.

He fumed that for all of Anna's damage control, he'd had plenty to deal with.

Cheryl hadn't returned his calls so he found himself camped out on her doorstep, waiting for her to open the door and let him explain. One of her roommates finally had mercy and let him inside but the sober mood in the place told him the pot was boiling and he was dangerously close to being cast into it.

Cheryl's roommates were gracious enough to stay in the back of the small apartment, making it clear with occasional appearances, that they were there for her support, not his.

He'd never seen anything but a smile on Cheryl's face and when she emerged with the puffy, red-rimmed eyes of disappointment he'd have rather been slapped.

"Can we talk?" he asked.

She nodded. He took her hand and led her to a flowery couch they both sunk into. Everything he had thought of to say sounded cliché and ridiculous. He could hardly think clearly through his brewing anger at Anna.

"You saw the news?" When she nodded, her icy blonde hair bobbed. "Cheryl, nothing happened except a lame campout in freezing weather."

"It's not any of my business, anyway," Cheryl sniffed. "I mean, you and I have no commitment. You can do whatever you want, right?"

When her eyes flickered with the hope to know more, he withdrew the urgency in his tone. A small part of him felt a lift that she saw their relationship as nothing more than close friendship, and the revelation confused him. "Cheryl, there's no one else I'm seeing right now."

As if she sensed his withdrawal, Cheryl eased away. "But that's more an issue of time isn't it?"

He shouldn't be here, defending something that he shouldn't have to defend, and another flash of anger at Anna pulsed through him. "Look. I know I haven't been the most attentive boyfriend," he used the word just to see what she did with it. Only a glint of light moved in her eyes so he continued. "But one thing I'd never do is screw around on one person while I'm with somebody else. I just wouldn't do that, Cheryl. I didn't do it in my partnership and I'd never do it in a relationship."

That she leaned toward him, he took as a positive sign. "I – I did find it hard to believe. I mean, you seem sincere."

"You have to talk things out," he told her. "It's something I do in my partnerships. If you're not happy with the way things are going, you talk about it."

A smile finally broke across her face. Flinging her arms around him, she rocked him with her laugh.

"Is this how you comfort your students?" He mumbled, his face burrowing into her neck. He took a deep breath, but when the layer of weighty guilt didn't vanish, suffocating confusion set in.

"When they're hurt, or when the bully gets mean." She angled her head at him. "So why did she do it?"

It was a question Jamie was still asking himself. A snooty princess does not drop everything for a night in frigid temperatures and no sleep.

"Maybe she likes you," Cheryl said softly, waiting for his far-off gaze to meet hers.

When it did, it was under tight brows. "What? No way." He moved back from her, the idea warming him more than he liked. And he didn't care for how it felt coming at him in Cheryl's embrace.

"You don't see yourself like women do." Cheryl snuggled close. "You're a great dancer, gorgeous, funny, honest—"

"Okay, stop."

She laughed. "It's true. When I first met you, I couldn't imagine why you weren't hooked up."

Absently, his fingers ran up and down her arm. The accolades embarrassed him. But he was too puzzled by Anna's motives to think about the compliments for long.

Cheryl cocked her head back so she could look at him. "I mean, how many really nice guys do you think she meets in her gilded circle, Jamie? She's probably hot for you."

Again he snickered. "We're dance partners – that's it. That's all it ever will be," he said aloud, hoping that by saying it, it would stay true. But the seed Cheryl had planted now took root beneath his skin.

They watched one of Cheryl's favorite movies, and Jamie dismissed the suggestion that Anna's interests were both personal as well as professional. It was the only way he could deal with the troubling idea. He forgot about dance. He didn't think about the campout or the press debacle. He watched the TV, kept his arm around Cheryl and had a few laughs.

Anna readied for the meteoric shower of disapproval she expected from her father. When Monday morning came and nothing happened, not even a phone call, she wanted to think her father had made great strides in his views of her life. Her nagging conscience warned her that the storm was only brewing. It was not because she had yet to see any real consequence for the act from her father, but that she had spent the entire weekend wondering and worrying about Jamie.

She tried to call Jamie but his answering machine was the only contact she'd had with him for two days. Using him and the campout to send a private message to her father was inexcusable. But her father had to understand that she had her own life. That she did what she wanted because it was right, and it was the progressive way, whether a campout or a marriage.

With her thoughts vacillating between guilt and determination, she oversaw the installment of the black-out window coverings Reuben had requested. She stood looking at them now, wondering what he planned to do in a pitch-black room.

She heard the front doors thud closed. It would be Reuben or Jamie, and as she stood waiting for one of them to be escorted in, her heart skipped. If Jamie were here, she could apologize again. That was all she would do because she could not jeopardize her future by telling him the truth.

Reuben came through the door. His smile reached across the room like a neon welcome sign. "That was some show this weekend." He let his duffle slide to the floor next to a chair. "You all right?"

She nodded. "Though I am afraid I have alienated Jamie."

"He doesn't stay mad for long." He sat, and changed his shoes. Both heard the door slam, but only Anna turned and watched Jamie stride across the floor with an edge that screamed warning.

Whatever had burrowed under his skin from Cheryl's suggestion had not left and Jamie was livid. Seeing Anna in the flesh, he was both irritated and fascinated with her.

Because he prided himself on keeping his word, he found his conflicting feelings disorienting to his very core. Uncertainty was not something he let linger in any part of his life. He was adamant about knowing just where everything stood. That was why Courtney's surprise exit had left him so shocked, and he'd had nothing but inconsistencies since he'd connected with Anna.

She was wearing white again. He would have laughed at the attempt at reconciliation had she not looked deceptively angelic. But she was far from angelic, he reminded himself as he ripped open his duffle, his gaze pinning her with all the anger he could muster. Anger would be the best way to keep her mystifying aura from opening him up and reaching where he didn't want her.

"Suppose you saw the circus Saturday," Jamie snapped first thing, his hard glare directed only momentarily at Reuben before he let it shift with obvious disapproval back to Anna.

"I saw it." Reuben smiled and strolled over so they could clasp palms in a show of greeting.

If only it had been nothing, Jamie thought, tying his shoes.

"You look good on TV, bro."

"You are still mad at me?" Anna didn't move one inch in Jamie's direction.

Jamie stood and shook out his arms, flicking his fingers. He crossed to her. "I woke up and some goon was outside my apartment snapping pictures and asking more questions." He stopped just inches away from her, and her upturned chin did little to amuse him.

"As I took the trash out my back door, I heard a click and what do you know, some other goon was stealing a picture of me by the dumpster. Can't wait to see the headline to that one." He extended his hand in the air as he spoke, "American treats princess like trash." It satisfied Jamie when her eyes widened and her mouth opened into a perfect O.

"It's fine for you," he continued. "You're sitting here in your fortress, with your pit bulls. The rest of us have to fend for ourselves. Tell me, Anna, how long can I expect to have the paparazzi on my back?"

"I will talk to them."

His laugh was halfway between a bark and a bite. "No thanks. In fact, if you'd let me do my own talking the other day, I could have told them I didn't approve of your little stowaway act. Instead, you left it convincingly ambiguous."

Her mouth dropped. Reuben slid close, placing a hand on each of their shoulders. "Kids…"

Anna jerked free and stepped back. "I did what was best."

"For you."

"For us. We are partners." A red flush crept up her skin. "I think it would be best to drop this subject and get to work, unless you intend to drag this out day after day."

"I can drop it," he nearly snarled, "as soon as you apologize."

Her angled head and hard eyes showed no sign of doing any such thing.

"I apologized. I do not have to apologize more than once. I have never heard of such a thing!"

"Yeah, I'll bet you haven't." Jamie strode away, body tight. She'd never have to grovel for anything. It annoyed and infuriated a man who'd been settling battles and putting out fires with siblings and partners since he could walk.

"I won't tolerate lies, Anna." He'd take the single apology for now, making sure she understood he was in charge of this partnership. "Either you trust me, and you trust Reuben, or this partnership is over."

She looked into his eyes for what grew to be an uncomfortably long time, forcing him to stare her down in another silent battle of defiance and compliance.

"All right."

Jamie nodded and looked at Reuben. "Reuben?"

"He's right. Might as well call it quits if we can't trust each other."

Anna's chin lifted but she nodded. It was harder pulling her from her throne than Jamie realized.

"Okay, time to work." Reuben looked around the room at the windows. "You done good, sis. Let's close them."

Each jogged around the room, closing the windows until any grey daylight was excluded. Only the lights overhead cast an ivory haze throughout the room. Reuben took Anna's hands and looked her in the eye.

"We're gonna do a little exercise. You aren't scared of the dark, are you?"

Anna shook her head. "But I do suffer from claustrophobia." She decided she would be honest even if it sounded silly and weak. She would prove she was holding nothing back.

"Do you?" Reuben swung her hands a little in his. "Well, Jamie will take note of that. Sometimes darkness can make you open up. Sometimes, not knowing what you can't see helps you cling to your partner. In rumba, it's all about conjoined movement. Movement so close, you can move with your partner without seeing him because you rely on every other part of your body and soul to feel."

An uncertain shudder pooled in Anna's belly. She looked over at Jamie, casually waiting. "Has he done this before?"

Reuben nodded. "It's a technique I use when my dancers need to connect."

Anna's insides fluttered as if filled with jumping crickets. "Oh."

"There's nothing to be afraid of." Reuben took her chin in his fingers, forcing her gaze from Jamie to him. "You just feel. Let those feelings take you through the steps. There are no distractions, no mirrors, no music, nothing. You won't even hear me. Just follow Jamie's lead." She didn't know why her legs felt wobbly. Why her breath seemed hard to find. Reuben led her across the floor to Jamie.

Anna looked at Jamie's outstretched hand. To be in complete darkness with Jamie's body directing her—she hoped that she could get through the exercise without him sensing just how deeply she felt about him.

His hand looked gentle and inviting, and though her heart began to skip, she took it.

She was looking at him as if he was leading her into the depths of the ocean without question and complete trust. It surprised and pleased Jamie. Faith flickered in her green eyes, latching onto his with an apprehensive urgency that humbled him.

"It's okay," he said softly, drawing her to the center of the floor. Something in her vulnerability stirred him. He didn't know why this would frighten her, but he was pleased to see the emotion nonetheless. For now, he would help bring her feelings to the surface where he could take them and teach her to use them.

Reuben had already crossed to the light switches and was waiting for Jamie's signal. Jamie looked down into Anna's face. "Ready?"

Her eyes never varied from his, as if her life depended on their connected gaze. "Will you be counting?"

He shook his head. "Just feel me, move with me."

It was embarrassing and undignified that her hands trembled, that her face burned with heat. When he slid his arm around her waist, she closed her eyes for a moment and took a deep breath.

The room went black.

Anna's first thought was to breathe. She'd had doubts that the room could become a dark cave, but it had. Her eyes strove to adjust, searching for Jamie's face. Relieved they were already in starting positions, she gripped his hands hard.

"Easy," his voice was a seductive whisper.

Not knowing what he would do, not sure where he would go, she tripped over his toes and cursed in Slovokian.

"It's all right," he said.

"But—"

"Shh."

She felt his hand firmly on her back, pressing her more deeply against his body. Then the doors flung open and light streamed a soft beam across the darkness of the room, startling them both. Jamie's arms fell away and he stepped back, leaving her feeling empty.

Anna squinted until the lights came on. Inessa stood in the door, her eyes huge behind her glasses. "I am sorry Anna, but Vladimir sent me. He must speak with you."

Anna's heart had leapt to her throat feeling Jamie so close in the strange darkness. Now, after such a bizarre intimacy interrupted, she had to clear her throat. "Tell him we must not be disturbed."

Inessa nodded.

"Hey, Nessa." Jamie sent a casual wave to Inessa that sent icy nails down Anna's spine. How could he so easily snap from something quiet and close to being friendly and casual?

"Good morning, Mr. Wilde."

"Nessa, Nessa, it's Jamie. Forget this mister stuff."

"Relay the message to Vladimir." Anna moved away from Jamie, irritated that she was jealous. "And see that we're not interrupted again." She was glad when the door closed and there was silence. The dark, mysterious mood brought on by the blackened room was near again, hovering around Anna with seductive whisperings.

"Ready?" Jamie's low, deep tone drew her to him.

When the room blinked black again, all she could feel was his hands. One hand, hot as an iron, slid around the small of her back, and once again pressed her into him. The other held her hand with the tender care of a bird in his palm. He started by spinning them both in a circle anchored only where their thighs joined. Her insides swam, and she clung with more urgency as the spin continued and they began to travel across the floor. His steps were large, aggressive, and she mirrored them, keeping her thighs locked with his. Every part of his body was tight and hard, a steady force she now took from as they branched out into the darkness. Afraid they were going to hit the wall, her fingers clutched, her nails dug into the hard line of muscles on his shoulders and arms.

"I – we're going to hit something—"

"Shh—" His face was near. Instinct turned her head toward his, snaking up from her belly with a need stronger than the need to follow his lead. Her cheek brushed his and the scent of his skin fired into her senses.

Suddenly he stopped, holding her so tight her breath wouldn't come. The fingers on her back spread wide and he began to lean his rigid weight toward her, pushing her achingly slow into a deep backbend. Though his strength whispered that she had nothing to fear as she inched further and further back, the strain in her body screamed for relief. Her limbs trembled against the stone power of him covering her.

When she thought she could arch back no further, as her body wept with sweat, mercy came. The gentle pressure from his hands urged her forward and soon she was upright against him, their chests heaving for breath aligned with each other.

Reprieve only lasted for a moment. He thrust her out into the darkness, their only connection now their hands, clasped tight. Emotion clogged her throat, forcing tears she hadn't known were there. After his body nearly covering hers, the emptiness surrounding her now was disconcerting in a way she had never experienced. She felt dependent on something her heart wanted and could never have.

The empty blackness he'd set her in swarmed around her as they moved until she could stand it no longer. She begged him near with her hands. He resisted at first, his arms stiff and unyielding. It sent a troubled tremor to her heart. In a flash that nearly had her falling over her feet he spun her, and her fingers dug into his for a lifeline.

Then he snapped her in, wrapping an arm around her while they moved in soft, gentle waves of possession. The whole of him again fused to her and the heat of his body dashed the cold being alone had brought. Without thinking, she laid her head in the crook of his neck, her cheek burrowing into firm, slick skin.

She wanted to cry, to dissolve the strange feelings of need powerfully roaming inside of her. There was a change in him then, as she lay against him in complete submission. His heart pounded beneath her cheek. But his hands didn't stay in the stance of dance. Like the wick of dynamite lit with a crackling flame, they traced her arms and lightly sketched her ribs slowly discovering every curve of bone, each stretch of muscle, leisurely finding their way up to her shoulders and neck.

His face was a breath away. Heat fanned her, igniting desire in a searing pull that began at her lips and now dangled with desperation somewhere inside. She slid her hands slowly up his chest, each muscle skimmed hardening in the wake of her touch. Her arms wrapped around his neck, her fingers groped the tense muscles there before dancing into his hair. She heard his breath hitch and whatever dangled deep inside of her pulled.

She wanted his mouth. Eager fingers gently drew his head to hers. His body tensed, like a fist clutching, contracting the full length of her. A low moan escaped his lips. So close. Blindly, her lips skimmed his cheek, the rough skin hot against her mouth. She pressed a kiss there and he shuddered. His breath was racing, she could hear it, feel it, and her head swam to the tempo.

Suddenly, he pushed her away.

Stunned, she stood alone in complete darkness, freshly torn from something so close, so deep, it had been severed from her very being. An involuntary whimper escaped her throat and she shoved her fist to her mouth to stop it. He would hear – he would know. His breath was heavy, erratic, moving in space somewhere in front of her. Stepping blankly his direction, she reached out her hands but felt nothing.

What had he done? Jamie paced wildly in the dark. He'd felt her heart—the need in it had reached out to him and he'd accepted it. No, he'd taken it. She'd been so warm, so aberrantly submissive in his arms. The scent of her hair, the feel of her skin had every part of him straining for more. Fine, he thought, knowing a body could react to a moment if it wanted to, whether or not the heart or the brain permitted. He'd done this before without crumbling. So why now?

Then she'd kissed him. His cheek still burned. He swiped the back of his hand across his face hoping to remove the brand but it did nothing but place the kiss on his hand.

"Lights," he barked.

He heard her rustling in the darkness. Part of him wanted to feel for her, to try and calm her. Guilt gutted him. It had been harsh to toss her away like that, but he'd been frantic with his own feelings spiraling so fast out of control.

Lights blared, blinding them all. Jamie looked over, embarrassed to meet her gaze, but knowing it had to be done; the dance had to be addressed.

She stood with her hands covering her face and Reuben was next to her rubbing her shoulders. Did she have to look so devastated? He'd barely touched her.

But he'd felt so much more.

He joined Reuben, his heart full seeing how tightly she pressed her hands to her face. Reuben's dark eyes met his with question. All Jamie could do was rub his jaw and try to navigate what to do next.

"Sis?"

Anna dropped her hands. There was only a trace of red rimming her eyes. She looked at both of them. "That was very hard for me."

"It can be," Reuben said quietly. "The first time can be like being naked."

Anna's eyes grew huge. "The first time?"

"Don't worry," Reuben told her, hands skimming her arms in comfort. "I'll give you plenty of time to gather yourself."

Anna looked at Jamie, her insides ready to collapse. "I – I don't think I can do that again." She hated that her emotions were so raw that when her voice hit the air, it cracked.

"Okay, okay. We'll talk about that later." Reuben's gaze swept her from head to toe. "Tell me what you felt."

She couldn't. She'd never felt so vulnerable and yet there was that sweetness of surrender. Jamie stood too near, his breath, his scent floated in the air, reminding her of where he had taken her emotions – from the vale of need to the peak of desire and back. Talking about it would be like stripping her of everything and leaving her emotions out in the open.

He would see, he would know.

But this was not something she could talk away. The dance demanded it. Indeed, she would never forget this experience. It was the most intimate she had been with a man, and because of that, she was both drawn to Jamie and apprehensive of him.

"What did you feel?" Reuben asked again.

Taking in air didn't help; she only wanted to float away on it. Uneasily, she glanced at Jamie. "I felt – it forced me to follow what was inside of me."

"Good, good." Nodding, Reuben's hands finally eased from her shoulders. "What else?"

"I had to let go. To open up. To put away my preconceived ideas, my…. pride… so that I could follow. That was very difficult."

"And you did it," Reuben said. "Remember these feelings. Draw from them now as you dance. Take yourself to that place, wherever it was when the lights were out and it was just you and Jamie."

Jamie moved to the center of the room and Anna's heart gulped in her chest. Her feet were rooted to the floor. Reuben nudged her. She crossed with all the trepidation of a toddler being forced into the arms of a stranger. His hand was out, awaiting hers.

"Try the routine from the top," Reuben told them.

Jamie brought her in and they stood ready for Reuben's count.

Moving through the steps with the steadiness of a metronome; continual, relentless, slower than water dripping from a stingy faucet, they danced. Jamie's dark eyes were focused, alive, dancing with as much expression as his body. His face went through stages of the dance just as his body did: need driven by desire. Joy. Satisfaction.

Anna didn't know if he understood what she was saying with her eyes and part of her didn't care. He'd opened up through the language of his face, and drawn her heart and soul to the surface. Now, she wanted to share it with him. Though she knew his expressions were theatrical only, her heart whispered to hope for more—to dream beyond performance.

He'd touched her. She'd felt want in it – more than rumba. Somewhere in the darkness, dance had shifted to something else. His fingers had trailed over her driven by desire and exploration, not obligation. Or skill. When her lips had touched his cheek, it had been she that had controlled the dance. She would remember that.

She hardly knew they finished. Wouldn't have, if she hadn't suddenly been standing still with Jamie holding her in their final position.

Reuben's face glowed. "Much better." He joined them in the center of the room, and Anna felt Jamie's arms slip away.

9.

Black-out shades no longer needed, Anna tugged the fringy bottoms and each rolled up in a crackling snap. She took her time. Reuben had gone, and only she and Jamie remained in the empty hall. She heard him changing his shoes. Highly aware of his every move, even with her back to him, she felt unusually awkward.

Few things intimidated Anna. Though it had been hours since their dance in the dark, she could tell that Jamie still had something to say about it. He'd worn the need to express those feelings on his face, drawn taut most of the evening. She was both curious and hesitant now to hear what was on his mind.

After she pulled up the last shade, she turned. Jamie stood with his hands at his sides, shoulders and arms poised as if ready to slug, scream, or both. His head was slightly lowered but his piercing gaze was like a black moonbeam aimed right at her.

Jamie intimidated her.

Still, she had learned some acting skill. She'd had to, being made to attend functions when she'd not felt like it. She was perfectly capable of pretending that her knees weren't wobbling, that her stomach was not in a fist of knots.

Silently, she crossed the floor to him. Though her heart boomed in her chest, she steadied her breathing. For a tortuously long silence, he simply bore his dark eyes into hers until she thought she would shrink.

"Today," his voice scraped raw, "was wrong."

Her booming heart tore. What had she felt in his fingertips if not desire? Through the dark drift he had taken her, forcing her feelings out into the open. Now, she felt ashamed that he knew them for what they were.

"What was wrong about it?"

"I shouldn't have touched you like that. It was wrong. It will never happen again, you have my word on it."

When she swallowed the hard knot in her throat, her heart went down with it. He was utterly serious. He might as well have laughed; it would have been less devastating than knowing they would never again go to those dark, seductive places.

He turned to retrieve his duffle and she took a step toward him. "What happened, Jamie?"

He didn't face her but lowered his head, and fingered the handle of his duffle. "We got carried away."

"We were dancing."

"We were at first."

"Are you ashamed of that?" Bravely, she came next to him, brushing his arm with her body in an attempt to remind him. His sharp gaze darted where she touched him before lifting to hers. She saw a fight there; shame battling with a natural curiosity that couldn't be denied.

"It's something I swore to myself I would never do. How do you think that makes me feel?"

That he would feel guilt over something she'd dissolved her soul into, upset her sense of truth. Men and women were made to find each other. This simple God-given right was a beautiful, if elusive gift that Anna held in as much regard as most people held her fairy-tale existence. It was the very reason she had come to America and left the confining chains of her homeland.

"You did nothing wrong. Please, do not feel—"

"I promised myself I would never allow personal feelings to interfere with my work. Today, I broke that."

Anna's heart fluttered with joy. She tried not to smile, tried not to let the admission thrill her, but it was too late. He had feelings for her. She had felt them in his arms and those feelings broke through his barrier whether he'd wanted them to or not.

"I'm not sorry, Jamie," she told him, her voice composed with pure elation. "My feelings were out there. Do you think that was easy for me?"

"But that was why we did the exercise. I expected that."

"Oh, and you are so strong, that you cannot respond to me as any other man might?"

His tone rose, and so did the fury in his eyes. "I'm not any other man."

"You mean to say that if Reuben had done that exercise with me, my reaction to him, his reaction to me, would have been the same? Who do you think you are?"

"A man who makes commitments and promises and keeps them." He practically shouted it. "Since you've come into my life, I've been nothing but challenged in my principles. I would have never found myself camping with a Princess. I wouldn't have friends questioning my motives. My family wouldn't be wondering what I'm doing." He finally stopped, heaving out a breath. Turning a weary gaze at her, he said, "It's not your fault. I don't mean to make it sound like it's you. It's me."

Fearing he wanted to dissolve the partnership, her mind scrambled with what to do. "I do not think you should torture yourself over this," she started, because he still wrestled with it. "I will do whatever you want, Jamie. Whatever. You tell me."

The moment stretched arduously long and Anna waited with her nerves on ice. The very thought of Jamie, her dreams and her future, perilously close to being altered, caused her to ache. She knew then that she loved him. She loved his strength, his commitment, his integrity. Whatever happened would only make her happy if it was what gave him peace.

Resolve closed the door to his heart – there was a change in his eyes when that door slammed shut. "I'll see you tomorrow."

She should have been overjoyed that he was willing to stay, but the finality of the slammed door echoed in her heart. It would be a one-sided love, this she knew. He would be even more determined to keep their relationship professional, and it would torment her, every hour of every day.

All that Anna knew was that she could not see. Afraid to move, unsure of where she was, she stood utterly still, surrounded by thick blackness. Her heart raced. Without light, without any sense of which way to go, she began to tremble. Though she was not cold, she sensed no warmth. No movement of air. There was no sound and yet space was filled, as there was no echo.

One step any direction could mean a perilous loss. Every part of her felt exposed. Her hands skimmed her body. Fabric. Relief did nothing to comfort her. In the dark distance, she heard a drum beat, slow and enticing. Her head jerked around, seeking where the sound came from.

She sensed someone.

Though her eyes widened naturally, nothing filled the black space between her and the presence. But the air around her changed. There was breath -- warmth. Scent.

She reached out and was not afraid when her fingers touched flesh. She knew Jamie the instant her fingers met his skin. She knew the tempo of his breath singing with the drum. She knew the fabric that clothed his sleeve, and she ran her fingers from his wrist to his shoulder. The angled bone where his shoulder joined his arm she knew, she'd laid her hand there countless times, marveling at the hand-carved beauty of flesh over bone.

Through the darkness she stepped toward him and felt his arms wrap around her. Willingly, she melded, resting her head against his chest, and he slowly began to move them both in a rock. Their bond was sure, tight. A spin came next. She was not aware if her feet were even touching ground, but air whirled at her legs, her hair, her face. His soft clothing flapped soundlessly against her. The beat of the drum intensified. Their bodies spun faster, the force pressing them closer together. Her lungs filled with such pressure she could only release it with a laugh, and she threw her head back.

They spun until her body was weak. It didn't matter that she was helplessly pinned against him, the vortex threatening to consume them both. His arms were her shield, his breath her breath, and his heart beat next to hers.

When the darkness suddenly shifted to grey, she heard whispers, hard voices and footsteps. The safety of Jamie's arms slipped away, leaving her alone and empty.

"Anna."

She opened her eyes. Her father stood over her bed.

Anna shot up, her body warm, flushed, she was sure. The dream of being next to Jamie lingered in her blood. Pushing the hair out of her face, she up pulled the blankets, securing them at her chest.

"Papa."

His grey eyes scanned her quizzically before he leaned over and kissed her forehead. "Get dressed." He turned, and she watched his dark-suited figure walk heavy- footed from her room.

Anna blinked, still unable to believe that her father had actually come.

Because it was Monday and she was scheduled to rehearse she dressed in an all-grey sweat suit with black stripes along the seams. Her hair she wore up. Her father preferred the conservative hair style to any other.

She came down the stairs to the sound of three deep voices and instantly glanced at her watch – eight forty. Jamie and Reuben weren't set to arrive for another twenty minutes. When the loud sneeze rumbled paintings on the wall, she stopped. Only one person sneezed like a tuba blowing a spit wad from its throat. Her heart stopped.

Lev.

The pinched-nose tonality of his voice rose up the stairway like a clarinet off-key, annoying enough for her to turn on her heels and run. It was too late. Lev, led by her father and Vladimir, was coming into the great hall, looking right at her.

Anna's stomach crimped. It never got any easier to look at the man her father wanted her to marry. A man she'd known since childhood, who was like a brother to her. Tall, spindly, Lev Geza stood, itching with eagerness just behind her father. His hair fanned from his scalp like unraveled brown yarn. Gaunt, his gold-rimmed glasses barely stayed put, in spite of a God-given hook centered in his nose. Skin, like the surface of the moon, covered his face and neck. She'd once counted fifteen craters of various size and shapes. He looked ready to wet his pants every time he saw her, reminding her more of a homely pup than a man promised to a queen inheriting a throne.

"Anna." He religiously carried a wad of white, monogrammed hankies in his tightly clutched fist. His face broke into a toothy grin, pulling and opening those craters that covered his face. They embraced on the last step. Over his bony shoulder, she glared at her father.

Trussed in his black suit, her father looked fresh from a board meeting rather than a twenty-five hour flight. His black goatee was sharp-edged over lips thinned with disapproval.

"You look great, Anna." Lev took her hand in his clammy one and kissed it.

"Thank you, Lev. Did you have a nice flight?"

"Oh, yes. Your father's jet is fantastic."

Stepping onto the tile floor, Anna removed her hand from Lev's moist sticky one. "How nice of you to surprise me." She turned an icy eye to her father.

"This really isn't much of a surprise now, is it?" Her father stepped forward, extending his arm. The disapproval in his lips was now in the air, a storm Anna had known was on the horizon and she would have to face.

"I have rehearsal in," she checked her watch before wrapping her arm around his. "Ten minutes." She felt the undeniable pinch of displeasure when he kept her against his side.

"Rehearsal will have to wait."

10.

Four official-looking black Expeditions lined the drive, along with two Provo police department squad cars. Jamie had a twist in his gut. What has she done now? One news van sat near the front door.

Jamie got out of his car and hurried past the two men sitting inside. He heard their doors open, and his rapping on the front door turned into a pound.

Ivan had never looked better than when the door finally opened and Jamie slid into the house. After the door shut behind him, he let out a sigh.

"Anna is in a meeting. Please wait in the dance room."

Jamie grinned. "Do you realize that's the most you've ever said to me, Iv? You have a great speaking voice by the way. You could be a sports commentator: boxing, wrestling, weight lifting – any of the killer sports."

The humor grazed Ivan without any reaction whatsoever. Jamie helped himself to the dance room. His eyes went directly to the windows – to the shades, now rolled into invisibility. A heated shudder pooled low in his gut. Anna.

He walked the room and flicked out his hands. It smelled faintly of sweat, Anna's perfume and of walls kissed with the heat of their hard work. He stopped, closed his eyes and inhaled deeply. Even when she wasn't there, she was there. She was everywhere.

The door opened and his heart skipped. He turned, thinking he'd see her. He was greeted not by the face that haunted him, but a toothy smile underneath bespectacled eyes.

"Hey. I'm Lev." The man flew at him, nearly tripping over gangly legs. Instantly, Jamie felt an electrical energy shoot like invisible lightening through the room. He knew if it struck him, he'd be drained.

"Jamie Wilde."

"The dancer. Anna's told me about you."

"Has she? So, you're a friend of hers? From Slovakia?"

Lev broke out in a laugh that wound into a snort. "You could say that, yeah. We're betrothed."

Jamie's breath held in his chest at the news. "You're—betrothed? To Anna?"

Lev's head bobbed. "Yes. Have been since we were kids. I'm surprised she didn't tell you, being that you're her dance partner and all."

To say he was stunned by the news was an understatement. Jamie's stomach still hadn't settled, and he found himself in a daze filled with flashing images of Anna, of their dance in the dark, all surrounded by feelings he couldn't sort out now with the revelation.

"Uh…yeah. Well, I'm just her dance partner."

Lev laughed again. "Yeah. I recognize you. She watched hours and hours of your footage. It was all she could talk about for years."

The words froze Jamie. "Years?"

Lev's head bobbed. "She even had me search for stuff about you. All I could find was a few snapshots. You know, the usual AP stuff. That didn't make her very happy. She wanted more, more, always more."

A knot formed in Jamie's stomach.

"Oh, and when I had my people dig up copies of your old high school yearbooks and town newspapers, you'd have thought I'd discovered plutonium. She went bozzles."

Jamie scratched his chin. "No kidding. How long has she been on this…this…quest?"

"Gosh, let me think here…About five years now."

Jamie's eyes popped. "Five years?" Sweat dribbled down his back. For a moment, he couldn't think.

"Maybe longer than that," Lev continued with innocent eagerness. "I mean, she's been fascinated with ballroom dance since she was twelve and started taking lessons."

Still swimming with the idea that his life had been studied for years without his knowledge, Jamie was distracted.

"Hey, you don't look like you feel good." Lev threw a concerned arm around Jamie's shoulder. "Need to be sick?"

"No." Jamie shook his head. But he headed for the chairs and sat himself down. Why this news astounded him, he was sure had to do with the whole fairy-tale aspect of their meeting; Anna had told him that first night that she had come specifically to meet him. Somehow, he'd not really believed it. Even with the castle being real, the guards menacing, and a moat filled with paparazzi. He'd not actually believed she'd spent royal time and royal money learning all about a little-known dance competitor named Jamie Wilde.

He buried his face in his hands to still his swirling thoughts.

Lev followed him to the chairs. Settling himself down in the chair next to Jamie, he looked around the room. "I'm surprised this place is so small."

Jamie dragged his face up from behind his palms. "Is it?"

"Oh, yeah. I mean, the royal palace is no Buckingham by any means. But she's got her own quarters, you know? She must be going crazy."

Crazy? As the royalty of her continued to settle in, Jamie's emotions rode a rollercoaster. From shock, he'd soared up to amusement. "Has it pretty good back home, does she?"

Lev nodded like a bobbing-doll on the dashboard of a car. "Oh, yeah. I mean, My pops spends his money on different stuff than Zakharov, but that's one of the reasons they've pushed for an alliance – strengths and differences. I mean, Anna and I, well, we've been pals since we were kids. I know everything good and everything not so good, if you know what I mean."

Jamie sat back and stretched out. "Really?"

"Oh, yeah. You have to check up on your intended. You know, make sure they're not screwing around on you or whatever. That's why we're here."

"You think Anna's screwing around on you?"

"Oh, I don't. Her pop is worried about – well," Lev looked Jamie up and down, pushed his glasses up his nose, "He's worried about you actually."

"Me?" Jamie sat upright, his gut churning.

"I really shouldn't say."

Restless, Jamie stood. More unreal, overblown misunderstandings – that was all he'd known since he'd started dancing with Anna, and the news about her betrothal…it still didn't seem real. But it was, and now, her father had flown half-way around the world to do who knows what. Images flashed in his mind: stocks under the noon sun, dark, smelly dungeons filled with chains and rats.

It was just what he didn't need – an angry king accusing him of distracting his daughter from her royal duties.

"You are her dance partner, so I guess I can talk to you about it," Lev began, standing next to him. "He's concerned about the alliance dissolving."

"Why?"

"Her press conference a few days back was a direct threat to her father's sovereign will. He's here to figure out why. Hey, has she said anything to you? I mean, you guys are close, right?"

After clearing his dry throat, Jamie shrugged. Their dance in the dark had been like looking through a crystal ball of sorts, full of colorful, real emotions vague with direction but all pointing to Anna's open heart. "Sort of. Do you dance, Lev?"

Lev shook his head, laughing. "I'm so uncoordinated. I know it doesn't look like it, but I'm a two-left-footer if there ever was one."

Jamie scratched his head, smiled. The guy was so honest it was brutal. But he had a child-like quality Jamie liked. "Well," Jamie started, "just because we dance together doesn't mean we know each other well." That was more than clear now after hearing this surprising bit of news. "It's like any other relationship. It takes time."

"You're sure right about that," Lev nodded, folding his arms across his scrawny chest. "I mean, as long as Anna and I have known each other, I still feel like I don't really know her. I mean, there's Anna the princess, and there's Anna."

Having seen glimpses of that, Jamie understood Lev completely. Still, if they had known each other since childhood, he wondered how the guy could have missed getting deeper. Maybe royals didn't play like other children.

"What was she like as a little girl?" Jamie asked.

"Oh, you know, about like other girls."

Jamie waited for more. He and his brother hadn't done more than tease and torment their younger sister Jocelyn, but he still knew that her favorite colors were black and purple, that she hated pizza and dresses, and liked boys too much. And he'd never let anything happen to little Jessica. Both he and Justin would do anything for the girls.

"She liked dolls, horses, stuff like that?" Jamie asked.

"I guess."

What had they done when the families got together, played queen and king instead of hide and go seek? Jamie couldn't help but feel sorry for Anna – for about a minute. She may be promised to a nice guy who was, well, even for guy standards, not good-looking by any stretch. But she stood to stay in her cozy royal spot, living the high life, having it all on a silver platter.

He didn't know much about the life of a royal but he figured, as with the life of a commoner, there was give and take, pluses and minuses. You never got everything you wanted, even if you had everything in the world.

He had to hand it to her. To accept marriage because of duty was admirable – strong. For her, it had its purpose. He was just glad it wasn't something he was required to do.

Reuben entered and both Jamie and Lev met him halfway across the floor. Jamie introduced the two men to each other and Reuben and Jamie changed into their dance shoes.

"Maybe I'll learn a few steps while I'm here – you know, to impresses the ladies," Lev snorted out a laugh.

Jamie looked at him, confused. "I'm sure Anna would think it was great if you learned how to dance."

"Oh, we'd never dance together," Lev said.

"Why not?"

"She told me she can't dance with somebody she's going to marry. I think her exact phrase was, 'you can't dance and make love.'"

Jamie wanted to laugh, but he also wanted to strangle somebody – Anna, specifically. "She said that?"

"Oh, yeah. She's been telling me that for the last year or so. I guess it makes sense. It might affect her performance."

"A lot of dancers feel that same way." Reuben concealed a grin.

The doors flew open again. Anna hurried in with her father and Vladimir. Jamie saw her differently now; an imported, exquisite doll, whose painted-on expression did little to reveal what was beneath the porcelain protecting who she was deep inside. She greeted Lev with a casual cheek to cheek embrace, then joined Jamie and Reuben in the center of the floor.

Her father stood near the chairs with Lev and Vladimir. Jamie looked at the man who was king with a smidgen of awe. Striking, imposing with his dark hair, painted grey at the temples. His brows and goatee were the same nearly-black color of Anna's mane of hair, accentuating grey-green eyes. Eyes that looked like spears – spears aimed directly at him.

"Anna." The man's voice was deep and strong, like the blade of a sword in swing. "You have forgotten to introduce me to your coach and your dance partner."

"Oh, yes. Pardon me." Jamie felt her hand slip into his. Her neck and cheeks flushed. He had the sudden urge to pull her close and tell her everything would be all right. At the same time, his troubled heart wanted to take her aside and ask why she hadn't told him about Lev.

She led him and Reuben to where the three men stood. Jamie extended his hand and they shook.

"Alexander Zakharov." His hand was as strong as his voice, but Jamie didn't back down from delivering a sturdy handshake of his own.

"Jamie Wilde."

"Yes." The man's eyes were looking at more than just the commoner standing before him: This was the guy who danced with his daughter, and Jamie met his censuring gaze equally.

After the introductions, Anna returned to the center of the floor as if it was any other day, any other rehearsal.

The three men sat, comfortable as three surfboards propped against a wall. Reuben ignored them, but Jamie felt the tension in Anna before he'd even touched her.

Anna stepped close to Reuben. "Today we work on standard."

Without a flicker of confusion Reuben nodded. "Viennese waltz."

Jamie stood ready for her.

Her body was tense. She looked over his shoulder, an acceptable conservative stance for the Viennese waltz, but he knew it was more about their audience than the fact that they had not yet done this dance together that caused her to remain anxious and aloof.

Floating over the floor, Jamie led them through the simple, five-step dance. He had momentary visions of her in a gown, dancing at some royal function, looking the princess that she was. He marveled at the simple way they flowed together – like two silk streamers on a breeze, their bodies, their movements flurried, yet beautifully controlled as the tinkering wave of the waltz rhythm.

There was nothing he could say except to squeeze her hand and smile when they finished – she had danced poetically. She accepted his gesture with a brief nod, returning her focus to Reuben as she awaited instructions for their next dance.

They covered tango, fox trot, and quick-step, flowing from one to the next with the expertise and ease of partners who had been dancing for years, not weeks. Because they had not talked or discussed sequences like they normally did during rehearsal, Jamie hesitated. She was editing her performance. Part of that bothered him. Why she was Princess Anna in front of her father and Anna when it was just the two of them? Sensing the integrity of the moment was vitally important to her, he held back. Later, he would ask.

Lunch was served in the formal dining room with Vladimir, who Jamie had never seen do anything more than wander in and out of rooms with the stealth of a cobra.

This meal was more lavish. Anna's usual salad was replaced with some kind of dark and meaty stew with crusty rolls and butter. Jamie enjoyed the rich sauce laden with chunks of beef, turnips and rutabagas. A tall glass of red liquid sat next to Alexander Zakharov's plate. Though the cook offered wine all around, only Lev and Vladimir partook.

"You like the stew, Jamie?" Alexander shot his smoky eyes across the table in a look that told him he was about to be on the firing line.

"It's good."

"It is an old Slovakian recipe. However, at home, it is made with our own beer. Cook has found a substitute, but I'm afraid Amstel, though hearty and flavorful, lacks the same intense flavor our Kiansk beer. You drink, Jamie?"

Jamie swiped the cloth napkin across his lips. "No."

"Wine?" This as Alexander brought his glass to his lips.

"No."

Alexander's eyes narrowed just a bit and he turned to Reuben. "You are very good with them. You have been coaching for years?"

Anna kept from rolling her eyes. Her father knew everything about these men: where they'd been educated to their moral habits.

"Eighteen years now," Reuben answered.

"Anna speaks very highly of you both. I look forward to seeing her progress under your guidance, Reuben, and in your partnership, Jamie. This is something she has desired for some time now, to dance competitively with an American coach and an American partner."

"She has a lot of talent," Reuben said.

"Anna is a hard worker," Alexander continued. "She has set her sights on this and is determined to be successful." His gray gaze slid to Jamie again. "Jamie, you share this determination?"

"Yes, I do."

"You would not have titles if you didn't. Nothing will get in the way of the goals you and Anna have set?"

Not sure where Alexander was going with that, Jamie paused from eating, his hand poised at the stem of his water glass. "Not as long as I'm her dance partner and we stay on the same page."

Alexander only gave a nod, but his critical gaze penetrated with warning.

The warning was a threat Jamie wouldn't back away from. "And as long as our goals remain in sync."

Alexander set his glass on the table with a clink. He pushed his finished stew away, resting his elbows on the table. "Tell me your goals, Jamie. Just what do you want from Anna?"

"I want to do the best I can. I wouldn't mind taking a few titles along the way. As far as what I want from Anna, I don't want anything from her except her commitment to do her best. And," Jamie looked at her, although her glance was nothing more than gracious, "I know that's what she's giving me."

"Her commitment to dance is all that you will get from her."

"Papa," Anna snapped.

Jamie refused to be intimidated. "I wouldn't expect anything more."

"Papa." Anna turned to her father, partly because she wanted him to see her displeasure, partly because she didn't want Jamie to see the humiliation on her face from her father's implication. "Jamie is a man we can both trust. If it were not true, you would not have approved of my being here."

"She is right," Alexander said. "I just want to make sure, Jamie, after meeting Anna, after seeing her, your intentions have not changed."

"This is not a conversation we should be having," Anna said firmly.

"I hide nothing from my daughter, nor do I hide anything from the people I have in her life to care for and watch over her. You and Mr. La Bate are two of those people now. I will be frank with you. My visit here is because I sensed things were changing in her life, that her goals for her future and her responsibilities at home were no longer what they should be. I came here to see for myself if that was true. Those are things that remain private to our family. But, as I am here anyway, I am inclined to see that all areas of her life are in order. You understand?"

"Papa, please, you make me sound like I am an incapable child."

"I am a concerned father."

"A concerned loyalist first," Anna said.

Alexander's right brow rose slightly. The tension in the room heated, silencing everyone at the table with the potency of poison.

"Hey, it was a great meal." Reuben stood. Jamie joined him. "Anna, we'll wait for you in the hall."

"I would ask you not to leave," Alexander stated boldly and both men froze at the request. "Please. Sit. Cook has prepared one of my favorite desserts."

Hesitantly, both Jamie and Reuben lowered themselves back into their chairs.

Alexander's staunch demeanor shifted into an easy smile. "Have either of you ever had rhubarb pudding?"

When neither Reuben nor Jamie could say yes, Alexander sat back with a robust laugh. "You are in for a surprise. A treat, eh, Lev?"

For the first time since lunch, Lev's animated disposition took fire. "It's awesome."

"Root vegetables grow prolifically in the islands," Alexander explained as small, white pots of pink-tinted cream were placed before each of them. "Over the years, our people have, for lack of choice, become very creative with their use. Originally, the pudding was made with goat milk, but cream is a much better choice. It makes the pudding very rich and thick."

"And the root of the rhubarb is quite potent," Vladimir added. "When used as a tea it renders the body useless for a time."

Alexander's spoon dipped into his pudding. "I believe that is an old wives tale, nothing more. Anna, have you not chosen rhubarb filling for your wedding cake?"

"I have not made any choice about my wedding, Papa – cake or groom."

As if some of the creamy pudding had lodged in his throat, Alexander coughed, tapping his fist at his chest.

The room was thick with tension and the pudding, though pleasant enough, went down Jamie's throat like tar. Taking the opportunity to watch Anna, the strain she had worn since morning was still plain on her face. He felt like a spectator at a chess game – with no knowledge of how to play, left helpless to sway the outcome whether he was welcome to or not.

It was clear that the betrothal was something unsettled between them. Anna's displeasure was as obvious as her father's, but Jamie was sure they stood on opposite sides of the issue. Anna was fighting her way out. Jamie sensed a pupae yearning to break free of its confining cocoon. He recognized, even after a few weeks of knowing Anna, the look in her eye, the hard-set of her jaw as she worked to control fiery determination.

"I mean to make my marriage decision myself," Anna stated at last.

Lev gulped, and the entire table heard it. His eyes were bright, his head twisted back and forth from Alexander to Anna.

Vladimir wiped at his mouth, then leaned over, whispering to Alexander. The act forced Anna out of her chair with a loud sigh of disproval. She threw her napkin to the table. Looking at Reuben she angled her head. "Shall we get back to work?"

Pleased she had voiced her thoughts, Anna let out a sigh that didn't help to ease the turmoil she felt inside. Her father was still in the dining room being cooled off by a steady stream of Vladimir's flattering words. No doubt, Lev was whining. She couldn't stand any of it, and was not going to live with her duty-induced manacle for the rest of her life. She was letting down the draw bridge slowly, but they still had a long way to go before the meeting place between her father and her could be found over a clean moat.

She continued to rehearse, forcing her mind to concentrate on perfecting steps. Reuben left her and Jamie to select some music, and Jamie stood close. She met his curious gaze. "I am sorry about that."

A moment dragged between them. "When were you going to tell me you were betrothed?"

His incisive eyes pierced her. "It's not what I want, and I do not intend to follow through with it. Therefore, it has nothing to do with our partnership."

"Except that your Father, the King of Slovokia, came all the way over to check me out because he thinks this…the arrangement between you and Lev is compromised in some way."

"It was compromised long before you came into my life, Jamie. That is the truth." That was all she could say for now, so she averted her eyes.

"Hey." His hand lightly brushed her shoulder. "You okay?"

Wishing she could tell him what really lay inside, she studied him for a moment, watching the gentle expression on his face shift to concern.

"I don't have any answers," he said in a voice meant to calm. "You are who you are, Anna. There are things that go along with that."

"And you think I should accept them, even if they are not right?"

"What is right for you and your situation can't be judged by what's right for someone else in an entirely different situation."

"But there is basic right and basic wrong, Jamie. It is wrong to force someone to do something, taking from them their freedom of choice."

"But your country, your father, your people don't see your inheritance as something forced. It's your birthright."

"I do not want it." In haste, she heard the words leave her lips for the very first time. She had thought them thousands of times, but had never uttered them to anyone.

She covered her mouth with fluttering fingers. Between them now was a secret he knew nothing about the consequence of protecting.

"I am just angry." Averting her gaze again, she hoped to stop the tears welling there without his notice. "This is my problem and I will deal with it."

"Wait a minute," he kept his voice private, "there's more to it than that, I can see it in you. I can feel it."

"Yes, perhaps that is true, but to tell you about it would infringe on your principles. You have made it clear to me that you don't want to do that."

"You don't give me any credit, do you?"

"You are the one who has these rules—"

"Yeah, to not become lovers with the women I dance with, Anna. But also not to shove my partner off into some convenient, dance-only corner. I would hope that our partnership would mean we would be friends."

Though the word was meant to comfort her, it did not. A friend was not what she wanted him to be, ultimately. But she would take it if that was all he offered. "I did not want to place you in a compromising position, that is all."

"I can be your friend without compromising my principles." He reached for her arm. "Okay?"

She nodded but as the music began to play, the soft, haunting lull of the waltz tore through her heart in a way that left her achingly empty. She went into his arms seeking solace through the dance, hoping it would last until tomorrow.

11.

Life had never been simple, Jamie mused, driving to his apartment. In his twenty-eight years he'd never run away from challenges, but he definitely saw a pattern as he got older; life got more complex. Children have it so easy. His little brothers and sisters face's flashed into his mind. Their days are storybook, their nights spent by fireplaces and campfires – with little thought for what it takes to create their picture-book existence, what it takes to keep logs on the fire.

Missing that care-free existence for a brief moment, Jamie thought of Anna, who, for all intents and purposes, still lived storybook days and campfire nights. Yet she was not happy with her life.

He pulled in front of his apartment and saw Cheryl's white compact car. Knowing she would be inside waiting, he checked his reflection in the rear-view mirror. He badly needed a shower and the stubble on his chin needed a shave.

Waving to his neighbor who was watching him from a front room window, Jamie thought the woman with the baby on her hip looked content. He didn't know the newlyweds well, only that they'd been married just over a year and they had a newborn. That every night she stood looking out that living room window, waiting until her husband drove up and was home with her.

It tugged on his heart.

That would not be Anna.

He paused outside the front door of his apartment. It was sad, painful even, to think Anna may never look forward to her husband's return.

He slipped the key into the lock, his hand poised before he opened the door. She'd shared something deeply intimate with him today; she did not want what life was forcing upon her.

The TV droned on with laughter and music just on the other side and he closed his eyes. He knew Marcus was glued to American Idol. Rather depressed by the telling events of the day, Jamie's emotions were in no shape to watch decent folks bludgeoned for entertainment' sake, not when real-life was just as harsh and condemning.

Opening the door, he was drawn to Cheryl's bright smile, but the sunny rays of her essence didn't penetrate his somber mood. With a grouchy kick he shut the door.

"Dude." Marcus' feverish gaze stayed on the TV. "They're merciless tonight."

Jamie scowled at the screen, at the dark-haired man making faces at a young guy who had offered his heart and soul on the alter in the name of singing.

"Hi." Cheryl got up and pressed against him before he could set down his duffle. Her kiss was too long, her arms too tight.

"Hey."

"Come sit down." She reached for his hand, took the duffle and set it aside. "I made you some cookies, they're in the kitchen."

As gently as he could he pulled his hand free and headed toward the back of the apartment, to his bedroom. "I need a shower first. Give me a second."

Without waiting for her comment one way or the other, he began peeling off his clothes, dumping them with more fury than he liked into the hamper once he was in the darkness of his bedroom. He stood naked, hands on his hips, and blew out steam.

Darkness brought Anna to his mind.

Knowing that she was over in her fortress, living unhappily ever after, ate at him. He wanted her to be happy. Every human being has a basic right to happiness. But she had said herself that her basic rights were not her own. He could see both sides of the scale, that the gold and riches of royalty would tip that scale in her father's favor and leave her empty.

Itchy to help, unable to, the shower did nothing to wash away the heaviness inside. Anna. As much as he wanted to help her, he felt inadequate. To try to deal with something as huge as her responsibilities versus her desires, was not something he felt was his place to do. His responsibility was to their partnership, to see that they could rehearse, perform, and compete with few handicaps as possible.

He turned off the hot stream, got out and grabbed a towel.

Jamie figured Anna had lived a fairly constrained existence. She was so beautiful, that it made the travesty of her life without love even more tragic. Surely, somewhere in her past, she had been in love.

His thoughts teetered dangerously close to a line he had drawn to ensure a healthy partnership and guard against trouble. He dismissed the warmth flooding his veins, tossed the towel on a hook and strode to his closet, where he snatched a pair of jeans and a crisp, striped shirt. He would be her friend, do what he could to help her and see to it that their partnership was in no way affected by what was going on in either of their personal lives.

He stood in front of his dresser, fingering his hair into place when he heard something and turned. Cheryl leaned in his door wearing a smile of black mischief.

"Hey." She had something in mind, and when she shut the door, her blue eyes stayed latched with his.

"You smell great," she said, coming toward him.

"Yeah?"

Nodding, she slipped her arms around his waist and lifted herself up on her toes. "I like you just out of the shower."

With a laugh he returned her embrace, lifting her off her toes so their mouths could meet. He kissed her, but the enjoyment that usually rattled his system was flat as a popped tire. She pressed her mouth over his, her hands played in his hair, but he couldn't muster anything.

She eased back and the look of bliss on her face instantly pinned him with guilt. "Do you have a lock on that door?" she tilted her head.

"Uh, no."

"Marcus is pretty distracted…"

And so was he. It would be unfair to profess feelings and desires that weren't in him at the moment. "It's been a hard day." He lowered her to her feet and felt confusion in her body instantaneously.

"Oh." She looked both irritated and hurt, and it didn't do much for his already stressed emotional state.

"Anna was…"

"You know, I'm sick of hearing about Anna."

"How can you be sick of it? I've never even talked about her with you."

"You don't have to talk about her, she's on your mind anyway. You don't think I've seen a difference?"

"You've – what?"

"You're just not the same." She zigzagged in front of him. "It's like you're not really with me when you're with me. I don't know."

He swam in guilt. He felt helpless to do anything for Anna, because in spite of everything he was doing to insulate himself, his heart was gravitating her direction of its own accord. Guilt went deeper now with Cheryl's accusations; accusations he could not deny had some truth to them.

"I'm sorry." Because he was, and he didn't want to hurt her, or to change something he had once felt would be good for them both, he reached out and touched her. Willingly, she snuggled against him and they stood quietly for a time, listening to the far off sounds of the TV.

"Do you still want me in your life?" Cheryl finally asked.

"Yes." He was surprised when desire still wasn't kindled by either the admission or because she was in his arms. He wanted her in his life because she was good for him. But the more alarming reason was because it would mean he wouldn't be alone, having to face Anna.

The only peace and respite Anna found at the end of each day was late at night in her bedroom when she was at last alone. That both Lev and her father shared the same floor with her was as stifling as a fox sharing a den with a gopher.

The oppressive air clouding the house only reaffirmed that her decision to change the course of her life was something she had to do. Even if she would enjoy Jamie on a strictly professional basis only, she was enamored enough with dance and the American way of life that shifting her dreams to weigh out in those areas would ultimately prove to be satisfying on their own.

Knowing her father sensed this shift troubled her heart. She loved him, but wanted him to want for her happiness as much as he wanted good for his people and his country. Their daily battles over the subject were just his way of showing her what he felt was best for her, as well as throwing his duty and power around.

The last two evenings he'd come to her bedroom to talk. She readied herself tonight, certain the relentless pattern could not continue, that her stamina would prevail and win her freedom.

"I need to go back home, Anna," Alexander began as he strode through the door, sending it into a slam behind his back. He wore his usual suit, trussed up like a royal cock.

"Why do you not change into more casual clothing," she sighed, both amused and annoyed.

He looked down at himself, surprise on his face for a moment. "This is what I wear."

"Don't you ever tire of the corset? I do not think I have ever seen you in anything other than a suit—oh, with the exception of your silk pajamas."

"This discussion is not about what I wear, Anna."

"But it is, Papa. Don't you see? It is about what you are expected to wear, what you are expected to do, to say. I don't want those things for me. I want to wear sweats, jeans—whatever I feel like."

"Your analogy is not overlooked, but will go unreciprocated. You have a duty to your heritage that cannot be dismissed with the simple change of clothing."

"Even if it means a lifetime of unhappiness?"

Silenced a moment, Alexander looked at Anna through dark eyes. Anna feared another screaming match but she was willing to risk it all if it meant he would truly see her side.

"You have a beautiful home awaiting you. A country whose good fortune it is to be one of the wealthiest, most prestigious in the world. You meet people, travel wherever, whenever you like. Every wish is granted—"

"Except the freedom to choose who I want to marry."

Alexander's palm rose to quiet her. "Every dream can be fulfilled—within the boundaries of your royal heritage. Anna, I was willing to allow you to pursue this dream to come to America because you wanted to do it. But I knew, once you shopped outside of the market, shall we say, there was a possibility you would find trinkets that would entice you. And you have. Does that make what you have done acceptable? No. Is it your fault you wandered beyond limitations I set in place to protect you? Yes. Should any of what you are required, and expected to do change because of this? No!" His voice boomed with the explosion of a bomb.

He would never see her side clearly. He was deeply embedded in their history, in roots he believed were severely entwined in a soil that had not changed for hundreds of years. His vision was blinded by the dirt surrounding him.

"I will abdicate my responsibilities to Nicki," she said firmly. His eyes opened wide—shock flashed in them, then anger. She had said what was really in her heart. She had already lost everything, having the opportunity to freely love forbidden from her; she had nothing left to lose.

Just as it was her opportunity to take the throne, it was also her decision to relinquish it. Now that she would soon be twenty-eight, the age at which a Slovokian royal was legally able to make such decisions, she knew it was her right to hand the title to the next in line.

"Impossible," Alexander scoffed.

"It is my right," Anna said, "one of the few I have."

Her father took four slow steps her direction, stopping in front of her. "You need to seriously consider what you are giving up." *It is what I am gaining that I am thinking of,* Anna thought, her eyes leveling with her father's. "Once it is in place, it will be irrevocable."

"I understand."

"Is Lev that unappealing that you would sacrifice everything not to be with him?"

"I would sacrifice everything to allow my heart the freedom to find its own love."

Her father's shoulders went back. "You are doing all of this for love?"

"I am doing this because I want real love, real happiness, real freedom. Not the love, happiness and life that people that lived centuries ago think I should have."

Alexander let out a sigh, his slate eyes taking in the full length of his daughter with disbelief. He shook his head. "I fear you are making a mistake you will regret when you wake up one day, next to a man you have let your heart choose, in some god-forsaken house, with four children at your feet. You will long for the finer things. You will yearn for the freedom only inherent power can offer. You will be in your sweats, as you put it, longing to dress up." Alexander Zakharov turned and took his erect shoulders, and all that he carried on them, out Anna's door.

All Anna could do was smile.

12.

Her father returned home almost immediately, but left her an electric dog collar in leaving Lev behind. Anna was not surprised. Her father was not giving up on his pursuit of what he thought was best for her – but then neither was she. If Lev remained to be an annoying reminder of what she was supposed to do, so be it. She was neither threatened nor angered by having him around. She would keep him pacified knowing that he would bark back only positive reports to her father.

Anna saw Lev as a brother more than anything else. She'd known him and his family long enough that any feelings she had for him were strictly sympathetic and Platonic.

Her mood was effervescent, even with Lev at her heels. As the days passed and she and Jamie rehearsed, talked, lunched, soon Lev was not just a nipping pup anxious for any pat or scrap of her attention, but the third party in their threesome.

Her decision to not make her political move common knowledge was a direct order from her father who, before leaving, asked her to consider carefully and gave her a six-month time period. She didn't need six months. She had decided years ago. But to send him off with a smile on his face, she'd agreed.

It was easy to forget she had made the promise, so elated at the hope of freedom that anything regarding her life as a royal began to drop further down her list of priorities as she focused on dance.

At Reuben's suggestion and with Jamie's approval, they entered their first national competition in San Francisco. Because Jamie had gone professional some years earlier and Anna was still under amateur status, they were competing for the Latin title he had won previously in his partnership with Courtney.

Grievances aside, Anna took some joy from the fact that her father had at last relented and was allowing her to compete in Latin. Anna yearned for the closeness and excitement she had come to love in Latin dancing.

Lev sat in a chair alongside the wall, eyes bright and attentive behind his glasses.

"Lev," she called to him before they started rehearsal. "Would you like to do some sightseeing? There is much to see in Utah."

"Oh." Lev fidgeted.

"I wouldn't want you to get bored."

"I could never get bored watching you dance, Anna."

Anna didn't bother to glance at Jamie or Reuben. She had no shame in her actions. "Nevertheless, I will have Ivan take you out." Immediately, she crossed to the doors, even though she heard Lev scuttling up behind her. She found the large bodyguard standing stoically beside the door. "Ivan. Take Lev on a tour of Provo, will you? He has yet to see any of the finer spots of this city."

With a nod, Ivan looked at Lev. Lev's mouth was open, ready to protest, but Anna slipped her arm through his and the tight weave made it impossible to move anywhere but out the door.

"We'll see you this afternoon," she called lightly over her shoulder when she left him. "Take him to the university; there are many lovely museums." Bringing the two doors together with a thud, she let out a sigh.

Both Jamie and Reuben stood with curious grins on their faces.

"You're smooth, sis." Reuben whistled.

"He needed to get out, that is all."

"Uh-huh." With a look of amusement peppered with chastisement, Jamie stood ready for her. "Something you're not telling us?"

Reuben crossed the floor toward the music system.

"You are my partner. I tell you everything."

Because she said it with a light air of jest, he snickered, looking down into her eyes. "Yeah, right."

They began with paso. "You don't believe me?"

"I know for a fact you have secrets, Your Highness."

He twirled her out and they mirrored each other. "That makes me more interesting." Her hands swung and played with a skirt that didn't exist and he stepped back, the matador circling and taunting.

Then he reached out, their fingers twined, and he brought her in. "You don't have to have secrets to be interesting, Anna." He threw her into a deep backbend and her head brushed the floor.

"You find me interesting?"

He jerked her up. "I never said I didn't." Again they circled each other in basic Paso Dobles steps. "It's just that you hold back." He grabbed her hand and spun her like a top.

"I – do – not."

He stopped her spin by slapping his palms firmly around her waist. She froze, and their eyes locked. Music pumped around them. "Then you won't mind answering some questions I have, will you?" Like a yo-yo on a string, he tossed her out in front of him, then back again. Her blood sung.

Without effort she spun with him, feeling the same euphoria she had felt in her dream, when they'd spun together in fantasy and her head fell back, a laugh escaped that wasn't theatrical but came from her heart.

After they stopped, Reuben signaled for them to come close. "For somebody who hasn't danced Latin in a while, you did good, sis. One more blind dance and we'll be there."

Her chest tightened. "Oh, no, I—"

"You're so close," Reuben insisted. "The summit is right there. You just need to be nudged over the top. It will take your performance to the next level, I promise."

"Not today." Jamie strode over to the chairs and sat.

"We are not done." Anna set two fists on her hips. Both she and Reuben watched Jamie take off his shoes.

"We are," Jamie began, slipping his shoes into his duffle. He looked at Anna. "Done dancing. But you and I are not done."

Reuben rubbed his hands together and got ready to grab his things. Anna stood alone in the center of the floor. "I had no say in this—whatever it is—that is going on. I just got rid of – or rather, excused Lev so that—"

"Change," Jamie's tone was firm.

"But we still have two hours left," Anna protested.

"Change."

She didn't want to be tickled by the prospect of being somewhere—anywhere, alone with him. She was learning to take their hours on the floor together in proper perspective.

Reuben left as quietly as an unwanted draft and Anna hurriedly changed from her dance clothes into a pair of slim-fitting camel slacks and a snug black sweater. Jamie was waiting for her at the door, standing as silent as Lukov. When his dark gaze locked on her like it wasn't going to let go, the nerves in her stomach bunched.

"I hope this is all right." She gestured as she came down the stairs. His eyes slid up and down the length of her and a warm shudder took her insides.

"It's fine, Anna."

Outside, she breathed in the bitter winter air and followed Jamie to his truck. The skies were clear without the blanket of clouds to hold in warmth, and frosty white coated every surface from rooftops to asphalt.

He opened her door for her, and she caught sight of Vladimir and Lukov coming out of the house, heading toward one of the black Expeditions. Her heart sank.

Jamie continued around to the drivers' side, slid in, and shut the door. "This time," he said, "it's all above board. I told them we had some things to do. Vladimir insisted they follow, for your safety."

Anna's head fell back against the headrest and she let out a sigh.

They drove in silence, heading north along University Avenue toward the gaping mouth of Provo Canyon. For a moment, she thought they might be heading back up into the mountains for another snow cave camp out. She laughed.

"What?" Jamie looked over.

"Just wondering what Vladimir would do in a snow cave overnight."

"Don't worry," Jamie grinned. "I'm not dragging you on another camp out."

Too bad, she thought.

He veered left. Normally, she insisted on knowing what was happening. But she trusted Jamie so completely; she knew at that moment, she would follow him into the depths of hell if he asked her.

She looked at him. She couldn't help that her body flushed warm, every thought of him insipidly breezy. She laughed again—at herself.

"What?" his dark eyes were curious.

"Nothing." You have it so bad, you are woozy with it. And he has absolutely no idea. Such is life. "Are you going to tell me where we are going?"

"You'll know as soon as I do."

They headed east, inside the deep crevasse of Provo Canyon. The sun hid behind the westerly mountains now, its fiery glow electrifying the snow-covered peaks in front like orange frosting.

"I want to talk," he said. "And because we're never really alone when we're at the house, I thought going out might be the best way."

She settled back against the seat of the truck, her body warm from the heater and the company. "All right." Whatever he asked, she would answer as honestly as she could.

Though Jamie had been holding back for days now since Lev had dropped the KGB-like news that his life had been carefully watched by Anna, it was all he could do not to start demanding answers. He had played this moment over and over, sure she would resist, even flat out deny answering him. But she'd been so happy the last few days, it had caused him even more concern. If she was happy, then that should be all that mattered. But it wasn't. Since learning that she'd studied him, he'd gone from shocked, to furious, to feeling violated in a remote way, to flattered, to fascinated. And all of the emotions kept whispering one question – why?

He'd torn his common sense apart trying to answer that question on his own, the answer she'd given him that first night just didn't jive. For her country's social benefit? He didn't think so. After meeting her father, that claim stuck about as well as water sticks to a wall. King Zakharov was interested in only one thing; to make sure his daughter's new dance partner wasn't after something he shouldn't be after.

Glancing at Anna, he found her eyes on him. The heat her gaze pushed through his body forced him to shift. He licked dry lips, found his gaze dropping to her mouth. It was always that crushed-mulberry color, always ripe for a kiss. He dragged his eyes back to the road, checking his rear-view mirror for the trailing black Expedition with a twinge of guilt for the lusty thought.

"Anna," he began, his voice scratching some. He cleared his throat. "Why are you really here in the U.S.?"

"There are things I will share with you that are confidential, Jamie. I must have your word that you will not share them with anyone, no matter how close they are to you." He nodded. "I am here because I plan to make the U.S. my permanent residence."

"You mean, you're not going to – to –" he stumbled for the right words, "to be queen?"

She shook her head. "I hope to pass that responsibility to my little brother, who, I think, will not fight it as much as I have."

He thrust his left hand into his hair on sucked breath. "Wow. Does your father know this?"

"It is part of why he came. He is doing everything in his power to convince me that my decision is wrong and that I will be sorry someday."

"That's smart."

"Why do you think that is smart? You do not think that I can make this decision and live by it?"

"I think anyone with such a life-altering choice would never really be able to fully comprehend the ramifications of such a thing, no matter how independent they were. It will only be years after the fact that you'll feel the effects of something so vast. He's right to insist you take a long look at this."

"I have taken a long look at it." Her voice was rising, matching her temper. "I have been looking across thousands of miles of ocean and land, to America, since I was a young girl and was old enough to understand that I wanted the freedom of choice, not the restriction of a crown."

"Yeah, I can believe that. I bet you check everything out under a magnifying glass before you do anything about it."

"You make it sound like knowing is a bad thing."

"Knowing is a good thing. Stalking is something I'm not sure is morally decent."

"Pardon me?" She sat pressed against the door, her arms crossed.

"You had your telescope aimed right at me, isn't that true? For the last, what, five years now?"

"I told you I studied you that first night we met."

"Studied is putting it lightly." Jamie grimaced. "Look, all I know is when Lev told me, it – it freaked me out."

A chirp escaped her throat. She turned from him so he couldn't see the horror on her face. "I see. Well," she kept her voice level, "you would have no reason not to believe him. Though it is blown extraordinarily out of proportion, I will not deny that my study was extensive."

They shot wary glances at each other across dark interior of the car. Suddenly, Jamie took a left and they were winding up a narrow road, higher into the mountains.

"Where are you taking me?"

"My family has a cabin at Sundance."

Though they wound up the steep incline in silence, Anna's head spun. Did he think she was some weirdo? Her search for American dreams had led her to the exciting world of competitive ballroom dance, which had led her to Jamie Wilde. After closely scrutinizing his competitions, she had decided she wanted to partner with him. Why did he make it sound so…so…underhanded?

Sure, she'd had fantasies about meeting him, and dancing with him, should he accept her offer. Any woman would. Perhaps her voracious appetite for information had been a little overboard, but it had been for valid reasons. She had to know that he was the right match for her.

Convinced her aggressive stance was nothing to be embarrassed about, she lifted her chin with restored dignity. Finally they stopped next to a dark, peaked cottage, setting like a brown Swiss clock on one of the sharp, snowy hillsides.

"This is it." Jamie shut off the car, got out and opened her door. Even in the moonlight, Anna caught the wariness in his dark eyes. It pierced her to her core. Just what did he have planned for her in this cold, secluded place?

13.

They crunched through thigh-high snow toward the steps, then stood on the darkened porch as he searched for the key.

"It's colder up here," she chattered. "I didn't know I'd need a coat."

He wasn't wearing one either. "You won't need one inside. But we have extras. We're the first up. Ski season doesn't start for another couple of months." He unlocked the door and thrust it open, and a stale, closed-up waft tickled her nose, bringing out a sneeze.

"You even sneeze like a princess," he tossed over his shoulder.

She dabbed at her nose with the back of her hand. "And what does that mean?"

He shrugged and led the way inside. Unable to see anything more than his silhouette in front of her, she stayed close behind.

"You'd better invite Vladimir and Ivan in." He flicked on a light and she squinted. "They won't last a half hour in the car." Annoyed that he would make her go back out into the cold, she huffed. "They're your pit bulls," he said hearing her complaint. He strode further into the cabin, turning on lights.

Anna stomped back down the path toward the car, mumbling, teeth chattering, bitter cold gnawing at her bones.

Vladimir rolled down the window.

"He said you can come in…or you'll die." Turning, she stomped back up the path, nearly slipping on the ice. Her squeal brought Jamie to the door but he made no effort to help her, rather, he remained in the jamb with a crooked smile. "Can't walk too fast on that ice, Princess—you'll end up on your, uh, rump."

Pounding her feet, she dislodged caked snow from her feet before entering the cabin and getting her first good look at the place. It was A-framed, with a generous loft upstairs. A large room with a pot-belly fireplace and two-story flue was the center of the cabin. A kitchen was tucked in the corner. One short hall led back to other rooms.

Jamie went about starting a fire, grabbing pieces of the wood stacked nearly halfway up the wall of the cabin. He didn't turn when he spoke, but artfully laid the logs in the cove of the burner. "Make yourselves at home. There should be food in the fridge. And there's a trunk of hot chocolate in the pantry. Go for it."

"What are you doing?" Vladimir stormed to Jamie without bothering to remove his coat, and glowered over his shoulder.

"This is called making a fire, Vlad. I'd have thought a strapping chap such as you would know how to make one of these pups."

Vladimir's black-gloved hands wrung each other tightly. "What are you doing here – with her?"

Logs in place, Jamie stood back, eyeing them before reaching over and adjusting one with a wrought-iron poker. "We needed a place we could talk," his eyes slid to Vladimir's. "Privately."

Vladimir snorted. "A man, a woman and an isolated cabin? I think you have more than talk on your mind."

Jamie rolled his eyes. "Sound's sexy, especially with you two along." He purposefully nudged the man's shoulder as he pushed past him. "The fire will be hot in about fifteen minutes. This place will be toastier than a Mexican beach at midday. What?"

None of them had moved since they'd come into the cabin, with the exception of Vladimir. "Look, Vlad, Iv, I know you have a job to do. But Anna and I need to talk, and we came up here so that we could do that without any distractions. If you stay, you need to be invisible, like real secret service guys." He pointed down the hall. "There are two bedrooms in the back, pick one or take them both, I don't care. I just don't want to see either one of you."

Vladimir's chest rose under his black overcoat, and he took a step Jamie's direction. "Just how long do you intend to be here?"

Jamie peeled off his sweater with a shrug. He wore a long-sleeved white tee-shirt underneath. Anna's insides fluttered. "As long as it takes."

"As long as what takes?" Vladimir demanded.

Jamie balled the sweater in two tight fists. His eyes hardened on the man. "That's between Anna and me."

Vladimir shook his head. "We will be in the back room, Anna."

The structure trembled slightly under Ivan's bulk when the two men lumbered begrudgingly to the back. Vladimir's Slovokian mutterings rumbled and finally disappeared.

Lowering himself down on the couch, Jamie sat, elbows pressed into his knees, fingers together at his lips, staring into the flames. "Sit down, Anna."

She didn't know why she felt like a little girl anticipating a reprimand, but she did. All of the convincing she had done in her mind to justify her actions now vanished, leaving no trace of sense at all.

"Please," she began earnestly, even though he did not look at her, rather kept his brown eyes steadily on the fire. "I don't want you to feel awkward about this. Jamie, it is important that you know my intentions for seeking you out were for professional reasons first. I saw in you qualities that I knew I could work with." She felt better when his dark eyes met hers.

Because he sat quietly, she continued. "I have always surrounded myself with the best in whatever I have done. When I studied under Tatyana, I played with her daughters. I knew that by playing with them I would change the way I danced, taking it into another sphere of my subconscious."

"You said your reasons for seeking me out were for professional reasons first," he said. "What else?"

The room suddenly felt like an inferno. Anna couldn't move, trapped by her own words. She couldn't admit her attraction to him. Not after the lengths he had gone to make clear what he thought the parameters of a partnership should be. Lying would be stepping backward, going against what she was striving for in their partnership – total honesty.

"You will not want to hear what I have to say about that. Please don't ask me to tell you."

He studied her for a long moment, pressing the tips of his fingers together under an intense gaze she couldn't interpret. "Try me."

She took a moment to ponder, knowing her cool, reflective demeanor was for show only. Her insides scrambled. "Me."

"You what?"

"I chose you for me." It pleased her that the dark in his eyes glimmered a little then. "But do not get the wrong impression. It was a necessary choice. Necessary in that I was – am, making a statement to my father about what I want from life, that I am not afraid to take chances. You, I saw as a risk-taker. You have done things I have always wanted to do but have not been free to – mountain climb, scuba dive, camping. See? I have already done one of those things."

Proud that she had kept her inner promise to stay within truth's boundaries, she waited for his reaction. When his eyes shifted back to the flames, she began to worry she had not been convincing. Wasn't the truth supposed to convince naturally?

"I can't say I'm not feeling a little bit like an object." All he had to do was think that he'd been analyzed then bought based on that analysis and he was seriously close to screaming at someone.

"But that's not at all how you should feel." Through all of my study, after all I've learned about you, I care for you very much, she thought, but wondered if she would further condemn herself by verbalizing those feelings.

Restless, he stood and crossed the room to the large window, his hands tucked in the front pockets of scruffy jeans. "Maybe you can look at people as a means to an end, but that's not the way I was raised."

That had been truth, in the beginning, and it sounded just as disgraceful as he made it sound. But Anna had come to hope that much more could come of their partnership than just the realization of life-long goals.

Rising, she dared take herself closer to him. He stared blankly out into white flakes now filming the air. "Be flattered, not offended, Jamie. It was not my intention to offend you."

His gaze stayed out the window, at the snow now falling in a thick veil. "You warned me I might not want to hear it." He'd toyed with different fantasies about what she might give as her reason, but never thought it would be because of what he could bring to the table in the name of extra-curricular entertainment for her.

He sure wasn't going to be her toy.

Shifting his body toward hers, he worked to not let out a shout. "So, just what are your plans with me, Anna, since I had no inkling that this years-in-planning-scheme of yours is going forward without any regard to what I think or say, now that I've signed that contract."

"If you are that unhappy, we will dissolve the contract." Though the words flew out, she had not thought herself capable of saying them. But they seemed to lift the clouds of anger in his eyes. He pondered her for a moment and she wished she was standing closer to the fire to warm the chill of rejection she was certain was next.

He'd made his point now, more than once, and battered whatever she held as important along the way. Jamie hated to compromise, but hated taking any part in someone else's compromise even more.

"Forget it," he said. "None of this was meant to be malicious, I can see that." In fact, it was clearer to him now as he stared down into those mysterious gray eyes that she had only followed her heart in what she'd done. She was a princess looking for life outside the fairy tale. Far be it for him to figure out why anyone would want something other than a storybook life.

Pressing his shoulder to the window, he casually leaned back. "So, do you think you'll find happily ever after here in America, Anna?"

Just the fact that she would be free from something she had no desire to take on was enough happiness for her ever after. Still, as they stood in the shadows of the cabin, the amber flame lighting their faces, heating their bodies, there could be so much more.

"I have already been given so much just being here, just dancing." With you, she wanted to add. "But America is the land of opportunity, is it not? I intend to have as many opportunities as I can."

"You really want to try mountain climbing?"

"Oh, yes."

His laugh filled the air with as much warmth as the fire. She liked it when he ran his hands through his hair, leaving it mussed. Desire gnawed in her belly.

"So you are giving up the crown so you can be a wild child? I don't know – you seem too afraid to break a nail to enjoy digging into the sides of mountains."

"Oh, I would love nothing more than to break all of my nails digging into a mountain. I have made a fire, have I not?"

After he laughed again, his eyes, dark with searching, leveled hers in a way that if she did not move, would give her pounding heart away.

The couch was a safer place for her, so she went to it, scrubbing her arms as she stared into a fire that was beginning to die. "Should I add another log?" When she looked over at him, something shadowy burned in the bottomless depths of his eyes.

In one fluid move he was away from the window and at the fire place, throwing on two gnarled logs. They hissed and cracked, shooting millions of fiery embers up the flu like electric gnats.

She'd picked him, Jamie thought now, chosen him. The idea wasn't as bizarre as it had been at first. Indeed, he was feeling flattered. A beautiful, royal, woman had chosen him out of every other schmuck to be her dance partner, yes, and to…he felt his body tighten…to what?

He shot a furtive glance over his shoulder at her and their eyes met – again. Still, he couldn't really read what was in her head and in her heart. He'd never felt her as open and vulnerable as that day they'd danced in the dark. Maybe it would take another exercise before he would have the rest of his answers.

She was holding something back, and like it or not, it was eating at him to know what and why. Tonight she had shared what she could, and he was satisfied with that.

"Well." His stomach growled so he headed for the kitchen. "We might as well get comfortable because we aren't going anywhere until this snow lets up. Want something to eat or drink?"

"What do you mean?"

He continued digging through shelves. "I mean, the roads would be too dangerous. I know you're anxious to live on the edge, but there's thrill and then there's stupidity. I try not to drive in these conditions. It's something I learned early on."

He had a box of graham crackers in his hand and held them out to her. Shaking her head, she joined him under fluorescent light of the kitchen. "I am sure Vladimir and Ivan will not want to stay here for the night."

"Then you can drive back with them." He pulled out a gallon of milk, took off the lid and sniffed. "But I gotta warn you, unless they've got chains in the back of that Expedition, you might find yourselves in that river alongside the road."

She let out a sigh as she watched him pour himself a glass of milk. "You are not at all unhappy about this?"

"Doesn't do any good to be annoyed by one of nature's occurrences. We need the water. Our snow pack's been low for five years. And it makes the skiers happy."

"But I have nothing. I didn't even bring a coat. I have no hair items, no makeup, no pajamas."

"Anna." He popped a piece of cracker in his mouth. "You can use one of our coats. You don't need hair or makeup stuff, and you don't need pajamas." Though he could imagine her in something flannel, the image of her in something less was what had that piece of graham cracker temporarily lodging in his throat. He coughed, sending it on its way.

"You are absolutely sure we cannot make it back down?"

"Absolutely." And it reminded him that his plans with Cheryl would be off. He dug into his pocket for his cell phone. "Tell Iv and Vlad they can get comfortable." He tapped Cheryl's number on the key pad. "And pick whichever room you want. I'll take the loft."

Knocking on the closed door in the back, Anna waited. Vladimir, now minus his coat, gloves and scarf, frowned at her. Ivan sat in the only chair in the room. Respectfully, he stood.

"We are staying the night here," she told them. "The snow is too deep to drive in."

Vladimir hissed. Striding to the window he tore open the shutters. Then he sighed. "Are there no snow plows?" He shot a steely glare at Anna.

"Jamie says it would be best if we didn't try, unless you have chains."

"He planned this. He wanted to get you up here—"

"Stop this instant," Anna demanded. "You will not insult him or accuse him. He brought me up here to talk. We talked. There was nothing underhanded in what he did."

"Then he will not mind when we insist on taking you back where you belong."

"It would be very dangerous, Vladimir."

"I am responsible for your safety. I will see to it that you make it back.

Come." Snatching his coat and gloves, he slung his scarf around his neck in a furious sweep and passed her.

Still on the phone, Jamie didn't notice the struggle of wills going on just a few feet away. When Anna heard his soft tone, she slowed so she could hear better.

"I know, I'm sorry...Yeah, it would have been fun. Hopefully we'll be out of here first thing tomorrow morning. She's -- I don't know, she's going to sleep in one of the bedrooms I imagine. Cheryl, come on, I—" Jamie caught sight of Anna, Vladimir and Ivan, dressing in their coats and outerwear and his brows synched tight. "I gotta go. I'll call you in the morning." He set the tiny cell phone on the kitchen counter, and nearly jumped around the corner. "What's going on?"

"Her Royal Highness will not be sleeping here tonight. I am taking her back." Vladimir buttoned his coat.

"Sorry, Vlad. Can't let you do it. It's too risky."

"She is my responsibility, not yours. She will come with me."

Jamie's lips twitched. He'd yell at the old loaf if he wasn't careful. "The roads are sheets of ice, Vlad. Unless you have chains—"

"I have chains!" Vladimir's voice boomed, leaving only the snap and crackle of the fire in the air. "Ivan, go install the chains!"

Ivan's bald head furrowed in confusion, giving away what Jamie was sure Vladimir thought would be an-air tight lie.

"It's not safe, Vlad." Jamie pinned the old man with one of his fiercest stares. "You'd be putting Anna's life at risk."

"If she stays here there is more at risk than her life."

The affront was meant to strike deep, and it did. Jamie forced out a laugh and set his itchy hands deep in his front pockets to keep from ripping off the man's glasses and pounding him. "You're getting close to asking for a new face, old man."

Vladimir's upper lip quivered under a fine layer of sweat. He leaned close to Jamie with a sneer. "So are you."

"Oh, stop it." Anna moved away from them both and looked out the large window into thick white quarters of snow falling with silent beauty. *God has opened his coin purse,* she thought. She meant to make the most of the blessing. "It's too dangerous, Vladimir. Jamie is right. We will stay."

Like that, it was done. Jamie watched Vladimir puff with anger, bulging tight at the very seams of his black overcoat. The scathing glare was meant to say more than the older man would dare say in the presence of his royal employer and Jamie angled his head at him in a smirk.

Ivan stomped back in covered with three inches of snow from his bald head to his booted feet. He shook his shiny pate with a look of impossibility on his face.

"You guys can take the bedrooms down here." Jamie ignored the anger bubbling from Vladimir. He turned, adding more wood to the fire. "I'll take the loft." The wood broke and Jamie let out a tense sigh. A slumber party with Ivan and Vlad…He could think of a lot better ways to be stuck in the cabin.

One appealed to him more than he liked, but she was off limits.

The first thing Anna did when she opened her eyes was dart to the window. It had stopped snowing but white capped every surface, from the drooping branches of evergreens to the cars out front, to the other cabins resting snuggly on the surrounding peaks. The road was still hidden under a blanket of white. She thought it looked as if everything, both living and inanimate, rose from a layer of snow, anxious to break free of the frigid frosting.

The sun was trying to break through clouds. There was no movement outside, and she imagined how silent and still it would be. The part of her that hated confined spaces also found complete silence hard to deal with.

Closing the shutters, she snuggled back under the covers. Her eyes roamed the room. Family photos decorated the walls and she crawled near the edge of the bottom of bunk she had slept in for a better look. Photographs taken through the years at the cabin showed little change in the house, but more in the family that occupied it. She saw all of the children, but her eye was drawn to Jamie, always the tallest, always next to his mother and father with younger Wildes surrounding him.

She didn't know Jamie's family well, but hoped that would not always be. As with everything she found admirable in American society, the structure and implementation of the family fascinated her. Though she had Nicky, she had secretly wished for more siblings. The commotion of endless noise and people were comforting to a person who struggled with quiet and small spaces. Family would fill in and fill out a life nicely.

Because she heard nothing, she got out of bed and decided to explore. Last night she had found long johns in every size and color stacked neatly in one of the drawers of a boxy dresser.

Figuring she would see no one, she crept out the door into the hall in the red pair that now clothed her. Coming from behind Vladimir and Ivan's closed door she heard two different tones of snoring and she squelched a laugh.

She tiptoed toward the kitchen, passing the bathroom. On the other side of the door, the shower was running. It was easy to imagine the lean, long lines of Jamie's body under a streaming spray of water. The picture made something low inside of her quiver and she decided to go to the window for a blast of cool air.

The view out the two-story glass front was stunning. Last night, she hadn't noticed the other cabins dotting the hillside. Some were buried with enough snow to signal they were shut up for the season. Others' chimney's streamed grey film into the clearing air above.

The Wilde cabin jutted out from the hillside leaving a steep pitch of hillside below for tubing and sledding. A redwood picnic table sat covered in snow. In her mind, she saw the family gathered there for summer dinners. How lucky Jamie was growing up surrounded by these beautiful mountains; sheltered by them, yet not held back by them.

"Quite a view, huh?"

She whirled around, startled. Jamie stood in the same jeans he'd worn yesterday, only minus a shirt. A towel was in his hands and he scrubbed it over damp hair. He crossed toward her and she drew in a long breath.

He stopped so close, patches of dampness on his shoulders and back glistened, calling out to her fingertips. She forced herself not to stare, even though the scent of soap, the smoothness of his skin snapped through her senses like a whip.

"It's beautiful," she said.

"Mmm."

Her admiring gaze lifted to his. Smiling, she tucked her hair behind her ears before remembering how she was dressed, that she'd not even glanced in a mirror. Her hands shot up to her face, covering it with a gasp. "I must look awful. Pardon me. I should have--"

"Anna, stop." Before she could say another word, he had one of her wrists and was gently pulling her hand away from her face looking at her through kind eyes. "Do you really feel like you have to look a certain way every moment of every day?"

"No. Well, perhaps."

"That's unrealistic." His gaze held hers in a comforting way she could not ignore, and she accepted what he told her.

"You're right," she finally said.

He leaned against the window for a moment. "I don't know how you've taken it for so long. I can see why you wouldn't like it."

She felt so much better knowing he understood. She followed him into the kitchen, enjoying the view of sharp muscles under tight skin. His jeans rode low on his hips, just at the angled cut where hip met belly and back. It was hard to drag her eyes away, and she was only able to when he faced her, dropping the towel on the kitchen sink. He leaned his weight on those wonderfully roped arms. "How about waffles?"

Her tummy gnawed but not for food. She nodded anyway, enjoying his every move as he opened the freezer, pulled out a box of frozen waffles, ripping the top, then the plastic that held the waffles inside. Each muscle moved in harmony, creating a captivating vision of shifting, silken skin.

"Sleep okay?" he asked, dropping the waffles in the toaster.

"Exquisitely."

He laughed. "In that old bunk? You must have been tired."

"I guess I was. I slept right through Ivan and Vladimir's orchestral attempts."

He pulled out syrup, butter, strawberry jam and sour cream. "Yeah, I heard them."

"I hope they didn't keep you awake."

"I grew up with four brothers and sisters. And my younger brother, Justin, snored like a woodpecker on Prozac." The first two waffles popped up and he set them on a plate, slid them her direction. "The works." He gestured to the toppings with an upturned palm.

"Sour cream and jam?"

"Heck, yeah. Butter, sour cream and jam…tastes great like that."

She reached for the sour cream. "It sounds Belgian. Ever been there?"

"Yeah, once." Snatching the wet towel from the counter, he balled it between his palms. "I'm going to go finish getting dressed. Help yourself to whatever." His easy generosity appealed to her. It wasn't exclusive. He was the same host, the same man, to whomever he was with.

The waffle tasted delicious. She enjoyed what she hoped was one of many Wilde family specialties.

His cell phone buzzed on the countertop. With water running again in the bathroom, she knew he hadn't heard it. She pressed her ear close to the door and knocked. "You phone is ringing, Jamie."

"Go ahead and answer it for me, will ya?"

She hurried back and opened the phone. The name on the caller ID read Cheryl. She debated for about two seconds. "Hello?" The long pause caused Anna to bite her lower lip. A smile worked its way on her face. "Hello?" she repeated.

"Is Jamie there?" Recognizable frenzy was in the tone coming through the phone. It pleased Anna, even if it shouldn't.

"He can't come to the phone. Would you like me to give him a message?"

"Have him call Cheryl."

"Cheryl? Cheryl the little blonde?"

"That's me."

"Cheryl, it's Anna."

"Anna the princess?" Cheryl snapped with a whip of sarcasm.

"That's me. You're up early. You're not checking up on him, are you?"

"Now why would I do that? I trust him."

Anna took another bite of her waffle with a giant grin. "He was quite the host last night."

"Was he?"

"As accommodating as any luxury hotel I've stayed in."

A low chuckle ended on a snarl in Cheryl's throat. "Been there, done that."

"Anyway, he's in the shower. Would you like me to take the phone in? I could—" Anna turned and stopped, bumping into Jamie's chest, now hidden under his black turtleneck sweater. Her eyes moved up to his. "You're in luck, Cheryl. He's standing right here." She passed him the phone, but he didn't move, wouldn't make way for her to escape by him.

He put the phone to his ear and kept her pinned with narrowed eyes. "Cheryl, hey…" Anna swallowed thickly.

"We'll talk about it when I get back down there…I don't know, I haven't had a chance to look at the roads yet…Cheryl. Chill." Jamie's tone sharpened and Anna averted her gaze. "All right, fine. I'll call you then." He clicked off the phone, stuck it in the back pocket of his jeans. Anna waited for him to move but he wasn't going anywhere. "You want to tell me why you riled Cheryl into a lather?"

Lifting her chin she finally looked into his eyes. Expecting displeasure, she was taken aback at the glimmer of amusement. "She does not trust you. I don't think you deserve that."

"But you didn't go out of your way to clarify that she could trust me, did you?"

"How could she not trust you, Jamie?" She ducked around him. "If she cannot trust you, than she deserves a wild imagination."

"Fertilized by you."

She sat back at the bar and took up her fork. "Look at it this way, she is jealous. That proves how much she loves you."

He came around the corner and stood next to her, close enough for her to feel his heated breath on the side of her face. "Love's a strong word, Anna. One I don't throw around lightly."

"I did not say that you loved her, I said—"

"I heard what you said and you're riling me now. Don't rile me about my personal life. It's something I protect like a bear." He went back into the kitchen, clearly annoyed, and dropped two waffles into the toaster.

She could not recall, even being a princess, when someone had made her feel worth protecting for anything other than what she stood for or what she would become. Because she was jealous, she couldn't leave it alone. "How lucky for her," she began. He was leaning on the counter, his arms tight underneath that slick, body-glove of a turtleneck.

"What are you talking about?"

"How lucky for Cheryl that you are so concerned for your relationship that you guard it with such passion." She took the last bite of her waffle but didn't taste it.

"I have to, for preservation's sake." His waffles popped up and he put them on a plate, dressing them just as she had, with sour cream and jam.

"Yes." She watched him lick a finger after red jam had smeared on it. The sight shot heat to her belly. "There are many wolves in the forest, Mamma used to say."

When he looked up at her, his eyes narrowed some. "Yeah."

He ate standing. "Speaking of wolves," he began after swallowing a bite. "You think Iv and Vlad will want some?"

The laugh that escaped her felt wonderful, releasing the hurt and disappointment inside. "I'm sure of it. In fact, I'll go wake them so we can be on our way." As she slid from the stool, breakfast and the thought of Cheryl lodged in her stomach like a pile of bricks.

Jamie stole the opportunity to eat while he didn't have the distraction of Anna sitting across the kitchen in those faded, red long johns. He thought he'd be able to taste, that he'd fill the hole in his gut. But it wasn't working. The hole was one of those below the belly, gnawing kind that come from a hunger not satisfied by something easily accessible like food.

How could puckered old long johns look sexy? The answer was easy: Anna. Anna could wear a plastic garbage bag and look hot.

She'd looked fresh, ruffled, and squeezable with her hair scattered about her face, her gray-green eyes rested. The kind of face he could spend the morning going over with leisurely detail, discovering every inch with soft kisses.

Get a hold of yourself, man. Jamie wolfed down the rest of his waffles so he could be done with the chore of eating.

He was glad she'd slept well. It had been a horrendous night for him. Between Vladimir and Ivan's snores rumbling the floor to the image of Anna sprawled in the bunk bed, he'd spent most of his night knotted in sheets. His fib about being able to sleep through anything only guarded the real reason for his insomnia.

Just when he thought he'd gotten Anna to a place in his brain where he could function, she crept into other areas with the stealth of that spicy perfume she wore. She was always doing something to make him take another look. Like that phone call with Cheryl. It had been at his request she'd answered his phone, he could take the blame. But hearing Anna push Cheryl's buttons just to provoke a reaction, well, it had been maddening as well as flattering, and he didn't want to think about why.

He cleaned out the fireplace and heard low murmurs from down the hall, followed by the shuffle of movement. He had to keep from chuckling when he glanced over; Ivan was crumpled, having no doubt slept in his clothes. Vladimir's hair stood up like Einstein's, shooting every direction but down. The old man was buttoning his shirt sleeves, clearing garble from his throat.

"Morning." Jamie stood, dusting wood powder from his palms. "You guys hungry?"

Finished buttoning, Vladimir shook out his suit jacket and slipped it on. "We need to leave this instant."

"Is there an emergency?"

"No. But we have been here long enough."

"Vlad, Vlad, relax." Jamie crossed to him on his way to the kitchen and lightly tapped his arm. "There's time for breakfast."

"There is no time. We must leave at once."

In the kitchen, Jamie held up the box of frozen waffles. "Iv, want some?"

Ivan remained still as a statue. Vladimir strode to the counter. "We will not be eating breakfast, we—"

"Vlad," Jamie interrupted cheekily, "you can't expect a big guy like Iv to keep an engine his size going without a little sustenance. Look at him. He needs food, don't cha boy?" Ivan's head angled and Jamie smiled at the attempted reaction. "Come on, guys, Anna's eaten, and she's not even ready yet. Have something."

"Oh, for goodness sake," Vladimir spit out. As he came into the kitchen, Jamie held out a palm and stopped him in his tracks.

"Sit. Let me. You guys do enough. Iv? How many?"

Ivan glanced at Vladimir before answering. "Four."

After slipping four waffles into the toaster, Jamie pulled out two plates. "Have a seat. They'll be up in, what, three minutes? Vlad, how many for you?"

Vladimir didn't move. His eyes bulged from their sockets and his lips quivered. "I said I would not eat!"

"Hey, that's cool," Jamie nodded. "Occasional fasting is supposed to be a great cleansing tool for the body."

"I am not fasting," Vladimir said through clenched teeth.

"I can make you eggs or something." Jamie poked his head into the fridge. "Actually, I take that back. No can do. But we have some great cereals." As he crossed to the pantry, Jamie whistled. "Let's see, there's Coco Crunchers, Captain Jacks—oh, and one of my little brother's favorites—"

"I will not be eating!" Vladimir boomed.

"No problem." Jamie grinned.

The waffles popped up and Jamie put them on the plate, handed them to Ivan who said something in Slovokian. "We Wildes like 'em with sour cream and jam." Jamie pushed the condiments toward Ivan.

"Yes, they are delicious that way." Anna came around the corner and went right to the sink. Gone were the baby-doll long johns. She had on the camel slacks and nubby sweater she'd worn the day before. Her hair was straight back in a pony tail.

"What are you doing?" Jamie asked. She had her nose under the sink, had pulled out a container of liquid soap.

"The dishes."

"You know how?"

"Of course." Anna turned on the water, poured the soap. "I played house once or twice."

"You mean castle?"

"And the first rule of castle was to leave it just the way you found it," she grinned.

"That was Mom's first rule of house as well," Jamie countered, standing next to her.

It was clear to Vladimir that there was more going on between Jamie and Anna than their professed exclusive partnership. He'd known Anna for too many years not to recognize the signs. The way her eyes lit, the perfect fullness of her smile whenever she looked at Jamie— not once had she ever looked that way at Lev.

Since the inception of this supposed socio-political move to the States, Vladimir had had his doubts. Assigned to do Alexander's search on Jamie Wilde, he'd discovered that Anna had been doing extensive research on the man for years. Though he brought this unusual finding to Alexander's attention, it had been lightly glossed over by Alexander with his usual pride. "She is like me. I would expect a detailed inspection with a decision such as this."

But Vladimir had suspicions that more than just a thorough check of character, talent and reputation was underway.

Suspicions were confirmed that day the young man had danced in the flesh and Anna could barely remain in her seat. It had grown since then. Now, he could see just where she was headed: to a permanent life in the United States, shirking her duties in her homeland, all because of a brainless infatuation.

He'd known for years that Anna's strong head and questioning nature would mean trouble as she matured and the responsibility for her to step into her father's shoes drew near. Anna was craftier than he'd given her credit for. Keeping what Vladimir believed was her real reason for coming to the U.S. a secret, she had positioned herself exactly where she wanted to be. Wasn't it just like a woman to manipulate a man for gain?

One reason Vladimir had never married was because he saw women as annoyingly high maintenance individuals that, given too much say, would have too much power – power that would then be lost because women thought with their hearts, rather than their heads.

The only reason he could accept Anna taking her rightful spot as heir apparent was because it was he that would step up as her chief advisor. He would be the one with the power. But if she jumped ship, he'd be left dog paddling in some low-profile administrative job.

Even if dance was not the only reason Anna was here, and Vladimir doubted it was, America's dream of fantasy fulfillment was hard to argue, and too big a battle for one man, loyal to the conservative, if not somewhat archaic way of life in the Isles of Slovokia. With a broken heart and no possibility for winning any of her beloved competitions, perhaps the rocky shores of home would be a more appealing place for Anna to mend wounds.

Ivan's laugh broke through Vladimir's heavy train of thought. He shot a glare at the bald man sitting at his side but it went unnoticed. Ivan laughed at something Jamie said. Vladimir's lips turned in a scowl. He stared at Jamie. "Enough. It is time we go home now."

Still on the tail end of a laugh, Anna took Ivan's plate to the sink. "We are almost ready, Vladimir."

The ease with which she dismissed his every command was the whistling top of a teapot left boiling too long. Vladimir stood and crossed to the big window. He didn't see the sun finally breaking free of oppressive clouds, the mountains, cabins, snow and trees charming and inviting as a mountainside in Switzerland. Anna was foolish; blindly led by her woman's heart to put down roots in a land that promised success, freedom and happiness by virtue of living on its soil. She belonged with her people, on her own soil. Mixing blood in the dirt of another country made for mud. He would not let that happen.

14.

"I don't know." Reuben sent a friendly elbow in Jamie's ribs. "Whenever you two get together after hours, you end up in these reality show situations."

Jamie finished tying the black laces of his Latin shoes and sat back with a flippant grin. Could he help that his eyes darted toward the double doors while he and Reuben waited for Anna to appear.

"Uh-huh. I see what's going on," Reuben smiled. "As plain as the skin atop my head, brother."

"You need contacts."

"And you need to take a good look at yourself."

Jamie stood, and began to do some warm-up exercises. One night and the time spent with Anna in the car and at the cabin, had brought him a clearer understanding of her. That was both good and bad. Good, because he liked to know everything. He couldn't possibly have a partner he wasn't intimately familiar with.

He let out a breath and walked a kink out of his left knee. The more he knew Anna, the better he would anticipate her moves in dance. All of that was good. The bad part was, unlike Courtney, with whom his short-lived, adolescent crush died and was buried without the possibility of resurrection, the more he got into Anna, the deeper the danger.

"Buddy, look." Reuben joined him on the floor. "I know you've lived by this dance-no-make-love thing you came up with when you were too young and stupid to know better. But have you ever noticed that there are three types of partnerships in this business? Married, dating or gay."

In the middle of practicing a spin, Jamie slowed, then stopped. Because he couldn't meet Reuben's grin, he walked the other direction, his face heating. Reuben was right. He'd been to hundreds of competitions over the years, had analyzed everything about every competing couple he'd watched. He knew their tricks, their strengths, their weaknesses. He knew which ones were so in tune with each other they danced as if only one shared breath strung them together.

He dropped his head to his chest and blew out a sigh. It hadn't dawned on him, who belonged to whom, because he'd been married, in a way, to Courtney.

"You and Gail didn't dance together," he said in his defense. Reuben's smile deepened.

"A weak answer. If you'd been a lonely runaway from an abusive home you'd have latched on to a pretty face and an open heart just like I did."

"My point is—"

"Your point is lame, man. I've seen the way you two are together, I watch it every day. It's like two exposed wires. Watch out when you finally connect, there'll be more sparks than the fourth of July."

Jamie rolled his eyes but the heat in his cheeks he could do nothing about.

"Let's face it, dance is limiting," Reuben continued. "You spend a lot of time with a few people. Your circle is close, but tight. There's not a lot of room for exploration. That's why so many couples end up together. And it's a good thing. Look at some of the greats, your old coach for one – Nic – she ended up with Breck."

Jamie averted stubborn eyes. The oversight made him look like a lughead, like the only one jumping upstream when the current pulled everybody the other direction.

The doors opened and Lev entered. He sent the two of them an animated, two-handed wave.

"Lev, buddy. You going to watch us today?" Reuben met him in the middle of the floor and shook his hand.

"Yeah, but, Anna's talking about Thanksgiving Point. She says it's really cool there. But I'm kinda touristed out."

"It is, it is." Reuben glanced at Jamie who had not moved, but was deep in thought in the corner of the room.

Anna came in next, wearing a tight, long-sleeved top and another pair of her hip-hugging knit dance pants in ballerina pink. Her abdomen was exposed, planes and muscle just hard enough to cause Jamie's gut to stir with want. His glance held. Her dark hair was down today, flowing around her shoulders. He swallowed a flash of desire and once again resigned himself to be neutral.

"Hello, everybody." She was so pleasant. Like nothing, especially none of this them – stuff, affected her. It boiled his blood just a little.

She crossed directly to Lev and Reuben while Jamie watched under crimped brows as she laughed and talked. With San Francisco their first competition together, he was determined to make a jaw-dropping show. Their standard routine was flawless; he couldn't be more pleased. Princess Anna would have everyone, including the judges, watching them as if they were a fairytale couple.

Latin still wasn't where he wanted it. He wanted it bold, daring, and just on this side of wild. It was something he'd always wanted to have with Courtney, but her look had never broken free from pretty-girl-next-door-dressed-up.

The beauty of Anna was that she was Princess and Vamp. He wanted her hair whipping in jeweled strands, her lips painted a luscious plum. He wanted her eyes dramatic and glittering. And her dress…he wanted… there were so many things he wanted to see her in, all of them showcasing her watch-me-move curves. Dipped in diamonds, rolled in rubies – she could wear anything, everything, or very little of anything and hypnotize with that exquisite body of hers.

He warmed uncomfortably fast, so he walked the room flicking nervous hands.

She laughed, and the light fluttering sound trickled through his insides. When she reached out and touched Reuben, Jamie felt as if her hand had grazed him. When her gaze crossed the expanse of the room and locked on his, he couldn't tear away. Inescapably drawn, his feet soon had him waiting for her in the center of the floor.

The laughter died.

Reuben took his spot nearby, and Lev scurried to a seat.

Then she came to him.

He looked down into her eyes as if he stood alongside a deep well from which echoed his own heartbeat. He wouldn't be satisfied until he'd gone to the very depths of the mystery that was there.

"Pull the shades," he announced.

Her eyes widened and it sent a hot spark through him.

"Good idea." Reuben began the process, enlisting an eager Lev to help. Jamie didn't let Anna's gaze go; watching emotions cross her face like wind over the sand – curiosity, fear, determination.

"It's what we need for Latin," Jamie demanded on a low whisper. "And we're going to use it as often as we have to until it's where I want it." She didn't like it. Good. There was plenty he didn't like he had to deal with.

"What are we doing?" Directing his question to Reuben, Lev pulled down the last shade. "Watching a movie?"

"It's an exercise." Reuben jogged across the floor to Jamie and Anna. "To fine tune dancers who just need that little extra umph." He grinned at them both. "You guys ready?" He looked at Anna. "Sis?"

She was so good at hiding what she really felt, Jamie found himself watching her closely just to catch any signs. She licked her lips, leaving them glistening. Her chin lifted, her shoulders went back. In her eyes, the dark flecks of grey opened to black discomfort.

"Of course I am ready." She stood in position for him.

"All right then. Close, but not so close that when I turn off the lights you can reach out and touch. Find each other. Then dance."

Jamie let out a slow stream of air. Part of him wanted, needed to go through with the exercise, knowing if he was going to burrow deep, he would have to have Anna right where he wanted her first, open and vulnerable. But he also understood that with his blood this ripe in his veins, it would be a struggle not to lose himself.

"You mean you're going to make them dance in the dark?" Lev asked, eyes huge behind his glasses. Reuben nodded, hand poised on the light switch.

"This is weird." Lev sat in one of the chairs. "What other things do you do?"

"We got all kinds of ways to improve technique, don't we?" Reuben smiled at Jamie. "We've been known to dance in the water, to dance on balance beams. We try it with our hands behind our backs, with our eyes blindfolded."

Lev's smile was huge, his Adams apple bobbed. "Cool. Do you play music?" Lev blurted. It tore through Jamie's fragile psyche. He stepped away from Anna, running his hands down his face.

"Sometimes." Reuben's voice softened. "For now, we just need total silence. Got it?"

Lev nodded and sat back, as if ready to observe a game.

Jamie's eyes latched on Anna's just before the lights went out. Wanting to be the first to make contact, he reached one hand through the empty air and found hers waiting He eased his fingers through hers before gently pulling her toward him.

His left hand found the soft heat of her hip. He closed his eyes, seeing the muscled curve in his mind, the sharp cut of female flesh. Lightly, he let his hand wander up the side until he found the firm nitch of her waist. Cupping there, he pulled, until she was pressed the whole length of him.

His heart pounded against his ribs, he was sure she could feel it. Her breath, hot and sweet, tickled his neck, shooting ribbons of fire through his body that demanded he move.

Slowly, he eased them through the measured turns, rolls, sways and bends of rumba. Her body was tight and hard brushing against his as thigh met thigh, chest met breast.

Silent at first, when his hips grazed hers, her breath hitched and the sound hammered desire through already ripened veins. He slowed them even more, dragging out the movements so every part of her had to strain in unison with him to stay fused.

Then he turned her.

There was no resistance, only complete willingness and trust. Bringing her back against his chest, he savored the feel of her rounded buttocks brushing teasingly against him. Her head fell back, and pressed into his shoulder. Her face was near, her breath caught between a moan and a whimper as her lips lightly grazed the side of his neck. Finding the delicate curve of her ear, he whispered, "Tell me."

He kept her pinned there, arms twined at their sides, bodies swaying in lulling rolls.

She took a shallow breath. Her ear was at his lips. He bit back the urge to nip at it with his teeth. "Tell me why you wanted me. Why you really want me, Anna." When she shuddered again, he took that nip.

It was she that moved then, separating them with the blackness of distance when she stepped away. Emptiness shot through him like a cold slap of unwelcome air. Only their hands were linked, and he held on tight.

There was fight in her now, resistance to his question. Every step she took away, he took back, until they were moving too fast for the constraint of rumba and it became a clash of wills. When he snapped his arms around her, she twisted free.

Both of their bodies were glazed with sweat. It was easy for her to break away and she did, leaving him standing alone. Anger shot through him first. This was his dance, his lead. He heard her frantic breath struggling for calm and stood perfectly still. The jagged sound led him back to her, inching with caution through darkness.

When he bumped her, she jerked away, but he snatched her like the tongue of a predator stanches prey, bringing her against him with a fury building with impatience.

Burrowing his head tight to her neck, his lips brushed the moist curve. "Tell me, Anna." He kept her close, unwilling to give her any freedom to move but what they did as one.

She struggled against him in a frantic effort to free herself. It didn't feel right, holding her against her will. A will, he was coming to realize, as stubborn as his own. And it wasn't easy to let her go, knowing black emptiness would surround him again, but he did.

He wiped his brow and ran his hands down his face. This time he didn't hear her. He had no sense of place from any sound at all and felt the utter helplessness of it. He'd wanted to break through her, to find truth and be settled with her secrets.

When she touched his back, he froze, every nerve end jerking upright. Her hands wandered across his shoulders and down, lightly touching his tense muscles fisting beneath her fluttering fingers. Her hands slid teasingly to his arms, along his biceps, to his chest, where her hand laid, palm open, across his heart.

A red-hot whip would have been more merciful. The line of fire where she'd touched him burned as if she'd carved him with a dagger. Now, his heart lay vulnerable under a hand he was not sure he should give it to.

His heart thudded for her whether he liked it or not, and he grabbed her wrist. But suddenly she was in front of him, her feet locked between his, her legs in perfect alignment with his legs. Slick heat throbbed with each bang of his pulse as she ran her hands over his chest, down the length of his arms, forcing both of their linked arms up over his head like a prisoner.

He could dissolve and die, he decided, right then, right there. At last he threw his arms around her. He could melt into her, body and soul at that very moment and not regret the submission. The unmistakable flutter of soft lips was at his collar bone. He couldn't allow it – another kiss – he would feel the brand for days. A lover's burn.

She slid up; her breath sweet at his lips. "Is this what you want?" she whispered.

Hot tremors ricocheted from his heart to his gut. He was dangerously close to pleading – desperately close to saying yes. His head swam in the deliberate way she now led him through the tortuous movements of rumba.

"Let me," she whispered on a slow turn that had her taking him in easy, controlled steps, further into darkness. He held one of her hands as if it was a lifeline, and, for the moment, it was. For the moment, he would go wherever she asked.

She took his hands and placed them on her hips.

He cursed the darkness. He needed to see her, wanted to drown in the mysterious wells of her eyes. To see if the answers he sought were there.

They moved as one in ribbon-like rolls, shuddering to release at their shoulders and toes. Over and over, they arched and curved. It was perfect. He didn't need light to see—he felt it, their wills had finally joined in purpose.

Jamie took the lead, slowing them both to their final position. He held her carefully in the darkness, taking in her scent, the wet feel of her for the last time. There was a pang of sorrow, knowing the moment would soon be gone and he lowered his head, coursing her neck with his lips. "This isn't over."

A light moan escaped from her. He wanted to wrap himself around her until that sound sung through his veins. Because he couldn't, he was frustrated with himself and he pushed himself away.

"Lights!" he barked.

The lights blinked on and for a few moments, everyone ducked behind their hands as eyes adjusted.

"Wow." Lev blinked big behind his glasses. "Whew. Wow. I couldn't see anything but I sure heard a lot of heavy breathing."

Jamie couldn't dislodge disappointment. He hadn't been able to get to her, and he was mortified that she'd turned the tables on him. He strode over so he could have a few words with her before Reuben started in.

"What was that all about?" he growled.

"I could ask you that same question."

The faint shimmer of sweat on her neck and arms reminded him of her slick skin against his. It was true, he'd used the exercise every bit as much as she had, so he couldn't say anything more. "You're still holding back, Anna."

"Let's try it with the lights on," Reuben announced, joining them. "I want to see where it got us."

Anna followed Reuben to the center of the room and Jamie swallowed bitterness. It hadn't gotten him anywhere but worked up and he wouldn't let that show.

Lev sat forward in his seat. "Did it help?"

Anna tucked a dangling hair at her nape back into her pony tail, keeping her lowered gaze on Jamie. "I think it did wonders."

Jamie's eyes narrowed when she turned that prim head his direction just enough for him to see there was a smile on her face.

Reuben jerked his head once. It was time to get back to work, and Jamie crossed to them.

It had taken their performance from great to spectacular, Reuben told them after. They'd connected. Anna had found "It." Reuben was confident the judges would be awe-struck by her princess performance in standard and would be equally wowed by the seductive change she brought to Latin.

It should have pleased Jamie that they'd reached a level he and Courtney had not been able to reach, but something wouldn't let him enjoy the small victory.

After the day wrapped, he headed to his car without even a goodbye, so tangled in his thoughts. Anna caught up to him at the front door. "Jamie, I have something to show you."

He didn't want to stay in her surroundings any longer than he had to. Her mystique, her eyes, her body, were all working to break him down into nothing but a love-sick servant.

Following her into the office, he noted that Lev had vanished. Her posse seemed to have as well. She went to the desk and opened the large center drawer. "I wanted to get your opinion on these." Pulling out a black, leather sketch book, she came around, sidling up close to him. The very feel of her pressed against his side pumped his abused system into agony, everything about her reawakening his senses.

"See?" She turned the large pages. Detailed, beautiful and elaborate drawings of her in the most stunning dresses he had ever seen lay before his eyes.

"Which is your favorite?" Her face tilted up, was just inches from his. He looked at her mouth, poised with a half-smile too lovely to cover with a kiss but he wanted to just the same.

He slid his envious eyes to the image of her curves in beads, just like he'd imagined; burgundy and black beads in a halter-style dress showcasing sharply-cut shoulders, rounded breasts and a tiny waist. The beads flowed over full hips, spreading out in a hem of dangling fringe.

"Wow." He swallowed. "That's – I think that's the one."

"And look." Eagerly, she turned the page where he saw himself sketched in black slacks and a burgundy shirt, sheer at the chest and back, cuffed and collared in black, the seams of the sleeves beaded to match the dress. "I am having them made."

He frowned. "You – what?"

"I had a feeling you would like that one. Everything I know about you told me you were tired of boring designs that didn't speak of passion. These costumes will be perfect."

"You went ahead and ordered our costumes without my approval?"

"Well, of course. All final costume design decisions are to be mine."

He dropped his duffle.

"You do not like them? We can use another design. I can draw—"

"You should have consulted me. They're our costumes, Anna."

"Jamie, I am so sorry."

"It's my reputation, my name," he growled out.

"Don't you mean our reputation, our name?"

"You're talking about being fair when you've circumvented my decision in the costuming?"

Bringing the book to her chest, she considered him for a moment. "You are right. That wasn't fair. I'm sorry."

The hard edge of his face softened some. "They're great designs. Really. You'll—you'll look beautiful in any of them."

"Thank you."

"Just – let me in on it next time, will you?"

Her eyes were round with sincerity and she lifted up on her toes, her face nearing his. Jamie stopped breathing. Every muscle froze in anticipation of what she might do.

She kissed his cheek.

Long, drawn out heat stretched between them. Jamie reached over and picked up his duffle. "What are you doing for Thanksgiving?" She blinked in surprise. "I know it's a random question. But if you don't have plans, bring the crew up to my parents.'" He figured Reuben was right, they all needed to stash their dancing shoes for a while and just hang. "Want to?"

Supposing it was his way of extending himself in a more personal way, Anna nodded. "That is most kind, Jamie. Yes."

His gaze lingered, sending a warm flush over her skin. "Great. I'll call you."

She walked with him to the door in silence. "I have never been to an American Thanksgiving dinner," she told him. He looked more relieved now, and she was glad for that, even if she wasn't sure of the reason.

"It's about food, football and fun," he said. They stopped at the door.

Why was he feeling awkward, like they'd been on a date and now he was saying goodnight? He stepped outside, looked at her again. That desire he'd felt earlier still dangled somewhere inside, and it pulled, when he remembered the kiss she left on his cheek. "Goodbye, Anna."

Jamie walked to his car counting the hours until Thanksgiving.

15.

Joyce Wilde was not an uptight woman. After baby number three was born, she'd easily scrapped everything glossy related to perfection for the matte of reality. If her children weren't dressed in matching ensembles, she counted herself lucky that they had clothes on at all. If her husband walked in and she'd managed to throw a makeshift casserole together instead of steaks and salad, she thanked God he'd been home early enough to bless the meal.

Through the years, her perfectly tidy house had become like a well-worn shoe, with plenty of nicks in the walls and stains on the carpets, but comfortable with familiarity.

Having a princess for Thanksgiving was changing all of that.

The day before the holiday she donned her sergeant hat. Every toilet seat joint got scrubbed. Justin patched walls, then painted. She enlisted Jessica with her small hands and eager spirit to scrub every baseboard. Jeff offered to perfect "Sweet Emotion," just in case the princess asked for a concert. She let Jocelyn attend to a deep dusting of every surface.

As the aroma of baking pies mixed with roasting turkey, the nerves in her stomach skittered. Royalty was coming for dinner.

The woman had seemed nice enough when Jamie brought her over after their campout. For the life of her, Joyce could not figure out why he'd taken her snow-caving. Sometimes the child had no sense when it came to women.

She smiled at a photo of him on the wall, running her feather duster across a frame Jocelyn had missed. She imagined Jamie's lack of sense was a result of never having to work for it. In a way, dance had made women necessary objects.

The front door swung open and Jamie walked in with a bouquet of yellow roses – her favorite. His grin took her back in time and for a moment, she saw him running, hair mussed, face smudged with dirt, wildflowers drooping in his grasp.

He kissed her cheek, set the roses in her hand. "Happy Thanksgiving, Mom."

When he'd been a boy, she'd run her hand along his cheek and felt the petal-softness of a child's skin. Today, she felt the roughness of a man and her heart hollowed some.

"Thank you, honey." She immediately put the roses in a vase of water.

The sight of his siblings busily engaged brought a grin to Jamie's face. "It's good to see you guys working."

Jocelyn stuffed potholders into a drawer. "We busted our butts for this princess pal of yours. She better be nice."

"She's nice." He strode over to the TV and snatched Jessica into his arms. "You'd better mind your manners or she'll order ye flogged, mite."

It was all Jessica needed to break into giggles, and all Jocelyn needed to snort. "I'm surprised she hasn't flogged you yet."

"I'm serious." Jamie set Jessica back down in front of the TV, went to Jeff next. "Better watch your step – she's bringing Ivan and Lukov with her."

Annoyed but curious, Jocelyn folded her arms. "And who are Ivan and Lukov?"

"Those huge guys that came looking for her that night," Jeff answered with pride.

Jamie slugged him playfully. "Glad somebody's paying attention."

"They're too old," Jocelyn mumbled, "and ugly."

"Is that all you ever think about? Boys?" Jamie asked.

"It's all any girl ever thinks about," Justin answered for her. He came in from somewhere, tucking a light-blue shirt into some baggy-enough pants. Then he shook his shaggy head of hair into place.

That his younger brother knew more about women than he did irked Jamie. "And you're the expert."

Justin honed in on a tray of perfectly displayed vegetables and dip. "Need we tally girlfriends? Let's see, I've had…eight in my twenty-six years and you have had…hmmm…zero?"

"That lie's as big as your face." Jamie joined him at the hors d'oeuvres'. Both were whisked away by Jocelyn when she saw the platter was about to be obliterated. "And we're not counting high school, of which you had – one, I think."

"And your life is so fast that you keep track of mine? You're pathetic." Though Jamie said it in jest, the reality stung deeper than he liked. Because he was feeling ornery about it, he shot back. "What does a guy your age know that still lives at home?"

The flash of mean in his brother's eyes reminded Jamie that the battle could get ugly – which took him back to his discussion with Anna. "Sorry," he muttered.

Everything in the kitchen stopped. Jamie looked from face to face. "Can't a guy apologize without it bringing the house down?"

Jocelyn cocked her head. "Not when that guy is you."

"Hey," he cleared his throat. "I could have used some of those jujitsu techniques a while back."

"Yeah?" Justin started opening cabinets in search of food since he'd gotten nowhere with the vegetable platter.

Jocelyn sighed loudly and everyone looked at her.

"What?" Jamie asked.

"Neither one of you gets girls. And you think you do. It's so retarded."

The fight to defend one's maleness was at stake and Justin forgot his stomach and strode over. "Hey, I know girls."

"What do you know? You take a different one out every weekend, you schmooze them on the phone, you—"

"You eavesdropping little twerp."

"No fighting," Joyce warned.

Jamie masked interest behind a stolen carrot stick. "What else, Joce?"

"You're even more pathetic."

"Hey." Jamie feigned being wounded. "You can massacre him but keep me out of it."

"Why should I? You should be married by now, or at least serious about somebody."

The room quieted again and all eyes were on him. Jamie shifted. "Why should I be married? I'm still young."

"You're almost thirty."

"In two years," he protested. "And who are you to decide what age is the age to get hitched?"

"It's 'cause she'd get married tomorrow if she could," Justin shot out on a laugh.

"She would not," Joyce chimed. "She's only sixteen."

"I still know what I want."

"And it's all in where he sits, right?" Justin taunted. "Every girl I know says she likes a guy with a cute butt."

Jamie stopped chewing. "Seriously?"

"You really are lost." Justin laughed. "You've been quarantined on that dance floor too long."

Jamie scratched his head, feeling stupid. "So," he managed as casually as he could. "What else?"

"A guy shouldn't be afraid to call and talk," Jocelyn spoke with all of the authority of her sixteen years. "Of course, the conversation should be equally spread between you and her. Girls hate it when guys go on and on about themselves."

"Well I don't do that," Justin said.

"Finding out what really turns her on is—"

"Hey now," Joyce piped.

"I don't mean physically," Jocelyn added, then shot her brothers a glance after her mother went back to wiping the counter. "I mean, if it's flowers, walks in the park, long drives—whatever—find out what she likes. Don't just do what you like or what you think she'll like."

Jocelyn continued to expound on the secret, inner workings of females. It surprised Jamie that in his mind, he saw Anna's face. He hadn't thought of Cheryl in days. Not since he'd invited her to Thanksgiving dinner.

His stomach dropped.

"You look ready to heave," Justin told him matter-of-factly.

"Hey, the house looks great." Jack walked in and took his ear-phone out of a very red ear and rubbed. "I'm hiding this for the next two days."

"Yeah, we've heard that before." Jocelyn rolled her eyes, went back to the oven and checked on the croissants.

When the doorbell rang Jamie didn't hear it. His head was swimming with his female dilemma.

"That'll be her, Jamie," Joyce nodded toward the front door. "Why don't you get it?"

Or Cheryl. His gut cramped.

He opened the door and Cheryl's blonde cap of hair, her cheery smile, was what greeted him. She wrapped him in a hug and placed a kiss on his cheek. "Mmm. You look as yummy as it smells." She leaned up and kissed him again, and his eyes stayed out the door knowing that Anna would be pulling up any minute.

"Cheryl?" Joyce looked surprised for only a moment before her hostess skills kicked in and she hugged Cheryl. Over her shoulder, she met her son's gaze. "How nice to have you here. Happy Thanksgiving."

"Thanks for inviting me. My parents wanted me to come home, but, with teaching, I couldn't leave."

"You want to shut the door, Jamie?" Joyce said before escorting Cheryl to the back of the house. Jamie pulled his sweater away from the beads of sweat gathering on his chest.

He shut the door, leaned against it for a moment, and closed his eyes. It wasn't as though he anticipated a problem. They were all adults. And women get along with other women, right? They could all be…friends.

When he opened his eyes, Cheryl was coming back toward him. He stood erect, stuffing his hands in his pockets.

"You invited her?" she whispered, but it sounded to Jamie more like a hiss. His back smacked flush against the cold metal door.

"Yeah," he shrugged. "It's Thanksgiving." He didn't like that he felt the need to defend himself. "She's millions of miles away from her country."

"She's not American. She doesn't celebrate Thanksgiving!"

"Then this will be her first. She's excited about it. Come on, Cheryl. She's my partner." He should reach out and touch her, the gesture would ease her. But something kept him from doing it.

He headed toward the kitchen, and heard her follow.

Anna had attended events with dignitaries, celebrities and other important people, but none of them had made her nerves itch like this. In her lap she held a wrapped gift for Jamie's mother. Anna had not given Inessa the assignment of picking something out but had taken it upon herself, spending hours until she'd found just the right thing.

No one had spoken on the short drive over. Anna supposed it was the fact that Vladimir had refused to come along and had made his displeasure obvious, and that she was still attending without him.

Of late, his behavior had been suspicious. Anna didn't like that she was watched and scrutinized by one of her own. Today, she'd try not to think about it. It was a holiday: an American holiday for giving thanks and she had much to be thankful for.

Anna shot a glance at Inessa sitting next to her. She looked remarkably pretty, wearing her mousey-blonde hair to her shoulders, flipped up at the ends. Her young assistant had dressed her face with just enough makeup to enhance features Anna had never really noticed before. And the dull gray she seemed to live in was replaced by navy slacks and a deep mint blouse.

"You look very nice, Inessa." The surprise in the young girl's face brought a smile to Anna's lips. "I am excited for this today, you?"

Inessa nodded. "Yes, Your Highness."

Both Ivan and Lukov wore dark slacks with sweaters rather than suits, a more casual look Anna liked, but it was at Jamie's insistence. When he'd called to tell her what time to arrive, he'd mentioned that they were going to be "laid back." It didn't stop Anna from dressing up. She preferred erring to the side of dressy than too casual. She'd chosen her favorite color— black, and worn it from cashmere sweater to snake-skin boots.

It was Jamie who greeted them at the door. He looked wonderfully handsome in a pair of light gray slacks and a tight, crew neck sweater in hunter green.

Anna's cheeks warmed under Jamie's smiling eyes. Not that he spent anytime studying her, she noticed with a small wave of disappointment. He cordially invited them in and hugged Inessa, his hands on her shoulders while he looked her up and down with a grin that Anna was ashamed to admit made her envious.

"You look awesome, Nessa. I have a little brother I want you to meet." Jamie shook both Lukov and Ivan's hands. "Guys, welcome. Glad you dressed down. No need to be in protector-mode today. Relax."

Then his dark eyes slid to hers and her insides melted. "Anna." He leaned and lightly kissed her cheek. She almost closed her eyes. The soft heat of his lips sent an even softer trembling through her and the faint scent of him taunted the ache in her heart. "Where's Lev? And Vlad?"

"Lev's ill," Anna said. What a lucky stroke that was. She'd only felt a moment's concern over Lev at home with a runny nose, his perpetual hankies stuffed up his nostrils like plugs. "Vladimir chose to remain behind." Now she could enjoy getting to know Jamie's family without either man looking over her shoulder.

Jamie gestured for them to follow him to the back of the house where the low-drone of a football game came from the television and mixed with laughter, voices, and the clatter of pans and dishes.

Everything quieted and all of Jamie's family eyed her. Anna took a deep breath.

"Anna." Jack stepped forward and shook her hand. "Welcome." The wary scrutiny she'd seen in his eyes during their last visit was gone now and it pleased Anna to see that he wasn't holding onto it.

Joyce embraced her with a friendly pat. "It is so nice of you to have us," Anna said. "Thank you very much. This is for you."

Joyce's eyes lit. She took the brightly-wrapped present. "My. Well. Look at this Jack."

With their mother opening a gift from a princess, the Wilde children gathered around. Anna noticed Cheryl for the first time. Bright and bubbly, dressed head to toe in soft pink, Anna couldn't help but think how very different the two of them were: all-American and dark foreigner. Sliding right up next to Jamie, Cheryl wove her arm in his with a possessive look aimed right at Anna.

Joyce gasped as she drew out the intricately cut Waterford crystal vase. "My goodness. Swarovski? It's been a long time since I've owned anything this nice. Thank you, Anna."

"I noticed you like flowers on your tables. I thought perhaps this would go nicely in your dining room."

Joyce nodded. Her eyes had yet to return to their normal size. "It will look beautiful."

"Take off your coats and make yourselves at home." Joyce tucked the vase into Jocelyn's nearby hands. "Jocelyn, put this in the dining room where it will be safe, would you please?"

After Jamie and Jack helped with the stowing of coats, the entire Wilde clan stood in an informal semicircle waiting for Anna to introduce her entourage. Anna found it especially amusing how impressed both Justin and Jeff were with Ivan and Lukov.

"So, you guys get into any real, you know, life-threatening situations?" Justin asked.

Having never been the subject of admiration or attention other than that brought on by the job, neither Ivan or Lukov responded, with the exception of a brief glance at each other.

"They're a little shy when you first meet them," Jamie piped, playfully slugging Lukov's bicep. "But they'll warm up. Just don't piss them off."

Anna gestured to Inessa. "This is my assistant, Inessa."

"It's very nice to meet you." Justin's eyes sharpened instantly.

Jamie slipped up behind him and gave a quick squeeze to his shoulders. "Nessa and I are buds. You be a good boy now, you hear?"

Justin kept his sparkling eyes and Jamie-like grin on Inessa. "I am a good boy."

The family dispersed, going back to the football game on TV, into the kitchen to help with the meal.

Anna went directly to Cheryl. "Hello, Cheryl." Cheryl's smile would have looked absolutely sincere if Anna had not been familiar with the look of black jealousy glittering in her eyes. "How very nice to see you again," Anna began smoothly. "Your family is not here in Utah?"

"No." Just as smoothly, Cheryl came back at her. "Arizona. But, Jamie's family is like my family."

It surprised Anna when Jamie shot Cheryl a startled look then.

"The Wildes are lovely people," Anna agreed. This was not a sprint, but a marathon, and Anna figured she had already been at it much longer than Cheryl. But it was also a family holiday and she knew better than to engage in anything that would cause any wrinkles for Joyce, Jack or Jamie.

Anna excused herself and headed to where Jack sat in front of the TV. She caught sight of Justin who had Inessa captured with one arm casually around her shoulder and was showing her Wilde family photos hanging on a nearby wall.

"You're beautiful."

The light, sweet voice had Anna looking down into the bright face of Jessica who held a very ornately dressed Barbie. "As pretty as her." She held the doll up for Anna's inspection.

"She is very nice." Taking the doll, Anna fixed a wayward ringlet then handed her back.

"She's a princess too."

"Oh?"

Jamie and Cheryl were in a whispered chat across the room but Anna didn't look for long. Jocelyn was making her way inconspicuously over. Anna could tell the teen wanted to talk.

"Will you play with me?" Jessica asked.

"Jess." Jocelyn stepped into the conversation by picking Jessica up. "Grown-ups don't play Barbies."

"I would love to play." It brought a smile to Anna's face when both girls' eyes widened. "I love dolls. I have an extensive collection from around the world at home in fact."

Jessica gasped. "In the castle?"

"In the castle, yes."

"You don't have to, you know," Jocelyn said.

"No, I'd love it. Really." It would be an excellent opportunity to get to know Jamie's sisters and see more of where Jamie grew up.

Within minutes they were up in Jessica's room. The space was pink and white and all girl. A canopied bed was on the center wall, piled with pillows and furry stuffed animals. A shelf ran the entire perimeter of the room where toys and decorations that Anna assumed weren't play things sat with a fine layer of dust covering them.

The room felt like a little girl's room.

Her own quarters had never looked or felt played in or used, she thought now, smelling the scent of child. The rooms had been too big to be cozy. Her parents had insisted she keep the areas looking as if they belonged to a princess. These toys had lost fur from cuddling, paint from play, and limbs were loose from hours of dressing.

And they looked to have permanent residence on the floor.

It was easy for Jessica to play; she began the moment she sat down in front of her toys. "Which one do you want?" she asked Anna.

Anna sat and crossed her legs. Jessica still held the pretty princess clutched tightly to her chest, a signal of ownership Anna didn't overlook. She reached for what she assumed had once been Jessica's favorite, now minus the garish clothing and mussed from love.

"I'll take her."

"She's one of my other princesses," Jessica informed her with gratitude in her eyes that the doll would not be left out. "How about you, Jocie?"

Jocelyn was still debating whether picking up a doll in front of a princess was a very good idea, so Anna set her doll down and began to dress her from the pile of clothing. She pulled out a hot-pink dress and noticed that Jocelyn reached for another well-loved doll and began to dress her. "What shall I wear to impress Ken?" Anna asked, changing her voice. "Do you think he will like this dress?"

"Oh, yes," Jessica piped. "Only, it's not Ken, it's Prince Ken."

"I see." Anna picked up a dark blonde and naked Ken. "We had better dress him, or he will not be permitted to see our princesses."

"What is your name, princess?" Jessica asked, lost now in play.

"Anastasia. That's my mother's name."

"Cool." Jocelyn looked at her doll. "Mine will be Gwyneth."

"Anastasia," Jessica's voice was pitched high, "who do you want to go to the ball with?"

"Why, Prince Ken of course—unless he is your beau," Anna replied.

"Bow?" Jessica giggled.

Jocelyn rolled her eyes with a careful glance at Anna. "That's royal for boyfriend."

"Oh." Jessica stopped giggling, clearly understanding her sister's expression of warning. "He's mine, but you can pick from any of those boys behind you."

Anna's eye caught a dark-haired, brown-eyed Ken that reminded her of Jamie. With a smile, she picked him up.

"That's Jamie," Jessica informed her.

"Is that so?"

"Uh-huh, and that one's Justin but you can change their names."

Anna smiled. "I think Jamie will do just fine."

"Do you have a boyfriend?" Jocelyn asked.

Anna was searching the pile to her left for doll clothes. "I have Jamie," she said absently.

"No, I mean in real life."

"Oh. No." Anna picked out a pair of brown slacks and a blue shirt and began to dress the doll with care.

"But you're a princess," Jessica's disappointment was plain.

Now dressing her own boy doll, Jocelyn stated, "Guys are stupid."

"It's not a matter of them being stupid necessarily," Anna began, searching through the pile for shoes. She found one. "Sometimes they are taken already."

"Taken? Like kidnapped?" Jessica asked.

Anna laughed. "No. They already have a girlfriend."

"But you're a princess," Jocelyn said. "How much better could it get for a guy than that?"

Anna shrugged. "Some men are afraid of that."

Jamie thought now might be a good time to jump in on the conversation. He'd come up to call them for dinner and stopped in his steps when he heard Anna's voice.

He'd managed a couple of sneak peeks. It brought a smile to his face seeing Anna sitting Indian-style on the floor with his sisters. His first thought was to rescue her from what was most likely an obligation she did not have to endure. But she looked surprisingly at ease, as if she was really enjoying herself. He was ready to step in when what Jocelyn said stopped him.

"Did it scare Jamie? You being a princess?"

There was a pause. It almost drove Jamie to take another peek but he kept hidden in the hallway, his heart pounding surprisingly fast as he awaited her answer.

"No. That's one of the things I like about him. He treats me just like any other girl."

"And you like that?" Jocelyn snorted. "He's so bossy."

Jamie grimaced.

"Oh, he's very bossy," Anna said lightly, and Jamie imagined she was smiling. "But I let him think he's getting his way. A smart woman will never let a man think it's any other way."

Jamie heard their laughter then, and as much as he wanted to go in and set the record straight, he couldn't interrupt what was proving to be a very enlightening conversation.

"Are you going to marry my brother?" Jessica asked.

The back of Jamie's neck bloomed in sweat. He peered in.

"Jess, that's personal," Jocelyn told her.

"No. It's all right." Anna's voice was soft with remorse Jamie wasn't sure how to interpret. "He's a very nice man, your brother. I like him very much."

"But he's taken, huh?" Jessica asked. "Cheryl has taken him."

Anna cleared her throat. "Shall we play?"

"Don't ask personal questions," Jocelyn hissed.

"It's all right, really. I've had every question you could possibly have asked, asked of me at some time or another."

"It must be hard being…you," Jocelyn said.

"Me?" Anna's pitch rose. "Why I'm princess Anastasia, and here is my prince. We're ready to go to the ball, even though he's a bit under dressed."

"At least he's dressed," Jocelyn quipped. "And better than my brother."

Leaning in the door, Jamie waited to be noticed.

Anna walked her dolls toward Jessica's. "Shall we put on some music and then we can dance?" Anna's voice dropped low, as if she were speaking for the man. Jessica giggled.

"I would love to dance with you," Anna then said in a higher pitch. "You are the best dancer in the world. I have come a long way to find you. I will only dance with the best."

Jamie grinned. "Is this imitating life?" He got a kick of pleasure when both Anna and Jocelyn jolted. Anna's face flushed.

Jamie stepped into the room with a smile. His gaze stayed with Anna. "Time for dinner."

Facing her dolls together Anna's pitch dropped. "We will have to wait for that dance, princess." She looked up, smiled. "Would you like to join us? We could use a good man."

Jocelyn snorted. "Don't ask him then. He doesn't have a clue when it comes to girls."

Anna cocked a brow Jamie's direction just as he eased a foot into Jocelyn's ribs. "It's time to eat. And you'd better watch it or I'll tell everybody you moonlight with Barbie and Ken."

"That's Justin and Gwyneth," Jessica told him matter-of-factly.

"I'm sure Justin would love to know that you've named one of your dolls after him."

Anna stood, dolls still in her hands. "Been listening have you? Of course you know that this is you." She extended her Ken doll his direction.

"At least he's better looking than Justin." He looked at Jessica. "You ready to eat, mite?"

Giggling, Jessica set down her dolls and flung her arms around Jamie, crawling up his side like a monkey. He scrubbed her head with his knuckles

"I got to play with Anna," Jessica whispered. "A real princess."

He waited until Jocelyn had gone, until Anna had put the dolls down with care on the floor. "That was nice of her to play with you."

Anna ducked by him, and their eyes met and held in the darkness of the hall.

Cupping her mouth, Jessica whispered in Jamie's ear, "I like her."

"Yeah." Jamie squeezed her and they took the stairs down behind Anna.

* * *

Conversation covered everything from the history of Thanksgiving to a similar holiday in Slovokia called Bonniskiwa. By the time the pumpkin and lemon cream pies were brought out for dessert, Anna had gotten a historical overview of the holiday from Jeff, whose fifth grade understanding was more accurate and fresh than anyone else's.

She learned that Jessica hated pumpkin. One year, Justin, going through a Hindu martial arts craze, tried to bust pumpkins with his bare hands and broke a finger in the process. The entire family spent that Thanksgiving in the emergency room. It seemed each Thanksgiving was about the stories surrounding it as much as the holiday itself.

Anna sat back, feeling fuller than she had in a long time. It wasn't just the food that added to her contentment. She couldn't deny the easy camaraderie quietly traded among Jamie's family. A fond glance, a teasing poke, the way Jack and Joyce smiled at each other across the length of the table surrounded by their children. She especially enjoyed watching Jamie interact with his younger brothers and sisters. There was no doubt that he carried the position of eldest with all of the responsibility required. It was obvious he would never expect anything from them he did not expect from himself.

For a moment, Anna saw her little brother's face in her mind. It would be terribly selfish of her to shift the heavy burden of her responsibility to him without his complete understanding and acceptance on the matter. At thirteen, he was still too young to really comprehend any of it. No one at home was preparing Nicholas for what might happen should the responsibility pass to him.

Lost in her thoughts, Anna stared at the lovely vase she had brought that now stood in the center of the table. It was filled with a dozen yellow roses.

Her mother favored yellow roses.

She was suddenly besieged with a wave of sadness she couldn't explain. She had lived away from home for stretches at a time. Indeed, her parents, her brother and she had lived such individual lives she'd never been prone to homesickness. She knew her parents loved her, but before their love for her, came their love of country. Part of that meant they would never accept her alliance with anyone other than blood fit her for blood. For them, it was unfathomable for her to fall in love with an American.

The thoughts threatened to submerge her cheer, and Anna forced them away. Discipline was no stranger to her. She focused on the smiling faces of a family she wished she could find herself a part of, a family whose relationships were sealed without compulsion by the simple bond of love.

She marveled at the way the family pitched in to clean up. Joyce cleared the dishes with Jeff's help. Jack donned an apron and then he, Justin and Jamie loaded dishes into the dishwasher, hand washing whatever didn't fit. Jocelyn swept, while Jessica made Popcorn, the fluffy white dog, a special Thanksgiving treat of dry food mixed with turkey gravy.

Of course Cheryl jumped in, keeping herself at Jamie's elbow.

Anna felt at odds with nothing to do. She stood with Ivan and Lukov and Inessa at the fringes of the kitchen. Cheryl was the only one who glanced over her shoulder now and again, simple satisfaction on her face. Everyone else remained absorbed in work.

"You relax, Anna," Joyce told her. "You're our guest."

Anna would have gladly swapped places with Cheryl, to be elbow-to-elbow with Jamie, doing domestic chores.

"I imagine you had help with things like this growing up?" Joyce brought in another stack of china and set it on the counter next to her husband.

"It is true."

"You've never done dishes?" The inquiry stopped Jeff, who held four crystal goblets in his hands.

"Well, I've done them, but not at home. When we went on good-will visits, often I would help in the kitchens of homes we visited."

"I've seen pictures of the royal palace in Slovokia." Jack scrubbed the roasting pan in elbow-deep suds, then handed it to Jamie who rinsed. "It's a pretty nice place. The grounds are what, twelve thousand acres of timberland?"

"Yes." Pleased Jack had some knowledge of her home, Anna continued, "It was built in the sixteenth century by Slav, Russian and Ukraine non-conformists who left their countries, formed an alliance, and fought for independence."

"The terrain looks very much like Utah from the pictures I've seen."

"Unlike Utah, we have very little change in season. It is mostly cool all year round."

"So you have yet to experience one of our sizzling summers?" Justin wagged his eyebrows. "Do you like the outdoors? Because there's tons to do here outside."

Anna shot a glance at Jamie. Cheryl was smiling, laughing and whispering to him. As he handed her rinsed plates she dried. Anna realized he had probably not been listening to the conversation. "There are many sports I would like to try," she continued. "I have not been permitted to—rock climbing, mountain biking, camping. I did enjoy my snow camping experience with Jamie."

Justin glanced at Inessa who instantly blushed. "You like to do any of those things, Inessa?"

She nodded. "Oh, yes."

"Jamie can do some of those things," Justin began, then, noting that Jamie wasn't listening, added, "but I can do them all."

Jamie's head jerked around. "Heard that."

"Knew that'd get your attention." Justin whipped his hand out and stung Jamie on the back of his ear with a snap of his soapy wrist.

Jamie ducked too late. Ditching the dishes, he took off after Justin. Sides were taken, all with the thud of grappling flesh as it smacked into cabinets.

"Can't you boys do that somewhere else?" Joyce asked as she came in from the dining room with six more crystal goblets artfully balanced in both hands.

Justin maneuvered Jamie onto the floor, face down, then straddled him across the back before quickly snapping his arm and neck into a lock. "See? This stuff really works, I'm telling you."

Jamie tapped the floor, signaling submission, and Justin jumped to his feet. He extended a hand and pulled Jamie up.

"Try that on Iv or Luk and let's see how well it works," Jamie told him, gasping for breath.

Without hesitation, Justin was next to Ivan. "I'm willing. You?"

Jamie grinned with pride and a measure of disbelief. "You're gonna get smashed, dude."

Ivan and Lukov exchanged unsettled glances then looked at Anna for approval.

"By all means, go ahead," she said with a shrug.

Justin and Jamie moved furniture back, clearing a space in the family room. Ivan pulled his sweater over his head and handed it to Lukov. The sight of busting muscles didn't faze Justin who just stood ready. Ivan and Lukov exchanged words in Slovokian with a laugh before Ivan rolled up his sleeves, revealing two massive forearms.

"He must outweigh you by a hundred pounds." Jack's voice held warning but he didn't say anything more.

Anna debated giving Ivan a warning of her own—in Slovokian, but didn't. It amazed her that Justin didn't hesitate, but dove right for Ivan's middle, taking him over onto his back like a pin hit by a bowling ball. Justin's smaller, leaner frame clung like a leopard on a struggling rhinoceros, as Ivan tried to shirk him free.

Within seconds, Justin had the big man underneath him on the floor. Justin's legs wrapped around Ivan's neck, his hands pinned Ivan's in a double choke-hold lock that had Ivan sweating out a grunt and tapping for release.

Applause and good-natured cheering filled the room. Justin reached over and helped Ivan to his feet. Jamie whistled.

"Very good." Ivan wiped his red brow. "He is very good." He turned to Lukov, and the two chatted animatedly in Slovokian.

"I believe that's the first time anyone has done that to him," Anna said. "He is very impressed, I can tell."

Justin beamed and shot a proud glance at Inessa. "The stuff's unbeatable."

With new admiration, Jamie gave Justin a firm pat on the shoulder. "I want to know those moves."

"Why, so you can throw Anna here around? I'll show her the moves."

"I would like that very much," Anna said with a smile. Jamie tilted his head at her. Something playful danced in his eyes Anna enjoyed for the brief moment it was there.

"Maybe we could talk trade." Justin sent a flirty grin to Inessa, still bashfully smiling. "You can finally teach me a few dance steps, if I teach you a few moves."

Pleased that her young assistant was garnering some attention, Anna said, "I would be happy to do that for you."

"You thinking what I'm thinking?" Jamie's breath was hot against her cheek and Anna's heart fluttered suddenly. Though she liked the warm tingle she felt when his body pressed into her side briefly for the whisper, she took a step away.

"You mean, Justin and Inessa? Well, yes."

"How cute." Cheryl squeezed between them. "They seem to like each other, don't you think?" This question she addressed to Jamie, ignoring Anna.

"I'd say Justin definitely has the hots for Nessa." He slid Anna a glance that held in spite of Cheryl being sandwiched between them. "If he's talking dance, then he's got it bad."

"Maybe it's time I learned some steps." Cheryl hooked her arm in Jamie's and ushered him away. Anna stood alone.

Ivan and Lukov helped move the couches back and then settled onto the fat, leather couches to watch the football game with Jack. In the kitchen, Joyce and Jocelyn chatted while finishing with cleaning chores. A wide-eyed Jeff sat next to Jack, but he spent more time staring at Ivan and Lukov than watching the game.

Anna strolled to French doors that opened onto a balcony. She would never assume to explore the Wilde home without permission, but Joyce had vanished and Jack was talking football with Ivan and Lukov. That left Jamie, who stood a few feet away. But he and Cheryl looked as though they were in a serious conversation. Jamie was tense, his face drawn tight. Cheryl's eyes were on the verge of tears. Occasionally, Jamie glanced over, and when he did, Anna gestured to the doors.

"May I?" she asked.

He nodded, left Cheryl briefly and opened the door for her. She had to brush him as she passed. "Thank you. I didn't mean to interrupt."

"It'll be cold out there. You want a coat?"

She looked up at him, just as Cheryl came behind him and slid her arms around his waist, peering around his arm.

"No, thank you." Anna went out and heard the door close softly behind her. In the quiet of night nothing but the lively, muffled sounds of life in the Wilde house floated on the air. It was altogether wonderful, that house, those people, his family. Cheryl was a lucky woman.

Anna wondered if things would be different between her and Jamie if she did not dance. But that is impossible. It is because of dance that I am here.

Knowing she and Jamie would be companions only in dance stung. She alone could make her dreams happen, she alone had brought herself this far. Just because Jamie would only play a stand-in part in her future did not mean she had to give up on ever finding real love. Perhaps there would be someone else.

The doors opened and the scent of something sweet and floral made her turn around. Cheryl stood in the opening, a petite silhouette. For a moment, she paused. Anna tried to see her face in the darkness. Cheryl closed the door behind her and slowly crossed the deck.

"So." Cheryl rested her forearms on the balcony and looked out over the bed of sparkling lights below. It was then Ann saw traces of red rimming her eyes. "What do you think of Thanksgiving?"

"It is a very nice holiday."

"Makes us count what we are grateful for."

Anna nodded. The lake looked like a giant silver mirror reflecting the moon, now centered in the open surface. "And you have much to be grateful for. Jamie is a good man, his family is so kind."

"You're right." For a moment, the women were silent. Then Cheryl sighed. "I would love them like my own. But he's not in love with me."

Anna's heart pounded against her ribs. There was resignation in Cheryl's profile. Her chin lowered, her eyes glistened with the moon's slivery light.

"But that is not true," Anna said. "I have seen the way he looks at you."

"When I first met Jamie, he and Courtney were partners," Cheryl said softly, still staring out at the lake. "I saw the way they danced together and thought there was no way two people could be so close and not have feelings for each other. But I was wrong. He was no more than a friend, a brother maybe, to her. I asked him why? How? I mean, for women, dancing's so intimate you know? At least it is for me. That was one of the things I liked about him, that he could engage in something and not lose his heart."

A valiant struggle he was determined to win, Anna knew first hand. That she had spent even a moment challenging his determination now made her feel guilty.

"I don't know if Jamie can ever love anyone," Cheryl shook her lowered head. "He's married to dance. It's what he loves best. His heart is in steps, his thoughts are in the music."

"I am so sorry if I have caused this."

"Oh, it's not you." Cheryl wiped a lone tear. "It's just a fact of life for someone who is driven to be the best at what they do. I know you understand. I just don't know if I can handle him being in the arms of other women all of my life."

Anna's heart sunk. She thought of the whispered talk she had seen between them moments ago.

"I came to say goodbye." Cheryl blew out a quavering sigh. "I'm heading home. There's no reason for me to stay."

"But his family cares for you."

"And I will miss them. I'll miss all of this." Cheryl's gaze followed the lines of the house to each window, finally landing on the door through which she had just come. More tears pooled in her eyes and she wiped them back. "But it's over, and it's just too hard for me to be around him and know he'll never be mine, you know?"

How Anna knew. She felt the slug of disappointment on Cheryl's face as if it was her own broken heart. But then she had come to accept that from Jamie, that she would only be his partner. She knew Cheryl's heartache well.

"It was very nice meeting you, Anna. I'm sure you'll be the first and last princess I'll ever meet. Good luck with your competitions. I hope you guys do great."

Anna's heart tore. Reaching out, she placed a hand on Cheryl's arm in a gesture of shared female understanding. "I do wish you the best."

Cheryl slipped through the door and was gone.

16.

Jamie needed a distraction. Not interested in football, sitting in front of the game wouldn't take his mind off of the hurt he'd seen in Cheryl's eyes after they'd talked. Argued, might better describe it. He'd been totally shocked by her possessive behavior all night and finally said something about it, only to find fiery tears in her eyes when she admitted that she loved him and wanted him to love her the same way.

Stunned, he'd only been able to tell her, to his own dismay, that he did not feel the same. Cheryl had been absolutely right when she'd said he was already in love – with dance.

That had been true for as long as Jamie could remember. From the first day he'd been coaxed by his mother to give ballroom dance a try and set foot on Nicole Dubois' studio floor, heard the music of Latin, he was captured. He'd spent week nights, weekends, and any spare hour taking everything from funk classes to—he hated to admit – ballet, fine-tuning his craft. He'd shocked his family who'd thought dance would be a passing interest and nothing more.

But he'd not won any hearts. There were no trophies or ribbons from women who thought he was a prize. He snickered. Some prize. All he'd done was go along with his head dancing in the clouds, stepping on hearts with neglect or indifference.

Would that mean he'd spend the rest of his life alone?

Partnerships were the closest thing he knew to relationships, and his partnership with Courtney had ended disastrously. Now he had to admit first to himself, then to Cheryl, that his heart hadn't really been in the fragile relationship they'd shared for some time now.

Heavy disappointment blanketed him. Would it be any different with Anna? He'd not seen her for a time and went in search of her.

Jamie strode to the French doors. He found her outside on the balcony.

She was clutching her arms, leaning against the railing. He stepped back inside and snatched his coat from the coat rack. He held it against his body to warm it and sidled up next to her. "Cold?"

As if he'd awakened her from a deep dream, she looked at him, startled. He held the coat out and she turned her back so that he could slip it over her shoulders.

"Thank you."

Resting his elbows across the rail, he looked out.

"You have a nice home and family, Jamie."

He nodded. The idea of sharing what had happened didn't bother him. They'd crossed boundaries, shared things important. He hoped that maybe by sharing, he could avoid repeating whatever had caused things to go sour with Cheryl. "Cheryl doesn't want to see me any more."

"Yes, she told me."

"She did?" He wondered what else Cheryl had said.

"She only told me she did not think you loved her." Anna turned to him, searching for remorse, for a broken heart, and was both saddened and relieved when she did not see either. "I told her I thought she was wrong."

"She was right."

Rather than be intimidated by his penetrating gaze, thrilled by his admission, Anna wrapped her heart in the thick cloak of her common sense. "She told me she didn't think you could ever love anyone because your first love is dance."

There was pain behind his eyes. He stared out over the stillness of the lake. To see him battle turbulent feelings was difficult. She so wanted to stroke the tightness in his jaw until it gave under her fingertips, to wrap her arms around him and tell him everything would work out. "Jamie, if that is what you want then you should be happy in that."

"It's what I thought I wanted," he began. "Truthfully, the contentment of my partnership with Courtney kept me from needing anything else. Or so I thought. Then—" How could he explain that since she had come into his life, he'd found the challenge of her, of all that she had brought to the dance floor, the most exciting yet frustrating time of his life. Dance had taken on a flavor he'd never tasted. Life had done the same. And, he was realizing, it was all happening whether he wanted to allow it or not. He was coming to enjoy it, would miss it even if it was suddenly gone, and that stirred feelings for commitment to more than a partnership. He wanted more of her, more from her. More for them both.

"When Courtney and I were young and had a short thing for each other, our act went on the fritz. I mean we bombed big time. Every competition was a disaster. After that, we decided it was because our personal feelings had interfered.

"A lot of partners are married. It works for them. But I was a scared kid when all this happened and I wanted to go places with my career. We both decided it would be in our best interest to keep our personal lives separate. The minute we did, the magic was back. I guess it freaked me out enough that I didn't want to play with it ever again."

Anna would respect his reasons, but in her mind, the passion of love would transcend all, illuminating performance with something that couldn't be feigned and would take a partnership, and its dances, to another level.

"I see why you separate those things now," she said.

A quiet chuckle left his throat. "Yeah, well, I don't know how good it is really. I may grow old and die without children, without a—" He looked at her then and the look lingered. "Without someone."

And that would be a shame, she thought. He looked thoroughly despondent there in the moonlight. Torn up inside. She placed her hand on his arm without thinking, and it drew his gaze there. Then his eyes shifted to hers, latching on with a need that broke her heart.

Her touch was more comforting than anything he could have imagined to ease the pain gripping inside. Jamie covered her hand with his. He ran his tongue along dry lips, his gaze lowering to her mouth. Impulse singing in his veins prompted him to kiss her, but he couldn't. What they had together was as near to perfect as anything he'd seen on the dance floor. They had yet to compete, to show the world, and he couldn't risk ruining that before they'd had their chance.

It didn't resonate. His body and heart had a mind of their own, and both were reaching out to her. It was in the way his breath skipped, the way his blood soared. His eyes all but devoured her, as if slowly going over her every inch would satisfy the need to feel, to touch, to taste. It didn't. Frustration bubbled inside of him.

Forcing himself to find control, he turned away, focusing instead on the view. "San Francisco's coming." When she turned and wasn't looking at him anymore, when her hand slid out from underneath his, his body relaxed. "I think we're ready."

"Yes, I think we are. Do not worry, Jamie. Everything will be perfect."

How could she be so certain? He studied her, hoping to somehow find the answer, but he didn't say anything more.

"Well," she began and turned as if she were heading inside, "I should go. We will be rehearsing early tomorrow?"

He nodded. "Reuben's off until Monday. It will just be you and I." The idea of it sent a pleasant thrumming through him.

"Very well." When she leaned up close, his heart nearly stopped. She kissed his cheek and the gesture forced his eyes closed. When she eased back, they opened, and never left hers. It was juvenile to question a kiss given only in gratitude for a nice day. His swollen feelings hoped it was more than that.

"Thank you for a lovely holiday. I had a wonderful time." He watched her, knowing he was expected to follow and see her to the door, but his heart was too vulnerable beating within his chest. If he followed her, he would be tempted to stop her and take what he wanted. He couldn't throw away years of sweat and work that had brought him to this point. He wouldn't rip her dreams of winning away before she'd had a chance to live them.

He turned and faced the lake and thought of the cold iciness, of deep, dark emptiness and soon his desire began to ebb. He was her partner. She was counting on him to lead them to a win. That was what he thought about. That, and the fact that within hours they would be dancing and he could, in a small way, have a part of her.

Characteristically cold in November, San Francisco was not an adjustment for Anna. Having grown up covered with coats, furs and mufflers, she donned them with the ease of royalty slipping on a crown or a string of necessary jewels.

Their first competition was just hours away. She was nervous, pacing alone in her suite on the eighteenth floor of the Drake Hotel. The view was stunning but not enough to distract her. From where she stood, the hustle of Union Square and busy shops buzzed. Muffled sounds of horns and brakes squealing snuck through the closed window. She could only enjoy the picturesque scene for a moment. Her brain was clicking off regular visuals of steps. Latin steps.

Though they had prepared for both standard and Latin, it was Latin Anna was most exited about. Latin was everything intimate and passionate she would ever share with Jamie.

Next door, he was getting settled. She wanted to rehearse, had told him that on the flight. He'd agreed. Now, she wondered if she dare knock or wait until he came to her.

He'd been distant since Thanksgiving. This was not something she was used to. He'd been so light-hearted and playful when they had first started dancing together. Of late, rehearsals had been business only, where steps were hammered out until they were as smooth as Jamie wanted them. Trusting his judgment, she had obliged him without any objections.

Reuben had videoed them countless times and they'd reviewed their work, picking out areas where they could improve with tighter moves, better spins, more succinct form. These critiques were done in place of their lunches and she missed the casual way he and Reuben used to talk with her over cook's fare.

It wasn't as though he'd been short or impatient, and for that she was grateful. He was a perfectionist. That left minimal attention to the personal aspects of their partnership. This competition was vitally important to them both but especially to her. The world would see that she was a serious competitor and their name as a couple would finally have its start.

The fast tapping at her door caused her to jump. Only one person she knew tapped like a woodpecker. Ivan came from the room he and Lukov shared just off her suite and opened the door.

"Hey, you ready?" Lev blinked big from behind his glasses. He wore mustard-colored slacks and a bold, paisley shirt. Anna felt a wave of compassion for him.

"I'm sorry, Lev. I need to rehearse with Jamie."

"Oh. Well, do you mind if I peruse the streets?"

"No." Lev's tenacity amazed Anna. Her hopes for him to be overcome with boredom died weeks ago when it became dreadfully clear he was content just to be wherever she was. "You go. It's a wonderful city."

"Yeah, I know. I was here ten years ago. I thought I'd hit the cable cars."

"That would be very nice, I'm sure."

"I'll have my cell phone if you want to call me when you guys are done. Maybe we could meet for dinner."

"Perhaps." It pleased her that he would choose an alternative activity to just sitting and watching. He was accepting that her life in the States, her devotion to dance, was not a passing whim but a serious commitment.

"Will there be anything else?" Inessa quietly entered from one of the adjoining rooms of the suite. She had a copy of the entry forms for the competition and handed them to Anna.

"No, Inessa. Thank you." Anna tapped the entry copies against the palm of her hand. "I'm going to be in practice most of the afternoon, would you like to do some sightseeing with Lev? If you hurry, you could still catch him."

Inessa's eyes widened. "That would be very nice, if you're sure."

Anna nodded.

After Inessa had gone, Anna stood again by the window and looked out. How romantic it would be to see the city with Jamie. She closed her eyes from visions of night walks down sparkling-lit streets bustling with tourists and vendors, of meals eaten at sidewalk cafes, harbor views, and lazy strolls through art galleries and cozy trips on crowded cable cars.

The banging at the door startled her, bringing Ivan from the room he and Lukov occupied and straight to the door. With his palm out, he signaled for her to stay where she was. He put a hand on his firearm, tucked under his coat, before he opened the door. Jamie leaned with both palms on the door frame, his face as tight as a drum.

Pushing past Ivan, Jamie crossed to her. "Anna." She looked over his tense shoulder to Ivan, and excused him with a nod of her head.

After the door shut, she turned, heading back to the window, expecting him to follow. He did.

"I went downstairs to check things out, say hi to a few old friends, and wasn't I surprised when they were all shocked to see me." He pulled her around by the elbow. "We aren't registered, Anna."

Her eyes flashed. "That's impossible."

"I'm afraid it's not." Zigzagging beside her, he flicked nervous hands. "I went in, saw for myself. How could this happen?" He let out a groan and drove his hands into his hair. "Do you know how stupid this makes us look? This happens to ditsy, brainless kids, not professionals."

"But, I—"

"You told me you would take care of everything. I should have never—" He spun away from her, walking a few feet before falling into a chair and closing his eyes. "I should have taken care of this myself."

Anna could not believe the news. She lowered into the chair opposite him.

"When Dancesport gets wind of this, they'll never take us seriously," he muttered. His hands gripped the arms of his chair until his knuckles bled white. "It'll go down as the shortest career on record—the princess and the pawn." He covered his face with his hands. "Unbelievable."

"Is there no way to register still?"

"Are you kidding? You don't just waltz in on the day of competition."

She shot up and snagged the papers Inessa had brought to her and looked at them. Holding them out toward Jamie, she said, "There has been some mistake, see?"

He grabbed them, looked. For a moment, his face lit, his lips looked on the verge of a grin. But it all flattened. "Where did you get these?"

"Inessa brought them to me just moments ago."

"Who gave them to her?"

"I don't know. I gave her the responsibility to register us. Jamie, she would never mess something like this up. She is very—"

"They're bogus." He shoved them at her, stood.

"What?"

"I've heard about stuff like this happening. Contenders get false forms, thinking they're registered, put out their money for hotels, costumes, coaches, only to get there and realize they've been duped out of their registration fee, but far worse, their opportunity, by some crack. Wherever she got these, they aren't the real thing and they aren't going to get us into the competition."

Anna lowered into the chair again. Her stomach rolled and knotted and she looked up at him. He was still uptight, holding himself at the window. The white sweatshirt he wore sucked all the color from his face as he stared out.

"I am so sorry, Jamie." Tears started in her throat, worked their way up to her eyes. She wanted to cry on his shoulder, to let him cry if he needed to. But she didn't know what emotions he was feeling; he had closed that part of himself off from her.

He blinked heavily, staring out. Rising, she dared to stand near, but he didn't move even an inch in acknowledgement of it.

"All our work." He shifted his eyes to hers and her heart tore. There was grief, disappointment, but the most frightening thing was the flicker of surrender.

"Can we not say that we came to observe and nothing more?"

"That would have worked if I hadn't already gone down and made a fool out of myself." He shook his head and looked back out the window.

"But you did not know."

"I should have handled the registration. I always handled this stuff with Courtney and me." When he looked at her again, his brows were a hard line, his dark eyes nearly black. The line of his jaw hardened to stone.

Suddenly, he strode across the room to the door.

"Where are you going?" Anna was right behind him, tailing him down the hall. When Lukov lumbered after them she held her hand up and shook her head so that he would not follow. "You cannot leave without discussing this."

"What's to discuss? We're screwed. We have to wait another year for this title."

He nearly punched the button on the elevator, waited.

"I will say something to them."

"There's nothing you could say that would get us out of this mess, Anna. These people don't bend rules for royalty, money, or influence of any kind. You dance by the rules or you don't dance."

"I will make a statement," she said as the doors slid open. He got in.

"You better let me handle that." He pressed his back against the rear of the elevator, hard eyes still holding hers.

The doors started to close but she stuck her foot in to block them. Eyes narrowed on him, she stepped into the elevator taking a safe spot directly opposite where he stood. "I do not know how this happened, but I will find out and I will deal with it. However disappointing this is to you, it is just as disappointing to me. But you do not think of that. No, you have closed me off, and so you are only thinking of yourself, of how this will reflect on you."

He gripped the brass rail lining the inside of the elevator. He'd had his share of fights with Courtney and never liked them. Now, here he was arguing with another woman and the same distasteful feeling was clawing his gut. With all that he, personally, had riding on this competition, he knew she was right.

That comment she made about him closing her off nagged at him. They dropped a few floors in hot silence staring at each other, and his stomach lurched with guilt. He had packed her away, and it had worked – sort of. He'd seen her only as Anna, his partner. He'd removed himself from anything personal, even going so far as to stop listening to her light, frivolous talk, protecting himself from being further drawn in to her.

But the disappointment in her eyes now could not be dismissed. They were in this together, yet not sharing the grief. Even in his worst moments with Courtney, he'd lent her his shoulder. Fighting pride, he kept his eyes on the numbers above the doors.

When they stopped at the lobby, Anna lifted her chin. "I am going to take care of this, Jamie." She tried to press the 'open' button but he snagged her other hand, twisting it around in a hold behind her back to keep her tight against him.

"Don't." His fingers dug deep into her arm and he tugged her flush against him. His other hand held the elevator 'close' button as he stared down into her eyes.

The demand sent a swirl of hot, fast sparks through her. His eyes moved like a whip across her face, finally stopping at her mouth. Inside, those wild sparks pooled low in her belly, and hummed. She deliberately ran her tongue along her lips.

The look on his face wasn't pleasure, rather it was taut pain. His dark brows knit together. He let go of her, and took a step back. It hurt, that he'd let her go, that she'd tempted him. She whirled, and tried to pry the doors open with her fingers. "Open these doors," she shot out.

His palm slapped over the 'close' button. "You're not going anywhere."

"I am going to straighten out this mess."

When the doors automatically opened, she strode from the elevator with all of the dignity of her noble upbringing. Determination rode on her shoulders, infallibility hardened her chin.

Jamie followed her to the ballroom where the competition was to take place. She stopped just inside the doors and scanned the room until her eyes lit on the judges table.

"You can't get us back in the game, Anna. It's over."

That infallible chin of hers only lifted higher. "Watch me."

It would have been an admirable effort, had he not known the rules intimately, been familiar with many of the judges from years of previous competitions. He was sure most of them had heard through the short, tight dance-world grapevine that he was dancing with Anna. What occurred to him was the fact that they might think he had sent her to do the dirty work, thinking they would be impressed by her title and make the first exception in the history of the sport.

He didn't like that idea one bit.

Only a handful of ladies and gentlemen, dressed formally, readying for the night's events, mingled around the judges' table. They quieted as Anna approached, turning their attention to her with mixed reactions.

Jamie was too far behind to hear what was being said but decided he'd better join her or he'd look like a weasel. In the short time it took for him to cross the wood floor, she was already using her arms and tilting her head in that very controlled, but undeniably feisty royal manner.

"But it is unacceptable that we cannot compete because of a simple thing like this. Can you not see that we were deceived?"

Jamie recognized the judge who was nodding, an older man with Santa-white hair and just as cheery cheeked as Santa, though at the moment, he didn't look all cheery.

"I understand, Ms. Zakharov. But you must see our position. Any competitor who was not timely enough to register by the due date, could then come back to us citing deception as you call it, and still compete. It would be unfair to those who were punctual."

"It would break the structure we must maintain for organizational as well as ethical reasons." The woman sitting next to him added. She was Genevieve Marceau, one of the greatest competitive ballroom dancers of all time. Jamie had never seen her dressed in anything less than a classic gown, usually in black, to accent her raven hair she always wore straight back. Upon Jamie's arrival, she smiled at him.

"Jamie, how nice to see you." Extending one of her hands, Jamie took the cue and kissed her jeweled knuckles. It was something he'd been doing since he was a young man, since Nicole Dubois, his first coach, had confided the older woman found the gesture endearing.

"Genevieve, you look wonderful." She tilted her head, her smile widening. "I see you've met my new dance partner." Jamie moved close to Anna. A few months ago he would not have been able to read her. But now, those gray flecks in her eyes were turning black, and he knew if she said much more the two of them would be invited to leave.

Looking every bit as noble as Anna was, Genevieve gave one slow nod before she turned her focus back to him again. "A very headstrong young woman."

"That she is."

"She told us of your misfortune. I am deeply sorry for it. I was quite anxious to see you two perform."

"We're ready." Jamie slipped his arm around Anna's waist and felt her stiffen. "But neither one of us is willing to jeopardize our reputation by asking for something we know you are unable to do anything about."

"You know I would if I could," Genevieve said.

"Will you be staying to observe?" the white-haired gentleman asked.

"That will depend."

Anna's tone was too threatening for Jamie's liking and he gave her a light tug, flashing the judges a grin. "We're still working out our plans."

Anna spoke again, "Are you absolutely sure that there is no possibility—"

"We've taken up too much of your time." Jamie began the gentle pulling he hoped would be enough to remove Anna from the room and keep her from saying anything further.

He wasn't surprised she wiggled and glared at him. What surprised him was how much he enjoyed restraining her – like he had in the elevator. The way the fury in her eyes stirred him deep inside.

He escorted her from the room with a wave and a smile to the judges.

She broke free just outside the door, but he snatched her hand tight in his before navigating them through a small crowd of competitors and other hotel guests beginning to gather.

She pulled one direction and he the other.

"Anna." He used his strength and in one snap, she was flat against him, breathing hard, looking up into his face. He couldn't explain why it sent a pleasant tremor through his system. He grinned.

"Let me go," she said through teeth.

"Let's take a little ride." The grin on his face remained in place as he all but hauled her toward the elevator.

"I am very angry right now."

"I can see that."

"It would be wise of you to leave me alone."

"It would be wiser if we left this alone and got on with it."

The elevator doors opened and she stormed in. Biting back a smile, Jamie let the doors close behind him. He decided then it was somewhat perverse that he got a kick out of her when she was irate. Was it his fault she looked beautiful whether she was fuming or agreeable?

They were silent as the elevator sped upward. Anna's heart was racing the vehicle. She looked into Jamie's eyes; saw the way they lingered over her face with admiration and…did she dare think she saw desire there? But it didn't quell her disappointment. "They should have made an exception for us," she snapped.

"Would you if you were in their position?"

She thought a moment and knew she would not. A few months ago, she might have toyed with the idea, but knowing Jamie, seeing his standards and how he strove to live them, had changed her. She realized then that going in and demanding they bend the rules had been the wrong move. Later, she would apologize. But Jamie was too smug for her liking.

"You are something else, Princess," he murmured.

"You would be wise to remember that."

His snicker was not at all meant to bruise, but to tickle, she recognized that, and ignored it. The car stopped at their floor but he placed his back in front of the doors, blocking any exit. He pressed his finger on the 'roof' button.

"We need to decide our MO," he started calmly. It was over now, he'd come to terms with the loss. Somehow, he could deal with it knowing she was as devastated as he was. "Do we stay, take the questions, the publicity and just go with it? Or do we get out of here, leaving a tidy statement in our defense?"

"You would like to stay."

It pleased him that she knew what he wanted to do. "I think it's better to face it with honesty."

"I agree. We have nothing to be ashamed of."

"No, but that won't be what's remembered when all of this hits the fan. It will be, how could Jamie Wilde overlook something as basic as registration?"

She would not let him take the blame, knowing how fastidious he was about details. "You are sure you do not want me to handle the statement to the press?"

"It's our problem. We'll talk to them together," he said. The elevator stopped and the doors opened. Holding his hand toward the open doors, he waited until she passed before going out.

They took the double doors labeled 'Roof' and found themselves on top of the world. Anna sucked in a breath and slowly turned, admiring the view of the city.

Horns blared below. Rumbling engines echoed through canyons created by towering buildings, filling the air with a sort of eclectic music. Jamie was already near the ledge, looking down. The wind whipped his hair into a dark tangle luring her to his side.

"And I thought the view from the room was good," he said. "This is amazing. Can you imagine what this would look like at night?"

With you, it would be magnificent. "I imagine it would look spellbinding."

He laughed. "Only from a princess." Leaning on the wall, he faced her with resignation in his sigh. "Let's go get this over with."

"It won't be over until I find out who is responsible."

"Those guys are long gone, Anna. Don't waste your time or energy."

"Someone should pay for this. It has ruined our chances for this title and has kept us from—"

"Anna." Moving close, his hands ran the length of her arms. Wind stirred her hair, the sun warmed her pale skin to ripe peach. Her eyes, shadowed with blue disappointment, now opened with something that called out to him. His blood skipped. Hands that had rubbed in comfort now slowed with the tenderness of a gentle caress meant to entice.

Her lips eased apart, her eyes blinked heavily fastened to his. Jamie's hands stopped caressing. His fingers dug, felt the firm muscles in her shoulders and he pulled her against him. He could call it comfort. He could say he needed it, that she needed it. But it was a lie. He wanted her. He wanted to touch his lips to hers and finally feel and taste for himself.

"Anna." Her name came from his tongue with the ease of one heartbeat. Her body moved against him like a cat begging for his touch, and so his grip fastened around her, his lips sought the curve of her neck where he whispered her name again. "Anna."

She was ready to soar, high up from the rest of the world in his arms. At last, he is going to kiss me. But first she enjoyed being in his embrace for no other reason than to soothe the loss they had both shared. Her arms slid around his neck, she laid her head on his chest. It was a dream, him opening his arms and his heart to her for something other than dance and she wanted that dream to last.

They both heard the door thrust open, and Jamie looked up. His features drew taut; his dark eyes latched onto something that caused Anna to whirl around, still in his arms.

Two hotel security guards stood with their hands poised on the weapons they carried in their belts, behind them stood Ivan and Vladimir.

"There she is." Vladimir pointed at them, his eyes locked on the way Jamie held her close. After a pause, the collective group of uniformed and black-suited men proceeded to cross to them.

"The hotel is crawling with security looking for you, Anna." Vladimir's disapproval was obvious.

"I have been gone but a few minutes. You jumped to conclusions."

Vladimir's eyes narrowed at Jamie. "One of you should have been smart enough to tell us of where you were going."

"I was in no danger," Anna's tone was sharp, hating that Jamie's arms loosened. "Jamie and I had some business to take care of."

Vladimir waved a hand at their bodies, close together. "This?"

"It's none of your business." Jamie stepped forward but kept an arm around Anna's shoulders.

Vladimir took four steps to the edge and swept his hand in the air. "Seventy-four floors up, alone?"

It was almost absurd enough to laugh at, and Jamie would have, if he'd not caught the undeniable glint of accusation in Vladimir's slit eyes. "I don't like what you're implying, Vlad."

"I do not need to worry about my safety when I am with Jamie." When Vladimir merely cocked his brow, Anna continued. "If that is good enough for me than it will have to be good enough for you. But enough of this. Something has happened we need to discuss."

They took the elevator down in heated silence. Jamie thought it best to keep his mouth shut, though something told him Vladimir was not going to be his friend, not even his ally, and to watch his step. He didn't like thinking he was going to spend the next few years with a man, and a system, that questioned his honesty, his character and motives every time he moved.

Vladimir's phone rang and he plucked it out of his jacket pocket. "Yes? Yes, we found them. Thank you, sir. I am sorry for the inconvenience. Her Royal Highness apologizes for any misunderstanding. It was not her fault." He glared at Jamie. "Yes. That is very kind. I will tell her."

After he clicked off the phone, stuffed it in his pocket, he looked at Anna. "That was the hotel manager. He was most concerned for your safety. He has offered any additional men to help if you would like."

"I am not anticipating any such need," she replied.

She was as frustrated as he was, and Jamie wondered if she and Vladimir had always shared such a turbulent relationship.

At her request, Jamie followed her into her suite, along with Vladimir and Ivan. Lukov remained posted outside the door. Anna strode right to the registration papers she had left on the table. "What do you know about this?" She flashed them at Vladimir who stopped, looked them over and shrugged. "We are not registered. That means we cannot compete. Someone fouled up. I demand to know who."

"You are asking me?" Vladimir's voice was void of concern, "I, who have never been privy to handle your private affairs. Was it not Inessa's responsibility to do that for you?"

"I will question her when she returns, to be sure. I would hope if she went for help, she was not misled."

Vladimir stiffened. "She came to me and I pointed her in the direction she should go, that is all."

"I see." Anna let out a breath and slowly crossed to the windows. "I would like you all to leave Jamie and me now."

Ivan left first, but Vladimir stayed, his suspicious glare darting between the two of them. "You must promise me that you will alert me when you are going to leave," he insisted.

Over her shoulder, Anna spoke to him, "I will tell you of my plans, yes. However, you can be sure that if I am with Jamie, I will not need you."

It was obvious to Jamie that Vladimir did not like that answer. His throat constricted, working at what to say next. When nothing came, he shot a narrowed frown Jamie's direction before finally turning to leave.

Anna feared Jamie would never speak to her again if he knew Vladimir had destroyed this opportunity for them. He would dissolve the partnership instantly. But there was no other explanation for what had happened. This was a simple thing: some lines filled out on a form, some money sent. Too many systems she had in place succeeded. Regardless, she would do what she had to protect her future and Jamie's career. "Come here, Jamie."

She felt him come up behind her, could see his reflection in the window. She thought for a moment she felt the heat of his eyes tracing the length of her neck. She hoped he might turn her, kiss her. It was what she wanted, but she would not ask.

She would wait until he wanted her enough to take.

She kept her eyes on his milky reflection. Before admitting her suspicions about Vladimir, she had to make absolutely sure. "I will arrange the press, you make the statement."

"I thought we were going to do it together."

"I will be there, but it shows my commitment to the partnership if you are the voice." She did turn then. The setting sun flickered in his eyes like a flame. "It shows that I am willing to submit myself to you."

His mouth opened as if to speak, but he said nothing, only covered her face with the singing intensity in his eyes. It tore her open, the look, as if he was toying with the idea of her – of them.

It was too much to bear, knowing she had to hold back and not desire him openly. "Find Reuben," she said. "Tell him what has happened and then we can meet, we can decide to stay or go."

"He'll do whatever we want, Anna."

"But he has a family at home. He may want to fly back."

Jamie nodded. "What about you?"

"I will leave what we do up to you, Jamie."

Again he searched her face with electric heat that threatened to consume. Because she could take it no longer, she turned and looked at the city. "Isn't that what you want?"

In the window's reflection, she saw that his intense scrutiny of her did not waver. He seemed to sense she would not face him again. "Leave a message for me at the desk when we're to meet for the conference," he said.

She nodded, wondering why he didn't answer her question. After he left, she reached into her pocket and pulled out her cell phone. "Yes, this is Anna. I need to speak to my father immediately."

17.

Jamie had never felt anything like what he'd just felt swarming inside of him. He hoped to walk off some of the pressure stretching every nerve towards some desperate release. He'd been ready to break his vow, ready to kiss her and toss resolve to the wind from the soaring heights of the top of the hotel. With his feet on lower ground now, he was glad he'd not given in to the moment. He wanted Anna, that was torturously clear.

That meant he was a deep trouble.

For now, he'd get his mind back on solving what could potentially be a media nightmare once word was out they'd screwed up, royally. He would have smirked at the irony of it, if Anna wasn't still lingering in his blood.

He searched for Reuben.

Reuben knew almost everybody in the dance world. Jamie would not be at all surprised to find him at one of the tables, kicked back in reminiscing with competitors or judges. With that in mind, Jamie realized there was also the very real possibility Reuben had already heard about the registration bungle.

He stood waiting for the elevator to take him down to the lobby and another jag of disappointment rammed through him. It was just so asinine. He still could not believe that the blunder had happened.

The elevator doors opened and he stepped in, for the first time feeling the presence of someone behind him. He turned, and found Vladimir. The doors shut. For a moment, the two men just looked at each other, the temperature in the confining place rising.

Vladimir remained blocking the door and placed his hands comfortably behind his back. "It is very enlarging to your ego to have a woman such as Anna insisting you can take care of her, I am sure," he began. "She is beautiful. Eye-candy, as you Americans have coined the phrase. But she is also very valuable. If anything happened to her while she was in your company…anything at all, there would be severe consequences for you."

"If this is your attempt at a threat, save it." Jamie leaned his back against the elevator wall, rested his hands along the brass railing and tilted his head up to look at the floor numbers as they lit.

"A smart young man understands warnings and takes necessary precautions."

This was all getting to be too much and for Jamie, having to deal with the day's disappointments, as well as tomorrow's foreboding, pushed him very near the edge.

"I could say the same to you, old man."

A hearty laugh, twisted with a bite of sarcasm filled the stuffy space. Vladimir took off his glasses and wiped them clean with a white handkerchief. "I will quake in my boots." Replacing the glasses, he aimed a final stare at Jamie.

At the lobby floor, the doors opened and Jamie left the elevator with his jaw tight. When he glanced back and saw that Vladimir had not gotten off, he flicked his hands until they cracked and popped. He hated being threatened.

Wandering the halls of the lobby, Jamie's mind was so ensnarled in the conversation with Vladimir he didn't see Reuben who had to grab hold of him when he passed.

"Where've you been?" Reuben asked. "I've been looking for you. Bro, what happened?" Taking him aside Reuben waved a hand in front of Jamie's distracted face.

"Hey. Yeah. What?"

"I heard about the registration." Reuben shook his head, set his hands on his hips. "How did that happen?"

"We're still getting to the bottom of it."

"I don't have to tell you how this looks."

Jamie nodded. "I know." He ran his palm along his jaw in hopes of loosening it up.

"Folks are talking about it." Reuben's gaze flickered around the busy lobby. "Everybody wants to know how you, of all people, could let something like this happen. And I gotta tell you, I'm pissed. Everything was so beautiful, so perfect. I've never seen a couple more ready."

"I know, I know."

"How's Anna taking it?"

"She's—" Jamie shrugged. Walking helped, so Jamie started—aimlessly. It had never been easy to be reprimanded, not by his parents, not by Nicole Dubois when he'd first started dancing. He hated it most coming from Reuben. "It was stupid, I know—all part of the contract. I'm telling you, I feel more like a possession than a dance partner."

"Without the perks." Reuben slapped a palm on Jamie's back, a sure sign that he was ready to get on with it.

Perks? Jamie wanted to laugh. He'd come close to taking a perk just moments ago and was glad he hadn't, wondering if just entertaining the thought had been the jinx that had caused this trouble.

He checked in at the front desk. "Any messages for Jamie Wilde?"

The man behind the counter was dressed in a deep burgundy suit with bright gold buttons. He tapped in the computer keyboard then replied, "No, sir."

Voices and commotion grew louder and both Jamie and Reuben looked toward the glass front doors flanked with security as well as doormen. Without warning, a small crowd came at them, led by a man with a microphone, towing a photographer.

"That's him," someone said, and before either Jamie or Reuben knew what was happening, the small crowd had surrounded them and was tossing out questions faster than a tape recorder in fast-forward mode.

"Where's the Princess?"

"Is it true she was in danger earlier today?"

"Are you or are you not dancing in the competition?"

"It's rumored the partnership is over. Is that true?"

"Is it true you were on the roof of the hotel with her and you were in the middle of a fight when you were discovered?"

Soon, security was around the outer circle of the congregation. Jamie held up both hands in surrender, but the crowd was being jostled by the commanding security guards and no one saw his attempt to speak.

Finally, an officer broke through, shouting at him. "You'll have to take this outside."

"You can't throw me out with these sharks."

"They're here to talk to you and we have no orders to do otherwise."

Ready to curse, Jamie looked helplessly at Reuben. Where was Anna? He didn't like being left on the lurch like this, especially after she'd made it clear they would share in this frustration together.

For a sickening moment, he had the thought that she'd done this to him on purpose. That she was letting him have it. Serves her right if I publicly blast her, Jamie thought as he and Reuben were reluctantly ushered out the front doors, left to fend for themselves. Jamie tried again to quiet the group by raising his palms. It amazed him when they hushed and stood ready.

He took in some air. If Anna can do this, I can do this. "Questions?" he asked. Flash bulbs sparked in his eyes.

"Are you speaking for Her Royal Highness, Anna Zakharov?"

"I am speaking for the partnership of Wilde and Zakharov, of which Anna Zakharov is a part."

"Why are you withdrawing from the competition?"

"We're not withdrawing," Jamie flicked out his hands. "We were never entered. There was a mistake in our registration. We're not able to compete."

"What kind of mistake?"

Jamie shook his head. "That's all I'm going to say."

"Is it true she got cold feet?"

Reuben shook his head and stepped forward with a little fight in his tone. "Not true. Anna's as prepared as any competitor I've seen. She's ready."

"Are you having second thoughts, being a championship winner? Do you still want to dance with her?"

Jamie shook his head, though he could ring Anna's neck right at the moment for leaving him to do this alone. She should be at his side. That's what partnerships were about. "No second thoughts. We're a committed partnership."

"What do you say to allegations that she was emotionally disturbed and threatened to jump from the roof earlier today?"

Jamie's face twisted into a smirk. He was ready to strangle somebody. "That's a full-on lie. You people have to get new binoculars. That's the most outlandish thing I've—"

"How about allegations that you didn't want her to upstage you?"

"That's ridiculous!"

"Have we answered all your questions?" Reuben placed a firm hand on Jamie's shoulder.

"So when will we see the princess in her first competition?"

"Officially?" Reuben kept Jamie securely in place. "At Blackpool."

That seemed to satiate the group, who turned collectively and began scribbling notes, talking amongst themselves. Jamie sighed, felt the cool breeze finally seep through his sweat shirt and do its job. Nervous hands drove through his hair, dragged down his face and he let out a groan.

"Jamie. Reuben." Lev bounded up the large stair of the hotel with Inessa primly skipping behind him. Lev caught his breath, and as he did, the foul stench of garlic filled the air. "We've been all over the place. You guys should have joined us. This city is awesome, isn't it, Inessa?"

Inessa nodded, smiled.

"We ate lunch at this place called Rinaldi's. It's right on the wharf. You can actually see them dropping the live lobsters into the boiling water." Lev glanced at the dispersing crowd. "What was that all about?"

"Just clearing up a little problem with the press," Jamie mumbled.

Inessa's face drained of any pleasure that had been there. "Is something wrong with Anna?"

"She's fine." Jamie reached out and touched her arm. "We discovered that the registration forms were counterfeit."

Her mouth dropped and she quickly slapped her hand over it under eyes huge with horror. Jamie brought her into his side. "Hey, it's okay."

"But I was – it was I that—"

"Nessa, calm down." Jamie led her through the glass doors and back into the hotel lobby. "It's okay."

"This is terrible, just terrible. After all of your hard work. Oh, this is such terrible news."

Her eyes glistened, bringing his heart to his throat. He squeezed her just as Anna emerged from the elevator, followed by Ivan, Lukov and Vladimir. Their eyes met across the hive of the lobby and Anna crossed to them. Jamie thought she looked ready to tear someone apart. Instinctively, he kept the small young woman tucked under his arm.

Anna stopped directly in front of them. "Inessa, are you all right?"

Inessa nodded but didn't meet Anna's gaze, which now shifted to Jamie. He thought he saw anger there, but couldn't be sure. She was smiling her princess smile because a small crowd had gathered and photos were being taken. "I thought something had happened to you, the way Jamie was…comforting you."

"I just found out about…about what happened," Inessa sniffed. "I'm so sorry."

Smoothly, Anna wrapped her arm around Inessa and led their small group to a more private area of the lobby, smiling and nodding at those watching. "Not to worry. I am about to make a statement right now."

"I already made the statement," Jamie told her.

Anna's arm slipped from Inessa and she stopped. "You did?"

"Yeah, I came down here, checked with the desk. You hadn't left me a message, and the—"

"But I did leave a message. I left one for you to wait for me, to—"

"Well I never got it, and there were all of these people everywhere, like a freaking feeding frenzy. I had no choice, they—"

"What do you mean you had no choice? Or was it that you didn't want to wait for me?"

"That is not it and you know it." Jamie took a step toward her. "You and I discussed this upstairs. We agreed that we would do this together. I wouldn't have gone back on that."

She knew that, her heart needed no more convincing. But she had to be sure she was doing what was best for the partnership before she took action as final as she intended. To her right, Vladimir rocked back and forth on his heels, a grin playing on his lips. She only needed a brief glance at the man to continue her attack on Jamie.

"So you took the opportunity to showcase yourself?" When Jamie's eyes brightened with shock, then darkened with hurt, she felt the accusation as if she had inflicted it with real malicious intent. "It was a very cheap shot, Jamie. It undermines my position in the partnership and now weakens my socio-political status."

As if he'd been struck by her hand, rather than her words, Jamie took a step back. "I can't believe you're standing there accusing me of—"

"You jumped on the opportunity to put me in my place," she bulldozed him. "Even after I admitted to you that I was willing to subject my place in the partnership to you. What am I to think?"

Reuben held up both of his hands. "Wait a second. I was right here, nothing like that happened, Anna. It came down just like he said. We were surrounded, and the security guys invited us to handle the situation outside – on our own."

She dug for the courage to continue, knowing she had to be even crueler to be certain. "I can hardly believe that you are in on this as well, Reuben. It disappoints me. You both disappoint me. I must think this over privately." She turned, and Jamie lost it.

He was at her side, her arm in his fist in one vengeful breath. "We need to talk about this."

Lukov ripped Jamie's hand from Anna's arm and tossed him a few feet away. Anna made no effort to stop him. "I will talk to you when I am ready, James. Until then—"

"You talk to me now, Anna." Jamie wasn't about to let a little thing like a two-hundred and fifty pound boulder get in his way. Agilely, he slid between Ivan, Lukov and Vladimir with pleading in his eyes. "Come on, Anna. You owe me this much."

"It is you who owe me," she snapped. "As long as that is the case, you will wait until I am ready to see you."

They were at the elevators now, Inessa with her head lowered, Lev watching each participant as if observing doubles tennis match. Reuben paced behind, rubbing his shaking head in disbelief and reigned frustration. Held back in Lukov's firm fists, Jamie struggled in vain.

Anna got into the elevator and lifted her chin. "This time I will send a messenger to make sure you get the message." She gestured for Lev and Inessa to join her. "Stay with him," she told Lukov. "I don't want him running out on this."

"Running out?" Jamie shouted. "Oh that's rich. I'm standing right here. You're the one that's running away from this, Your Highness."

The doors slid closed and Jamie wrenched free of Lukov's grasp. On a curse he slammed both palms on the face of the elevator before pacing the floor, ignoring patrons slowly passing around him, staring with curiosity.

Finally, Jamie slowed. His head lowered to his chest and he bent over, both palms on his knees. The gesture brought Reuben to his side, had him patting his back. "We'll get to the bottom of this, bro."

It was just Anna and Vladimir in her suite and that's what Anna wanted. Coolly, she went to the kitchen area looking for a drink even though her stomach was synched tight. "I am not sure what to make of all of this," she began carefully. Vladimir stood a distance away watching her every move. She opened a bottle of water and drank.

"I think he has already made something of it, Anna."

The bottle clunked on the granite counter. "He did it on purpose, after we had just decided we would handle the press together."

"As you said, he was only looking out for himself."

She strode to the window, pretending to look out, but keeping her eyes on Vladimir's reflection. Gathering his arms behind his back, he continued to observe her in condemning silence.

"I am disappointed in him," she said.

For a long while, Vladimir remained quiet and pearls of sweat dripped down Anna's neck. She had purposefully accused Jamie and Reuben in hopes Vladimir would come out from behind the veil of concurrence he was standing behind and align himself with her views. Then she would see if it was him who was trying to destroy this competition for them. It was bold move, intended to draw Vladimir out so she could then send him home. But he stood without words, and she began to panic. All she could think about was how hurt Jamie had looked. Tilting the bottle back, she drank again.

She turned, shrugged. "Oh, well. I can overlook that." She took a sliver of pleasure when his eyes widened a bit. "I will look at it as a test." She kept the cold water bottle in her hand—it gave her something to hold onto, as she crossed to the front door. Vladimir stopped her.

"A test?"

"Of course. I wanted to see how he would handle it. I thought he might speak despairingly of me, given the chance. But he handled it with dignity."

"How can you defend him when he went against your wishes?"

"You know how relentless the press can be. He did the right thing by taking care of it quickly and discreetly. I am very proud of him." Taking a step toward the door, she felt Vladimir's hand around her bicep tighten.

"What if he is not as forgiving as you think he will be? You accused him."

"When I explain that I was merely testing him, he will understand." She was banking on it, in fact, hoping the spontaneous actions would not do irreparable damage. "Now, if you will excuse me, I need to go to him."

Vladimir released her with a nod. He looked at Ivan. "Take Anna down."

Her heart beat fast as she stood in the elevator. Cat and mouse, she thought. Vladimir was playing with her. It was so deceptive; she realized then that she did not need to catch Vladimir in the act of something mischievous to confront him face to face. Yes, Vladimir would resist when she excused him without any further notice. But he could do nothing except follow her wishes until he returned home and plead his case to her father. By that time, she would be closer to being free of all of the entanglements that could still drag her back home, and have that much more evidence to condemn Vladimir's behavior, keeping him out of her life for good.

Rather than go down to the lobby, she looked at Ivan. "I want to go back up."

* * *

Lukov pressed his ear piece to his ear and nodded. "You are to come with me," he told Jamie.

Both Reuben and Jamie had settled themselves on the dark wine-colored couches in the lobby to wait. They hadn't said much. Jamie was too coiled up inside.

Reuben patted Jamie's arm. "Find me when you two have worked this out."

Jamie followed Lukov toward the elevators. It hadn't even been a half hour since Anna had unjustifiably lashed out at him, but he didn't need anymore time. He already knew what he was going to say to her.

Lukov held the door open, and Jamie entered the shiny, gold vehicle and stood toward the back. A woman and her two children tried to ride up with them but Lukov blocked the door with his body and a shake of his head. "Private car." Then he stepped back in and the doors shut.

Jamie's eyes narrowed. "They could have ridden with us."

"Orders." Lukov stood at the doors, his massive back blocking any exit.

There was a little twist in Jamie's gut as the elevator soared upward and he watched the numbers light. They passed the thirty-fifth floor. "Why aren't we stopping?"

Lukov didn't acknowledge him in any way. The numbers continued to climb until they reached the roof and the car sighed to a stop. Then Lukov stood aside, waiting for the doors to open. They did, and he held his palm out. "This way."

It was ridiculous to even let the skittering of fear linger. Anna probably just wanted to move their meeting to the roof so they could speak privately. Jamie went out, boldly taking the lead to the doors that led to the roof.

It was getting dark, the sun was setting, but the giant ball of fire was hidden behind the other tall buildings that surrounded the hotel. The wind whipped, and Jamie chilled, burrowing his hands in the pocket of his sweatshirt.

"Where is she?" he asked.

"She is not coming." The voice had him turning. He felt stupid then, that he'd not expected the man.

Vladimir looked comfortable and toasty in his black overcoat and gloves. "She has asked me to relay this message to you, but before I do that, let me relay a message of my own."

Slowly, Vladimir advanced. "Your behavior does not befit Her Royal Highness, treating her as if she were just any woman, without any regard to her royal birthright and her imperial heritage. You have placed her in danger with selfish abandon. You have treated me, Ivan and Lukov with no more respect than a wild street urchin would. And today you did the unfathomable by placing her position below yours. She finds it unforgivable. It is with great satisfaction that I inform you that your partnership is over."

Jamie was willing to throw out her strange behavior if it couldn't be explained by temporary insanity. But he never thought it would come down to this. He expected the final blow to come from Anna herself.

"Where is she?"

A smile curled Vladimir's lip. "That is no longer your concern."

Jamie turned to storm right down to Anna, and found his face in Lukov's barrel chest. So he turned again, and forced grin. "You can tell Anna she can relay the message herself. Until then, the partnership remains intact."

"She no longer wants to see you."

"Too bad, old man." The injustice continued to pour over Jamie like quicksand. He wasn't about to let it swallow him up without a fight. "She owes me an explanation."

"She owes you nothing!" Vladimir shouted. Then he worked to regain his composure. The wind whipped and hissed, the cold of it bit and stung his skin to crimson.

"If she wants me gone, fine, but I want it from her lips, not yours."

"Mine will have to do, because that is all you will get!"

The obvious pleasure the man was taking in delivering the news made it hard to look him in the eye without wanting to slug him. Jamie kept his gaze out over the city, at the lights springing on like scattered stars underfoot.

He refused to believe Vladimir. Hours earlier he'd seen real sorrow in Anna's face that they had lost their opportunity to compete. He'd felt oneness between them sharing that grief.

"Yours isn't going to cut it, Vlad." Jamie headed back to the doors, flinging them open with the determination to find Anna and hear the dismissal from her. When he heard frantic scuffling behind him, he glanced over his shoulder to find both Vladimir and Lukov bowling his direction.

He took off. He didn't have the luxury of waiting for the elevators, so he opted for the stairs. Both Lukov and Vladimir were on his tail, but his chances of outrunning them were good. Lukov wasn't very nimble with all of that bulk and Vladimir was just plain old.

The cement stair chamber echoed with frantic feet, panting breath. Jamie glanced up, saw he had a two-flight lead and sped faster. He only had three more floors before he was at thirty-five.

He took the last flight by leaping over the railing, an entire set of steps down. He threw open the door, glanced at the room number on the nearest door to get his bearings and fled down the hall toward Anna's suite.

Banging on her door, he waited, gulping in air. His eyes were poised down the corridor, waiting for Lukov and Vladimir to come tearing around the corner.

"Anna." He pounded again, but the door remained fixed, and Jamie realized she indeed did not want to see him. Pressing his brow to the door, he strove to breathe. It seemed unreal, the last few hours. He refused to believe everything was over and pounded again.

When the door opened, Inessa stood with white fear on her face. He gripped her shoulders. "Ness, is Anna here?"

The thud of footsteps down the hall had Jamie's head jerking left. Vladimir and Lukov were at a full run headed right toward him.

Jamie pushed past Inessa. "Anna?" He darted into the back bedrooms, heard voices, commotion, and didn't have time to call for Anna again before both Lukov and Vladimir descended, toppling him to the floor of one of the back bedrooms.

Somebody screamed. Jamie figured it was Inessa, but wasn't sure. He'd been pinned by Lukov. One of the man's big hands was plastered on his head, the bulk of his body straddled his and Jamie's face burned, ground into the carpet as it was.

Vladimir stood and brushed off his black overcoat. He looked down at where Jamie laid pinned, shook his head and made a light tsk-tsk sound.

"Keep him here," he told Lukov.

Calmly, Vladimir left the room and went in search of Inessa. He found her, trembling in the living room of the suite. She was ghost-white.

Vladimir smiled as he crossed to her. "Inessa. You should have been with Anna." He stopped directly in front of her, meaning to intimidate. Her eyes were large and blinking, her mouth barely open, her chin quivering. It sent a surge of power through him that he caused such a reaction. "Your loyalty is to Anna and her safety is it not?"

Inessa nodded.

"Indeed, that is all of our concern. Jamie was going to hurt Anna. That is why Lukov is holding him. We are going to remove him from the room now. You needn't be afraid. In fact, if you would rather, you may go to your room as we do so. In may get ugly."

Inessa looked over Vladimir's shoulder to where she had seen all of them disappear.

"He meant to do you both harm, Inessa. You must believe that." He looked down at her, waiting for her to nod.

She only looked over his shoulder again at the closed door.

Vladimir placed both hands on her shoulders. "I will explain all of this to Anna. It will be very hard for her to understand and it would not be acceptable coming from you. Do you understand?"

"Yes," Inessa's voice quivered.

"Good." Vladimir dropped his hands. "Now go to the bedroom."

Inessa did not move.

"Very well." It would only strengthen Vladimir's case if he could get Jamie in enough of an uproar that Lukov was forced to restrain him with the spill of blood. The sight would terrify the timid girl, sealing her mouth shut.

Vladimir found Lukov still straddled across Jamie's back. Jamie's face was tomato-red from Lukov's heavy-handed pressure, applied, quite nicely Vladimir thought, over Jamie's smug face.

Squatting down, he tilted his head so that he could meet Jamie's eyes. "What, no humorous quip Mr. Wilde?"

Jamie's head felt pressed between sandbags. He could barely breathe, and decided Lukov was all muscle underneath that black suit he wore. All muscle that felt like a two-ton rock. His shoulder burned, his hand and arm no longer had any sensation and he figured he could squeeze two, maybe three more breaths in. If only Justin had taught him some of those jujitsu moves, he might have a fleeting chance at tipping old Lukov from his back.

"You have brought this upon yourself," Vladimir continued.

Jamie tried to wriggle, hating that he was pinned, hating that he was forced to take the ridicule from Vladimir. The one thing he could still move was his mouth. "This is illegal." He mumbled because his face was smashed, cheeks and mouth distorted in such a way that he could barely form words.

"What's that?" Vladimir cupped his ear, started to laugh. He sat upright and nodded at Lukov who lifted up just enough that when he came back down again, it caused Jamie to grunt, forcing whatever air had been in his lungs out. With his lungs compressed, he could barely suck in a stream of air. Panic clutched his oxygen-deprived throat. He was sure he would die right there on the spot and was preparing himself, even as Lukov leaned over, bringing more crushing body weight down over him.

Vladimir jerked his head upward at Lukov, signaling for him to bring Jamie up. In one violent yank, Jamie was on his feet, albeit wobbling. Lukov held Jamie's arms tight behind his back.

"Let us be civilized," Vladimir said simply as he slipped off his black overcoat. "Sit."

Lukov moved Jamie to a chair next to the picture window and sat him in it, staying directly behind him as Vladimir crossed to the door and called to Inessa.

"Before we discuss what we did not finish upstairs, we will have some tea."

Jamie sputtered out a reply, "I don't want any tea."

Inessa stood in the door, wide eyes on Jamie first, then on Vladimir. "Bring me some hot water and two, no, one cup for tea."

After a nod, she disappeared.

Vladimir let out a sigh and slowly crossed back to Jamie. "You are making this more difficult than it has to be. Anna needs to go home, to face her responsibilities there. Her father demands it." Vladimir paused, allowing Jamie to react. When his firm glare didn't vary, he continued. "He has asked me to make sure she understands that this fantasy of dance, of America—of you—is just that. A fantasy."

Because Jamie's eyes darkened, Vladimir smiled. "Yes, you have been a part of this since the beginning. And now she finds herself in love with you." He let out a sigh. "A foolish, empty, irresponsible thing, as it can have no course. She is Anna Zakharov, you are…" Vladimir's lips thinned. "Nobody."

Jamie blinked hard and averted his eyes. Love. The idea pleased him in spite of Lukov pressing behind him, in spite of Vladimir's threatening stance. It filled him with a surge of power and he struggled again and was again met with forced restraint when Lukov pinched back his shoulder blades.

Inessa appeared with a tray of delicate tea cups clattering in her grip. She glanced at Jamie and set them down on the table. He sent her a crooked smile, seeing that she was ghostly white. Vladimir waved a hand to dismiss her and she left.

Vladimir pulled a small, white packet from his pocket and dropped it into one of the teacups. "Anna cannot think for herself when her heart is wrapped up in the foolishness of love. Her father has asked me to remedy the situation." He lifted the cup, swished it once and extended it toward Jamie who stared at it with wide eyes.

"I'm not drinking that."

Vladimir's smile spread like a snake uncoiling. "You may drink it willingly, or Lukov will hold you while I pour it down your throat. Your choice."

Jamie shot to his feet but was met with Lukov's weighty palms, pulling him back into the chair.

"Come on, you can't be serious."

"You have made the situation most serious," Vladimir hissed, voice rising.

Jamie squirmed under Lukov's hands until he saw Vladimir nod, and then felt the big man's arm slide around his throat in a choke-hold. Instinct had Jamie's hands grabbing at the trunk wrapped around him. "You learn this from my brother, Luk?" he squeaked.

Lukov nodded. Jamie would have laughed at the irony of it, had the rest of him not been filling with dread. The man of steel had him by the throat and another man was now coming toward him with what he was sure was some sort of poison.

"I would have waited until the tea cooled but your insolence will give me great pleasure in pouring it down and watching it burn." The teacup came closer as Vladimir leaned near with perverse thrill in his eyes.

Jamie's gaze fixed on the cup. He pinched his lips. He waited until just the right moment, when Vladimir's sickeningly satisfied face was close, then lifted his foot, shoving it in Vladimir's stomach. It sent the man toppling back, the mysterious concoction in the tea cup flying into the air before shattering on the floor.

Lukov still had him by the throat but with the surprise of what had happened, his grip loosened enough for Jamie to slip away. Vladimir sat up, adjusting his skewed glasses before reaching out and snatching Jamie's left foot, bringing him down to the floor.

With a growl, Vladimir jerked his head at Lukov. "Get him."

In a flying leap, Lukov came down on Jamie's back, putting an abrupt end to any attempt at escape.

"What is this?"

It sounded like Anna, but Jamie couldn't be sure. The sudden pressure of Lukov's weight had sent the wind out of his lungs. Just as he began to see stars and blackness in the back of his eyes the only thing he was sure of, was that he was going to die, squashed like a bug.

Suddenly, the weight was off of him and he was able to breathe. But he could barely move.

"Must I repeat the question?"

It was Anna's voice, Jamie was sure of that now. He rolled onto his back. Anna was there with an annoying amount of composure on her face. Couldn't she see he'd almost bitten the dust? Inessa was right next to her, still white-faced and trembling.

Jamie forced himself to his feet, rubbing his neck. "Vlad here wanted me to drink some tea."

Anna looked from face to face before Lukov bent over, picked up the white tea bag and handed it to her with a look of sorrow on his face.

She took it, sniffed it, and angled her head at Vladimir. "Rhubarb root tea? Not quite poison, but nearly as potent. It temporarily paralyzes the body with the exception of the lungs, heart and the brain."

Jamie looked at Vladimir whose face showed no sign of remorse. "Jeez, Vlad."

Anna tossed the tea bag and in two steps was in Vladimir's face. "You're going home."

"You can't dismiss me."

"I can and I have."

"This is my rightful place!"

"You lost your rightful place when you took it upon yourself to interfere with my plans and threaten Jamie's good health."

"I did what any patriot would do to save their country—"

"Our country is in no danger. It is especially safe now that I will see to it you no longer have a place in its leadership."

Vladimir bled red from the neck up. "Lukov, Ivan, see that Her Royal Highness does not leave this room!"

Anna held her head high, the air around her filled with the aura of who she was. Jamie stood in silent awe. "Ivan. See Mr. Petrenko to his room. See that he packs and take him to the airport. See that he gets on a plane and then call me when that plane is in the air."

Vladimir huffed and stormed from the tight confines of the bedroom and out into the living room. With one jerk of her head, Anna had both Ivan and Lukov take him in a vise grip, holding him like a captured insect.

"Know that as you are in flight," she began steadily, "I will be bringing my father up to date with your vicious activities. Inessa, would you fetch Lev, please?"

On a nod, Inessa left. It was suddenly quiet. Anna took in a deep breath before she went to Jamie, her eyes searching his face, his neck and body. Her heart had not slowed since she had been summoned by Inessa, since she had feared for Jamie's welfare. When she'd come in and seen him pinned underneath Lukov, her heart had stopped. "Are you all right?"

He nodded, enjoying the intense way she was checking for injury.

"I am so sorry about—"

He silenced her by grabbing her and pulling her close. Whatever just happened had been bizarre and too close to something he was sure could have ended dangerously.

When she melded into him, her head burrowing into the crook of his neck, he knew where he wanted her – right next to him, for the rest of his life. A flush of comfort sunk to his bones.

"That was my fault, I'm so sorry, Jamie," she murmured against his shirt.

"How was it your fault? The guy's got major wires loose somewhere, Anna."

"No." She eased back so she could look at him. "I planned it. I got angry at you on purpose. The press conference, the false documents—they were all

Vladimir's doing, Jamie. I had no proof but what was in my heart. I had to catch him. So I pretended to be angry with you downstairs so that I could trap him."

He brought her against him again and kissed the top of her head. "You made me crazy down there. I couldn't understand what the heck was going on."

"He meant to hurt you."

"And he ended up with my foot in his gut instead," he said with a half-grin.

Her relieved gaze danced from his lips to his eyes. "Something you learned from Justin?"

He shook his head, laughed. "Luk's the only one who was smart enough to do that." His hands ran up and down her arms. "You're shaking."

It was true. Anna felt no shame in it. So what if she had been taught to control such things. The man she loved had been in danger and she'd been a part of it. It was inexcusable and something she would never do again.

"I am so sorry. I should have told you from the beginning and we could have worked this out together, it is only right with the partnership."

"I imagine letting someone help you is not part of that royal blood that runs in those veins of yours."

"I will admit I am used to everyone doing what I say."

"You'd like that from me, wouldn't you?"

She shook her head. One of many things she did not want him to change for her sake.

With his finger he brought her chin up, her eyes to his. "Vladimir said some things." He thought about what Vladimir had told him, that she had fallen in love with him, that her father wanted her home. "Your father asked him to bring you home."

"I know."

"You do?"

She nodded. "It was a lie—all of it. Papa and I talked this afternoon. I told him what I suspected. He wanted me to be sure, and then if I was, to send Vladimir back. He was shocked at first. Vladimir's family has served in one way or another for many years." But he'd not questioned her, he'd trusted her, and that had given her hope, and the confidence to follow her plan. "When I told him what he had done with our registration, he was appalled and told me he would call you personally to apologize."

It made Jamie uncomfortable. Then he looked down into her face. Her father had entrusted her to him. His arms, still around her, gave a tug so she was tight against him.

"So what does this mean for old Vlad?"

"He will lose his position, but will not be utterly disgraced. Though I told Papa I thought he should be put in prison."

"There really is a dungeon isn't there? See, I knew it."

She laughed. "Yes, but it's used as an office now."

He cringed and she wrapped around him, her whole body finally beginning to relax.

"I am so glad you are all right," she whispered.

She felt so good. Everything comfortable and familiar reached in and drew his heart to hers. He could easily spend the rest of his life like this. Then it occurred to him, maybe Vladimir's lie had included her feelings. Because the idea was disappointing, he eased back a little.

Neither heard the door open, or saw Lev when he suddenly appeared. He stopped short, staring. "Lev."

"You…" His wide eyes darted between her and Jamie. "You and Jamie?"

"Something happened," Anna began, breaking free of Jamie. "I was just making sure he was all right."

It didn't relieve the angst on Lev's face. Jamie averted his eyes with a slug of guilt. "It wasn't what it looks like, Lev."

Anna's hand went out to stop Jamie from any further explanation. "Let me."

Jamie nodded. "I'll wait out in the hall." Jamie left the two of them alone.

It wouldn't be easy confronting Lev with her true feelings, but it was time. Lev didn't say anything, his head bowed momentarily before his gaze met hers. There was understanding there, mixed with disappointment anyone who'd had feelings for another could see.

"We must talk, Lev," Anna began.

"I saw it," he began, his throat wobbling," I just didn't want to believe it."

"I'm so sorry."

"No. I'd rather you just say it. Nobody says things to me. They think I can't see what's really going on and then they act like I'm some idiot. But I see everything."

"Have you seen my feelings for long?"

Lev shrugged. "Oh, yeah. I mean, we've never really been anything more than pals you and I. I feel the same way as you."

"You do?"

He pushed his glasses up his nose with a big nod. "Oh, yeah. Sure, I held onto the dream, but it was father's dream more than mine. We both know how that is. Gotta make father happy, gotta keep everything just so, you know? But really, I mean, you're beautiful and I do like you Anna, but," he swallowed, his Adams apple rolling up his throat. "I've had it for Natalia Broski for a long time." His face broke into a smile that confirmed he was as relieved as she was.

"How wonderful for you." Anna pictured the dishwater blonde girl with glasses and thought she and Lev were a much better match. "She feels the same?"

"Oh, yeah. It's just that we've been waiting to see what happened between you and me."

"So you'll be all right with this?"

"Father will flip out, but I'll handle him. Don't you worry about a thing." He took her hand in his and swung it.

"I need you to do something very important."

"Sure, whatever you want."

"Vladimir has done something disappointing to me. Because of that, I am discharging him."

"Seriously?"

She nodded. "I need you to make sure that he goes directly to my father. I need you to accompany him home."

"You're really sending Vladimir back?"

"Yes."

"Wow. That's…wow, big news."

"Yes, well, he deserves it."

"Did he do something to Jamie?"

"Yes. And to me."

"I'll take him back for you, Anna."

"Thank you."

"Anna." Lev took her hand again. "I won't be coming back. There's stuff I need to do at home, you know, with Natalia."

"Of course."

Once Lev left, Anna's heart resumed fluttering. The bridge was slowly lowering over a moat she had only dared dream would be crossable. She went to the window and looked out at the darkening sky, the twinkling lights of the city. "Lukov, will you find Jamie and bring him to me please?"

18.

Jamie sat on the floor of the hall with his back against the wall. He let out a long sigh. The passage was empty now. He'd seen Lev and Inessa leave the suite and wondered why Lev looked so happy after getting the royal brush off from Anna. The guy had made a beeline for his room. Curiosity had him running ideas through his mind. But his stomach churned when he thought of one—that the man had finally gotten Anna to say yes.

Vladimir's words rung with an air of truth that had Jamie hoping. He was at odds, unsure if he should trust his feelings or bury them once and for all and be settled with simply being Anna's partner, like he was contracted.

Just hours ago, he'd thought he'd almost lost her when she'd feigned anger at him. He'd thought all they had worked for, every teasing possibility he had toyed within his mind about the two of them was forever gone. It had nearly driven him mad.

He heard movement to his right and his head snapped up. Lukov towered over him. "Her Highness will see you now."

Jamie decided at that moment he could live with her being a princess. He could live with her calling for him, like she owned him. He could even live with the risk of what might happen to their dance career if the two of them became personally involved. He walked behind Lukov to her suite, his heart beating hard. It meant giving more of himself than he'd ever given, but only he knew what that cost.

She stood by the window, gazing out, but she didn't turn when he came in. In the reflection of twilight, he watched her eyes move to him.

He'd take being her possession. She was worth the price.

"The competition's going," he said after a time.

"I'd like to see some of it."

"Yeah." His nerves jittered when she finally turned. Her eyes were lit with what he so wanted to be desire. Vladimir's words echoed in the back of his head, "She finds herself in love with you."

Tonight he'd know for sure.

He crossed the suite and stood beside her in front of the window. "First, there's something I need to know." Jamie's gaze locked on hers. "You said you talked to your father. Did you talk to him about this? About dance, being here? About your future?"

"Everything is the way it should be."

"That's all you're going to tell me?"

"Papa loves me. He wants me to be happy and he sees that I am. Here. Doing this with you." There was truth in her eyes, and openness. "I am free to do as I please."

He took a deep breath that shuddered as her words sunk in. "That's great news. So, the title, the throne – what about that?"

"When Nicholas is older, Papa will relinquish that to him. Papa was happy, actually, that he'd been made to think about it. He thinks it is the progressive way."

Jamie nodded, astounded at what he had yet to learn about her curious existence. "And will Iv, Luk and Nessa stay on?"

"So many questions." The taunting lull of her voice sent his blood into a low hum. Her head titled and the slow smile creasing her lips was his undoing.

"Can I help it if I want to know everything about you? You're my partner."

"They work for me. They will stay."

"That will make Justin happy."

She nodded. "And Inessa as well."

"What about you?" He stepped closer.

"I will follow my heart, like I always do."

"Was that what brought you here? To America?"

"That's part of it," she said, bringing her body flush with his. His chest brushed hers, teasing her heart into a throbbing pound.

His face drew tight in anguish and in a snap he had both hands wrapped around her upper arms in a grip that sent hot fire blasting through her system. "Don't do this to me."

"What? Jamie—"

"Keep things from me. Not after everything." His tug was fast, sharp, and brought her lips near his. "I want it all. I want all of you."

Her heart skidded to a stop. "You do?"

He nodded, and in his eyes she saw desire ripening.

"Talk to me, Anna. Tell me everything."

Her heart hammered against her ribs. It didn't seem right to admit she had fallen in love with him in this manner. It wasn't at all what she had envisioned. "This is not a set of steps we're discussing, Jamie." His grip softened, his fingers skimmed her shoulders and arms.

"Yeah, okay. So?"

"So, this is…it's important to me. It's part of my heart."

"Anna, what is it?" He shoved his hands into his hair and stepped back. "You're making it more than I'm sure it is."

"How can you say that?"

He planted his hands on her shoulders again. "I'm sorry. You're right. Just…now you've got me itchy. Tell me." When she paused he squeezed. "Trust me."

"Promise me you won't hate me."

His brows crimped with confusion and he paused for a thick moment. "Okay. I promise."

"And promise you won't leave the partnership, no matter what."

He swallowed hard. "Jeez. Anna what is it?"

She took a deep breath and held it for a moment. "I love you."

She expected flickers of anger, of betrayal or shock to shadow his face. Her heart stopped after the words left her tongue and was slowly beating again now as his eyes brightened. The corners of his mouth lifted.

His fingers dug into her shoulders for an instant before a glorious smile broke on his lips. Then she was next to him, pressed so tightly she winced for breath.

"You are not mad at me?" she asked.

She felt the soft chuckle in his chest under her cheek and closed her eyes. He didn't speak, but she felt him shake his head.

"You scared me." Softly, he kissed her brow, then framed her face in his hands. "Why didn't you tell me?"

"After all you said about not mixing business and pleasure? I could see how hard you were trying."

He shook his head. "It was a losing battle."

"I didn't want you to lose it because of me."

All his fighting had been vain, wasted effort. He could never fight fate. The universe had brought them together the minute she chose him, and he'd been unable to resist the force. "You blow me away," he murmured. "I guess that's what first struck me about you."

"Does this upset you?"

He shook his head. "Not at all." There was such vulnerability in her dark eyes. Those deep wells were clear and promising now as he looked into them. He would find part of himself if he dove deep enough. The part of him that would make his life complete.

"You've snagged me, Anna. I don't know, I think it was when I saw you playing with my sisters."

She smiled, lifted to her toes and wrapped her arms around his neck. "Art was imitating life then. I wanted you."

"Oh yeah? You've had me since day one, since I signed my soul to you in that contract."

"I intend to hold you to that contract as long as it pleases me."

He grinned. "An indentured servant, hmm. I could think of a lot worse ways to spend the rest of my life than pleasing you."

She didn't want to think he really meant it – to spend the rest of their lives together, but the words went straight to her heart. "The rest of our lives?" she asked carefully.

Something in his face changed then. "Yeah. But that'll require another contract. I think it's called a license."

Anna smiled. "I like that contract," she whispered next to his neck, then kissed him there.

"We can talk about that later," he said drawing back. He kept hold of her hands, and his hooded gaze swept her from head to toe. "There's something I want."

Anna swallowed the fluttering in her throat. "And what is that?"

"Your dress. I want to see you in it." He wasn't making a wish, he was telling her, and the demand sent a hot thrill through her system.

"All right." She gave his hand a squeeze before she went into her bedroom.

The beaded dress hung on the door to the bathroom. Slipping it on over her head, the cold beads and icy sequins rolled down every inch of her skin, fitting into each curve with perfection. The mirror held her reflection. A sensual sight, she mused with the smile of desire. Nude fabric held each tiny, glittering bead to her body as if she had immersed herself in colorful gems. The fringed hem shimmied and shook with every step.

He liked her hair up, he'd said that once before, so she pinned it up and sprayed some perfume at the nape of her neck. Then she slipped on her dance shoes.

She could hear music, the slow, sensual beat of a favorite song. Her system thrummed. Jamie wanted to dance with her.

He stood in front of the elaborate stereo system housed in the entertainment armoire. He'd taken off his white sweatshirt and now wore what she liked him in best – a white tee shirt with his jeans. She didn't alert him to her presence. Instead, she took the moment to enjoy the sight of his strong back, tapering down to his tight waist. His arms were magnificent extensions of a body she had come to admire for its ability as well as its beauty.

Suddenly, his arms fell to his sides. His head cocked enough for her to know that he'd sensed her. When he turned, his eyes widened at first, then narrowed with trapped desire.

"Is this what you wanted?"

His eyes swept her from head to toe like a brush fire. He shook his head. "It's what I want."

They met in the middle of the room. For a moment, he only stood close, his eyes taking her in as if he had finally completed a journey and she was the prize. She enjoyed the way his gaze admired, lingered and held, ramming her insides with building need that pressed against her skin.

A lonely whistle echoed from the speakers. The rumba beat began with a tentative thud of drum, the tap of a synthesizer. A violin plucked, a guitar strummed. Jamie's hand slipped around her waist and he jerked her against him, stealing her breath. Then he took her to a drop, forcing her to arch back, her body submitting to his.

Need was in his hand, clasped tight at her waist. Urgency was in the tension she felt from his body straining against hers. When he brought her back up, it wasn't with gentleness or even finesse; but with exigency she'd only felt when they had danced in the dark.

Anna expected him to slide them both into another move, but he stood still as the guitars sang and the lyrics demanded that whatever happen, not to let go. She wouldn't. His hands shot up to her hair, angling her head just right for capture. His eyes locked on her mouth. As if he had to place his mouth on hers for his next breath, his eyes sharpened. She feared any breath shared would ignite them both when their lips finally joined.

She couldn't wait any longer, the pull deep inside ready to snap. Her anxious hands fastened around his neck, her fingers dove into the soft hair.

"Anna."

She melted from the heat of him, but when he said her name, her knees nearly dissolved. She forced herself to wait. He would kiss her, and she would know it was his need that had done it, not hers.

She kept her gaze fixed on his mouth, that wonderful mouth that spoke her name and fought her will, that laughed and teased, and broke into a smile, and never ceased to cause her heart to shudder. As he neared, she closed her eyes, her heart skimming so close to the surface she was sure he would feel its pulse in the kiss.

Softly he pressed his lips to hers. The taste of him sparkled through her in quenching liquid. Jamie. As if she would never get enough, each cell inside awakened as he poured, filled and drenched her. Cupping her head, angling it, he began to explore. With the eager tug of his neck, she urged him forward.

His fingers dug and fisted as he deepened the kiss, his lips fluttering, sliding, and wetting hers. At last his hands lit the sides of her neck, tracing her shoulders, the kiss moving along her face.

"Finally," he murmured against her jaw.

Everything around them seemed to whirl. Jamie drew back. There was something different in her eyes. What was once foreboding gray was warm now, as if he stood over that endless wishing well and suddenly saw a glimmering of flame beckoning him. He would go there and beyond if she would have him.

It seemed fitting to show her what she had become to him, to give his heart to her as they danced. It was where their steps came together, their hearts joined for one purpose. A purpose that would celebrate without restraint now, as their partnership fused into companionship.

The light touch of his fingers lit sparkling fires, moving down her arms until they found her back and he brought her against him again in another crushing lock. "This dress," his lips traced the side of her face before coming again to her mouth, "is incredible."

Anna wanted him to know everything, and so her heart turned inside out. She eased back and held his heavy gaze. "From the first time I saw you," she admitted, "I wanted you. That is why I came here to the United States, Jamie. From the very beginning, it was you." She reached out, tracing the quiver of his lips. When the look in his eye snapped from brown to black, her heart pounded.

His dark eyes shifted from taut desire to soft contentment. His lips broke into a smile. He shook his head. "Then I guess that makes us equal." The familiar hard and strong length of his body filled her with a blast of fire. "I love you, Anna." His lips skimmed her jaw, traced the pulsing vein down the side of her neck, shuddering that fire to every cell under her skin. With his other hand, he reached around to the back of her dress.

About the Author:

Katherine Warwick writes women's romance
with the spice of ballroom dance.
She is married and lives in Utah with her husband,
six children and five cats.

You can read more of her work at one of her websites:
www.katherinewarwick.com   and   www.ballroomdancenovels.com

Read an excerpt from
SAVAGE
the next book in the dance series:

He hated dancing. Couldn't do it, for one thing. Besides, the seductive ritual of foreplay was a waste of time. Why not just get right to the good stuff? To counter his feelings with the only thing that would subdue them, he waved the bartender over and slapped a palm on the top of the bar giving his order for another beer.

To his right a little blonde bumped into him, sending a smile. Of course he smiled back. She kept nudging him; nearly causing him to spill the beer the bartender had just slid his direction.

"Hey," he said, smiling down at her.

Her eyes brightened, though he couldn't tell the color of them at the moment. She turned, facing him, exposing a low-cut, tight blue tee shirt. The pale tops of two rounded breasts peeked up at him.

"I'm Missy," she said.

He thought she wasn't missing anything. His gaze purposefully began at her breasts and lingered up her pale throat, finally landing on her face. "I'm Chance."

Her head tilted in surprise. It was the reaction he had been getting to his name since he was old enough to decipher the language of facial expressions. To know they could be just as enlightening, just as damning as words could be.

She eyed his mouth. It sent a warm thread through his blood. "You have a great smile," she said. Another thing he'd been hearing since he'd known he could smile and get anything he wanted -- except what he really needed. "I love your dimples."

Chance raised his bottle. "Thank you." Then he drank it down. He still hurt inside. Another bottle would do him some good. With a clank to the bar that was swallowed up in the noise, he waved to the bartender.

"You've had a lot of those." Missy glanced at the empty bottle.

Leaning his elbows against the soft padding of the bar, Chance avoided his reflection in the mirror that ran the length behind it. "You going to be my mother or have a drink with me?"

"Sure, I'll have a drink with you."

The bartender was waiting. "She'll have a…"

"An Amstel light," Missy answered, edging even closer to him. She crossed her arms, resting them on the bar so that her breasts pinched in the center, giving them more fullness. His gaze fell back to them.

"Quite a shirt you have on there, Missy." Chance dropped his bottle back for another swig.

"Glad you like it."

What's not to like? he thought, taking her in. She had it all -- handfuls, from what he could gather -- a study in feminine flirtation.

Even though he didn't particularly feel like indulging in company at that moment, he'd learned that if getting completely wasted didn't dull what was raging inside of him, being with a woman could do the job.

He lifted the bottle to his lips in hopes the desired effect would drown him soon. This time he caught his reflection in the mirror. And hardly recognized what he saw.

The young man staring back at him looked older than his twenty-seven years. Rough, scraggly, with dark smudges under two angry eyes. When was the last time he'd had a haircut? He couldn't remember -- the fog in his brain too thick. But the damned hair was everywhere, dark curls and waves that had never done anything but what they wanted to. He thought he'd shaved. Maybe that was the other day. The shadow along his jaw made him look like he'd been holed up somewhere -- neglected.

But then he had been.

It was hardest to meet his eyes. To look at them and know he couldn't escape what he saw: Chance Savage.

A roll of self-disgust started low in his gut and he dropped his head to the counter. He took deep breaths, the sour stench of his own inebriation nearly gagging him. Then he felt a soft hand on his back, a soft breast pressed into his arm.

"You okay?" Missy asked.

He closed his eyes, kept his face buried in his crooked arms for a moment. "I'm fine." The music drove through his head like a boxer pounding a heavy bag. He was sure she hadn't heard him. And she was a stranger. She didn't really care about what was wrong with him.

She just wanted him to take her home.

Thrusting himself up, he faced his reflection in the mirror with a determined scowl before jerking toward Missy with another smile. "Hey." He was beginning to think she was just what he needed. Yeah, he could bury himself in all of those soft, round curves. That would do it, at least for tonight.

He'd worry about tomorrow later.

"How about we dance?" Missy asked. He could see it in her eyes; she wanted to get him away from the bar – for his own good.

He resisted. Resisting was his middle name. "I don't dance." He finished the bottle he'd been drinking with a thud to the bar.

"We can just rock." Missy took his hand in hers. It was soft, warm -- inviting. Like the rest of her.

Rock? He could rock.

Chance let that warm hand lead him through the crowd. He scanned for his friends, saw them scattered and called out to them with careless abandon.

The dance floor of Bruisers was lit from underneath and the pulsing lights hurt his eyes. He stopped a moment, reeling from the flashing colors. He was feeling a little better now, lighter, giddier. He laughed at his own discomfort, at his being there. Wondered why he couldn't just shove everything clawing at him aside and lose himself, like everyone else around him.

Missy tugged him deep into the center of the crowd and slid her arms up around his neck and since he had no idea what he was doing, he did just what she'd suggested – he rocked. It was incredibly dull and he was ready to ditch the dance floor when his roommate, Justin, elbowed him with a look meant to chide because he'd sworn he wouldn't leave the bar.

The look of sheer happiness on Justin's face struck Chance's belly as if he'd been slugged. He was envious. In the years he'd known Justin, the guy had never let life tear him apart. Chance admired that. But then Justin came from a solid family, not a lion's den.

The music slowed to a thudding, sensual beat. A couple caught Chance's eye. They were talking to Justin as they danced in the center of the floor. Chance had never seen the guy before, but he wasn't concentrating on him, his eyes fastened on the woman with him.

She looked completely out of place, like she'd just been plucked from the pages of Town and Country or Society News. There was nothing of the midriff-baring, provocative attire he saw on most of the women in the place. She wore one color – a soft shade of lavender – from head to toe in a suit with the careful fit of someone tuned into a sense of self rather than to please an onlooker. Her dark hair was long, a mass of soft curls she made no excuse to straighten like so many women did.

But her face was what captured his eyes.

Classically sculpted, like a seventeenth century aristocrat. Her smile was as fresh and innocent as a virgin on communion day. Her eyes, though she was a distance away, were big, expressive, the color of which he strained to see.

Determined to see the woman up close, he moved through the crowd.

The man and the woman in lavender danced with perfect movements Chance suspected had been learned. Since the two of them had been talking with Justin, he figured they were part of that dance group Justin hung around.

Like a statue in the middle of the floor, Chance stood watching the stunning couple as bodies moved all around him.

"Hey, where'd you go?" He heard Missy's bright voice but didn't look down at her.

"I told you, I'm not much of a dancer." His eyes were still caught on the elegant woman in the arms of another man. She held that head of hers with a tilt that whispered untouchable. In fact, everything about her looked entirely out of reach and Chance's eyes narrowed. Stirring deep inside was the all-too familiar feeling that clutched at him when he felt challenged and in need of proving himself.

"You know them?" Missy asked.

Not yet, he thought. He took Missy's hand and led her near them. His heart pounded as he saw the woman more clearly.

"You're staring at her," Missy said, breaking free of his bear-hug.

Chance looked at her for a brief moment. "Maybe this dance is over."

Her eyes widened and she sneered at him before she disappeared in the crowd.

Chance dodged couples as he trailed the picturesque couple. He tapped the guy's shoulder and they slowed to a stop. Because he was so close to her, he barely glanced at the man who held her, enchanted by her face. Her skin was pale, smooth, the blue of her eyes startlingly dark. "I'd like to cut in," he said, still not offering more than a glance to the man.

Her partner hesitated and looked at her with question. She seemed too taken aback to reply, and Chance's itch to touch her intensified.

Finally, she nodded and her partner left the dance floor. She stood waiting for him and he had to blink hard, sure this was just a figment of his ripe brain.

Never at a loss for words when it came to women, Chance couldn't think, let alone speak. She was looking at him so intensely, he was sure she could see right through him. *She'd run if she saw what was inside. She'd certainly never let me touch her.*

"Are you going to dance with me?" Her voice had an air of confidence that instantly set him on guard. But he nodded, taking an unsteady step toward her.

She had the body and bones of a polished ballerina. Everything about her was refined, yet he'd just seen her dance with remarkable presence. He felt the first stirrings of incompetence fight with his need to prove to himself he was still alive inside.

"I'm Chance."

She extended her hand to shake his and he studied the delicate perfection of it. Then he slid his fingers around hers.

"Avery."

Chance held out his arms, even though he had no idea what to do with them other than to wrap them around her. But that would be enough. He'd be able to feel those bones move, close his eyes and see her muscles working. He was disappointed that she kept her arms in the traditional dance position.

He'd never learned how to dance.

As they moved, she looked off over his shoulder so he stared at her. The perfection he'd first seen was not a figment of his inebriated mind. The luminous glow was real, radiating from features that looked to have been hand carved by Michelangelo.

She knew he was watching her and he was glad. "What are you doing here?" he finally asked.

"Dancing -- like everyone else."

"But you're not like everyone else."

Usually, a stare that intense spoke of only one thing to him, but not with her. He saw no lust in her eyes at all. It relieved him, and he pulled her closer.

"Your eyes are incredible," he told her.

"Thank you." Her response was smooth enough to tell him she was used to being complimented.

"Is that your boyfriend?"

"He's my dance partner."

"So he's not your boyfriend?"

Her smile was too brief. She looked at his mouth, then back at his eyes before she turned her head away.

"You're a professional dancer, right?" he asked.

That she kept her cordial gaze over the crowd instead of looking at him, bugged him. He wanted to memorize the flecks in her eyes, the smooth contours of her face. More than anything, he wanted to let his hands roam her lovely limbs, trace her ribs, and explore hidden places.

Not used to being ignored by women, he turned her in what he hoped would be a deft move, but ended up twisted in a toe-stepping embarrassment. She shot him a look then, slightly annoyed as her brow lifted.

"What? Can't professionals dance with ordinary folks," he asked, more snap in his tone than he intended. "Or are you too good for that?"

"I happen to teach ordinary folks to dance."

"Teach me something."

The song had changed. He felt her draw back as if she was ready to leave him and he held on, not ready to relinquish her to her partner, now standing at the fringe of the floor, watching.

Chance moved, blocking her view of the man.

"I have to go," she said, craning to find her partner. It lit Chance's frustration, brittle as it was, and he was just careless enough to pull her against him, sending a fast, hot thrill through his veins as he felt her resist.

"Not until you teach me something," he said.

"This dance is over."

"I thought you said you were a teacher. Teach me, damn it."

"Let me go now," she said, looking him straight in the eye.

He let out a laugh of feigned indifference meant to cover up deeper bruises. When his eyes met hers again, he could see she was furious. He was acutely aware of her warmth, of the hard, long line of her body next to his.

Within seconds she would be gone.

"You are too good for me." He pushed himself away with more force than he intended and instantly regretted it, reaching out to snatch her back, but she kept herself out of reach.

Chance braced for a slap -- he deserved at least that. She merely tilted her head, and the pity in her eyes stole his breath.

Without a word, she turned, leaving him in the middle of the floor. Her lavender form weaved through the mass of bobbing bodies and he tried to follow her with vision losing its clarity. She went directly to her partner who shot Chance a nasty glare before the two of them were lost in the mass.

He'd been an idiot, he knew that. He'd had no business touching a Michelangelo when he was no better than street scum.

The room swayed as he turned around. Pushing his way through the crowd, he kept his eyes on the bar.

Chance could barely move. Each limb felt weighted with iron. Leftover echoes of music still jack hammered into his brain from Bruisers the night before.

He was in bed -- his bed, fully clothed. But he had no idea how he'd gotten there. Though familiar with the aftertaste of a night like last night, it still coiled his stomach. Still brought his body into a shadowy place he knew only time and dark quiet would ease him out of.

Somebody had drawn the blinds, God bless them. Whoever it was had also kept the place silent. Forcing himself up, he scrubbed the roughness of his face with both hands and let out a stale burp.

Faint rustling on the other side of his closed bedroom door hinted that Justin had been his designated driver last night. Justin didn't drink. For a second, Chance wished he didn't either. But he knew of no other way to rid himself, even if only temporarily, of what tore at him.

Stumbling to the shower, he peeled off his clothes as he went, dropping them along the hall with the carelessness of a child. He heard voices, looked, and saw Inessa whose hands flew to her mouth as she whirled away from him with a shriek.

Realizing he was standing in the hall naked, his delayed reaction made him chuckle as he scratched at his chest and head. "Sorry, Nessa."

Justin suddenly appeared, dish rag in hand, a smile on his face. He shook his head. "Sorry, man. I should have given you a woman warning."

"It's your own fault now if she can't look at you after looking at me."

Justin sneered good-naturedly. "You wish. Get your rancid self cleaned up. I want to talk to you."

Though Chance shot him an indifferent jerk of his head, Justin never wanted to talk unless it was serious. He stood underneath the hot shower with his gut hollowing. What would he want to talk about?

Scrubbing the towel over his face, he looked in the fogged mirror, wiping a circle so he could see himself. Sooty smudges pressed under his eyes. He needed to shave or he could be classified as growing a beard.

He leaned on the sink. His eyes locked in the mirror, the dark gray of them swirling with the uncertainty of a ferocious storm. He sighed, dropping his head to his chest. He'd shave another day.

Pulling on a faded shirt and some old jeans, he headed out to the living room of the apartment he shared with Justin Wilde.

He had still to button the top button of his beaten jeans and when he did, he stopped, noticing how he could pull the waistband from his waist a good inch. When his thumbs dropped, so did his pants, settling lower than normal on his hips.

"You look scary, man," Justin said.

Chance looked up, tugged at his waist band and shook out damp hair. He'd never been good at taking criticism, his delicate defenses shooting up with the efficiency of porcupine quills. But he had spent the last year living with Justin and knew that he was one of the only people on earth who really cared about him. Which made taking whatever he had to say a little easier.

"You're just jealous that Inessa's seen a real man." Chance glanced around for Inessa. "Where is she?"

"She had to go." Justin moved from the kitchen into the living room.

"Hey, I could have stayed in the back."

Justin shook his head. "She had to." Crossing his arms, he leaned against the back of the couch and looked at him steadily. "You're a mess, man."

Friend or not, the hair on the back of Chance's neck prickled at the comment and he stood erect.

Justin saw the resistance. "Just hear me out."

It was respect that kept Chance's feet from moving. He'd learned that moving could prolong the inevitable. Itchy hands that would normally lash out in physical defense hid deep in his pockets. He waited in silence.

"You're—" Justin stopped himself, rubbing the back of his neck in a frustrated sigh.

It wasn't like Justin to mince words. He said what he felt, whether you liked it or not. That was part of why Chance was getting better at taking it. Watching him stumble over them now caused that hollow inside to deepen.

"You were so out of it last night I had to drag you in here, dude. Do you even remember that?"

Chance shifted uneasily. "You didn't have to." But inside, Chance was scrambling through his memory trying to recall what had happened.

"I couldn't leave you at that table." Justin stuck his hands in his pockets but Chance knew he was reaching out. "You okay?"

"Yeah, of course."

"Things settling down between you and Kurt?"

The muscle in Chance's jaw contracted but he kept his gaze level. "As settled as two rattle snakes in a box."

Justin paused a moment that was long and tense. "If you need any help—"

"I don't," Chance broke him off with a bite. "Thanks."

It relaxed Chance when Justin's lip turned up on one side. "Yeah. Hey," he rubbed his hands back and forth, "I got a proposition for you."

With the serious talk over, Chance crossed to the kitchen in hopes of digging up something to eat. "What's that?"

"I made some waffles this morning, there's a few left on a plate."

Chance reached into the refrigerator and pulled them out. "Still warm." His fingertips lightly touched them as he took the plate to the microwave. "We got any sour cream and jam?"

Justin nodded. "A Wilde staple. Now, as you're between jobs, I was thinking you could take a short gig at the high school. Our art teacher's out on maternity leave."

"Yeah? That'd be cool."

"Figured you'd like that. There's one catch."

Chance pulled the waffles out of the microwave and began dousing them in sour cream. "What is it?"

"You gotta enroll in this ballroom class Nessa and I are taking."

"No way."

"It's one night a week."

"I can't dance, no way."

"It's a steal for your return, man."

"An impossibility. I can't dance."

"I couldn't either when I started, but the teacher's awesome."

With a firm shake of his head, Chance cut into his first waffle. "Nope."

"Consider it."

"No way."

"You mean you'd give up sharing your creative brain with all those squiggly kids because you aren't man enough to try a dance class?"

"That's cutting low."

"You know that's it," Justin taunted. "I saw your balls today man, they're nothing."

Chance laughed in spite of himself. His mouth was full so he shook his head. His eyes glittered with warning. "You've forgotten that I know jiu-jitsu, dude."

"Only because I taught you."

"I can cream your ass anytime."

"I'd pulverize yours first."

Chance didn't doubt Justin would pulverize him in a one-on-one. The guy could take down a sumo wrestler in five seconds. That was why he'd been stealing lessons here and there so that he could learn how to finally finish someone.

It was a well-meaning bribe. There was nothing but real goodness in Justin. Silently Chance thanked God he'd not kicked him out with all the crap and instability he'd put him through.

The life of an artist was anything but predictable.

Still, he had hopes of money on the horizon now that he'd been left his parent's earthly belongings -- if Kurt didn't kill him first.

"Just come once, and I'll forget what happened last night." Justin grabbed his briefcase, glanced at his watch. "Tonight. Seven – at the studio."

"Good try but no-go." Chance took a mug from the shelf and filled it with tap water. "What did happen last night?"

"You really don't remember?"

Chance tried to be amused but the shadowing in Justin's eyes sobered him some. Setting the buttons on the microwave for one minute, Chance turned and faced him.

"Man, you—" The shadowing darkened before a mischievous grin broke out on Justin's face. "I'll tell you tonight -- after class." Chance shook his head. Justin was half way out the door. "See ya tonight. Seven, at the studio."

"No way."

"See ya."

"Won't be there."

The front door shut and the microwave dinged, the hot water was ready.

Printed in the United States
79786LV00003B/69

9 781933 963952